Marius' Mules XIV

The Last Battle

by S. J. A. Turney

1st Edition

"Marius' Mules: nickname acquired by the legions after the general Marius made it standard practice for the soldier to carry all of his kit about his person."

For Michelle, sorely missed

Cover photos courtesy of Paul and Garry of the Deva Victrix Legio XX. Visit http://www.romantoursuk.com/ to see their excellent work.

Cover design by Dave Slaney.

Many thanks to the above for their skill and generosity.

All internal maps are copyright the author of this work.

* * *

Published in this format 2021 by Victrix Books

Copyright - S.J.A. Turney

First Edition

The author asserts the moral right under the Copyright, Designs and Patents Act 1988 to be identified as the author of this work.

All Rights reserved. No part of this publication may be reproduced, stored in a retrieval system or transmitted, in any form or by any means without the prior consent of the author, nor be otherwise circulated in any form of binding or cover other than that which it is published and without a similar condition being imposed on the subsequent purchaser.

Also by S. J. A. Turney:

Continuing the Marius' Mules Series

Marius' Mules I: The Invasion of Gaul (2009)
Marius' Mules II: The Belgae (2010)
Marius' Mules III: Gallia Invicta (2011)
Marius' Mules IV: Conspiracy of Eagles (2012)
Marius' Mules V: Hades' Gate (2013)
Marius' Mules VI: Caesar's Vow (2014)
Marius' Mules: Prelude to War (2014)
Marius' Mules VII: The Great Revolt (2014)
Marius' Mules VIII: Sons of Taranis (2015)
Marius' Mules IX: Pax Gallica (2016)
Marius' Mules X: Fields of Mars (2017)
Marius' Mules XI: Tides of War (2018)
Marius' Mules XII: Sands of Egypt (2019)
Marius' Mules XIII: Civil War (2020)

The Praetorian Series

The Great Game (2015)
The Price of Treason (2015)
Eagles of Dacia (2017)
Lions of Rome (2019)
The Cleansing Fire (2020)
Blades of Antioch (2021)

The Damned Emperors Series

Caligula (2018)
Commodus (2019)

The Rise of Emperors Series (with Gordon Doherty)

Sons of Rome (2020)
Masters of Rome (2021)
Gods of Rome (2021)

The Ottoman Cycle

The Thief's Tale (2013)
The Priest's Tale (2013)
The Assassin's Tale (2014)
The Pasha's Tale (2015)

The Knights Templar Series

Daughter of War (2018)
The Last Emir (2018)
City of God (2019)
The Winter Knight (2019)
The Crescent and the Cross (2020)
The Last Crusade (2021)

Wolves of Odin

Blood Feud (2021)
Bear of Byzantium (2021)

Tales of the Empire

Interregnum (2009)
Ironroot (2010)
Dark Empress (2011)
Insurgency (2016)
Invasion (2017)
Jade Empire (2017)

Roman Adventures (Children's Roman fiction with Dave Slaney)

Crocodile Legion (2016)
Pirate Legion (Summer 2017)

Short story compilations & contributions:

Tales of Ancient Rome vol. 1 – S.J.A. Turney (2011)
Tortured Hearts vol 1 – Various (2012)
Tortured Hearts vol 2 – Various (2012)
Temporal Tales – Various (2013)
A Year of Ravens – Various (2015)
A Song of War – Various (2016)
Rubicon – Various (2020)
Hauntings (2021)

For more information visit www.sjaturney.co.uk or www.facebook.com/SJATurney or follow Simon on Twitter @SJATurney

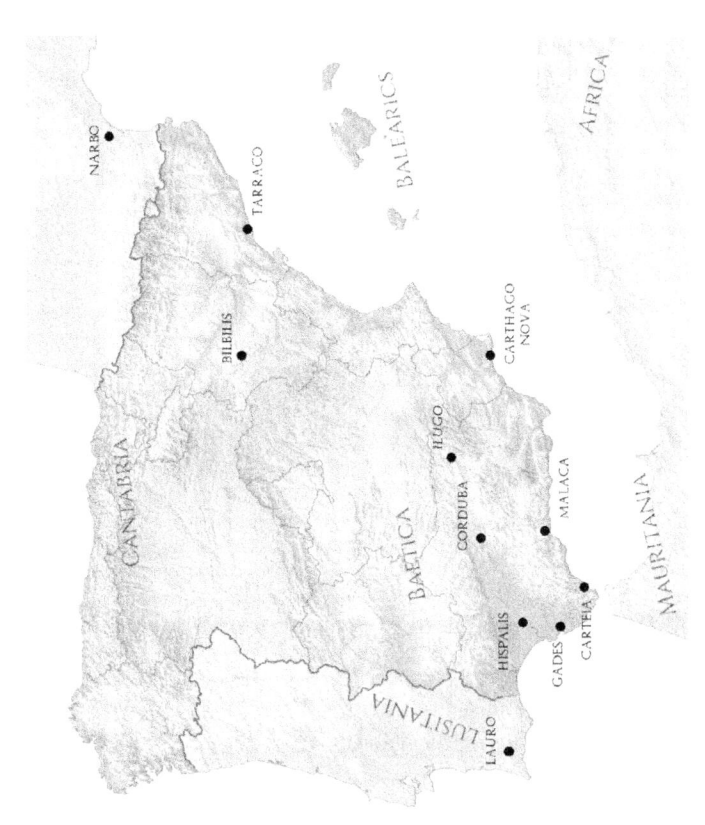

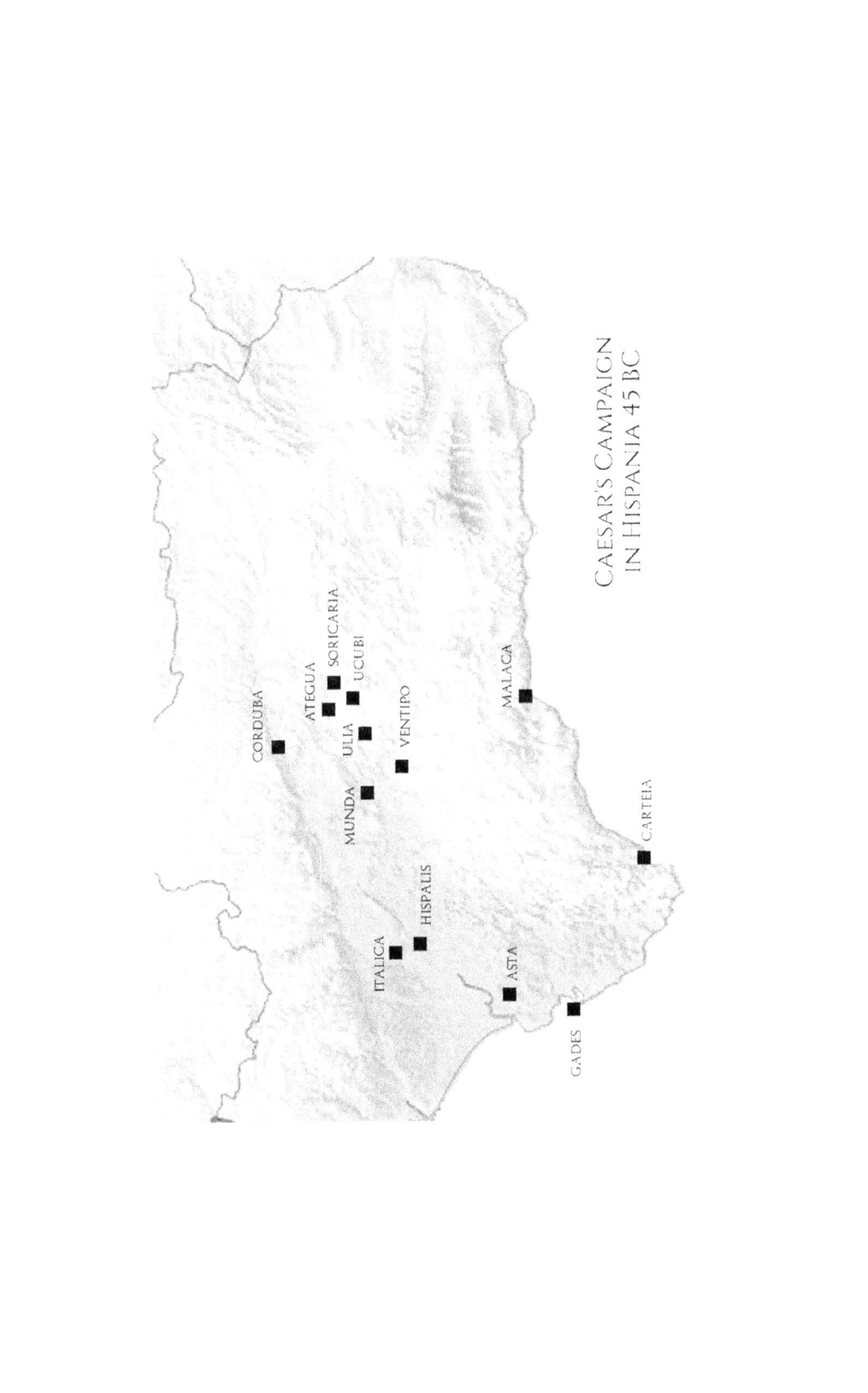

PART ONE

ROME – TRIUMPHS AND TRIBULATIONS

"So great was the calamity which the civil wars had wrought, and so large a portion of the people of Rome had they consumed away, to say nothing of the misfortunes that possessed the rest of Italy and the provinces."

- Plutarch: Life of Caesar

Marius' Mules XIV: The Last Battle

CHAPTER ONE

June 46 BC.

Plains by the Orontes river, east of Antioch

Sextus Julius Caesar chewed his lip as he peered out into the morning light, tense. The battle raged fiercely, and it was difficult to predict how it would pan out as yet. The roar and din of men crying out in rage and pain, overlaid with the whinny and snort of horses, the thuds of blows landing on wooden shields, the rattle, clank, shush and ding of metal meeting metal, the whole thing wove itself into a blanket of sound that filled the plain from hillside to hillside, echoing across the miles of farmland.

He was no novice to battle, for all his youth. Though, as Caesar's great nephew, Sextus had been kept away from the heart of the civil war, posted to peripheral and less volatile positions, he had served his military apprenticeship in a time of strife and battle could not be avoided. He had seen war as a tribune, and then as a commanding officer, first in Hispania before the civil war truly kicked in there, and then at Nicopolis against the armies of Pharnaces II. Like young Octavius, and even younger Pinarius, in Rome, Sextus had envied their cousin Pedius, the eldest of the four, who had served with the general on campaign. Now, however, he was beginning to understand why his powerful great uncle had kept him away from the civil war for so long.

Watching Roman kill Roman was an affront to civilization, and that was what was happening all across the plain. The legions of Quintus Caecilius Bassus had marched north from Tyrus with such suddenness and speed that it had taken a masterful logistical mind to mobilise an army to meet him. Fortunately, that was one thing Sextus shared with his great uncle, and the army he, rightful governor of Syria, had managed to field was every bit the match for the rebellious Bassus and his legions. Pedius, he suspected, would never have found himself in this position, for the man was always ready for whatever life threw at him, and for all his youth, Octavius would undoubtedly have managed to find a way to remove Bassus from command long before he'd managed to march with an army. Sextus, though, was a straightforward man. A clever one, yes, but without his cousins' guile. He liked to think himself a traditional Roman, though unfortunately he seemed to be living in a very untraditional Roman world. Rather than craftily avoiding conflict, he had met it head-on, and would secure victory the old fashioned way.

'Bassus rides with his cavalry,' one of the senior officers noted, pointing out across the plain. Sextus peered into the dust and the spray of blood to the left flank, where the cavalry forces were contesting for control of the field. It was an important position. Many officers, he knew, would write off the cavalry as a lesser force and concentrate on the struggle of the legions in the centre, thinking that the heavy infantry would be the ones to decide the day. Sextus knew differently, as, apparently, did Bassus. Whoever won the flank would manage to bring their cavalry round to the poorly-defended rear and would stand a good chance of breaking their foe. As such, Sextus had made sure to field sufficient horse on both flanks to match the riders of Bassus. He would not make such a simple mistake. He was heir to the greatest general in the world, and it was important, here, when the might of Rome met in battle, to show that he was up to the challenge.

'He is over-confident,' Sextus said, nodding. 'He believes his army will win, and he believes it will happen on the flank. He is wrong.'

'His men fight like lions,' another officer supplied. 'They believe his lies. Our men struggle. Perhaps they do, too.'

The lies… the rumours that Caesar had perished at Thapsus in Africa mere weeks ago, racing across the republic in advance of official word. Rumours that Sextus entirely disbelieved, and that he felt certain had been manufactured by Bassus in Tyrus to secure his anti-Caesarian revolt. He shook his head, addressing the officer. 'It is not in the will, but in the experience. Our men do not believe my great uncle to have perished. They know they still fight for him and for the strength of a new Rome, uncorrupted by the old pedagogues. They struggle because our army is a ragtag force of secondary garrisons, green recruits and near-retirees, all we could gather to face the battle-hardened legions of Bassus. Yet see how they hold, and it will change nothing. We will win on the flanks, for I have my secret weapon.'

He turned and looked over his shoulder. Here, on the low rise which had become his command post, he could see past the tents and the corral of officers' horses, the standards and the wagons, and saw the unit he had kept in reserve, out of sight of the enemy, hidden from view.

Gauls and Germans. Almost a thousand riders, veterans of war from the first days of his great uncle's campaigns against the Helvetii and the Belgae. Men who Caesar had left in Syria as part of the garrison, for they were riders the general could trust. Sextus knew damn well that Bassus would have reserves, too, and likely even cavalry. But Bassus would have *poor* riders in reserve, allies from Pontus or Judea, or perhaps Galatians. Nothing like the savage force Sextus commanded, which waited in the shadows, champing at the bit.

His gaze played across the field once more. The struggle really could go either way at the moment, though he was confident that one signal would change all of that. But it was important to give the troops he had already fielded the chance to win the battle themselves, to give them heart and to enhance their reputation. Yet he would not hesitate to field the Gauls and Germans, and the time for such a move was fast approaching.

He could see the centre, still struggling. Bassus had gained the edge there, his iron-hard veterans slowly pushing the governor's forces back, but still they were not breaking, and they held well. The right flank was immobile, contested by equal forces, and little was likely to happen there. The left flank, though…

He could see the standards there, marking Bassus' position among the riders. The man had committed to the fight in person. He was a fool. Scores of generations of Roman generals had learned that the best place for a general was safely at the rear where he could see the entire field and adapt and move as required. Bassus had instead put himself in danger. Sextus made the decision, then. He'd given his army long enough to prove their mettle and, even if they weren't the men who won the battle, they would be proud they had held long enough for victory to be secured. Now was the time to break the left flank and, with Bassus himself among the cavalry, there was a good chance the enemy commander would perish in the fray. Everyone knew how easily an army lost its heart with the death of its general. Sextus would commit the Gauls and Germans, turn the flank, kill Bassus, and break the enemy infantry with a harrying cavalry action to their rear.

'Aulus, give the signal. Deploy our reserves on the left flank.'

The adjutant gave a curt nod of the head and stepped away across the dry, dusty mound, gesturing to a messenger on his pony. The attack of the reserves would be a surprise, no standards waved or horns blown to warn Bassus what was coming. Just word of mouth setting the riders free.

Sextus looked back only once, checking that the messenger did his job. Sure enough, the trousered, braided mass of riders were beginning to move without the need for signals. He turned back and concentrated on the field before him. The last thing he wanted was for some astute officer among the enemy to see him looking back at a hidden reserve, and send out the alarm.

The riders burst into view like a flood shattering a dam, a mass of colour and metal, bright shields and gleaming helmets, banners shaped like fierce animals, horses racing, swords out, spears levelled. As they emerged, their war cries began. No longer needing secrecy, they now called upon their strange northern gods to aid them in the fray as they rode straight at the left flank.

Sextus nodded his satisfaction. His prefect of cavalry had been briefed well, and even as the reserves appeared in sight and the bellowing began, the man sent out the orders to his beleaguered riders on that flank. In a perfectly choreographed move, the Armenian and Pontic cavalry broke off their hard fought attack carefully, peeling back to both sides like a pair of curtains opening.

The Gauls and Germans filled the gap like the bright rays of the sun invading a dark room between those parting drapes. The effect was impressive. Sextus had never seen these men in action, but those few men on his staff who had served under Caesar across the republic had given him cause to trust in their efficacy. They had been right.

The battle changed in a heartbeat. The two cavalry forces had been struggling to make headway, battering at one another in a press where men and beasts fell together, only to become a carpet of writhing flesh to be pounded into the dust by their compatriots. Suddenly, Bassus' cavalry were being forced back and savaged. A unit of Germans, howling their gods' names and cursing in their strange tongue, cleaved into the tired and battered enemy like a blade into soft flesh. They met not a wall of steel and muscle, but a weary mass that gave in an instant. By the time Sextus' regular cavalry had pulled aside and then reengaged in support of the fresh Germans and Gauls, the new force had penetrated deep into the enemy ranks. There, Sextus watched them at work with astonishment.

They were acrobats. Even from a distance he could see them vaulting from the saddle where they could gain no headway, using knives and shorter blades to gut the enemy horses from beneath and then grabbing their reins once more and leaping back onto their mounts before the stricken animals had even hit the ground. Others had stopped using their hexagonal shields to block blows and were instead using them as weapons, lifting them so that they were horizontal and smashing the hard rim into nearby riders, even as they swung their swords at the far side. They seemed to have little care who was in the way of their blows. Their swords were considerably longer than those of the enemy, which could have been a disadvantage in the press, and yet they swung those massive blades wide, smashing riders from their saddles, cleaving limbs, crushing the necks of horses with the sheer strength of the blows, heedless of how they might catch their allies in the chaos. Oddly, despite the seemingly careless violence, the incidents of harming their companions seemed to be rare.

It was fascinating. They were the very antithesis of a Roman unit. There was no order or discipline evident in their attack, and they moved not with the purpose of ants but with the crowded ferocity of locusts. And yet despite the lack of organisation or order, they worked together like a troupe of acrobats, ducking and leaping, avoiding their own, lancing out with spears, swinging with swords, stabbing with knives and battering with shields, even using their mounts as weapons to force the enemy into more vulnerable positions. They were chaos, but gods they were *deadly* chaos.

In moments the battle was theirs. The enemy cavalry, completely unprepared for this onslaught and unable to effectively counter it, especially tired and abused as they were, began to break. Bassus had given an order somehow, and a fresh unit of cavalry was coming forward in support, but it was too little and too late. They never even managed to engage, for their entry to the fight was blocked by the fleeing riders from the rear of the flank. The cavalry had broken.

The enemy cavalry crumbled. The prefect in command of Sextus' riders desperately called out to his officers, telling them to hold position and not to chase down the fleeing horsemen. This was a critical point. If an enthusiastic cavalry unit decided they were not done with the broken enemy and gave chase, then the won flank was worthless. For a heart-stopping moment it looked as though that was precisely what would happen, for the Germans and Gauls, their bloodlust at its height, seemed to be ignoring the order to re-form. Instead, they pressed forward against the increasingly angry calls of the prefect.

Then Sextus realised what they were doing, and the prefect did too, a moment later. The fierce allies were not chasing down their fleeing victims, but meeting the reserves head-on, even as the riders attempted to navigate their panicked companions. The prefect gave up trying. His orders were going unnoticed, but it seemed that the Gauls and Germans commanding their units had their own plan. They broke into three wings now, the largest smashing into the terrified enemy reserve and ruining any chance of their regaining the flank. A second, slightly smaller, wing turned and began to smash into the side of the legions of Bassus. Where the heavy infantry had been struggling, Sextus' legions desperately holding them back, now the dynamic changed. The enemy, pressed from both sides, lost heart even as fresh energy surged through the forces of Sextus.

The third wing of Germans, a smaller unit, yet still strong and fierce, made straight for Quintus Caecilius Bassus where he attempted to rally his men, protected by his bodyguard. Sextus found himself willing the riders to butcher the enemy commander. He bit down on that desire. It was unseemly. Bassus might be the enemy, but he was still a Roman nobleman. Caesar had always made a great show of clemency, especially among Romans. In the best of worlds, Sextus would accept a surrender from an unharmed Bassus. In reality, he would be quite content to see the man trampled beneath German horses, for all the vaunted clemency of his great uncle who he preferred to emulate.

He almost had his wish. He saw the Germans unable to penetrate the mass of Bassus' bodyguard as the enemy commander gave up hope of victory and began to withdraw from the field. He saw one particularly fierce specimen rise in his saddle. He saw the javelin hefted and then cast. He saw it pass across the heads of the defenders and punch into Bassus. The enemy commander folded over in the saddle as the javelin broke and fell away. Sextus saw the man's sword fall from agonised fingers. For a glorious moment, he thought the man was dead.

Then Bassus pulled himself up in the saddle, though he was clearly wounded, and badly so.

There was a moment then when through the incomparable din of battle, across the writhing press of men and horses, somehow Sextus saw and heard his opponent. Bassus' finger shot out towards Sextus and, as he swayed, clutching his side where crimson flowed in a torrent, he yelled a command. Sextus didn't quite catch all of it, but he heard the words 'despot', 'villain' and 'republic.'

Quintus Caecilius Bassus toppled from his horse, grabbed by men of his guard. Sextus watched his wounded – *mortally wounded?* – opponent heaved across the back of another horse as the bodyguard fought to pull away from the field.

Something new was happening, though, and Sextus' brow furrowed in disbelief.

The battle had been won. The enemy had been beaten and even those veteran legions had been routed and were fleeing the field. Yet the danger was apparently far from over. A few of the units of Sextus' infantry had turned from their victorious pursuit and were coming this way, weapons still out, shields up. As he stared, unable to truly comprehend what was happening, some of his officers were calling out, attempting to counter the new peril. While some of his men seemed to have defected to Bassus even in their moment of victory, drawn in by his impassioned dying words, others remained loyal and attempted to stop them.

A new battle was breaking out between his own troops, even as those of Bassus fled to the east. Sextus turned, his heart beginning to beat louder and faster now. This was wrong. He was the rightful governor of Syria, installed in the position, admittedly, by his great uncle, but ratified by the senate. Bassus was just an army commander, spreading malicious rumours and trying to resurrect the spectre of his former master, Pompey. Sextus was in the right, the gods on his side. Bassus was a rebel and a traitor to the republic. And Sextus had played the battle correctly. He had made the right tactical choices and had correspondingly won the battle. Bassus was not only beaten but badly injured and probably dying. Everything had gone right. So why was it all coming undone now?

A true fight was being waged amid the slaughter of his victory, between his own men. And now, as he turned, he could see that other units among his reserves were moving to betray him. Aging veterans he had kept as his third line were struggling, sword in hand, against the loyalists among the wounded. His command position was coming under siege by his own men.

How could Bassus have so thoroughly suborned Sextus' army with just a short phrase, barely heard over the battle? How could such a thing have even reached the reserves on the other side of the hill. Either Bassus had said something that cut deep into the Roman soul and turned Sextus' men against him, and that sickness had spread like wildfire across the plain, or this had been planned.

He felt shock now. The former was surely impossible, and so this had to be a deliberate move being played out. But if there were traitors in his own army serving Bassus, why had they not moved earlier and saved the battle for their master? It was all so strange and unbelievable.

He took a deep breath and straightened. Reasons had to be brushed aside. He would get to the bottom of this odd betrayal later. Now he had to concentrate on a second victory, and he had to win here before the fleeing enemy realised what was happening and turned, committing once more.

He spun, slowly, taking it all in and nodding to himself. It had been a shock, and he had almost panicked, but now he looked at the situation in detail, detached, he could see success yet. His loyal infantry were roughly on a par numerically with the traitors, but he had five distinct advantages.

The first was the German and Gaulish cavalry, who were still putting down the last resistance in the field, apparently unaware of the new trouble. They were loyal, he was sure. They had been his great uncle's men, and would never side with Bassus. Indeed, even as he watched them, they were moving, aware of the danger and racing to assist, engaging the traitors in the midst of the battlefield.

His second advantage was his bodyguard. His praetorians had been drawn from the legions, including, admittedly, those now commanded by Bassus, but they had been chosen as the best of the best, with an unblemished record, each of them a decorated man, and they had taken a new, fresh military oath as the governor's bodyguard. Each man here had declared his loyalty on the altar of Apollo, and no Roman would break that. Sure enough, the eighty men surrounding the command post had remained steadfast and alert during the battle, and had displayed no sign of trouble. Even now, as the traitors tried to mass against the small hill, the bodyguard stood ready, waiting, blades out, protecting their governor.

Thirdly, he had the terrain and the position. Sextus and his staff occupied the only rise for half a mile in any direction, and it had been fortified with a fence of sudis stakes just as an added precaution. He had a makeshift rampart guarded by fierce, loyal men, and even if the traitors managed to assault it, they would be at risk of being hit from behind by harrying attacks from the Gauls and Germans, which would end them easily enough.

And if he needed any more advantage, it would come from the gods. His line, the line of the Julii, sprang from the lap of the gods. Venus herself lay in his ancestry, and his great uncle had already begun work on a temple in Rome to Venus Genetrix to honour her and celebrate the connection. Sextus was an honoured son of Rome, ratified by the dictator and the senate, and was fighting for the republic against its enemies. The gods would be on his side.

And finally, a fifth advantage sat on the crest of the hill. Sextus himself, for he was resolute and unyielding. He would withstand this and he was not afraid. He had taken the field at Nicopolis and had fought the withdrawal alongside his men. A general should command from the rear, but if the fight should come to Sextus, he would not shy from it. He was not afraid. Moreover, he could have faith in every officer supporting him in this camp. Each man here was a loyal Caesarian. A number of them were distant relations of the Julii themselves, three had served with the general in Gaul and at Pharsalus and were as loyal as a man could be. Two were of the Junii, the family full of Brutuses who were loyal to the Julii entire. Even those he could claim no relationship with were either men assigned by Caesar himself before Sextus had taken up the post, or arrived from Rome since then, assigned by Marcus Antonius or Decimus Brutus. Every man on this hill was a loyal follower of the general.

The fight on the plain had not gone his way. As he scanned the field, he saw that his loyal men had been overcome, and the traitors among his infantry were even now rushing for the hill and the defences. They were relatively few now, though. They could not hope to break the praetorians guarding the fence. Even when the evocati veterans to the rear finally overcame the injured and pressed for the hill, still there would not be enough to break the praetorian chain. And now the Germans and the Gauls had split into several units and were racing around the entire fight in circles, slowly tightening the ring until they could pick at the rear of the attacking traitors, abrading them until there were too few to achieve anything other than a horrible death.

The numbers and the tactics were still on his side.

His mind wandering, Sextus applied his thoughts once more to how this had come about even as he watched his second victory taking shape.

The evocati had reached the stake fence, but they would come no further. Two of them made a rush at the defenders, swords stabbing, shields up, but the praetorians were the best the army could provide, and much younger, stronger and more agile than the retirees. The two men managed to land one sword blow on a praetorian shield before both were efficiently dispatched and thrown back into their own ranks. More came, cutting and bellowing, but the guards at the fence held them back with ease, using the slope to their advantage, stabbing, hacking, chopping and punching, using shields as a weapons, smashing iron bosses into the old warriors' faces. A few of the praetorians who had taken up position as a second ring inside the first were taking pila from stacks around the slope and hurling them over and between their fellows, picking off attackers with simplicity and ease.

Sextus watched, satisfied that the attack there was doomed.

It could not have been Bassus who did this. For all that the timing made it look like his work, even Cicero himself could not have filled a dozen words with enough vim and bile to turn an army against its commander in twenty heartbeats, including those out of earshot. Moreover, if Bassus was capable of such a thing, why would he wait until the battle was lost? For certain that last impassioned cry had been a plea for all to move against Sextus in the name of the republic, but it had been a desperate last attempt, not part of a grand plan. Bassus had fully intended and expected to win the battle today.

He turned. The survivors from the main battlefield were now at the fence, trying to break through the praetorians, and yet they stood no more chance than the traitorous veterans, and already they were beginning to lose. Tired men, having already fought a battle against Bassus, then a battle against their own, made slow, exhausted strikes at the fresh men at the defences. Even as Sextus watched, two men fell away, blood fountaining from half a dozen injuries.

Why would traitors be sowed among his forces, but the order for them to move not be given until the battle was lost? What was to be gained there? And if there was some undiscovered and convoluted reason, who would have given the order? If it were a prearranged signal, it would have to be simultaneously given among those men in the ranks on the field of battle, and at the rear of the hill, among the veterans. How could traitorous officers coordinate such a move?

The riders were here now, the Gauls and the Germans, charging in even as they circled the hill, delivering brutal attacks to the rear of the traitors even as they failed to make any headway. Every attack saw another traitor down, another bloodied corpse in the dust.

He was about to win his second victory. He still couldn't understand what had happened, but he would work it out. He was Sextus Julius Caesar, heir to, and great nephew of, the great dictator, Gaius Julius Caesar. He was of the Julii, a child of Venus, protector of the republic and son of Rome. He would prevail and have Bassus' head sent to his great uncle to prove that the east remained loyal.

Victory was his.

The gods held their breath…

Sextus gasped with unexpected pain. He looked down with some difficulty, as his neck suddenly did not have its full range of movement. It was with some difficulty and shock that he spotted the hilt of the throwing blade sticking out of his throat. He blinked. He'd not seen it coming, and it had to have come from directly in front of him to be sticking out under his nose like that. It could not have been thrown. He would have seen it.

He called out for help, but no words emerged. Just a strange bubbling noise and an odd wheeze. Reason filtered through the shock. The blade had punched through his windpipe, preventing any hope of shouting for help. But the reason he couldn't properly move his head was because it had lodged in his spine, hindering all movement. With that realisation came a second: that there was no help that could come, even if he could shout. This was a mortal blow and there was no denying it.

And that brought something else. The shock and the confusion subsided, and in their place came agony. Pain the likes of which Sextus had never experienced, could never even have imagined to exist. It felt as though his entire body burned with intense fire from the inside out. An inferno raged along his veins and arteries from the blow in his neck all around his body. He cried out in horror, but the damage once again transformed his shriek into a mere bubbling hiss.

Through the pain, he heard someone shout 'The governor is down!'

And then someone was grasping him, lowering him to the ground. He stared, hissing and bubbling, up at the face of the man cradling him. One of his own officers, Lucius Gellius, arrived a month ago from Rome, a personal appointee of Marcus Antonius. One of the most trusted men on this hill.

Sextus looked into Gellius' eyes and felt the shock return. There was no surprise in those black pupils, no shock or horror, no sadness or pain. Nor was there glee or triumph, admittedly. Those eyes were as dead as Sextus would be in mere moments. Emotionless. Glassy and empty. He realised as he saw his stricken body reflected in those eyes, that it had been Gellius. Sextus had not seen the knife coming because it had not been thrown at all. It had been stabbed by a man who had calmly walked up to Sextus' side where he had every right to be. And with all that was going on around this hillside, no one had seen him strike the blow.

Sextus gasped again, as other figures came rushing across the hill. Gellius gave him a barely perceptible nod, a confirmation that he knew Sextus understood.

'For the republic,' Gellius said quietly, and even as he died, Sextus was not sure he believed that.

His world went black.

Syria rose.

Marius' Mules XIV: The Last Battle

CHAPTER TWO

25th July 46 BC

Rome

Fronto set foot on the dock with a good deal of relief.

'You look pale,' Galronus said, somewhat unnecessarily.

'If man was meant to cross the sea, we'd have been given gills. Hate it.'

'The sea was the calmest I've ever seen it. Like marble.'

'Marble doesn't slam you against the rail and make you throw up until you see stuff coming out of you that you ate when you were still at school.'

Galronus smiled benignly, which simply made Fronto more irritated. 'Plus of course,' he said, 'this is a complete waste of time.'

'We've been over this. Caesar…'

'Caesar is increasingly suffering from a medical condition we call "stupidity".'

'He has his reasons for coming to Rome. You know that.'

'Oh yes, I've heard it all spouted. We must delay Hispania until Rome is secure. The people need triumphs. The troops need a few months to breathe before we put them through another war. I was there for all the briefings. But every man in those tents was thinking the same thing every time. Caesar wants to see his son. That's all it is. And so we sail from Utica to Caralis. We sail from Caralis to Ostia. We sail from Ostia to Rome. And once Caesar's been reacquainted with his queen-on-the-side and met his baby boy, I'd lay you bets we'll sail to Saguntum for the next war. Probably late in the year when sailors start to get nervous. I'll have to stop eating at least a month in advance this time.'

Galronus' smile widened a little.

'I've never seen a triumph. From what Hirtius was telling me it's quite a sight.'

'Boring,' Fronto snapped irritably. 'I watched Pompey triumph three times. You know that's why Caesar's making a point of this. That and Caesarion, anyway.'

'Because...' Galronus began.

'Because Pompey got three triumphs,' Fronto interrupted, grunting. 'And now Caesar gets four. He's determined to prove he's better than Pompey. Why? Pompey's been dead for years now.'

'But his sons are still very much alive and controlling Hispania with Labienus.'

Fronto snapped a narrow eyed look at his friend. 'Four triumphs. Ridiculous. And spurious at best. Gaul I accept. If ever a general deserves a triumph it's for what we did in Gaul over eight years. I'll even accept Pharnaces as good reason, though I don't think Caesar meets the death toll requirements for a triumph there. Still, Zama was a fight I wouldn't rush to repeat, so fair enough. I'd even concede Aegyptus, despite the insufficient numbers and the fact that we fought alongside Aegyptians too. But Africa? It's being claimed as a victory over *Juba*, man.'

'Juba *was* there. We beat him. He died.'

'But he was just a tool of the rebels. Africa was a war against other Romans, and everyone, right down to Gaius Nobody the baker knows it. He's going to ride in a chariot behind a score of African slaves, but the public aren't going to see that in their mind's eyes. They'll see captive Romans. It's folly. Just folly.'

'You'll feel better when you're less sick.'

'Probably not while we're in Rome then,' Fronto snapped angrily. 'Forty days of thanksgiving. Forty! The senate is falling over itself to kiss Caesar's boots. Of course, that's because it's *Caesar's* senate these days.'

Galronus gave his friend a hard look, a warning. Fronto clamped his mouth shut as the general came ashore nearby with Aulus Hirtius. Fronto was irritated, but he also knew he'd picked up a tendency to complain in a most Cassius-like manner. He didn't want to pick up a reputation as one of Caesar's detractors, but equally, it *was* irritating. The senate was throwing honours at Caesar by the bucketload to see which ones stuck, and now, completely ignoring the whole 'sea journeys' thing, they were in Rome for the foreseeable future while Labienus and the Pompey brothers built up their army and secured Hispania. That was exactly what Cato and Scipio had done in Africa, and the result had cost them dearly. Did Caesar not learn from his mistakes? They should even now be landing in Hispania with the army and preparing to finish the job for good.

And, if he were to be truly honest with himself, Fronto would admit that in addition to grand annoyances about the fate of the republic, a small but very real part of his irritation was the fact that he had hoped that Hispania would see him reunited with his family. Lucilia and the boys, Masgava and the others, his sister, everyone had spent the past few years safely locked away in the villa near Tarraco, away from the trouble of Rome and the civil war. Now, with Hispania under enemy control, though they were far from the trouble zone, he was starting to think about their safety, and had hoped to visit them on the way to Hispania and make sure all was good. Indeed, when Caesar had been insistent about sailing for Rome, Fronto had petitioned the general to let him skip the triumphs and spend the summer in Tarraco, joining up once more when Caesar moved on Hispania.

No. The general had been adamant. Deep down, Fronto could understand it. Of the men who had served on Caesar's staff since they marched into Gaul fourteen years ago, very few of the great names remained at the general's side. Plancus, Hirtius and Fronto, really. Brutus too, and Marcus Antonius, though the pair of them had spent the last year in Rome, away from the war, playing Caesar's political games for him. Caesar was to have triumphs for his four great victories, and Fronto was one of the few men still with him who had been instrumental in all four. Of course he was required to attend.

Bitter thoughts slid to those enemies now lost too. Cato, suiciding in Utica, had been a loss to the republic, even if he had recently been Caesar's opponent. And Scipio too, who fled after Thapsus, but had been caught by Caesar's pet pirate Sittius in the city of Hippo, and had killed himself there. There were few of the great men left on either side these days.

'You look morose, Fronto,' Caesar said almost genially. That the man's mood was increasingly light as they neared home just made Fronto all the more irritable.

'Seasick.'

'Of course. Well I shall not keep you long.'

'Keep me? I was going to my townhouse to lie down and feel like shit for a while. It'll be cold and cobwebby, but there's no shit place like home.'

Galronus chuckled, and Caesar smiled widely. 'But I have need of you, Marcus. The people will be gathered in the forum awaiting our return. I want my veteran officers by my side as I address Rome. This is an important occasion. A lot of the coming months' civic attitudes will be determined by how the crowd see our return. We must not be beleaguered warriors in the midst of a campaign, but victorious sons of the republic, returning to our heartland.'

'We *are* beleaguered warriors in the midst of a campaign,' Fronto grumbled.

'All the more reason to let the people see that we are not. And after that I want you, as with the others, to come with me to my villa across the river. We have much to discuss.'

'We've discussed everything to the tiniest detail on the journey and in Caralis. I was at the meetings. Throwing up half the time, I know, but I was there.'

'There will be new matters to consider, and new plans to make once we have gauged the mood of Rome and caught up with the latest news. I will need my officers in attendance. We might be in Rome, but I still require my staff on hand.'

'I feel like I've been turned inside out. I haven't shaved in twelve days. I think something is living in my hair. I cannot remember the last time I had a clean tunic. I need new boots.'

'And all that makes you look like a veteran of war. It will remind the people that we have been fighting for them, not enjoying the African sun.'

Fronto fell into a grumpy silence. Clearly he was going to lose this argument, and besides, he had little energy left to fight it after a month of stomach contractions. He stood on the dock, silently ruminating on the many things that were getting on his nerves while Galronus chatted enthusiastically about what would happen and what the triumphs would entail. Would there be chariot races?

He liked chariot races. He'd heard that some bakers baked special free treats to distribute to the public. He liked Rome's sweet pastries. And so on.

As they stood, one silent, the other chatty, Caesar gathered his familia and staff around him, and, once they were prepared and looking a careful combination of battle-worn and triumphant, musicians were brought forth, the standards and eagles of the legions and all the pomp of a returning general, and, climbing onto their horses, they began to make their way into the city. Bucephalus was surprisingly steady and calm after the voyage, far more so than his rider, who groaned and drooled with every lurch of the beast, not yet recovered from the sea himself.

Still, despite feeling appalling, and not wanting to be there at all, Fronto couldn't help but feel just a little smug as Galronus nudged him and he looked up. As they rounded the building works where Caesar's new complex of temples and basilica were almost complete, the forum came into view. The place was packed with the populace of Rome, from filthy street beggar to toga'd senator being kept safe by private bodyguards with clubs. Every temple's steps resembled a theatre stand, occupied by people, while children clung to columns, trying to see over the crowd. As the horns blared to announce their approach, the crowd fell into an expectant hush, which then exploded into cheering as Caesar himself came into view on his white mare.

Fronto tried to sit straight and look slightly less green as the general was escorted up to the rostrum and, once the crowd had subsided into silence, given them a speech that was as rousing as any he'd given. The crowd cheered and whistled, and once he was done, lictors came forward. Fronto blinked at that. He'd not seen the general with his appointed number of lictors now since Aegyptus, and yet somehow he'd acquired them between the ships and the forum. The lictors cleared a space, and legionaries, disarmed within the city's limits, brought forth a cart with a chest on it and began to hurl handfuls of coins into the crowd. Fronto happened to catch a stray one and turned it over, looking at it. An image of Juba, the Numidian king on the obverse. Clever old bastard, but Caesar was giving the people the spoils of war, and this very gold proclaimed his victory in the hands of the greedy populace.

He sat patiently as it all happened, but if he'd thought it over then, when the coins were gone, and Caesar stepped down, he was sadly mistaken, for a small deputation of white-clad men made their way forward. At the head were Brutus and Antonius, urging Caesar to address the senate as well as the people.

The general, a carefully-formed look of casual worry on his face, greeted them, and then admitted 'I have prepared no speech, my friends, but I shall see what I can do.'

'Bollocks,' Fronto hissed to Galronus.

'What?'

'No speech my hairy arse. I heard him reciting it on board yesterday. Politicians,' he spat irritably.

Galronus just smiled. 'I should have a toga really.'

Fronto snorted. His friend, of course, was officially one of those very senators, but today he would be better served in his battle gear like the rest of the officers. Fronto followed on with the staff and familia as the general made his way into the senate house. The rows of stuffy looking old men awaited in respectful silence, sitting on their banks of seating, carefully arranged in order of importance. Fronto remembered visits here during the war in Gaul, when Caesar was still struggling to stay out of the courtroom, seeking his consulship. Hardly any of those old faces remained. In fairness most of them had taken up arms and had faced Caesar across the field in Greece or Africa. This was a new senate. *Caesar's* senate.

Moments later they were settled, Fronto standing at the back and hoping the equisio outside was looking after Bucephalus. The senators invited the general to speak, and Caesar stood forth and placed a palm on his heart as he thrust out his other arm in an oratorical gesture.

'Let none of you, Conscript Fathers, fear harsh proclamations or cruel deeds from a returning conqueror. I am, as always, a servant of the republic. Marius and Cinna and Sulla set a dreadful precedent by promising great things to achieve their commands, then returned as triumphant generals only to renege on their promises and institute a rule of fear.'

There was a careful pause then, to let the senate digest this.

'I am no Marius, or Cinna, or Sulla. I have never dissembled with this august body, never pretended anything I am not, and so I have no dreadful truth to reveal. I was your servant as a senator myself, and I am still your servant as a triumphant general. I shall be dictator, for you have twice voted that most crucial of roles to me, and shall be so as long as you see a need, but I shall never be a tyrant.'

There was a murmur of satisfaction at this. Fronto nodded his approval. A bold statement, especially when he had just promised the senate no lies nor dissembling. To then denounce the ways of kings and despots and openly distance himself from them would go a long way towards mollifying those who feared Caesar's increasing power.

'Fortuna has favoured me,' the general said, then spread out his hands to take in the rest of those with him. 'Has favoured *us*,' he corrected himself. 'But I seek nothing more from her other than the continued success of our critical endeavour. For that is my one great goal and the reason for which I have risen to such heights: to punish the enemies of the republic.'

A murmur of approval from the senate. Fronto smiled. He remembered half of this from its memorising on the ship. It was a good speech, he had to admit. This was Caesar's pet senate, but this might even have won over the *old* senate. His eyes picked out Cassius, seated somewhere near the back, one of Caesar's more recent detractors, and even the noble Cassius was nodding his approval.

'I stand here your servant in all I do. I shall not be like those same enemies we seek to remove, and I shall not imitate them. I am no Pompey to revel in war, nor a Cato to sit in judgement of the morals of my peers. I am Caesar, your warhorse, protecting the republic. Good fortune, if joined to self-control, is enduring, and authority, if it maintains moderation, preserves all. I seek your love and respect as a representative of this great council, and not some foe of the republic to be secretly plotted against.'

Fronto smiled to see how the general managed not to look directly at Cassius at this point, though he felt certain the comment was meant for the senator and still Cassius shifted slightly in his seat.

'The whole world, including his nearest associates, both suspects and fears a man who is not master of his own power. This is my vow to you all, and not some sophistry carefully constructed, for I had no speech prepared for you today. This is from my heart and of the moment. Be reassured for the present, and hopeful for the future. I will be not master of this body, but its champion. I shall be not tyrant, but leader. As you vote me, I shall be consul and dictator to preserve the republic, but to you all, I shall also be a private citizen. I will see no proscriptions even among my enemies, just as I always offer clemency to my noble opponents.'

'*Bollocks*,' whispered Fronto to Galronus, earning a warning glance from his friend.

'Let us, therefore, Conscript Fathers, confidently unite our interests, forgetting the past and respecting each other without suspicion. Fear not my armies, for they are *your* armies, the preservers of the republic, and while they cannot yet be stood down, and their ongoing support requires your continued goodwill, even with increased taxes, they fight to remove the last enemies of Rome.'

There was an uncomfortable silence then as the words 'increased taxes' filtered across the senate.

'Rest assured that any extra funding goes straight to the legions who seek to secure the provinces for the senate, and that none of it is for private gain. Indeed, I vow to you now that all such funds raised will be used for the security of the republic, and those new buildings that I even now dedicate in the city come from my own purse. So, Conscript Fathers, this is my oath to you. I am, as always, your servant.'

Fronto tried not to roll his eyes at the senate's reaction. Faced with increased taxation to pay for the upkeep of the legions, even Caesar's supporters had been ready to complain openly, and then the general had smoothed the way as always with a seemingly selfless act. The fact that the buildings he was paying for out of his own purse were for public use was popular, but that those buildings gloried the Julii and further enhanced his popularity went apparently unnoticed.

He waited patiently with the others while the senate applauded the general and half a dozen other speeches were made, fawning around the returning hero and offering further honours and concessions, and was quite grateful just to be moving again when finally they departed the old senate house and moved on, Brutus and Antonius joining them now.

'This will probably be the last meeting of the senate in that building,' Hirtius said conversationally as they mounted outside once more.

'Oh?'

The man smiled. 'Among Caesar's planned works is a new curia building, fitting for the new assembly. The old one is to be demolished this summer and work begun on the new.'

'And where will the senate meet in the meantime?'

Hirtius' smile jacked up a notch. 'In Pompey's theatre. It sends a fairly clear message, don't you think?'

Fronto rolled his eyes again as they set off, still a sizeable column and led by the lictors marching along with their bundles of sticks on their shoulders, setting a stately pace. From the forum, down to the markets and the river, across the Sublician Bridge and out past the boundary stones marking the sacred city limit, they finally entered the grounds of Caesar's grand villa. This was a massive affair set within acres of gardens with neat lawns, fountains, arcades and topiary. Down a gravel drive they crunched until the lictors finally spread out and came to a halt, and the horsemen reined in and dismounted, slaves hurrying out to take the reins without looking at their masters. Caesar rubbed his hands together and gestured for the others to follow as he marched to the door, more slaves hurrying out and bowing low, lining the approach on both sides.

Fronto carefully allowed several of the others to take the lead in Caesar's wake, falling in somewhere partway along the line. Galronus dropped in next to him, frowning.

'You don't look happy?'

Fronto nodded. 'Keep your head down. This could get messy.'

'Why?'

'I recognised some of the staff out front. Unless I missed the mark, Calpurnia is here. Atia too.'

Galronus' furrowed brow remained. 'I don't follow.'

'Caesar's wife. In the same villa as Cleopatra and Caesar's son.'

'Oh.' Galronus pulled a face. 'That could be uncomfortable.'

'Atia's a scheming bugger too, Caesar's niece and Octavian's mother. She'll be stirring things up, guaranteed.'

Galronus nodded and shrunk back into the crowd with Fronto as they made their way through the villa, and out into a pleasant peristyle with a bubbling fountain, and box hedges that could grant privacy to those sitting on the delicate marble benches. A small gathering at the centre of the garden near the fountain broke off what sounded like a rather heated conversation, and turned as they approached.

Caesar stopped; the three figures in the garden were clearly not those he had been expecting. Calpurnia, Fronto had not seen for years. A stoic and eminently sensible woman, she took all of Caesar's extremes in her stride. She had aged a little but was still a handsome woman. Her face maintained a carefully neutral expression, and the reason was perhaps standing close by. The second figure Fronto recognised all too well. Cleopatra's husband, and fourteen year old brother, Ptolemy, was unlikely to be thoroughly welcome in Calpurnia's home, though more so surely than his wife, of whom there was no sign in the garden. The third figure was Atia, who Fronto remembered very well. Atia looked focused, tense.

Even as Caesar stepped forward again, a fourth figure emerged from behind one of the hedges. Octavian had grown immeasurably since the last time Fronto had seen him, and a quick mental calculation confirmed that he wasn't a boy any more. At eighteen, Octavian had become a lithe but well-proportioned young man with the smooth jaw and intense eyes of the Julii. Standing close to both Caesar and Atia there could be no denying his lineage. The young man's mouth twisted up into a smile at the sight of his great uncle, very different from the expression Atia maintained.

'I expected there to be a two-year old here as well,' Caesar said, his surprise and disappointment robbing him of much needed subtlety.

Calpurnia gave him a meaningful look, which he ignored, as Ptolemy looked faintly panicked and Atia remained silent. Octavian spoke, and the youthful squeak gone, his voice was so similar to Caesar's that Fronto was momentarily taken aback.

'Auspicious timing, Caesar,' the young man said. 'Had you arrived last night the house would have been in chaos. Young Caesarion was extremely ill. We have had physicians in attendance half the night, dealing with his vomiting and gastric troubles. I investigated and discovered that it appears the boy had been left alone too long in the gardens and had decided to try oleander as a new taste. Fortunately it appears he stopped short of a fatal dose, and is now recovering, though he will be weak for a few days, the physicians tell us. Cleopatra is with him.'

Caesar's face paled at the news, but if he had hoped to then visit his infant son, he was mistaken, for Atia stepped forward, in front of Octavian. 'I need to speak with you, Gaius.'

Caesar, brow creased with concern and now thoroughly on the back foot, nodded and followed obediently as Atia led him away from the group. Away, Fronto suspected, from Ptolemy and Calpurnia, specifically. Hirtius struck up an exchange of polite small talk with Caesar's wife, and the gathering of officers began to murmur in quiet conversation. Fronto and Galronus shifted slightly to the side, away from the gathering, and, as they stopped beside a hedge, Fronto realised with a touch of guilt, that he could now just hear the voices of Caesar and Atia on the far side of the green barricade.

'…and she is less than comfortable with that woman staying here, even with her husband. In truth, I cannot blame her. Calpurnia and I rarely see eye to eye, but your eastern whore has no place in Rome, and the people are beginning to mutter the same.'

Caesar's reply came in cold tones. 'I do not have to explain my relationships to the populace. Calpurnia and I have always had an understanding. She is my wife, not my love. She has always been perfectly content to look the other way.'

'Not when there is a child, you fool,' Atia spat. 'That boy is the walking, gurgling proof of your affair with that Aegyptian heifer, and he is under Calpurnia's nose every waking hour. Gods, but when the boy nearly poisoned himself last night I almost blamed Calpurnia. She would certainly not weep over your loss.'

'Atia…'

'Anyway, that is not the matter I wished to discuss, though it has some bearing.'

Galronus, looking somewhat embarrassed, jerked his thumb, suggesting they move away, but Fronto shook his head and waved his friend to stillness, listening intently.

'Did you register your new will?' Atia asked in a meaningful tone.

There was a pause. Then: 'No.'

'So your original will stands. Sextus inherits all?'

'Sextus is my closest relative, the only one of my great nephews descended through a male line. The rest are all through sisters, and you know the way of this, Atia. He was always going to inherit.'

'Then you've not heard.'

Another pause. 'Heard what, Atia? You speak in clipped riddles as always. Speak plain.'

'Sextus is dead, Gaius. He died in battle against one of Pompey's old soldiers out in Syria. Word arrived in Rome yesterday. It is said that Syria is in open revolt.'

Fronto closed his eyes, wincing, and clenched his teeth. The news of Caesar's great nephew, one of the four, and one of the better blossoms of the Julian tree, was bad, but the news that Syria had revolted was appalling. Yesterday only Hispania remained before Rome was quelled. Now there were two trouble spots, on opposite sides of the republic.

'Your will is null and void, Gaius,' Atia went on. 'Worthless. And you keep launching yourself into stupid wars where I half expect you to get yourself killed. Do you really want the courts to settle your estate? You told me more than half a decade ago, when you were still invading Gaul, that you planned to alter your will in favour of Octavian. You *promised* me.'

Caesar's tone hardened. 'Who I make my heir is my business Atia. I have – *had* – four great nephews, and now I have a son to consider also.'

'You cannot make that half-Aegyptian your heir. Son he may be, but he's illegitimate and you know it. *Everyone* knows it. You pass your estate to Caesarion and you will be the laughing stock of Rome. You would be pelted with rotten fruit in the streets. No one wants an Aegyptian ruling Rome.'

'I do not rule Rome, Atia.'

A snort. 'You can play whatever word games you like with the senate, Gaius, but I'm no drooling old fool. I know what you are, and I know your ambitions. I know what you would be. You cannot name Caesarion, and you know that even if you won't admit it. Sextus was a good, true Roman, but he's gone. Pinarius is too young to take on such responsibility, younger even than Octavian. Pedius is brave and noble, but he's not got a political bone in his body. He's good with your troops, but can you picture him dealing with the senate?'

'No,' admitted Caesar. 'No, Pedius is a worthy nephew, but he will never be a good politician.'

'But Octavian is old enough and you *know* him. You know he's clever, wily, ambitious and strong. Gods, but he reminds me so much of you it makes me sick some times. When I say you promised me that will, I mean it. You know Octavian is the prime choice.'

Caesar sighed. 'He is clever. I'm not sure he's a soldier. If he cannot command the army's respect then he is no better than Pedius. One a general, the other a politician. Perhaps I should take him to Hispania? Test his mettle?'

'You put him on a ship to your war, Gaius, and I will follow you and claw out your eyes. He may be a grown man, now, but he is still my son.'

'Atia, he is of the age. A tribune's position is appropriate now.'

'Yes, but somewhere safe. Send him to Illyricum, or Narbo, or Greece. I will not have my uncle and my son both putting their necks on the line on the same battlefield, Gaius.'

'I cannot name him if he is untested, Atia, any more than I can name Pedius. Whoever takes up my mantle when I meet my end has to be an accomplished politician and general both. Without that sort of hand on the steering oar, the republic will founder and fail, Atia.'

'Then you had best hope you live forever,' Atia said acidly. 'Look to your safety in Hispania. If you will not make good on your promise, then the courts will split your estate.'

'Atia…' Caesar began, but she was already walking away.

Tactfully, Fronto and Galronus shuffled back towards the chatting gathering as first Atia and then Caesar returned to view. The general's face was dark, his mouth a thin, tight line.

'Change of plan, gentlemen. I must visit my son and spend time with him. I will send for you all when there is better need for a consultation. For now, thank you for your ongoing service and enjoy a much needed rest in Rome. Hispania can wait for a while.'

Dismissed, the group scattered, mostly returning to the drive out front and finding their horses and slaves, Hirtius, Brutus and Antonius remaining in the villa, speaking to Calpurnia and Atia as the general disappeared indoors. Fronto and Galronus slipped quietly from the villa and found their horses. For a quarter of an hour they rode through the city, back across the bridge, discussing what they had heard, and finally climbed the street on the Aventine and closed on the Falerii's town house in Rome. As they neared the door, Galronus pointed to the smoke curling out from the roof. 'Your slaves must have known you were coming and started warming the baths.'

Fronto nodded. Good. He'd hoped they were still maintaining the place and that it wouldn't be cold and unused. Reaching the door, he rapped on it and waited until the door swung gently inwards. An ebony face with flashing white eyes and shining teeth appeared in the gap.

'Well bugger me,' said Masgava.

CHAPTER THREE

11th August 46 BC

Catháin paced alongside Fronto on the gentle incline, tablet in hand, one eye on the road, the other on the list he was perusing. Masgava and Aurelius moved ahead, parting the general crowds of the street simply by their armed presence, while six slaves hurried along behind, carrying the sample wines Catháin had chosen. Fronto felt faintly irritated, content that he could have done all this without the entourage, and with a couple of strong servants and no slaves, but Lucilia had been insistent that in Rome, Fronto would at least try and act like a man of his status. He had drawn the line at riding in a litter, but that had been her only concession.

Still, for all his irritation, it made him smile. He had not realised just how much he'd missed her gentle nagging. It had come as more than a little surprise to enter the townhouse a few weeks ago and find his whole family in residence. It had been his sister's decision, apparently. She had reasoned that they had all confined themselves to a villa in northeast Hispania to stay away from the war, but since the war had now moved to Hispania, while Rome was secure, a move back to the capital seemed sensible. Fronto had agreed entirely, but had still been surprised. Apparently Lucilia had sent him letters while he was in Africa, three of them, the last explaining their plan to return. Not one had reached him. But then, he supposed, it had been winter, he had been overseas, and she had been reliant upon private couriers rather than the cursus publicus, as she'd had no access to the government postal system.

It had been a nice surprise, and a startling one in some ways. That evening he had enjoyed a slightly drunken reunion with the three remaining members of his former singulares, Masgava, Aurelius and Arcadios. In addition to those three, the forthright

Hibernian merchant Catháin joined them, and, surprisingly, Lucilia's servant-cum-guard, the Gaulish woman Andala, still carrying knives at her side and drinking like a man.

The real surprises had come before that, though, in how much people had changed. Not Lucilia, who was still stunning and very much the woman he had married, and not his sister, who had greeted him briefly and then disappeared for a more personal liaison with Galronus. The boys, though, Lucius and Marcus. The last time he had seen them they had been toddlers. Now they were both eight years old, rangy and outspoken. Both had been educated thus far by Lucilia herself, but would be placed in the care of a proper tutor this year. The boys had been guarded at first, harbouring only hazy memories of him, which had hurt rather more than he'd been prepared for, but it had not taken long to draw them out, especially with tales of his exploits in Greece, Aegyptus and Africa. By the end of the evening they were his boys entirely, and they had complained bitterly when made to retire to their rooms. His mother, the elder Faleria, seemed frail now and venerable, which, of course, she was. Yet when he put a foot wrong in conversation she had proved quickly and easily that her mind was still sharp, and her tongue more so.

Then there had been Balbus. His father in law, and his sister in law Balbina, too, had become part of the extended familia. Balbina was no longer the child he remembered, but a woman, now looking for a suitor in Rome. Balbus seemed as old as Fronto's mother now. It was becoming hard to remember the old man as the legate of the Eighth who had stormed Gallic fortresses alongside Fronto. Age had not been so kind, and he seemed more of a husk than a man these days. Balbus had greeted him warmly enough, but when he asked after the campaigns of the past two years, they carefully set the subject aside before disagreements over Caesar arose. Indeed, the general's name never once came up that night, and they had not spoken of such matters since.

In all, though, it had been a happy few weeks of readjusting to life with his familia, and he had become comfortable languishing in Rome and ignoring the still-growing danger in Hispania. In fact, he had only attended Caesar's meetings three times since they'd arrived. The general was currently busy enough with his strange, discordant family and the business of civic administration, and had displayed little time or interest in the future of the campaign. He had been involved in land acquisitions, colonial settlement, taxes and finance, keeping the senate on side, and so on.

'I need to know tomorrow,' Catháin said, 'which of the wines you prefer. If I delay, prices will rise, and our profit margin shrinks accordingly.'

Fronto nodded. 'I'll go through them with you later, when Lucilia isn't looking. She still thinks I drink too much anyway. Perhaps you should just choose yourself? After all, you know wine better than me, and I'm from patrician blood. It's not done for patricians to run businesses. Own them, yes, but not run them.'

'They are all good wines, Fronto. I favour them all. That is why I give you the choice. After that, I will deal with everything.'

Fronto nodded as they reached the house and the door opened for them, Arcadios smiling from the alcove just within. The slaves hovered outside, looking at their feet until the other four were in and passing through the atrium, then shuffled inside and disappeared to their various locations. Fronto watched them go with mixed feelings. He had nothing against slavery, of course, at least not on ethical grounds, but he knew that some slaves were only one opportunity away from revolt, and a servant had more incentive to work hard than a slave. Still, Lucilia liked to have a body slave and the various others for her hair and makeup and clothes, and Balbus had brought his own contingent into the household. Indeed, Fronto had never seen the place quite so busy.

Inside, Masgava and Aurelius went to change out of their 'city bodyguard' gear, and Catháin disappeared after the slaves to see that they settled the wine correctly. Left alone in the atrium, Fronto turned to Arcadios, who had closed the door behind them all.

'Where is Balbus? I need to talk to him about the arrangements for the play tonight.'

The Greek nodded. 'He's in his office with his guest.'

'Guest?' Fronto frowned.

'Yes. He's not been here long. Don't know him, but Balbus seemed to.'

Intrigued, Fronto left the guard to it and paced on through the house, leaving a trail of city street murk that Lucilia would grumble at, were it not for the fact that a slave appeared from nowhere and began to scrub the marble behind him. He heard the muffled voices before he reached the door, and complimenting the deep tones of his father in law, the other voice was lighter, more elegant. He faintly recognised it, but couldn't quite place it. He paused as he approached, ears pricked.

'…a return to monarchy.'

Gods, but not that again. Steeling himself, he approached the door and rapped on it. The voices stopped suddenly, and there was a long pause before the door crept inwards and the lined, pale face of Balbus appeared in the gap.

'Marcus?'

'I need to talk to you.'

'Now is not a good time, Marcus.'

Fronto's face slid into a grimace of irritation. 'Because you're busy undermining Caesar as usual. Who's your latest confidante?'

Without warning, angry at this behaviour in his own house, Fronto suddenly pushed the door. A decade ago, Balbus would have held it solid, but age and a faltering heart had stripped him of bulk and strength, and as the door jerked inwards the old man staggered back into the room. Fronto stepped inside, eyes seeking out the second occupant.

Anger gripped him as the other speaker rose from his chair, holding up conciliatory hands.

'Paetus? You've got a fucking nerve.' He turned to Balbus. 'I'm surprised that even *you* would let him in the house.'

'He is here as my guest, Marcus. Does xenia mean nothing to you?'

'There are limits to hospitality. Conspirators, traitors and murderers don't meet the list for me.' He turned back to Paetus, once one of Caesar's officers before a long fall from grace. 'Get out of my house.'

'Fronto, don't blind yourself to possibilities,' the thin officer replied, taking a step forward. 'Can you not see the way things are going?'

'I will not have treachery and conspiracy under my roof,' Fronto snapped.

Balbus cleared his throat. 'Marcus, we are not talking plots, nor crimes. We are discussing the philosophy of governance. The dangers inherent in dictatorship and the perils of monarchy against the value of democracy. We are a republic, and have been since the last king fell centuries ago. There is no treason in talking of Rome's rightful government and the history of our early failures.'

Fronto nodded. 'I know. You and I have such discussions. This man, though, is something different. This is a man who would kill to prevent a mere possibility, and don't be fooled by whatever morals he's spouting. Caesar saw him for what he was from the start, and it is because of that he fell this far. Paetus is no hero of the republic. This is all revenge for him, nothing more. I won't have him here.'

He turned back to Paetus. 'You have until I count to twenty to be out of my house. After that I will shout for my singulares and they will kill you. The law is on my side. You are an unwelcome interloper.'

Paetus faltered for a moment, and Balbus rounded on Fronto. 'He is not an interloper, Marcus. I invited him.'

'When you're in your own house, you can do as you like, Quintus,' Fronto spat, 'but while you're in mine, my rules stand. Get out of my house, Paetus.'

The thin man nodded his head. 'Very well.' As he made for the door, he gestured to Balbus. 'You know where to find me.'

'I'll bet he does,' Fronto snarled. 'Out.'

As Paetus stepped into the corridor, Masgava and Arcadios appeared, apparently drawn by the shouting. Fronto waved to them. 'Good timing. See him out. Quickly.'

Arcadios frowned. 'Fronto, you've got a visitor.'

'What?'

'Caesar is here.'

Fronto felt his heart lurch. Paetus and the general in the same building was an inferno waiting to happen. Of course, the general hadn't seen Paetus for some time, and probably wouldn't recognise him, but Fronto couldn't take the chance. And having the bastard in his house would look extremely bad.

'Take this prick and see him out through the gardens and the slave gate near the baths. Just get him off the premises.'

Masgava nodded and hustled Paetus away along the corridor. Left alone for just a moment with Balbus and Arcadios, Fronto turned to his father in law. 'This was a poor decision, Quintus.'

'You demeaned yourself there with your behaviour, Marcus. There was a time, not so long ago, when you were as opposed to Caesar as he is.'

'That was before I had my eyes opened to the alternatives.'

'The alternative is a return to the right and just republic, stripping this dictatorship away and stepping back to what made Rome great.'

Before Fronto could reply, they were interrupted by numerous footsteps. A slave appeared at a hurry, bowing as he ran, and behind him lictors appeared, falling into place along the walls before Caesar stepped in with a smile. Fronto forced his pulse to slow, calming himself. He bolted a welcoming smile onto his troubled face and noted with irritation that Balbus had not done so, his expression still angry and dark.

'Marcus,' the general smiled.

'Caesar. Perhaps we should head for my office?'

The general was looking past him, his eyes on Balbus. 'But ho, Marcus, I see an unexpected old friend. May we not remain here?'

Balbus nodded to the general and indicated the recently vacated seat with a sweep of his hand. His expression had not warmed, though. Caesar hadn't seemed to notice, as he waved away his various attendants and entered the room, sinking into that seat.

'This is unexpected,' Fronto noted, closing the door and sealing the three of them in, with just the slightest warning glance at his father in law. 'We have an appointment with the theatre this evening, and I thought our next meeting was planned for the Ides?'

Caesar nodded. 'I won't keep you that long, Marcus. Indeed, I am attending the same performance, I suspect. And this is no official meeting of my concilium. I am seeking advice individually. There are those among my familia whose strategic sense is less than impressive, and some of them are empty vessels rattling loud. I have a quandary, and I'm looking for the advice of a few of my more intuitive commanders. In fact, it is fortuitous to have found Quintus Lucilius Balbus here, for there are few men I trust more in tactical discussion. I am blessed with two valuable opinions for the price of one.'

Balbus' face finally lost a little of its edge, warming as the familiarity of the three of them insisted itself, years of such discussions ranging across the war in Gaul, overriding his current worries. The general took a breath.

'You will both be aware of the situation, I'm sure. I don't know how much detail you have, so I'll map it out for you. My attention is divided. I am in Rome for the summer, for the celebrations and a few administrative duties, and then I must move in the autumn to finish putting down insurrection, so that the republic can return to a semblance of peace.'

Fronto glanced at Balbus. The man's expression was troubled, and Fronto knew why. His father in law would despise listening to further advocating of civil war, but the notion of a settled republic was enticing, even to him.

'Where I previously faced only one last battle, now I face two,' Caesar sighed. 'Hispania has been under the command of the Pompey brothers and Labienus for months now, and is slowly becoming a fortress of resistance. I have little regard for the military talents of Pompey's sons, for they are not even a shadow of their father, but Labienus we all know. He was my second in Gaul, and there was no man whose strategy I trusted more. The longer I leave Hispania, the more work it will be to take it. I know what I face in Hispania. It will be a hard fight, and will require everything I can throw at it, but I know what we face and I know it can be done. And until Labienus and the Pompeys are vanquished, this war cannot end, and peace cannot be brought to the republic. I can't lay down the dictatorship until then.'

Fronto chewed his lip. 'Or Syria.'

'Quite. Syria is too important to ignore. Strong legions are based there. It is within striking distance of Aegyptus and the grain trade, and politically it influences every province from Cyrenaica to Greece. It appears that in the battle against my nephew, Quintus Caecilius Bassus was wounded, but has survived to take control of the province. As yet he has made no further move, simply consolidating his hold on the place. Syria is something of an unknown quantity. I have no idea what Bassus plans, and what we might face there. And herein lies my problem. I have two warzones to attend to. One critical but known, and the other completely unknown but with horrible potential. I am undecided as yet as to my preferred course of action.'

Balbus folded his arms and leaned back. 'Not everything needs to be resolved with steel and blood, Caesar. Syria need not be your fight. From my understanding, the trouble there arose through rumour of your demise in Africa. Now that that rumour can be seen for a falsehood, perhaps Syria can be settled in peace. Speak to the senate. Offer Bassus terms. Offer him the Syrian governorship. It may be that Bassus can be brought back into your fold.'

Caesar shook his head. 'Under other conditions, I would perhaps heed that advice, Quintus, but while I maintain clemency as my watchword wherever possible, Syria is personal. Sextus was my heir. He was my great nephew and in some ways a friend beyond mere blood ties. He was the most valuable of my nephews, the one who showed the most promise. Bassus had him killed. Bassus is not merely carrying on Pompey's legacy. That I could forgive. No, Bassus was targeting the Julii. He has stripped support away from me and then deliberately killed my direct heir. I will not offer him peace. The question is whether his threat is important enough to rise above Hispania or whether he can wait.'

Fronto straightened now. 'Can you not move on both? Send a deputy either east or west while you go the other way. Tackle both problems at once and be done with it all within the year.'

'The legions have been settled,' Caesar replied with a sigh. 'These wars have gone on too long and they are costly. The senate continues to agree with the taxes to cover the armies until the republic is safe, but they await the time the legions can be stood down and the taxes reduced once more. Labienus and the Pompeys have the silver and gold mines of Hispania, and they continue to raise legions rapidly. It will take every man we can spare to finish Hispania, and we cannot press the senate to pay for more legions. Similarly, Syria is close to Aegyptus. It already has strong veteran legions in residence, and if Bassus reaches out and takes Aegyptus while its queen is in Rome, he will have the gold to do the same as Labienus, fortifying the east. We have the manpower to take on only one. The question is which is more important.'

Fronto slouched back into his chair. 'Then it has to be Hispania. Syria is an unknown, and might be dangerous, but it could yet amount to nothing. Labienus is clever, though, and the Pompeys carry a name that will draw support. Plus your army has been twitching to finish the job they began in Africa.'

Caesar nodded slowly, then looked to Balbus. 'Quintus?'

Balbus shifted uneasily. Fronto knew how uncomfortable his father in law would be with all of this. Finally he rubbed his bald pate. 'I concur. I loathe this war, as you know, but if it must be fought, it should be finished as quickly and decisively as possible. Hispania has to be your target. Once your blood has cooled over the slight to your family, Syria might still be settled without war. Finish Pompey's legacy and be done with it, Caesar.'

The general closed his eyes for a moment. 'Antonius disagrees with you, favouring Syria, but Brutus thinks west. It seems that Hispania must be our first priority. There is still much to do in Rome, but I think two months more will be sufficient. In October we can move. It saddens me, Quintus, that you will not be with us.'

'It saddens me less, in truth, Caesar.'

The general gave a hollow laugh. 'Ever the voice of reason, eh Quintus? But when this is over, and the republic can settle, perhaps you and I can reacquaint ourselves a little.'

Balbus nodded, eyes narrow. 'In a settled republic, yes. A republic controlled by the senate and the praetors, where two consuls and a censor make our critical decisions, and no man rises above the governance of Rome.'

Caesar let out a laugh, then. 'You sound like a campaign slogan, Quintus.'

'And you sound like a king, Caesar.'

There was an uncomfortable silence. Finally, the general sighed. 'I do what I must to keep Rome safe, Quintus. I have taken nothing that was not offered. I am the senate's dictator, appointed to see us through the crisis.'

'I wonder if there would be a crisis, were you not dictator.' Balbus scratched his chin. 'I was your man upon a time, Caesar. And upon a time I saw in you a Scipio Africanus, and not a Sulla. That has changed, though I live in the hope that you will prove me wrong. One more year, Caesar. End this war and bring peace to the republic. And when this is over, you will lay down your extraordinary powers.'

Caesar fixed him with an unreadable look. 'You think I seek dictatorial powers for life? I was granted a ten year term to settle it all, but I tell you now, Balbus, that I pray it need not take that long.'

'I remain unconvinced,' Balbus said. 'But I hope to be proved wrong. When you return from Hispania and Syria is settled, if you are content to accept a last consulship and then retire from such power, I will adjust my opinions. You will have proved yourself a Scipio Africanus, not a Sulla, after all.'

Caesar smiled. 'In my triumph I will have a laurel held above me, but its bearer will be reminding me of my mortality and humility. Maybe my visit this morning has prepared me a little for that. Thank you both for your brief hospitality. Another day perhaps I may call upon you for a more sociable reason, and share a cup or two over old reminiscences. For now, I have work to do, and preparations to make. Perhaps I will see you at the theatre tonight.'

With that he rose, shaking Fronto's hand. There was an awkward moment when the general thrust out his hand and Balbus looked at it, unsure whether to shake. Finally, however, he did so, and smiled, albeit guardedly. With farewells exchanged, Fronto opened the door, and Arcadios, still standing in the corridor, escorted the general back to his entourage.

Once all had descended into silence, Fronto sagged and turned to his father in law. 'There are days when peace is more nerve-wracking than war.'

* * *

Fronto shuffled miserably under the weight. He hated togas. It was one of the reasons, a lesser one, admittedly, but one of the many reasons he had assiduously avoided a political career, shunning the usual cursus. It weighed the same as a small carthorse, certainly more than his armour ever did, it was itchy and coarse from lack of use, and the worst thing was that it was more balanced than fastened. Once it had been wound and draped, it would unbalance very easily. All it would take was a violent sneeze, and he'd be half-dressed again with several yards of heavy white wool lying in a pile at his feet. He'd have been happy to attend the theatre in a simple tunic, but the girls had been insistent.

The men were of senatorial rank and would wear a nice white toga, since the play was being attended by the cream of Rome's crop.

He smiled. If he thought he had it bad, he could only imagine how long it had taken Galronus to don the garment, even with plenty of help. Now, as the others gathered in the atrium, Fronto paced down to the door of Balbus' bedroom and tapped on it.

'We'll be late. Your daughter is about to start beating us if we don't move.'

The fact that this comment was greeted with only silence made the hair stand proud on the back of his neck. Something was wrong. Without preamble, he lifted the latch of Balbus' door and pushed. It was locked. Balbus had the ring-key for the door, and he was inside. What if he had collapsed? The old man had suffered three small heart problems since that day that had removed him from the military, and each time Fronto had worried that this would be the big one that finished his father in law off. He wasted no time. Stepping back, he ran at the door, shoulder forward. The door was only a light interior one, and it burst open in splinters in a heartbeat, Fronto staggering into the room, trying to stop. Even before the fuss kicked up in the atrium outside at the sound, Fronto stumbled to a halt and stared, taking it all in.

Balbus lay on the floor at the centre of the room. He was on his back, lying on the twisted folds of his toga. A jagged rent was evident in his chest, and the white of his tunic and the white of the toga were lost beneath a claret sea of blood, soaked into the wool.

Fronto gasped. His eyes focused on the body. The hands were clenched at the sides, and the face was tight, pained, eyes scrunched shut, jaw firm. He had died in extreme pain. Fronto's professional eye picked out the details. From the position of the tear in both material and flesh, the attacker's weapon had been thrust inexpertly into the chest, between the wrong ribs for an efficient kill. Indeed, amid the red-soaked tunic, Fronto could now see two more distinct tears from earlier blows. The attacker had been an amateur, perhaps desperate, panicked...

...and he had to still be in this room. Fronto was suddenly on guard again, eyes raking the shadowed corners. The door had been locked from the inside and the shutters were similarly latched. He heard a gasp behind him, and turned.

Lucilia stood in the doorway, her face white, eyes wide with horror. Galronus was there now, too, staring, and the others were coming along the corridor. Fronto fixed his gaze on his friend and pointed at his wife. 'Get her out of here.'

The Remi nobleman did not need to be told twice. In a flash he had grabbed Lucilia's shoulders and turned her, marching her away and telling the others to go back to the atrium. To prevent any of the children slipping past their elders and seeing the body, Fronto quickly shut the door, and then paced around the room. It took only moments to find the killer. A figure lay behind the bed on the floor in a pool of blood. Fronto reached down and turned it over. It was a slave, in a simple grey tunic and cheap sandals, a young man of perhaps fifteen. His hands were covered in blood that had splashed up as far as the elbows. By the time he had finished with Balbus, he had clearly learned where the heart was, for the kitchen knife, still in his grip, was jammed straight between his ribs in a quick suicide.

Hurrying back to the door, Fronto threw it open. He had been about to shout Masgava, but the man was already there, reaching for the door.

'The master?'

'Dead,' Fronto replied. '*Very* dead. A slave killed him then did for himself. Come in.'

Fronto led the Numidian around the bed and pointed down. Masgava tore his eyes from the body of Balbus and settled them on the killer.

'Who is he?' Fronto asked.

'I don't know.'

'You've been here for months with them. Is he one of the ones Balbus brought with him?'

Masgava shrugged, frowning. 'I don't know, Fronto. No one remembers a slave's face. He's wearing the same tunic all the slaves wear. That's all I can tell you.'

'Count the slaves,' Fronto said.

As the big man ran out, shutting the door behind him, Fronto began to work, moving the body to the bed and stripping the bloodied tunic in the process. Finding the old man's wash bowl on the table, he used a wet towel to wipe off the blood from his father in law's body, then found a second towel. This he placed over the man to prevent too much leakage. He found a dark blanket in the cupboard and drew it over all but the old man's face. He was no expert at this sort of thing, but sooner or later his wife was going to come back, and he needed the old man to look as peaceful as possible. He prodded and probed the face to try and make it look less pained, though even in grief and anger he had to admit that the look he'd finally achieved could only be described as 'constipated.' Finally, he gathered up the bloody toga and tunic and bundled them into a chest in the corner, using the bowl and more towels to clean the floor.

He was trying to decide what to do with the slave when Masgava reappeared, entering and shutting the door behind him. 'The house has fourteen slaves, all accounted for,' the Numidian announced.

Fronto huffed. 'Then this was not one of ours. This man was somehow sent here deliberately to kill Balbus.'

Masgava sighed. 'Sadly it would be all too easy to slip an extra slave into the house, perhaps on a return trip from the markets.'

'And unless someone complains of a missing slave in the morning, the chances of finding out where he came from are miniscule.'

The big Numidian clapped a hand on his shoulder. 'You need to console your wife. I'll take over here. I don't think we'll be going to the theatre after all. Besides, I can't see anyone being in the mood for tragedy tonight.'

CHAPTER FOUR

16th August 46 BC

Fronto straightened his cuirass, fretting at his scarf to get it in position, preventing the armour rubbing his neck as he rode. It felt odd to be decked out for war, but pristine clean and with no blade in the sheath at his side. They would be moving through the city's heart, though, and even on a day like today, no weapon of war was permitted to be carried within the boundary. Fronto had approached the general the morning after his visit, and had petitioned to be released from the triumph's personnel. After all, his father in law's murder was no small matter, and it would be some time before Lucilia felt able to even face the outside world. The general had been adamant. Fronto had to be here. A selfish little part of him had to admit that after days of protracted mourning and all the unpleasant organisation, of Lucilia sobbing and moping day and night, of the children wailing, and of having to hold everything together, it was something of a relief to be guaranteed half a day of family-free time.

The triumphal procession was long, stretching out both before and behind Fronto, who sat astride a freshly groomed Bucephalus at the head of Caesar's officers, the corps riding four abreast. To his right sat Brutus, to his left Hirtius and Antonius, all similarly attired. Galronus was directly behind him in the second row of officers. Slaves scurried around the whole procession, checking everything, making sure not a thing was out of place. The triumphal procession would depart any moment, and the general was determined that everything would be perfect, the whole thing going off without a hitch. As one of the college of pontiffs for the year, the general's great nephew Octavian had the responsibility for the preparation of all aspects of the triumph, and the young man, determined that nothing would go wrong, had employed a veritable army of high quality slaves to double and triple check everything.

Caesar stood in the four-horse chariot in front of them, motionless and somehow managing to look austere despite the gold and purple ritual toga and the brilliant red paint that covered his face and neck in time-honoured fashion. Everything had to be right this time, and Fronto knew damn well why.

The general had four triumphs lined up over several weeks, and this was the second of them. Originally, Caesar had planned to celebrate the triumphs in the order of the victories they represented, in Gaul almost a decade ago, then in Aegyptus two years earlier, then Asia, and then finally the last year's success in Africa. Octavian had been adamant that his great uncle was foolish in that respect, and that the last thing he should do was leave as a grand finale the people remembering the war that was mostly fought against other Romans. He needed to plan accordingly. Octavian's order made a great deal more sense. First would come Aegyptus, for certain sectors of Rome bristled with discontent over Cleopatra's presence and importance, and a reminder of the fact that it had been Rome that settled that ancient land and that Cleopatra was little more than a client queen of the republic would help soothe the people. Then would come Asia, for it was connected in ways with the Aegyptian war, and was the least well-known to the people. Then Africa, which would rely heavily on two hundred dark-skinned desert nomad slaves that Caesar had purchased slyly a week ago, to take the emphasis off the war being a civil one. And then finally, Caesar would celebrate Gaul, which was, of the four, the one victory the general could be content that the people would cheer and be thrilled over, and which, as the last of them, would be the one a generation of Romans would remember.

The first triumph had gone well enough, but there had been a certain grudging acceptance and somewhat muted cheers as the prisoners had slogged past in their chains. A hundred Aegyptians, including several officers, would have been well received, and the wagons bearing their arms and armour following would have drawn raucous cheers, but the problem was that the enemy leader, the elder Ptolemy, had died in the battle and his body never found, and some bright spark had come up with the notion of parading the second best captive at the front in pride of place. The second best captive had been Arsinoë, Cleopatra's younger sister, who had sided with Ptolemy and defied Rome. Unfortunately, she was both pretty, demure, very regal, and the sister of the general's infamous mistress. As such rather than eliciting the desired response from the crowd as the procession passed, Arsinoë in fact engendered a great deal of sympathy. Rome, it seemed, disliked watching the queen, once of a house allied to Rome, dragged through the streets in chains. After the triumph, Octavian had found the man whose brilliant idea it had been, and had him flogged within an inch of his life, vowing not to let anyone but he or the general make the decisions from then on.

Today was the celebration of the Pontic war in Asia. One hundred and thirty two Pontic slaves were chained together ahead of the chariot, but Octavian had been insistent that no similar mistake would be made today. They had four Pontic senior officers, in uniform so as to be recognised as such, chained together at the front, but pride of place had gone to Pharnaces. Of course, the king of Pontus had died on a different battlefield up on the coast of the Euxine Sea months after his loss to Caesar, and his body had been interred in his homeland, but Octavian was insistent that the mob of Rome couldn't tell one Pontic slave from another, and had no idea of the fate of foreign kings. Consequently, the young man had had one of the slaves made mute, just in case, and then had him attired as a glittering, gold-clad eastern king, then slapped the chains on him and thrust him out front. All the people would see was King Pharnaces, enemy of Rome, getting what was coming to him. Every other slave and attendant in the triumph who knew of the subterfuge was under no illusion what troubles awaited them if word of it leaked out.

And so today there would be a procession that the people could properly cheer, dissipating the spectre left by Arsinoë's display. Fronto sat quietly, trying to look dignified while surreptitiously scratching his crotch in the saddle. Four hours, it would take. There would be a whole day of festivities, but at least in four hours the procession itself would be over and the sacrifices performed. Then, Fronto could get out of both the saddle and the public eye.

A signal was given. The slaves left the column and scurried back into the various buildings of the villa publica, the structures themselves lost in the shadow of Pompey's great theatre. Slowly, the procession began to move. Fronto couldn't see that far ahead, but the lead element would be fake Pharnaces in his beaten gold crown and eastern silks, dragging the chains in misery and trying not to choke around the stubby remains of his severed tongue. Behind him would come the Pontic generals and then the swathes of military prisoners, all in chains. He heard a rumble from ahead as the wagons began to move, weighed down with the weapons, armour and standards of the defeated armies, as well as supposed treasure from the beaten king. In actual fact it was little more than an array of gold-plated dining ware and a number of coins scattered atop a load of sacks to give the impression of great depth. Then came a procession of exotic animals supposedly brought from Pontus, though in truth obtained from a merchant in Ostia a few days previously. A number of senior senators came next, all those who had been at the heart of Caesar's camp from the beginning, and were consequently deserving of a share in the glory.

Fronto could hear the animals moving now, and then behind the senators came Caesar's lictors, clad in their war robes of crimson, and at last Fronto could see the line moving. He braced as Caesar's quadriga began to move, the four horses stepping in perfect time, bred for this very purpose. Behind the general stood Salvius Cursor, the head of his praetorian bodyguards, holding the wreath of victory over Caesar's head. Fronto knew the law, and no man in this procession was immune from the prohibition on weapons of war. A picky man might, if he wanted to, argue that the kitchen knife sheathed at Cursor's side was a little long for a culinary tool, and rather contravened the rules, but Fronto also knew that Salvius Cursor took his duties very seriously.

Another heartbeat and the officers began to move, each concentrating on keeping his mount in position and moving at the same pace as the others, so as to maintain the form of the column. Twenty rows of horsemen, four abreast, formed of all the more senior officers who had taken part in the Pontic war. Behind the officers came the two white oxen for the sacrifice at the procession's end, and then finally the impeccably-dressed yet unarmed men of the Sixth Legion, the Thirty Sixth, and the soldiers inherited from Calvinus, with the cavalry bringing up the rear, a total of some fifteen thousand men. Fronto had learned from tedious experience at the last triumph that the sheer scale of the column meant that the officers and the general would be standing waiting at the temple on the Capitol for well over an hour while the column of soldiers arrived and fell into ranks, singing their usually crude and ribald songs.

Slowly, the column left the villa publica, Octavian watching them go with his attendants and staff, and passed from the shadow of the great theatre out among the neat grass and tended hedges of the Campus Martius. Fronto could hear the change in tone, even over the cheerful singing of the legions behind, as the slaves, carts, animals and men ahead passed from the springy turf of the campus into the paved area before the ancient and crumbling walls. The Porta Carmentaria which, on days like this, also went by the name of the Porta Triumphalis, marked the edge of the city proper, and the column slowed to a crawl as the masses filtered through the chicane of the gate into Rome. Here was where the celebrations really started, for the journey across the campus was little more than preparation. At the gate, as Fronto had expected, they began to pass the crowds and the roadside stalls. Everything from food vendors taking advantage of a lucrative event to the strange souvenir stands that seemed to spring up at times like this, full of busts of the general, commemorative medallions, statues of Venus as the origin of the Julii, and even childrens' wooden toys in the form of collections of Roman legionaries and Pontic villains.

And around the stalls the crowd surged, roaring their delight. The populace may have been unimpressed with the parading of the unfortunate Aegyptian princess, but this defeated and chained golden king of the east and his hardened generals in fetters was another matter entirely. The crowd howled and cheered, throwing rotten fruit saved for this very purpose at the dejected enemies of Rome. Fronto, even mourning his recent loss and faced with the tedium of the long procession and the interminable wait at the end, found it hard not to smile at the sheer exuberance of it all.

There were ominous creaks from the general's chariot as he managed with no small skill to pass beneath the central arch of the gate with a four-horse vehicle, but then he was through, and the officers filtered in after him, dropping down to two abreast for ease, and then widening once more on the far side. Moving into the

Velabrum region, they were tantalisingly close to the Capitol and their destination now, though Fronto was wearily aware of the fact that there was a long way to go yet. Turning away from the Capitol, they moved towards the great circus at the southern edge of the Palatine, the next step of a snaking route that would carry them through many streets and past as many of the citizens of Rome as possible. Octavian had planned a different route once inside the gate for all four triumphs, in order to allow the maximum exposure possible to the city. Today's would cover much of the Caelian and Oppian hills before returning to the forum and arriving at the Capitol.

Barely had Fronto left the shadow of the arch when disaster struck. As one of the riders closest to the general, he saw it unfold in moments, though he was unable to do anything in time. As the general turned his chariot across the wide square inside the gate, turning his back on the Capitol and the temple of Fortuna, there was a loud crack from the vehicle. It happened in no more than a heartbeat, but for Fronto, watching in shock, it seemed to last for hours. The axle beneath the general's chariot snapped. As the great beam struck the street and bounced, the wheel attached to the longer section broke and tipped to a strange angle. The axle became wedged in the deep groove between two paving slabs and the entire vehicle halted instantly, though the momentum of the horses yanked the traces forward and tore the whole front of the chariot apart. Salvius Cursor, only holding onto the side of the chariot for balance as his other hand held the wreath above Caesar, slammed forward and to his knees, smashing his head against the inside of the chariot. The general was less lucky.

Standing at the front of the vehicle, he was not holding on, using one hand to wave indulgently to the populace while the other held the reins. As the chariot jerked to a halt he lurched forward, and the horses, still moving on, pulled the reins taut and yanked the general over the front of the chariot into the wreckage of the yoke. Fronto kicked his horse in an instant, leaping out to one side and forward, rudely shoving Brutus out of the way as he tried to get round the crippled vehicle. He had a heart-stopping picture for just a moment of the general, still gripping the reins, being dragged along the ground between the legs of the now panicked horses. Just a single stray hoof from a horrible demise, the general bounced and rolled, but somehow, before Fronto could get to him to help, Caesar managed to save himself. Letting go of the leather strap, he timed it perfectly and rolled between two stamping legs out to the side, continuing to roll until he was several feet from the chariot.

Now, Salvius Cursor was standing once more, jumping from the stricken vehicle, blood pouring from his nose. He ran to the general's side and helped Caesar up. The general looked shaken, dazed even, for a few moments, and then straightened, squared his shoulders, and gave an odd smile.

'Hundreds of miles from Pontus, and Pharnaces is still trying to kill me,' he announced, granting the crowd a grin and a wink. The people of Rome, who had been shocked from their cheering into a sudden, distraught silence, suddenly erupted into joy once more, cheering the general and bellowing his name. Someone cited that Fortuna herself must have been looking out for the general from her temple across the road.

Fronto dismounted, as did Hirtius and Antonius. As Caesar dusted down his toga and Salvius Cursor helped him array it properly once more, the general continued to make light of the situation and joke with the crowd, much to their delight.

'See that?' Marcus Antonius said, crouching and pointing into the wreckage beneath the chariot.

'What?'

'The break in the axle?'

'Yes. Saw it happen, in fact.'

'That's no accident,' Antonius said, still pointing. 'When a piece of good hard wood like that breaks, it's jagged, all splinters and torn timber. This one's almost neat. At least half the break is a straight line. That axle was sawn half through before it left the villa publica. It was almost guaranteed to break once we left the soft grass and started to bounce across the flagged streets of the city.'

'Someone cut through the axle?' Hirtius blinked.

'I'd say so. These things are a death-trap at the best of times. I had a cousin who died when one tipped over and his neck broke. To have one with a weak axle is asking for trouble. Whoever did this must have wanted to hurt Caesar.'

Fronto frowned, but before he could say any more, Salvius Cursor had crossed to them. 'There are spare chariots at the villa publica. Get back there fast and have them harness four new horses. Get the replacement chariot brought here as fast as you can and have some slaves come to take the frightened horses away and clear up the wreckage.'

Fronto tried not to be irked that he seemed to be receiving commands from someone rather junior to him. The man was correct. This needed to be put right very quickly. The general was a master of self-promotion, and, while this had the makings of rumoured bad omens, Caesar could still turn it to his advantage for certain, as long as the procession could be continued with as little interruption as possible.

In a trice, Fronto and the others were back in the saddle and racing across the square, Galronus kicking his horse into speed to join them, hurtling through the arch to the fascinated murmur of the crowd, and off into the Campus Martius, making for the villa publica. The turf churned beneath their hooves as they hurried. Every moment the parade was delayed would add to rumours that would swirl around Rome for months to come, and the faster Caesar could be back, seen in full glory by the plebs, the better the result for everyone.

As they reached the villa publica, a collection of almost a dozen buildings within a low compound wall which served as the city's extra-mural census base, embassy, staging point for military recruitment and, of course, base for all triumphant generals, already the staff were hurrying out with interest at the drumming of approaching hooves. By the time the four riders, some of Rome's most important men, reined in outside, two dozen slaves were in attendance, along with half a dozen free administrators, and as Fronto slid from his saddle, Octavian too appeared.

'What's happened?' the young man asked, voice taut, likely because the responsibility for this triumph being a success rested squarely on his shoulders.

'Chariot broke outside the temple of Fortuna,' Brutus told him in short order, while Antonius pointed at one of the administrators.

'Have a second quadriga fitted out and put four horses in the traces as fast as you can. I want a replacement chariot under Caesar's boots before he can say Saguntum.'

'And send your best men to the temple to clear away the wreckage while the replacement is fitted,' Brutus added.

The administrators hurried inside, and Brutus went with them to chivvy things along as fast as he could. Octavian had gone pale at the news, and he and Marcus Antonius moved aside so that Antonius could give him more detail. Fronto, frowning, waved at the young man. 'Where was this chariot made ready?'

Octavian pointed at the building into which Brutus had run. 'There are eight carceres in there, each with its chariot. Caesar's one came from the third stall, I think.'

Fronto nodded and beckoned to Galronus. 'Come with me.'

As they ran inside, through the great arched gate and along one of the wide, basic corridors, the Remi nobleman grabbed at him. 'What are we doing? Shouldn't we be getting back?'

'There's plenty of men in armour riding around and looking important today. Someone cut through that axle, and if there's any evidence, I reckon it'll be in the stall the chariot was prepared in.'

Understanding, Galronus pounded along at his side and they turned a corner, passed through another large gate and found the chariot stable block across a courtyard. Eight large doors faced them, a numeral above each, and the pair hurtled across the open to the one marked with a III. Pulling the door wide, Fronto ran inside. The stall was a single large room with subdivisions created by low, shoulder height walls with half-doors in them. The main space was clearly where the chariot rested from the oil stains on the ground. Two of the low doors led off each side into other ante-rooms. Fronto gestured to Galronus and pointed right, as he moved about the room making sure that the main space was as empty as it looked. Apart from various pieces of replacement equipment hanging on the back wall, the place was perfectly clean. Fronto frowned. *Too* clean. No member of the public was going to come in here, so why was the floor so recently swept?

As Galronus ripped open the first door on the right and began to search inside, Fronto scoured the back wall until he found the broom, then pulled it from its rack and examined it. It was covered in dust, the odd bent piece of straw, animal hair and, finally, the confirmation he needed, tiny fragments of sawdust. Galronus emerged from the first room, grumbling and shaking his head, and went into the next.

Fronto looked at the wall again, replacing the broom. It did not take him long to find the tools, and it came as no surprise when in the midst, a nail in the wall hung empty, its usual burden absent.

'This is the one,' Fronto shouted into the other room, where his friend searched. 'Someone in this room sawed halfway through the axle. They were thorough enough to sweep up the sawdust afterwards, but there are signs of it on the broom, and the saw is missing.'

'Not any more,' Galronus replied, stepping back out of the second room on the right, his expression dark.

'What is it.'

'I was going to say you're not going to like this, Marcus, but on second thoughts, you actually might.'

As the man disappeared inside once more, Fronto followed, ducking into the small anteroom, frowning as his gaze played around, searching for...

He straightened in shock and with a whispered curse.

In the corner of the room, a body lay in a pool of blood. For a horrible moment, Fronto was right back in the bedroom of his townhouse, looking at the bloody corpse of his father in law. He would lose less sleep over this body, but still, it brought everything flooding back, especially since that same night had been the last time he'd seen *this* man. Aulus Caecina Paetus, once camp prefect for Caesar in Gaul, and now for many years a shadowy figure plotting the general's downfall, lay on his back, sightless eyes staring at the ceiling. The man was as pale as alabaster, his blood run out swiftly thanks to the chisel wedged in his neck. A pile of empty sacks had soaked up much of the crimson flood, but not enough to prevent Fronto and Galronus having to step through it to approach the body.

'He was surprised,' Fronto said. 'The angle of the chisel and the position of the grip. Someone jumped him. But they were using the chisel not the saw.'

The saw lay nearby, half submerged in the pool of red.

'This is getting serious,' Galronus murmured. 'Is death catching? I think you might be a carrier.'

Fronto glared at him. 'So what was this? Paetus found someone messing with the general's chariot and they fought? But Paetus is unarmed, unless the killer took the blade with him. And it looks like Paetus was jumped, so it seems unlikely.'

'Paetus broke the chariot,' Galronus said in a matter-of-fact voice.

'It seems the inescapable conclusion. Paetus has wanted Caesar dead for years. The only time he was ever going to get to him was in Rome, and most of the time the general's surrounded by lictors, officers, senators and the like. Something like this was the only way he could do it. So what have we got here then?'

'Paetus saws half way through the chariot axle and prays that it will be enough to give Caesar a messy end. Nicely public, too. No stab in the dark.'

Fronto nodded. 'But then who kills Paetus?'

With a frown Galronus nodded. 'If someone caught him doing it, why wouldn't they raise an alarm? Why let it happen?'

Fronto crouched, his boots making sticky noises in the thick blood. He held a palm over the pool, close to the ground, sensing the heat still in the liquid, then put it on Paetus' white forehead and felt the same.

'They didn't catch him doing it. They caught him here afterward. He's only been dead for a very short time. We were probably heading into the arch across the campus when it happened, I reckon. So someone finds Paetus here, maybe works out with the saw what he's done? Or maybe he just recognises Paetus anyway?'

'Maybe he even followed him here?' suggested Galronus.

A nod. 'And he jumps the man and kills him. Leaves the body to be found and disappears.'

'He might be findable. A neck wound creates a spray. Lots of blood. Might have caught some of it on his clothing.'

Fronto shrugged. 'Probably not if he did that from behind. Besides, this place was chaos this morning, and it still is now. Slaves and servants everywhere. A killer could very easily get lost in this place, especially with fifteen thousand soldiers massed around the place waiting. And I didn't spot a lot of security around the perimeter, did you? Whoever it was could probably easily slip in and back out.'

'Then there's not much chance of finding him.'

'First Balbus, then Paetus. That's the start of a pattern.'

'Don't forget the chariot. Caesar.'

'I don't think that's part of it. Balbus has been a vocal opponent of Caesar's dictatorship, and Paetus has been out for the general for the past decade. Someone is protecting Caesar, quietly removing his opponents.'

'I don't know about quietly.'

'And whoever it is,' Fronto continued, 'is clever. They used a slave to get to Balbus, and the slave killed himself before he could get caught.'

'I didn't understand that,' Galronus admitted. 'Even a slave surely wouldn't volunteer to kill himself.'

'There are ways of applying pressure. Slaves often have families in the same household. If he had the choice of doing what he did or his daughter or wife being killed, for instance...'

Galronus nodded. 'So someone wealthy enough to have families of slaves, who supports Caesar strongly enough to contemplate murder.'

'I don't think this was a slave's work,' Fronto said. 'Not this time.'

'Oh?'

'A slave wouldn't have the skill and training to jump an ex-soldier and stab him in the neck from behind. One blow and an instant kill.'

'Unless he was a gladiator. Masgava could do it, and he was a slave.'

Fronto nodded slowly. 'Maybe. Come on.'

He rose and padded from the room, leaving sticky red footprints that faded as he returned through the chariot stable, along the corridor, across the courtyard and out to where a new chariot was receiving the final touches before being sent off to the general. Antonius and Brutus were both overseeing it, while Octavian directed the slaves. They rushed over to the young man.

'What security do you have on this place?'

Octavian frowned. 'There are guards of Caesar's own choosing on the gate in the perimeter wall, but the column gathered outside. Not enough room for twenty thousand men and a menagerie of animals in the compound, so people were in an out all morning. Hard to be overly secure.'

'Have they been stopping people who clearly shouldn't be here?'

'Who knows,' Octavian shrugged. 'It's been chaos here since before dawn.'

'I thought you were in charge.'

Octavian gave him a level look. 'My priority was getting the procession out on time and in perfect order. The fact that even that failed is galling enough without you bothering me over my great uncle's guards.'

'Why are you asking about guards?' Brutus asked, swatting away a panicked slave and turning to Fronto.

'We just found Paetus dead. He seems to have been responsible for the "accident."'

'What's a Paetus?' Octavian asked, looking back and forth between the pair.

'Former soldier with a grudge against Caesar.'

Antonius snorted. 'After three years of civil war, there's no shortage of such men.'

'A dead end, I suspect,' Fronto sighed. 'The guards will be able to tell us nothing. If it was a gladiator bought for the job, he could easily slip in and out along with all the other slaves. The mind behind this is sharp. He chooses his times and places well.'

'So who's next?' Galronus asked.

Now both Brutus and Antonius turned to them. 'What?'

'Balbus and Paetus,' Fronto replied. 'Both men opposed to Caesar. Both dead a few days apart. Who's next?'

'Again, you're not short of choices,' Antonius noted. 'The most vocal opponent now, I reckon, is Cassius. He's been getting ever closer to Cicero, who's another potential target. The two of them have spent the past few months endlessly spouting republican slogans and calling for Caesar's dictatorship to be curtailed from ten years to one.'

Fronto nodded. He remembered Cassius in Aegyptus. 'Slightly higher profile than Balbus or Paetus, but I think we need to warn them to be on their guard. Things are starting to get dangerous here. In a way, I'm looking forward to going to Hispania. A blatant enemy in front of you is a lot easier to deal with.'

CHAPTER FIVE

28th August 46 BC

'What about funeral games for my father?' Lucilia snapped angrily. 'Why was *he* less important?'

Fronto took a deep breath. 'It's not like that, Lucilia. Your father was seen off in a good, traditional ceremony. Understated and noble, and with anyone he ever really cared about in attendance. That's precisely what he would have wanted.'

The funeral, just a few days ago, had been costly and quite lavish, in truth, yet it looked positively Spartan compared with what was to come. Balbus had been laid out in the house for visitors, then cremated and interred with the family in their vault close to the second mile marker on the Via Flaminia. Fronto had hoped Lucilia would perk up with the closure that would bring, and she might have done had it not been for the overshadowing of a much more important funeral.

That Caesar had stepped back from the preparations to pay his respect for Balbus had impressed Fronto, given the rift between the pair, but it had done little to console Lucilia. And then Caesar's great funeral games began. Like his delayed triumphs, held back until there had been sufficient time and opportunity, so too had the general held off any real acknowledgement of the passing of his daughter: Julia, wife of Pompey. To have held such celebrations while being currently at war with her husband would have been hypocritical to say the least. Now, however, things were different. Caesar had given Pompey every honour he could in death, for they had once been friends and relations, and the loss of the great general had been dimmed with the passage of years. Now, then, while Caesar was in Rome for the summer, and while there were already great triumphs every week or so, the general had organised the funeral games for his only daughter.

The games had begun in grand style with naumachia, a sea combat performed in a great circular basin that had been dug out for that very purpose on the far bank of the Tiber. The city had seethed with excitement, still awaiting, as they were, the final of Caesar's triumphs. Following that there were gladiator fights in the Circus Flaminius, chariot races, and a series of plays.

In some ways, it was heart breaking for Lucilia that her father's passing be so overshadowed by Caesar's daughter, but Fronto had slowly tried to reason with her. Her father had died a few days ago. Julia had been gone for years. Balbus was her father, but Julia was Caesar's daughter. It must have hurt, he reasoned, for Caesar to have spent so many years with that door of grief still open. And despite all that, Caesar had come to pay his respects to his old friend. Fronto had thought his reasoning had laid matters to rest. Until this morning, while Caesar's last triumph was carried out, and once again Lucilia became more than a touch bitter.

'Your father wouldn't have wanted funeral games, Lucilia. And if he had they would have been low-key and personal. Two men fighting over his urn. But I don't think he'd even want that. Balbus was sick of fighting. Gods, my love, but we're *all* sick of fighting.'

As she slumped into dismal silence, he left it, content that he'd be ready for her next wave of grief in the evening. He watched it all, trying to ignore the shriek and thud of sacrificed animals as the general made his final offering of the triumph. Fronto's eyes instead played across the gathered masses. Vercingetorix, once chief of the Arverni, perhaps even king of the Gauls before it all went wrong, languished in chains at the head of the triumphal column, bruised, bleeding, and covered in shit and rotten food. Rome never forgot that Gauls had raided her sacred places centuries ago, and Vercingetorix was the symbol now of everything they both feared and despised. Fronto could only see the 'what-if', instead. A man who was almost king of a united Gaul. Had the man been a few years sooner in his uniting of the tribes, Caesar would have lost within the first season. That was Fronto's opinion. Still, if there had been any way for the two to meet in peace, what might have happened with Gaul and Rome as close allies? Certainly many thousands of Romans, and *millions* of Gauls if the estimates were true, would still be alive. Oddly, even after six years in a dank room the size of a latrine, covered in shit and mess, chained and cowed, still Vercingetorix radiated power and a certain regal honour. If Rome had had kings like that, maybe the republic would never have happened.

A figure moved in the crowd near the prisoner and for just a moment, as Fronto tried to spot it once more in the mass, he thought it had been the Gaul Cavarinos, another man from among their enemy that Fronto found it hard to see as anything but a friend. Though the figure was gone in an instant, a small smile crept over Fronto. It had been Cavarinos. He was sure. The slick bastard was still alive, out there, somewhere.

His attention was drawn back to the Capitol as Caesar completed his sacrifices. The general had ascended Rome's most important peak with only his close attendants, allowing space for the sacred rites that closed the triumphal ceremonies and marked the beginning of an afternoon and an evening of games and entertainments at the great man's expense. Only his lictors and those senators forming part of the parade had climbed with him, and stood in attendance before the great temple of Jupiter. Octavian, of course, as one of the college of priests, was there already, awaiting him. It was a credit to the young man's organisational skills that he managed on each occasion to get the procession off and away from the villa publica, and then moved across to the Capitol while the triumph was in progress in order to await the general at the temple.

Down below, looking up at him, the commanders and men of the procession's legions stood in their ranks on the southern side of the forum, awaiting the expected announcements, and eagerly anticipating the amusements to follow. The masses of Rome filled every open space, all across the northern side of the forum, up the steps and among the colonnades of every temple, the viewpoints from the corner of the Palatine hill, and every street nearby that offered even a partial view of the Capitol. Only a short space separated legions and crowds.

Four triumphs completed. The general's principle reason for returning to Rome before continuing the campaign, or at least, that and Cleopatra. Fronto found himself wondering what the general's home life was like this summer, between great events, with Calpurnia and Cleopatra in the same house. He winced. In truth his own home life was tense enough this summer, walking on eggshells around his grieving family. The general had insisted that Fronto join his cavalcade on each of the four triumphs, and by the last, though it had been the one with the most meaning for Fronto, Lucilia had been equally insistent that if she were to plaster some visage of excitement over her features and attend the ceremonies, then Fronto had to be at her side. He'd tried to get out of it all, on all counts, but both general and wife had refused to budge. In the end, he'd done the only thing he could, compromising subtly. He had ridden with the officers to the very end of the procession, but as Caesar had climbed the steps to the temple, all eyes on him, Fronto had quietly dismounted, handing his reins to Galronus, and hurried across to where Lucilia and Faleria stood, falling in beside his relieved spouse.

'When this is over, you'll go and fight for him again.'

Not a question, and a subject Fronto had been dreading coming up.

'It is my duty. But it's almost over, Lucilia.'

'It's always almost over. Every year. You've missed the boys growing up chasing after that man.'

'I promise you, Lucilia. I'll place my hand on the altar of Apollo as I promise, if you like. One more season. Hispania will end it. Syria is troublesome, but it can be resolved politically. I need to see the end of Labienus and the Pompeys. But that'll be over by next summer. In fact, I hope to be back by the Dies Natalis festival in April. And then I will finally lay down my sword.'

'And what if Hispania ends *you* as well? You're not an energetic teenager any more, Marcus.'

'Believe me, I'm becoming more and more aware of that. I think I ruptured something getting off my horse. I think one of my balls is somewhere up near my armpit now.'

The glare she gave him suggested his humour had somewhat missed the mark.

'Shh,' hissed someone behind them.

'I promise to come back safely by summer, and that this will be the last campaign. When I get back, we'll get out of the city for the summer and head down to the coast at Puteoli, eh? I give you my word I'll be back. You know I keep my word.'

Lucilia nodded, saying nothing, as the crowd burst into cheers around them. Fronto looked up at the hill. Caesar had cleaned his hands in the ritual bowl, Octavian's servants clearing away the remains of the sacrifice as the young man stood, silent and serene by his great uncle's side. The general was raising his hands now to quieten the crowd. There was a positive buzz among the soldiers, in anticipation of what was to come next. Fourteen years of warfare, and many of the soldiers present had seen most of those campaigns. They had been paid, and they had received shares of loot, but the great bonuses Caesar had continually offered them had yet to appear. That fact had caused a number of troubles, and even the odd mutiny, for while the wars were ongoing, Caesar had neither the time nor the resources to satisfy the army. This was no longer the case. Though the general had made no promises openly since their return to Rome, he had spent much of the past month working with the treasury, and there was an expectation of generosity now. Here, at the end of the triumphs, if Caesar was going to make good on years of promises, now was the time.

The general waited, arms raised, for the crowd to subside, and finally cleared his throat. When he spoke, it was with the deep and strong voice of an orator. It was a good distance from the temple front on the top of the Capitol down to the men in the forum, but somehow the general's words echoed out into the silence across the waiting ranks, carefully placed men repeating the speech back to those too far away to hear clearly.

'Half a lifetime of service all across the world,' Caesar said. 'More than a decade of conquest and victory concludes here, in this hallowed place, on this feted day.'

A cheer arose, and the general had to wait, hands still raised, for it to die away once more.

'The legions of Rome have a right to feel unparalleled pride in their achievement. In *our* achievement.'

Another surge of noise, and another pause.

'In that time we have added our most ancient enemy to the republic as a new and lucrative province. The peoples of Gaul, who had once sacked our city, now stand behind the eagle of Rome.'

Another cheer.

'The unsettled and troubled land of Aegyptus, which has long gifted Rome with gold and grain, but which fell into strife and civil war, is calm once more, and those commodities flow into Rome from that ancient ally.'

The general paused for noise once more.

'And the great enemies of Rome, who took up arms against the senate, Pompey and Scipio, Cato and Domitius, have been defeated and the fractured lands brought back into the arms of Rome. Only one small faction remains, and they cower now, for the republic is whole once more, and strong, and they know their time is come.'

This brought a smaller cheer, but still Caesar paused, then continued.

'You have been loyal through good times and bad, serving the republic with honour and strength, and such devotion is deserving of reward.'

Now, the cheer could have stripped the roofs off buildings, so strong was it.

'I hereby pledge to every living soldier in the armies of the republic, whether they actively serve this season or have been settled in retirement after serving their time in these wars, the sum of five thousand denarii.'

There was a moment then of absolute silence. Fronto stared at the general. *Five thousand?* Where was such a sum to come from? How could Caesar have possibly amassed enough to cover such a fortune? Five thousand denarii represented more than any legionary could hope to earn in a lifetime. The stunned shock among the soldiers lasted for only moments before the cheering began, and this time it lasted so long that Caesar had to lower his aching arms. Finally, as the wave of noise subsided, the general gave the army a benevolent smile.

'For the centurions, who made all of this possible, whose bravery knows no bounds, for they are ever at the front of an attack, trampling the enemies of Rome and giving heart to their men, I decree the sum of ten thousand denarii.'

This cheer was smaller, but just as heartfelt, for the centurions were fewer in number. Fronto shook his head. There were limits to largesse. This was ridiculous.

'And to the tribunes and prefects who helped strategise a decade of wars, who held undefendable positions against powerful enemies with their men, who served with me, and who risked all for Rome, I vow the sum of twenty thousand denarii.'

The roar was astonishing. The money Caesar had just vowed would happily purchase a kingdom somewhere. The sum was simply staggering. The legionaries were no longer standing in neat lines, but had become a seething mass, cheering and pushing each other around, arms in the air. Yet it appeared that Caesar was not done. As the crowd realised this and slowly quietened once more, Caesar turned, away from the soldiers, to the great mob of Rome. Fronto frowned. The general had covered his donatives, crazy though they were, for all the officers and men who had served him. What was he up to now?

'For the people of Rome, too, I have gifts.'

There was an odd silence now, and Fronto could feel the strange dissonance. The silence arising from the people of the great city was surprised, expectant, hopeful. That from the gathered soldiers carried a strange resentment. Fronto winced. The general was going to woo the people to his cause, but in doing so, he might slightly estrange the army he had so exalted just now.

'To every man of Rome, be he high-born or low, I give one hundred denarii, to be accompanied by a double public ration of wheat and of oil for the period of three months.'

Fronto felt the tension rise to breaking point.

The crowd exploded with cheers and whistles. The mob of Rome was to be enriched by the general, and they would leap through flaming hoops for Caesar at that moment, which, of course, had been the point. But Fronto's eyes were not on the exultant populace. They slid across to the soldiers.

'Why?'

It was just one voice from somewhere in the middle of the crowd of soldiers, and yet Fronto was not the only one to hear it. Others around him focused on that collection of uniformed men, and Caesar, atop the hill, turned too.

'Why them?' the soldier demanded again, just one face in the crowd. 'Your legions shed blood across deserts and swamps for you. We earned our bonus, time and again. We waited patiently when it didn't come, and still we shed our blood. Why these people, though? How have the mob of Rome served you with their life to deserve a share?'

Caesar frowned. He'd clearly not been expecting something like this. Fronto found himself willing the general to do something, and quickly, before this got out of hand.

'That's *our* money,' called another voice, close to the first, and Fronto clenched his teeth. There was a twang to the voice that suggested perhaps the owner had been partaking of badly-watered wine before today's procession. Of course, half the soldiers here had been in their cups for much of the week. 'We *earned* that gold,' the man snapped, 'with our blood. And you give it to the people who sat home in peace, eating their free bread and playing games while we fought?'

'That's enough,' bellowed a centurion nearby, clearly thinking on his feet and seeing the potential trouble unfolding.

'Oh I'm sure it is for you, mister twenty thousand denarii,' snarled a slurred soldier.

'You're on a charge, that man. Report to me when this is over.'

'Piss off.'

Fronto watched in horror as the centurion turned and began to wade through his men, vine stick raised to chastise the foolish soldier. Taking his eyes from the centurion, he looked up to Caesar, but the general was silent and wide eyed, staring down in shock at what was happening. Fronto turned back in time to see the centurion disappear under a mob of angry soldiers with a cry.

Small scuffles were now breaking out among the soldiers. Finally, the general was addressing them, saying something with a flat and dangerous expression, but no one could hear him. The Roman mob's voice had risen in a wave of anger at the soldiers, while the army was roaring as men battered one another in the press. Fronto tensed. They were a single blow from disaster. Currently the citizens of Rome were shouting their derision, while the soldiers fought among themselves, a few angry idiots rising in violence while the majority tried to control the few. All it would take was one blow struck between the army and the people, and all that would change in an instant. Caesar would have a full-scale riot on his hands.

Fronto looked round. Masgava, Aurelius and Arcadios had moved forward, protectively, gathered behind Fronto and the two ladies. He waved to them. 'Get them out of here. Somewhere safe. Home, for preference.'

For just a moment, Lucilia looked as though she might argue, but her eyes slid past Fronto to the unfolding disaster, and she nodded. 'Stay safe and come home soon,' she said, then turned and left in the protective huddle of the three warriors. Watching his wife and sister leave, Fronto took a deep breath and then turned back. Galronus had extricated himself from the army now and was cantering across to him, leading Bucephalus.

'To the general or away?' the Remi asked.

Fronto was about to reply when a new voice cut across the din, and his eyes slid past Galronus to the speaker. The Remi noble turned to follow his friend's gaze. A man in a clean white toga, one of the senators who had been part of the procession, had descended from the Capitol and stood on the rostrum at head height, where he was addressing the shoving and arguing soldiers.

'…the army of Rome, but remember the Mos Maiorum. If you cannot comport yourself with dignity and pride, then you are less than that, and less even than those civilians you chide. Be ashamed, soldiers of Rome. Have shame for your deeds.'

He continued to harangue the men, and Fronto could see a fresh disaster in the offing now. The anger the soldiers had been showing one another was gradually turning on the white toga'd speaker. Fronto peered, squinting, and realised that he recognised the man even now thrusting out accusing fingers at the legionaries.

'Ah, shit.'

'What?' Galronus frowned. 'Who is it?'

'That's Lucius Pinarius. One of Caesar's great nephews. He thinks he's doing his great uncle a favour, but if they touch him, this'll get a lot worse really quickly.'

'Come on, then,' Galronus said, turning his horse. Fronto pulled himself up onto Bucephalus and joined his friend as the pair raced away from the mass of citizens and towards the rostrum, where Pinarius continued to shout haughtily and more and more soldiers were turning his way.

'We're not going to get to him,' Galronus said, and Fronto could see the truth in that. There was no way they would reach Pinarius from here without riding down the soldiers between them.

'Distraction,' Fronto said.

'What?'

'This all started with the two noisy bastards over there,' Fronto replied, pointing ahead.

He could see the two men who had voiced their anger over the gifts Caesar had offered. Like most rabble rousers, now that they had set this trouble in motion, the two had prudently stepped back out of the way of the danger they had caused. The majority of the soldiers present were still trying to contain their more troublesome friends, and a full-scale riot could still be avoided by the application of common sense. But just as one thrown missile between soldier and civilian would change it all, so would a single blow landing on Caesar's great nephew. The only thing they could do was distract the army long enough for someone sensible to pull Pinarius away from danger, and an example might just help bring things back into order.

Galronus nodded, and the two men approached the press, slowing. Fronto spotted a centurion and leaned close as they neared. 'May I borrow your vitis?'

The centurion looked doubtful for a moment. His vine stick was the symbol of his authority, but as he struggled, his innate sense of duty won out, facing a senior officer. He bowed his head and held the item up. Fronto grabbed the stick. No one here was armed, but the centurions' vitis was a symbol, not a weapon of war, so they were all in evidence.

Armed now, Fronto started to push his way through the ranks, men panicking and shoving their way out of the path of the horse and its important rider. Somewhere in the path through the army, Galronus had similarly acquired a vitis, and as they neared those two soldiers, who were now on the steps of a temple, watching with a certain wary satisfaction, Fronto glanced back to make sure Pinarius was still intact. Caesar's nephew had staggered back across the podium, now attired in a rich tunic, for his toga had been pulled away in the crowd. Salvius Cursor was hurrying down to reach Pinarius with two of his praetorians, that not-weapon-of-war huge kitchen knife in his hand. Pinarius would probably be alright now, as long as he didn't do anything stupid.

Heaving his way out of the far side of the press of soldiers, Fronto fixed his gaze on the man who had very vocally claimed his right to all the money Caesar had offered the plebs, while Galronus made for his mouthy companion. Finally, the two men, drawing their attention from the swarming soldiers at the rostrum, noticed the riders coming for them, eyes widening, realisation dawning, and turned. They ran.

One raced around one side of the temple, his friend the other. The two riders veered off in pursuit, and Fronto lost sight of Galronus then. The panicked legionary before him was doomed. He was running, but there was nowhere to go where his pursuer could not catch him. Leaning out in the saddle, Fronto pulled alongside the running soldier and swiped with the vitis stick. The vine wood was extremely hard and unyielding, polished to a club-like state over years by its owner. The soldier caught Fronto's blow on the back of his helmet, a strike that sounded like a bell in the open air.

The man went down like a sack of grain, tumbling to a heap on the ground, and Fronto reined in Bucephalus a few paces further on, then turned and walked the horse back to the fallen rioter. The man was out cold, and it took a few moments for Fronto to dismount and check him over. After four abortive attempts to lift the man up and throw him over the horse's back, he was about to give up, puffing with the effort, when Galronus appeared around the back of the temple, leading his own horse with a struggling, cursing soldier tied over the back.

With the younger man's help, Fronto heaved the unconscious soldier over his horse, and the two men turned and hurried back to the forum proper. The various struggles were ongoing, though fortunately it had yet to turn into anything worse. As they approached, side by side, slowly the gathered men became aware of them. First Caesar and the others on the hill spotted the two horsemen returning with their burdens, and then Salvius Cursor and his men, busy hauling Pinarius away from danger, laid eyes on Fronto. As they all turned to look, gradually the seething mass of soldiers followed suit, and the pushing and shoving slowly subsided as everyone realised what had happened.

As the potential riot gradually sank into wary and nervous stillness, silence fell upon the gathering, and the sound of the two horses' hooves clopping across the paving echoed weirdly around the forum. Fronto led, with his friend at his heel, and they skirted the mob, with difficulty climbing the steps behind the rostrum and making for Salvius Cursor and Pinarius. As they reached the rostrum, Fronto none-too-gently shoved the unconscious rioter from the back of his horse, the man landing on the wooden platform with a thud. Galronus and he then lifted the second, struggling, man down.

'This fiasco is over,' Fronto bellowed across the gathered crowd of soldiers, using the vitis to gesture at the men. 'Caesar's largesse is his affair. He wishes to relieve the burdens of the people of Rome, and you and I are not the only ones who have suffered over years of civil war. These people are your families, and they need to be cared for. Be grateful that Caesar has been beyond generous to you with his gifts, and forget petty jealousy over a small excess.'

He paused. Silence reigned.

'The next man,' he announced, eyes narrowing dangerously, 'who raises a fist or pushes another, will join these two, who are guilty of insurrection and inciting a riot.'

He let this sink in, and was relieved to see the men begin to separate and settle back. Similarly, the gathered civilians were calm now, no angry arms outstretched. The soldier with the bound hands on the rostrum, realising that he was now in real trouble, suddenly tried to make a break for it, staggering past them to throw himself from the platform.

He had not reckoned on Salvius Cursor. The head of Caesar's personal guard stepped across to intercept him. Fronto saw a momentary flash of steel in the sunlight, and there was a cry of pain. The beleaguered rioter turned, and Fronto could see the blossom of dark blood below the man's waist, torrents of crimson pouring down his left leg from where Cursor had stabbed him in the inner thigh.

The soldier fell. Fronto heaved a deep breath. He'd meant for this to be a peaceful arrest of two criminals, not an execution. Salvius Cursor, though, had never been a man to let sense get in the way of a good bloodbath. Fronto looked from the stricken legionary who now collapsed to his knees, keening gently, to Cursor, who was calmly wiping his knife on a rag, and then up to Caesar. The general's countenance was stony. There would be no reprimand for Salvius Cursor, Fronto realised. The general had no intention of going easy on the two men who'd started this. As the mortally wounded soldier slumped to his side and sobbed hopelessly in the growing pool of his own blood, Caesar gestured to the remaining figures on the platform.

Fronto and Galronus reached down and grabbed the unconscious soldier by the shoulders, lifting him with difficulty. Caesar looked from them to the mob of soldiers and back.

'Who are you to deny the people of Rome?' the general asked, darkly. His eyes fell on the unconscious soldier who had almost started a riot, and then he turned back to young Octavian, who stood close by, still in his priestly regalia, head covered piously. 'Is it not an ancient practise to appease Mars with blood?'

Octavian nodded sagely. 'It is rarely invoked.'

Fronto nodded. He knew why. There was a fine line between executing prisoners and human sacrifice. One was an accepted practise, the other abhorrent and forbidden by Roman law. The rite of offering the blood of executed prisoners of war to the god to stave off further violence had long since fallen out of use for its dubious nature. It seemed it was to be revived today.

'That man,' Caesar said, pointing to the unconscious soldier, 'broke his oath as a legionary, and that alone condemns him, but he also turned on the people of Rome, offering them violence. He is less than a mere criminal. Take him out of the city, to the Campus Martius, and strike off his head. Bring it back to the forum for display as a reminder that no man, no matter what he has suffered, can put himself above the people of Rome. Then dedicate the rest of the body to Mars.'

There was a grudging acknowledgement from the army, then. Two men had been sacrificed on the altar of peace, and while no one would like that, each soldier present knew how close this had come to something unstoppable, and each of them would be quietly grateful it wasn't *them* being carried away.

The crowd of citizens suddenly began to cheer and to chant Caesar's name. Their dictator had condemned his own men to save the people. It was mere moments before the army was beginning to cheer once more, albeit with a hint of humility and embarrassment in their tone.

Fronto looked to Galronus. 'I am so looking forward to getting safely back to the war.'

CHAPTER SIX

The Kalends of September 46 BC

'You are wasting one of your greatest opportunities,' Octavian grumbled.

'No, this is the way,' Caesar replied, meeting his great nephew eye to eye. Fronto had never seen two men so evenly matched in both wit and will. The tense exchange of silence was broken by the younger man.

'That near disaster at the end of your Gaulish triumph could have been avoided. If the soldiers and civilians alike had watched the Gaulish king die, the mood would have been so jubilant you could have given the peasants a *farm* each and no one would have argued. Rome needed to see Vercingetorix die.'

'No,' Caesar replied. 'No, they did not. They needed to see him beaten, and that happened at the triumph. No matter how much a Roman might say he hates the Gaul for his barbarity and his history, the truth is that Rome has always been a little fascinated with our ancient enemy. It is distinctly possible that watching him die would have been worse than watching the Ptolemy princess in chains.'

'I think you're missing a different trick,' Marcus Antonius muttered. 'While you've been off kicking rebels in Africa, I've been mopping up your political messes, and every missive I've had from Gaul in the past year has been a shit show. You conquered the place, yes, but no Gaul seems to want to stay conquered. Every few days sees a newly-built Roman installation mysteriously burned down, a Roman merchant strung up from a tree on a supposedly safe road, or a popular demonstration against Rome in a town square. Gaul might just benefit from being given a gift, from your vaunted clemency. Strike a deal with Vercingetorix now and send him back to Gaul to tame his own people.'

At this, Fronto felt Galronus flinch at his side, and the Remi stepped forward. The man rarely interrupted without being invited, and yet now he took centre stage.

'No.'

'Oh?' several men said, looking at Galronus.

'No. Caesar has the right of it. A quiet death, out of the public eye.'

'And why is that?' Antonius snapped.

'Yes,' Caesar said, though he had an odd smile that suggested he already knew what was on the Remi's mind.

'If you had killed him in public, you would have opened an old wound once more. Half of Rome's territory across Italia and the Province was once the land of the tribes, who you call Gauls. You have given citizenship to many. Watching in the streets of Rome were Remi, Aedui, Carnutes and more. They suffer a triumph at their expense because they are hopeful that their war is over and that Rome will bring them prosperity if they embrace it, but pushing them further is asking for trouble. What Antonius is describing is natural in a land so recently annexed. You cannot expect defiance to go away in an instant. It will take time, and careful management. You put "Gauls", men like myself, in the senate to give you the edge. Would watching their own die really help? You could not kill him in front of everyone, as it would undo everything you've achieved since the war ended.'

Caesar gave a knowing nod.

'And you cannot let him live, either,' the Remi added.

'Why not?' grumped Antonius.

'Because he is not some tribal leader, a petty chieftain or even a prince. He is Vercingetorix. The moment you strike his chains he will begin to build a new Gaul. Some men will never accept defeat. He is one such. If he lives, he will find a way to raise Gaul against you once more. Within the year he would be king again. Oddly, Caesar, I think he is a little too like you in many ways. Had you been beaten, Vercingetorix could never have afforded to let you live. From what I hear of your youth and that escapade with the pirates, that much is clear.'

If the barb in the comment about kingship was intentional, Caesar ignored it.

'You are right, my Remi friend. And that is why things have come out the way they have.'

As the officers and statesmen fell into quiet conversation, Brutus and Plancus arguing the future of Gaul, a yellow-tunic'd administrator appeared from the door of the carcer, the infamous prison that remained the home of Rome's political enemies as they waited for death.

'Is there an officer here called Funt?' he asked, uncertainly and with a frown.

There was a long pause as men looked at one another before Fronto sighed and held up a hand. 'Fronto, I suspect. Marcus Falerius Fronto. Gaulish is an accent that takes some getting used to.'

The servant shrugged. 'The prisoner asks to speak to you privately before what is to happen, happens.'

'Me?'

'If you're "Funt",' the man pointed out archly.

Fronto turned to Caesar. Given the situation he was far from certain of the wisdom of encountering their old enemy in private, and he wasn't at all sure Caesar would approve. However, the general merely gave him an intrigued shrug, and nodded. Fronto turned to the administrator. 'Lead on.'

He had not been prepared for the powerful emotions that struck him as he stepped into the infamous prison. He had set foot here twice, the first time ten years ago, when the place had been full of unpleasant killers being groomed for trouble by Pompey. That particular visit had led to one of the less pleasant episodes in Fronto's life, and images assailed him from the darkest parts of his memory as they made their way into the deepest, dingiest part of the prison. The second had been to stop Gaulish rebels trying to free this very prisoner. Fronto had almost died that day, had Cavarinos not helped him in defiance of his own king.

The Gaulish rebel was in a large cell at the furthest recess of the prison, far from the others who were being kept here, and through several doors that would deaden all sound but the occasional scream of despair. The man's cell contained a hard bed with a single blanket and a shit bucket in the corner which, going by the smell, had not been emptied in some time. Fronto tried not to let sympathy rise for a man who had been all but a king six years ago, and had spent those years in this place. Sympathy came naturally, but then Vercingetorix, for all his strength and nobility, had cost the lives of hundreds of thousands of men, both Roman and Gaul, raising a land to revolt that might have been settled in peace so much earlier.

As he came to a halt, Fronto looked around. As well as the man in the yellow tunic, one of the guards paid for by the generals and senators who filled the cells sat on a stool in a corner, clutching a stout ash stick.

'Leave us,' Fronto said.

'It is common policy to…'

'Leave us.'

Sharing a look, the two men shrugged, and left the small corridor outside the cell. Fronto lit two extra oil lamps with a taper from the first, raising the level of light considerably, and then pushed the door to the outside world closed, leaving him in a sealed corridor with just iron bars separating him from the cell and its occupant.

'On the assumption I am "funt",' Fronto said, 'you asked for me.'

'Fronto,' the Gaul said in an interested tone. 'Marcus Falerius Fronto. I remember you. We probably did not meet in battle in person, and I had other things on my mind when it was over, but I remember you from this very place a year later.' His Gallic accent was still thick enough to confuse someone who had not spent time among the Gauls, but despite the accent, his Latin was good, and Fronto was used to the strange twang.

He sighed. 'You remember me? That comes as a surprise.'

Vercingetorix stretched and stood, approaching the bars. Fronto stayed still, refusing to step back out of any perceived danger, as the Gaul looked him up and down. 'Fronto is a name that was often on the lips of Cavarinos, even before that day. There was a time during the war when he suggested that our troubles could have been avoided if you and I were to come to an arrangement. Unfortunately I had set something in motion that I could no longer realistically stop, and from what I now understand, no matter what you might have wished, Caesar would still have done what he did. War was inevitable. And yet I remember the name of a man who might have been thought a potential peacemaker. Cavarinos was one such, also.'

Fronto nodded. 'I liked him. He was a good man. There were many good men before the war.'

'And that attitude is precisely what draws me. Did you know that he came to see me after that day, only a few years ago, in fact? I have no idea how he managed to secure access to this pit, but he did so. He came to apologise for what he did, for saving you over me. And he brought me fresh fruit. The first I had tasted in a long time. I wonder what happened to him.'

'He was well when last we spoke,' Fronto said, wondering with an odd sadness where the man was now. 'He was heading east, to Galatia, where cousins of your people had carved out a kingdom centuries ago. Sadly we were at war in Galatia recently,' he realised suddenly. 'I hope he made out well.'

Vercingetorix nodded. 'You would be surprised, I think, at how well informed I am, despite my circumstances. I know, for instance, that I am now living out my final hour. But I have also come to know your world with a certain grim fascination. I have learned your tongue well, have I not?'

'I am impressed. You speak Latin like a native.'

'I have had the luxury of time. And the guards here are often as bored as the prisoners. I had a number of teachers over the years. Sometimes,' he added, almost conversationally, 'they leave the interior doors open to allow a little circulation of air, and occasionally they move us into a holding area while the cells are cleaned, Perhaps twice a month I have had the blessed opportunity to spent an hour or two in the company of fellow prisoners. I was surprised at who they were. Of course, they have come and gone, while I remain.'

Fronto nodded. 'This is not a place for common criminals. This is where dangerous political enemies are held.'

'Which is why I was rather surprised to discover that most of them were Romans.'

'We have always been our own worst enemy,' Fronto smiled oddly.

'They are often important men, nobles and senators, generals and the like. I have heard much of the events of the past six years direct from the mouths of some of Rome's greatest men. Men who know you, who know Caesar. As you say, it appears that Rome is unable to achieve concord and harmony every bit as much as my people. Had we been of one mind, Alesia would have seen our victory.'

Fronto folded his arms. 'It was a close thing anyway. Why am I here? Surely not to pass the time of day with you?'

Vercingetorix's expression became serious. 'As I say, I have learned much. And whether I like it or not, it appears that my people's fate now lies in the hands of Rome. Without me, they have become part of your empire.'

'Our republic,' corrected Fronto.

'In name, perhaps. But even though I will no longer draw breath tomorrow, I still have a care for my people. Their destiny is no longer in my hands but in yours. And for the first time, I find myself caring about the future of Rome, because the future of Rome *is* the future of my people now.'

Fronto frowned. This was starting to sound awfully familiar.

'Rome would not let me become a king of an independent nation, what you call Gaul. You would not allow it because I would have become too powerful. Under me, that nation would have presented a very real threat to Rome; a threat to rival Hannibal and his Carthaginians. Rome could not allow it, and *would* not, because you hate kings. You had your own, and they left a bitter taste in your mouths to the extent that you don't even like kings of other nations.'

'And?'

'And what is Caesar becoming if not a king of Rome?'

'I've heard this argument many times,' Fronto replied in a bored voice.

'From your own people. I am an outsider. I can see it without the bias of one of your own. The man has become dictator twice now, the latest I gather for ten years. He cannot be vetoed by your politicians, he has all but absolute power over the military and the state in the pursuance of his civil war, even the consuls would have to fight to supersede him in any way. He is, theoretically, answerable to your senate, but he has filled the senate with his people, and mine, strangely, and so they will continue to vote him whatever he wants. There is no one in Rome who can tell him what to do. He has all the power of a king, and now he seeks the trappings of one too. He has a queen for a mistress. It took me a while to understand the purpose of your lictors, but now that I do, I am surprised at what I find. Even a consul is allowed only twelve lictors. You know how many Caesar currently has, from what I am told?'

'More than twelve,' admitted Fronto, who hadn't actually counted, though they appeared to be everywhere and formed a small cohort of their own.

'Seventy two,' Vercingetorix said. 'Seventy two lictors. An entourage six times that of the highest official in your republic.'

Fronto greeted this with simple silence. He had no answer to that. When you thought about it, it was utterly excessive. Oh there were reasons. It was all to do with how many triumphs he had, how many times he'd been consul and so on, and a politician would be able to explain it all, but the simple answer was still that it was excessive, and should have been entirely unacceptable in Rome.

'So what would you have me do?' Fronto sighed. 'I am assailed often by those warning me that Caesar will make a bid for complete control. This is nothing new to me.'

'Protect your king,' Vercingetorix said.

Fronto blinked. 'What?'

'Your state will seek to see him fall. They hate monarchy. Caesar will become a target, and soon.'

'You're not warning me against this? I thought you'd come to see me because I was a republican.'

'No, you fool,' the Gaul snorted. 'Why would I want your republic to endure? A king is what my people need, even if it's a Roman one. And although he conquered our lands, already Caesar fills his senate with my people. We can recover from being conquered. Our tribes have been conquering one another since the world was young. They will be surprisingly receptive even to a Roman king.'

Fronto scratched his head. 'Why come to me?'

'Cavarinos spoke of you. I understood that you were close to Caesar, one of his most important men. And those to whom I spoke in here seem to think you are Caesar's man through and through. Have you not fought for him across the world even against your own people? Who else would I warn to look to Caesar's safety?'

Before Fronto could fully process this, they became aware of approaching sounds beyond the door, and then there came a rapping on the wood. A muffled voice addressed them.

'Time is up, sir.'

Fronto shook his head. A man who was almost king of Gaul, the one man in the past ten years who had almost beaten and humbled Rome in general, and Caesar in particular, was charging him with protecting the general. An unhappy memory of a vow made in a quarry in Hispania rose to meet that realisation. A promise that Caesar would die. Gods, but how did he get himself in these messes.

'It is in the hands of the gods,' Fronto said, uneasily.

'No. It is in the hands of men,' Vercingetorix replied as the door opened, and the administrator in yellow reappeared, a small entourage of hard-looking men behind him.

'I am sorry for what must happen now,' Fronto said to the prisoner.

Vercingetorix shrugged. 'It is how enemies of Rome end. It will be painful, but I will enter a list of famous men and go to the next world in esteemed company.'

Fronto laughed darkly. 'Farewell, king of Gaul.'

He turned away from the man and made his way back through the unpleasant, dank corridors and rooms of the carcer, emerging into fresh air and daylight with no small amount of relief. The time he had spent inside had been put to good use, he noted as he passed through the last room, the large hall at the entrance to the prison. The garrotte had been made ready, and buckets of fresh water and brushes put to one side to clear up the mess afterwards. The room had been cleared to allow space for observers.

Barely had Fronto recovered in the open air before someone gave an order and the gathered officers and senators made their way inside that prison. Fronto gulped down a few last breaths of clean air and then returned to the dim room, where his peers were gathering around the edges.

Once everyone was in position, the door was closed behind them and the gloom insisted itself. This was not part of any great public event. It was a ceremony, in its own way, and of the most ancient sort, but it was a private one, witnessed only by a few important men, those who had reason to be here. Even Octavian, who had no connection to the prisoner or the war he'd lost, was here in his role as high priest of Jupiter, witnessing the end of a man who had defied Rome and almost defeated her armies. As the door finally shut out the daylight, it did not escape Fronto's notice that a small army of lictors were gathered outside.

Fronto felt the odd sympathy welling up once more as the small, subdued procession entered the room, two men with ash cudgels leading the way. Then came half a dozen of the men who controlled the carcer on behalf of the state. Behind them came Vercingetorix, hands bound tight, and then two more club-wielding guards.

Seen in better light, Fronto was impressed with the Gallic rebel. Six years of languishing in this place had stripped him of fat and muscle, leaving him not so much lean as lank and cadaverous, his cheek bones prominent, his hair wild and filthy, his beard more so. His clothes were limited to a shapeless coarse wool smock of dirty dun colouring. He looked dreadful. Until you saw his eyes. In his eyes, Fronto could see everything that might have been. A glorious Gaulish king with a torc of gold, clad in bright colours, standing atop one of their oppida and calling for his people. There was an undiminished pride and defiance still within, and Fronto realised that the man had been speaking truth and from his heart just now. He was still thinking of his people. He would never be their king, but he had been bested by a man who could.

Vercingetorix caught Fronto's eyes for just a moment, and might have nodded. It was hard to tell. Then the guards were standing him in front of that vertical timber slab. A leather thong was tied around his ankles and pulled taut, heaving him back against the wood. The same happened at his midriff, pulling his bound hands to his belly and tying it and them to the timber. Finally, the cord was looped around his neck and fed through the two holes in the board, then fitted to the capstan behind.

'There is no trial here,' Caesar said. 'No accusation. No defence. This is not even an execution. This is the removal of a threat to Rome. Witness this, men of the senate. Witness this, priests of Jove, of Juno and of Minerva. Proceed.'

As the executioner stepped out to the rear of the board, the condemned Gaul fixed Caesar with a look. 'Were it not for the treachery of my nobles, Alesia would have been mine, dictator of Rome. This would have been *your* fate.'

Caesar said nothing, remained still, watched as the executioner began to turn the wheel behind the board, the cord around Vercingetorix's neck tightening with a series of squeaks and creaks. The rebel leader managed to maintain a look of dignified defiance for the first four turns of the wheel, his eyes fixed on Caesar. Then with the fifth turn, his air supply failed, the cord digging into the flesh at his throat. On the wheel went. Slowly, and deliberately so. A turn. A pause. A turn. A pause. The man began to make gasping, retching sounds, and Fronto could see an increasing discolouration of the skin around the tightening cord. His lips darkened, his tongue swelling to fill his mouth and make the gasps little more than odd burbling sounds. The blood vessels burst in his eyes, which gradually became an unpleasant red. He was shaking, twitching, living out every moment of agony as he died. Another turn. Another pause. Another turn.

Fronto watched every moment, refusing to turn away. The man was in some ways as heroic a figure as Fronto had ever met, yet he was also an enemy and the man responsible for years of violent war, and a massive death toll. Sympathy and satisfaction, both together.

It was almost a relief when the man died, sagging limp in his bonds, the cord having bitten so deep into his neck that veins had been severed and blood sheeted down the hanging corpse to mingle with the filth where the rebel had involuntarily defecated and urinated. The smell was appalling, though nothing new to those of them who had fought battles.

'It is done,' announced one of the administrators.

Caesar nodded, expression grave. 'Have him cast into one of the pauper pits beyond the Esquiline.'

Fronto took a deep breath and then rather wished he hadn't. 'It's over at last.'

Octavian frowned. 'At last?'

'Gaul. The war.'

'That war was over six years ago.'

Fronto shook his head. 'The last battle was fought then, but as long as this man lived, the war was never truly over. For the more defiant Gauls there would always be some hope of his return. He was a symbol to rally behind. He was the last hope, though. With him gone, the tribes are no more. Now they are all just Gaul, a province of Rome.'

'I don't follow. He was just one man.'

Fronto gave Octavian a look. 'No. He was a lot more than that. You weren't there. You don't understand. One day you will, though. One day you'll have fought wars of your own, and you'll remember this. The war is finally over.'

'What about Hispania or Syria?'

'Different. And inevitable.'

'All the enemy leaders from the triumphs should have had this,' the young man said quietly.

'Oh?' This time it was Caesar who questioned him.

'Just as this man was, those you let go will become symbols of opposition to Rome. Better to suffer a little unpopularity and remove the threat for good. The people are fickle. Give them bread and a chariot race to distract them and that unpopularity will vanish.'

Caesar nodded his approval of this, but still he responded to his great nephew. 'The same fate cannot be applied to all cases. Each one requires its own consideration. Sometimes the death of someone like this can be more damaging than freedom. Release risks creating an opponent, but death can sometimes create a martyr, and it is much harder to fight a martyr than a rebel. Arsinoë would have been one such.'

Octavian chewed his lip, thinking on the wisdom of this.

'So if that is the end of the war,' Fronto said, 'and only Hispania stands between us and peace, assuming Syria can be bought off, why delay further? Your triumphs are done, all our old enemies exiled or dead. Are we ready to finish this?'

Caesar turned to him. 'Almost. Another month or so. The new temple and forum are almost complete. It would be remiss to leave them to be dedicated by someone else. I will see them opened and ready, and then we will prepare to depart for Hispania. We shall leave by the end of November, but I will have the legions mustering ready at Narbo with Trebonius while we wait, and Didius can take the fleets to Hispania and begin the process of blockading and putting down Pompey's own admirals. I have Sittius at work undermining enemy presence in Hispania's ports already, and with a little work and a little luck we can keep the enemy off balance until we are on their doorstep. That way when we move we can go straight on the offensive. It will be late in the year, but with all in place, I am confident that we can conquer and settle Hispania and return to Rome before the summer.'

Fronto nodded. It was still an unhappy delay, but he could see the sense in it. Two months, and then they would fight the last battles of the civil war.

'You will need to assign positions on your staff,' Antonius said. Fronto pursed his lips and kept silent. Marcus Antonius was pushing for a fresh command and not to be left in Rome this time. Indeed, Fronto could see both Brutus and Octavian perking up now, paying attention.

'The time for that will come,' Caesar replied noncommittally, and with a nod to the administrator he turned. The door was opened and the general led the room's occupants out into the relief of blessed fresh air. The various soldiers, politicians and priests separated, their task complete, and went their own way. Caesar mounted his horse, his lictors gathered around him in a huge crowd. Salvius Cursor, his role as commander of Caesar's bodyguard rendered currently obsolete with the large number of lictors, watched the general set off back towards his villa. Fronto waited for Galronus, who had remained inside for some strange exchange with his fellow Gaul, and gradually the others departed. He crossed to the far side of the paving, looking down across the forum, and a moment later Salvius Cursor was next to him, leaning on a railing.

'I've been thinking,' the man said.

'In your case that's usually dangerous.'

'There's something deep and unsettling going on.'

'There always is.'

'No, Fronto. You know there's something happening. Your father in law? Paetus?'

'Yes, someone appears to be protecting Caesar and removing his opponents.'

'No, it's more. I've been casting my net wider and I think this is more than that. I can't figure a motive, yet, but think beyond those two.'

'What?'

'The more I learn about what happened to Sextus out in Syria, the more it sounds like a deliberate assassination rather than the loss of a war.'

'That's reaching, and there's no obvious connection,' Fronto replied. 'Paetus and Balbus were arrayed against Caesar. Sextus was Caesar's heir, entirely on his side. It makes no sense.'

'Exactly. But think on our return from Africa. The day we arrived Caesarion had almost died. Are we to really believe that the boy had decided to eat poisonous plants in the garden?'

'What? You think someone tried to poison him?'

'I'm certainly not ruling it out. It seems a little too suspicious to me to be coincidence. Two of Caesar's potential heirs in a row. I'll grant you that I can see no connection to Balbus and Paetus, let alone to any attempt to kill Caesar with his chariot. But I'm sure that there is a connection, even if we can't yet tell what it is. And that means that this might not yet be over. There might be more deaths to come. My job is hardly fulfilling right now, since Caesar is surrounded by a mob of lictors most of the time and I can't arm my men in the city, so I think I might devote some of my time to investigating, trying to find out more.'

Fronto nodded. 'Sensible, and it is protecting Caesar in a way, too, so it could be said to be your job. I can't see how it can all be one plot, but I have to admit the timings are all a bit suspicious. I shall be interested to hear what you come up with. Keep me informed, will you?'

Salvius Cursor nodded and rose from the rail, stepping away. Fronto remained in place for some time, trying not to think, cleaning the air in his lungs with deep breaths, and only stepped back as Galronus approached.

'Enemy or no enemy, it was not fitting to send a chieftain to his grave without certain rites.'

Fronto nodded. At long last, the war with Gaul was over.

Now the war in Hispania could begin.

CHAPTER SEVEN

Mid September 46 BC

Marcus Antonius swooped past with a nod to Fronto, plucked a delicacy from a bronze platter, and then disappeared into the crowd, making for the arbor, where Caesar was busy holding court in the peristyle garden. Fronto wondered where Galronus had gone, and wandered across to the doorway where he'd last seen the Remi trying to extricate himself from conversation with a Roman matron who had flailing arms and a voice like a harpy. Briefly he felt guilty as his eyes slid to the other corner of the garden where Lucilia and Faleria were similarly caught in a conversation. They had been ensnared by Cleopatra and then flanked by her husband-brother even as they tried to escape. Fronto hoped they hadn't seen him leaving them to their fate as he moved into the house once more.

He had never been in the domus of Marcus Antonius before, and had half expected it to be a debauched pit of machismo, given his experience of the cavalry general. That it very much was not came as a surprise. The place showed no hint of a woman's touch, though, despite the number of women who must have touched it. In addition to an overwhelming love, and seemingly boundless capacity, for drink, the man was perhaps the only nobleman in Rome whose exploits among the fairer sex had outstripped Caesar. Two wives down, Antonius was supposedly on the prowl for a third, even as his three mistresses kept him occupied.

As he passed into the wide vestibule, it occurred to Fronto that the place probably did look more like a brothel crossed with a tavern most of the time, but had been redecorated from ground to roof over the past week. So recently, in fact, that even the myriad perfumes, food smells, sweaty guests and more, could not quite hide the odour of fresh paint and recently-dried plaster. Fronto rolled his eyes at the décor and wondered if Antonius' rather childish and blatant attempt to woo the general had escaped *any* of the guests.

A mural to his left was one of those common copies of the Apelles painting of Alexander's army at the battle of Issus, the ones that appeared on wealthy house walls wherever their owners wanted to show off their martial aspect. The clever painter, and he was good, Fronto had to admit, had managed to make Alexander the Great's features look suspiciously like those of Marcus Antonius. The effect was to remind the passer by that Antonius was a great general. The other side held an array busts and death masks on pilasters, and it was no surprise that of Antonius' ancestors on display, each had been a general in his time. The fact that each of them had been involved in some kind of moral or social embarrassment seemed part of being of the Antonine lineage. His father had failed to rid the sea of pirates and had resorted instead to a little plundering of his own. His grandfather had been accused of violating one of the Vestals. His great grandfather had won a battle and earned a victory, but had lost so many troops in doing so that he had carried a stigma to the end of his days. Antonius' décor seemed to Fronto a little misguided.

An atrium held a pool with an impressive bronze centrepiece of a Gaul, busily plunging a blade down into his neck while water fountained from the wound to fill the basin speckled with rose petals. The fact that the original statue after which Antonius' Gaul was modelled was actually a Galatian from the east would escape few. The décor went on as he strolled around the house until he found Galronus, who was standing and examining a mosaic on the floor of the summer triclinium being decked out ready for the meal by dozens of scurrying slaves. The room was barely-organised chaos, with platters being carefully placed, and drapes straightened.

'It's a battle,' Galronus noted, sensing his friend's approach, eyes still on the mosaic. 'That I can see. I can't see the purpose of it here, though.'

Fronto examined the heroic looking figures at the centre and rolled his eyes once more. 'Another piece of Antonius' subtlety. 'It's the Roman general Quintus Sertorius soundly thrashing Paccianus near Tingis in the last civil war about thirty years ago.

Sertorius won, and he was allied to Marius, a distant relation of Caesar. He was the propraetor of Hispania. If ever there was a blatant reminder that war in Hispania loomed and that Antonius was a general at a loose end, this is it.'

Galronus folded his arms. 'I'm trying to understand a man who would pay huge amounts of gold to have his home turned into a campaign for a further military career, as well as organising an expensive party for hundreds of people, all in the hope that Caesar will give him a command.'

Fronto nodded. 'Truthfully, I understand him. He's spent time in Rome dealing with squabbling senators while we won wars in Africa. He's wanting to get back in the field where he can do what he likes to do... apart from the drinking and fornicating.' Fronto snorted. 'Actually he always did that on campaign too. He doesn't want to spend another year holding Caesar's political centre together. I understand, as I would hate it too. I'd be desperate to get back in the field.' He tried not to think then on the promise he'd made Lucilia that this would be his last campaign.

'The difference,' he said, 'is that I would argue for my place and wear Caesar down, not try something as blatant and ostentatious as this.'

Galronus chuckled. 'Everywhere I look there's a picture of some Roman general wading in body parts. He's not subtle, is he?'

'My worry is that Brutus will take the opportunity to one-up Antonius. Brutus is as desperate to do something worthwhile as Antonius is. Will we be in Brutus' house next week, surrounded by similar images?'

'And yet Caesar seems to always take you and I without the need to ask.'

Fronto laughed then. 'That's because for all his faults, Antonius could sell sand to an Aegyptian. He's the best choice of us all to keep in Rome and have holding Caesar's political enemies in check, despite that unfortunate incident with Dolabella.'

They both winced. Antonius had failed to halt a law of Dolabella's last year. Little would probably have come of it had not Dolabella then had the lack of foresight to sleep with Antonius' wife, leading to a messy divorce, a public display of bile, and then more or less open warfare in the forum. Caesar had not been pleased.

'And Brutus is politically astute, too,' Fronto added, moving on quickly, 'and with a name respected by the old guard. He and Antonius are both men who are at least as useful in Rome as they are on the battlefield. Conversely, in the senate I would be a true liability. And your only real senatorial value is to occupy a seat and support Caesar. We all know that. You and I are of value in the field alone.'

'Ironic.'

'When did you stop being a Gaul. When I met you, you'd have had no idea what irony was.'

Galronus chuckled again. 'I was never a Gaul. There was never such a thing as a Gaul, Fronto. You know that. I was Remi. Still am, but I've grown to appreciate the finer things.'

'Like wine, and my sister.' He sighed. 'Speaking of which, if we don't save them from the queen, life won't be worth living for a few days.'

Galronus nodded and the two men strolled back through the political and military statement of a house into the garden, where the two women were still trapped in a conversation with the Aegyptian guests. Fronto managed to drop in to a part of the conversation reflecting on Caesar's "heroics" in Alexandria and steer the subject away to Antonius, deftly leading Ptolemy to wanting to meet their host and dragging his sister-wife away.

'Thank you,' Faleria said, once they had gone, looping her arm into that of Galronus. 'What an insufferable woman. I cannot imagine what Caesar sees in her.'

In actual fact, Fronto could, but he prudently decided not to mention it, instead turning and smiling at Lucilia. She gave him a weak smile in return, which he treasured. They still mourned, and home was not the joyous place it should be, but in recent days he had seen something of a recovery in her spirits, and for that he was truly grateful. Of course, those spirits would plunge once more when he left for Hispania, but he would do what he could in the meantime.

The two couples passed their time in the garden, carefully steering clear of the various persons of importance who might try to trap them into dull conversation, and enjoying the warm evening air. A troupe of acrobats cavorted around the lawns with fiery hoops and flaming torches, performing feats of incredible skill, while a trio of musicians played pleasant melodies. How many people, Fronto wondered, would recognise the acrobats and the tunes as all of Hispanic origin?

The cooling relationship between the general and Antonius was never more evident than in this desperate display of trying to claw his way back into Caesar's favour.

Another half an hour saw the great gong clanging and calling them all into the triclinium for their dinner. Faleria expressed her distaste at having to eat a meal while looking at an image of bloodshed on the floor, though it bothered few. Fronto was grateful that his social position had granted him a place somewhere halfway down the room, far from both the important guests at the top table and the irritating empty-headed senators who had to be invited for the look of things, but who no one wanted to talk to, at the other. The head of the table saw Antonius, of course, with Caesar and Calpurnia on one side of him and Brutus and his mother, Sempronia, on the other. Cleopatra and her husband were tactfully some way from the general, though it made Fronto laugh that rumour had Sempronia also as one of Caesar's conquests in his time. No matter where one looked in this room, one's gaze would inevitably fall upon the wives and mistresses of Caesar or of Antonius so numerous were they. Fronto's gaze idled around the table until it fell upon Octavian, seated next to his mother, Atia, who nodded a greeting. Octavian was not the only nephew of Caesar present, either, for Pinarius, recovered from his ordeal in the forum, sat close by.

Conversation murmured across the room throughout the meal as courses came and went, wine mixed in great kraters and distributed copiously to the guests and their host. Fronto and Lucilia spoke of the boys and of the possibility of spending the winter down at Puteoli, Galronus and Faleria speaking of possible plans for finally exchanging their vows once the situation in Hispania was resolved. In fact, Fronto was starting to enjoy himself, and had even begun to relax, when he suddenly realised that not everyone was as content.

The raised voices broke through the general hum of conversation, and Fronto and Lucilia, like every other guest in the room, trailed off into silence as Antonius rose, his face red.

'You insult me, Gaius.'

Caesar gave Antonius a look that Fronto knew well. It was more of a warning than anything else, a single range-finding shot preparing for the glares that were to come.

'Sit down, Marcus. You are embarrassing yourself and your guests.'

'I am to be your caretaker once more?' Antonius spat.

'For the last time…'

'No. This is my house and I shall not be silenced in it.' Antonius thrust out an angry finger even as his other hand closed around his delicate wine glass and lifted it for a hearty gulp, probably unwatered, at that. 'You charge around the edges of the republic finding new enemies to get rich from, making a name for yourself as a conqueror and sending me messages to nudge the senate into granting you more and more honours for it. Four fucking triumphs. Four! And once again you drop me into the side lines. It's not good enough. I won't be your mouthpiece in the senate this time.'

'No,' Caesar said with quiet menace. 'No you won't, Marcus. You have proved yourself incapable of such a thing. That mess last year could have been avoided by a novice. Instead you escalate it to the point where senators are being clubbed senseless in the forum. You have no idea how much I had to work to heal the rifts you opened up. I left you to control Rome as my trusted lieutenant and right arm, and you played the whole game poorly.'

'That,' Antonius spat, 'is because I am in my element on the battlefield. I should have been with you, not in Rome. And what do you mean no, anyway,' he said, suddenly realising what Caesar had suggested. 'You drop me from your familia entirely now?'

Caesar leaned back. 'You are drunk, Marcus, and fractious, and that is precisely why I cannot rely upon you. You are a wild onager shot, loosed blind, and we have no idea where you will land and what damage you will do. I cannot put you in command against Labienus. He is a tactical genius and quietly competent. You are a borderline drunk with a talent for mishaps. As such, I equally can no longer trust you in keeping Rome in line.'

While Antonius made furious gasping noises, Caesar folded his arms. 'You are my friend, Marcus. You always have been, and you will ever be part of my familia, but you are your own worst enemy. You have true talent, but you submerge it behind anger and drown it in wine. I suggest you sit out this winter as a private citizen and look to your future. Then, next year, when the consuls have been elected, we will see what new positions open up if you can keep yourself out of trouble that long.'

Antonius was shaking now. The wine glass in his hand shattered, shards of colour digging into his palm as blood spattered to the table and floor.

'Gaius, this is too much. I have supported you when the whole world wanted you dead. You forget just how loyal I have been. And healing rifts? Is that what you call it? Trying to secure the consulship for that philandering shit-tip Publius Cornelius Dolabella? The bastard proposed laws in opposition to you and slept with my wife. Have you no honour? I've stopped you making him consul twice now and even as a private citizen I'll find a way to do it again. He is my blood enemy, and you have no right to try and mollify him.'

Caesar's face became even colder. 'You will not have to worry about that, Antonius. Dolabella will not be proposed for consul this year. I have not yet decided who I would like to join me in that role, but it will not be Dolabella.'

Antonius glared at the general, eyes narrowed suspiciously, blood dripping from his wounded hand.

The general steepled his fingers. 'Dolabella will be in Hispania on my staff.'

Fronto winced. That had been a low blow. Antonius' face shifted through a number of shades and settled on a sort of puce, as he trembled. He cast the broken glass to the floor, Brutus edging out of the way, and reached out his hand. A slave plopped a full glass in it, and Antonius drained the contents in one mouthful as he fought to control himself. He was still a funny colour, but had at least stopped shaking when he spoke again. 'Explain.'

'You stopped me making him consul, which would have brought him and his allies back on to our side, and so I had to find another way. Dolabella is a competent officer. He acquitted himself admirably at Pharsalus. He will be honoured with a position on the staff and perhaps in command of a legion. Thus will the political rift you caused be healed, and his friends pulled back into our cause.'

'You take insults to a new level.'

'Brutus,' Caesar said, deliberately ignoring Antonius and looking past him.

'Caesar?'

'With the influx of Gauls into Rome, I have a mind to install you as Praetor Peregrinus this coming year, settling the foreign populations, perhaps with a tie in to an appointment as propraetorian governor of Gaul afterwards.'

Fronto tried to drag his gaze from the angry figure of Antonius to that of Brutus, who was having trouble controlling his own expression. Fronto watched with fascination. The younger man was trying to appear pleased and grateful, for the appointment and the promise of the governorship were truly an honour, but beneath that look was an echo of the disappointment he was trying to hide. Like Antonius, Brutus had equally been hoping for a command in Hispania. Brutus brightened for a moment. 'Perhaps if the appointment is next year, Caesar, I can be of use to you on campaign in the winter beforehand?'

'No,' Caesar said with a smile. 'I have tasks for you in Rome. There is still much to do.'

Brutus' face fell, but he nodded his acceptance anyway.

Antonius, however, was still furious. 'You claim to be my friend, while you promote others past me, deny me a rightful command, and push me into virtual retirement? You claim to be my friend while you grant a legion to a man who cuckolded me. What friendship is this, great Caesar? Where is your vaunted clemency and generosity towards *me*, one of your oldest friends and strongest supporters? I warn you now, Gaius. Push me away and watch my support and my friendship drain like sand through the hourglass.'

Caesar and Antonius' gazes met in icy silence, Brutus tactfully having retreated from conversation. The whole room was silent in shock and embarrassment, and Fronto suddenly discovered he needed to sneeze. With trouble he forced the urge down, refusing to be the one to break the tense silence.

He was saved that particular worry, though, for a cry tore through the triclinium, and all eyes except those of Caesar and Antonius shifted to the top end of the room, where colourful drapes were lit by braziers and flickering oil lamps.

Caesar's lictors were not present here, but Salvius Cursor had brought three of his best men, and the four of them had been carefully positioned not far from the general all night, no matter where he had been. In the triclinium, they had taken up positions at the room's edge behind the top table. Fronto's eyes scanned the recess, looking from one tunic'd guard to the next, then the next, and then to Salvius Cursor himself. The man was clutching at his throat and making gagging noises.

Fronto and Galronus were up in an instant, rushing around the rear of the tables to their stricken comrade. As they ran, others now rising from their chairs, Salvius Cursor was starting to shake, and suddenly collapsed like a pillar in an earthquake, smacking hard on the marble floor at the room's periphery.

As Fronto reached the man, one of the other praetorian guards hurried over to help, the other two closing protectively on Caesar and on Octavian, who sat not far away, watching the exchange with surprise. Even at first glance Fronto suspected there was little they could do without the knowledge of a clever physician among them. Salvius Cursor had begun to vomit, and what was coming out was yellow and frothy, while the rising odour made it plain that he had also shat and pissed himself. He was shaking wildly, and his eyes had rolled upwards.

Fronto and Galronus grabbed him and tried to hold him still, as his head kept clonking on the marble floor with the shaking.

'Is he choking?' someone called, rising from the table. 'Smack him on the back.'

'I hope it's not the wine,' suggested some callous wag, earning angry remonstrations.

'Poison?' Galronus asked as they looked at the man in their grasp. He had stopped shaking so wildly now, but had settled into a rhythmic jerking. The stink of urine, faeces and vomit was overwhelming, and Fronto pulled his tunic up over his nose, then returned to holding Salvius still.

'I never thought I'd see you running to save his life,' Galronus said. 'Time was, you'd have killed him yourself.'

'Not like this,' grunted Fronto.

Cursor suddenly stopped shaking. He went very still, though yellow fluid continued to pour from his mouth and his eyes were white, pupils rolled up.

'Is he dead?' Brutus called quietly.

Fronto checked. 'No. He breathes, and his heart is pounding very fast.' He frowned. Poison meant stomach contents, and if anyone knew anything about the removal of stomach contents, it was Fronto. Perhaps they did not need a physician after all. He turned to Galronus. 'Hold him tight.'

As the Remi did so with the help of the praetorian, Fronto ran across to the table. Grabbing an empty jug, he filled it with water, then scoured the condiments on the platters. To the intrigued frowns of the guests, he tipped an entire bowl of salt into the water, and then another bowl of mustard powder. Putting one hand over the top, he shook the jug, then ran over to Salvius Cursor with his container of murky, swirling yellow water. With the help of the other two, he dragged the stricken man across to a pillar and propped him up in a seated position.

'We need to make him throw up.'

'He's already throwing up, sir,' the guard noted.

'That's just leaking out. We need him to properly empty his stomach.' As the others held the man, Fronto poured a little of the acrid water into Salvius' mouth, and then tipped him forward a little, allowing the yellow liquid to clear. Then, with the man's throat empty, he tipped the head back and poured more in, massaging the throat to make him swallow, even unconscious as he seemed to be.

'How did you know to make that?'

Fronto snorted. 'When you've been seasick as much as I have you learn a lot about emetics and anti-emetics. Salt water is enough to make you hurl, but mustard just makes it more immediate and violent.'

Sure enough, a moment later, Salvius' body jerked, and in a spasm the likes of which Fronto had never seen, he vomited. Not just throwing up, though. The fountain of stomach contents came forth like a burst dam, soaking both Fronto and Galronus. They held him as it came, seemingly endlessly, and when the flow finally abated, Salvius collapsed in their arms like a limp rag. Fronto looked him up and down. He was still breathing.

A medicus seemed to have been found somewhere, or at least someone with a little medical knowledge, for a man in a green tunic was next to them now, looking Salvius over.

'He is comatose, but I think your emetic likely saved his life. Sharp thinking.'

'Will he wake up?' Fronto asked.

'Perhaps. It is too early to tell.' The man gestured to a small gaggle of slaves who had gathered nearby. 'Find something to use as a stretcher. Take him to a cold, dark room and clean him up as best you can before laying him in a bed. I will be along shortly.'

Fronto and Galronus stood and watched as the slaves worked, carrying Salvius Cursor away. Others brought mops, buckets and towels, and someone was addressing the two of them, suggesting he show them the way to the house's private bath, where they could clean up and be supplied with fresh clothing. Fronto waved the man away, and held up a hand to the cleaners who were about to go to work. Among the mess, he was looking down at the vomit. 'Mushrooms,' he said, pointing.

Galronus nodded. 'We *all* ate the mushrooms, though.'

'Did we?'

Fronto stepped away, looking around. 'Salvius Cursor wasn't a guest. He wasn't seated at the table. He was not eating with us. But these are barely digested, so he's only just eaten them, while he was here, in the house.' It took mere moments to find what he was looking for. The four guards were not partaking of the meal, but small platters stood on tables at the back of the room with bowls of delicacies to allow the guards to nibble even while they stood on duty. A bowl of mushrooms sat near where Cursor had stood, half eaten.

'He had his own mushrooms.'

He turned and walked across to the tables, stopping near Antonius, who recoiled from the smell. 'Who would have provided food for Caesar's guards?'

Antonius shrugged. 'Slaves. From the kitchens,' he added helpfully.

Fronto nodded. Of course, Antonius would not have been involved in such minutiae. In a moment, he and Galronus were making their way back into the kitchen area, where slaves scurried this way and that. All ducked, frightened, out of their way, though many did so with wrinkled noses. In the centre of the kitchen, it was easy to find the man in charge, for he was better dressed than the others, and held a wax tablet full of lists, throwing out a finger and ordering the slaves around.

'Who supplied the food for Caesar's guards,' Fronto demanded as the man turned to face him in surprise.

The slave blustered in panic for a moment. Word of the incident had already spread through the slave areas. 'I arranged it myself. Paro and Artus delivered the platters. But...'

'Where were the mushrooms from?' Fronto asked, holding up the half eaten bowl of brown lumps. 'Where is the store?'

'We didn't supply mushrooms, sir,' the slave said, trembling a little. 'We were short of them, so they were only supplied with the main feast. The guards were given only the foods we had in excess. No mushrooms.'

Fronto frowned. 'You're sure?'

'Quite, sir.'

Leaving the man, Fronto led Galronus back into the triclinium. As he walked around the room, he confirmed a suspicion. The bowl the mushrooms sat in was dissimilar to every other piece of tableware in the room.

'This was deliberately placed next to Salvius Cursor, and not by the kitchen slaves.'

'How could anyone have done such a thing?' Galronus murmured. 'Surely he would have seen them.'

Fronto shook his head. 'No. We watched the room being prepared, remember? While we were discussing the floor. The place was chaos. Slaves everywhere. The food for the guards will have been put out then. They might even have done it while we were in the room. And it needn't have been a slave that added a bowl of mushrooms. If you and I happened to wander in and it raised no comment, then anyone else could have done so.'

'Do you think the slaves will remember who came into the room?'

Again, Fronto's head shook. 'The slaves will have been coming and going constantly. And their kind do not register the identity of Roman nobles. Other than their master, they'd be as unlikely to recognise a guest as the guest would be to remember the slave.'

'Then we're unlikely to find out any more.'

'I won't have such things happening in my house,' snarled Antonius, who they hadn't noticed approaching. 'I will have every slave tortured until we find out who is responsible.'

'You won't find out,' Fronto said. 'You'll just ruin your slaves and learn nothing. Whoever did this is clever. They've been on a campaign of death recently.'

Galronus frowned. 'You think this is connected?'

'I do. Salvius Cursor spoke to me the day Vercingetorix was strangled. He thought all the recent deaths were connected, even Sextus Caesar over in Syria. He was determined to investigate. It occurs to me that he might have come close to uncovering something. *Too* close.'

Galronus nodded. 'Makes sense. If he recovers, perhaps we will learn something.'

'But,' Fronto noted, 'soon we'll be on our way to Hispania. Might be too late, then.'

'It will be interesting,' the Remi noble replied, 'to see what happens with these deaths while we're on campaign.'

'Oh?'

'Well if they continue in Hispania, we'll know someone there is behind it. If they continue in Rome, then we can discount anyone who's with us.'

'Good point, although if Sextus's death was part of this, then it would seem that distance is no problem for our killer. We've only got a week or so until the general consecrates his new forum, and not long after, we're off. With luck, this will be the last time something like this happens, and then we can get back to good, simple warfare.'

He winced as he caught the expression on Lucilia's face as she overheard this last comment. Tonight was going to be a grumpy night.

CHAPTER EIGHT

25th September 46 BC

'Oh, Gods, I cannot watch,' Lucilia said in a breathless whisper.

'Mmmm,' replied Fronto, absently patting her reassuringly on the shoulder while he failed to take his eyes off the spectacle below. Marcus and Lucius, the two scions of the Falerii, rode out onto the turf of the Campus Martius along with the rest of their turma, proud as peacocks, lances held high. Fronto had to admit to a certain base nervousness. After years of absence, he had spent the past few months reacquainting himself with his sons, inveigling his way back into their affections, and they had responded well. He felt like a father for the first real time. And here they were taking part in a potentially lethal display. And yet, as long as everyone performed correctly, there was no real danger. Still, he knew why his wife was so worried, glancing at those sharpened points borne by each rider of the twelve-man turma.

The celebrations had begun yesterday, with ceremonies and sacrifices in the new forum, a public feast in the open, and in the evening theatre performances and poetry recitals in every available space, each related to the history of the Julii in some way. Then, this morning had been a naumachia in the great basin across the Tiber, re-enacting the battle against the Veneti. Fronto had not been able to spot Brutus among the crowd of luminaries given the best seats, but the man had every right to beam with pride as he watched his own victory played out before his eyes, with a handsome young man taking the role of the heroic admiral. It had been propaganda of Caesarian greatness, of course, but Fronto had rather enjoyed watching events he remembered, and was surprised at how well they had managed to recreate the battle, given the limited space and scope.

Then, this afternoon, came the horse sports, before the gladiatorial conflicts tomorrow that would signal the end of the celebrations, closing with the dedication of the temple to Venus Genetrix. The horse sports were divided into two categories. In a few hours' time, in the Circus Maximus, the chariot races would take place, to which Galronus in particular was looking forward. Before then, here on the edge of the Campus Martius, banks of temporary wooden seating had been raised around a wide space to make an arena for the Ludus Troiae, the Game of Troy. Where the races were limited to adult contestants, and Octavian would be there, taking part, finally of an age to allow such displays, the Ludus Troiae was devoted to the younger scions of the noble families.

The turma of twelve containing Fronto's two eight-year old boys rode out from the right hand side of the field, keeping surprisingly in formation, given their youth. Each rider was required, of course, to have some skill on horseback, and fortunately, Aurelius and two of the servants had trained the boys from an early age in the villa near Tarraco. Then, for the past month, they had been practising every day for this very display, at the expense of all other lessons and activities. Each rider wore a green chiton of Greek style and decoration, riding with only a green saddle blanket, and the head of their turma, the oldest and most experienced rider among them, wore the panoply of a Greek hoplite, taking pride of the competition as the embodiment of the hero Theseus.

As their turma settled into place in neat rows, another horn blew and the second turma appeared, similarly clad, though with red chitons and saddle blankets, their leader clad in a black pelt with bull horns affixed to his head, the embodiment of the Minotaur destined to face Theseus. Once the red turma was in place, the third and final unit rode in from the far side of the field, clad in blue and with their leader bearing a gleaming golden crown and a blue cloak, representing Minos, King of Crete and master of the Labyrinth.

All three turmae now in place and ready, Caesar stood and made his speech, opening the display, then signalled the musicians, who began the calls. In response, the three turmae started to move. Fronto watched with bated breath, a smile on his face, as the manoeuvres began. Once the calls had been given, the rest of the following half hour was all down to the skill and memory of each and every member of the teams. There was no winner at the Game of Troy, for every tiny move was already planned and choreographed in advance, and yet competition remained, for prizes of gold, of silver and of bronze awaited the three teams, granted by Caesar as the games' editor to the three turmae based on their level of excellence.

Beside Fronto, Lucilia continued to twitch and whimper with every manoeuvre, worried for her boys. Fronto felt his nails bite into his palms as his fists tensed at the first near disaster. The reds of the Minotaur and the Greens of Theseus hurtled in perfect formation towards one another. At a moment where even Fronto, who had watched cavalry at work on the battlefield scores of times, believed there must be a collision, suddenly both units changed simultaneously. The Minotaur team thrust out their spears as their mounts thundered to a halt, while the Theseus team fanned out wide and wheeled their horses in an incredibly tight space, turning their backs to the gleaming points as they rode away. One of the Greens, however, was a little slow in turning his mount, and the spearpoint of a red Minotaur came horribly close to impaling him, tearing through the tunic at his side as they separated.

Lucilia gave a little shriek, even though she knew neither of the children involved, but Fronto simply huffed in irritation. That cock up would cost their team vital points in the scoring.

They continued to watch with increasing tension. The Ludus Troiae was not held often, and this was only the second time Fronto had ever seen it. If he'd thought that first near-collision was to be the worst of the game, he had been mistaken. He winced, drew sharp breaths, joined the crowd in their worried 'oohs', and clenched white knuckles throughout as the teams danced their units in intricate patterns, often coming so close as to invite disaster, on occasions spreading out and filtering through the other team as they came the other way, spears flashing, riders whooping. Half a dozen times there were panic-inducing moments, particularly when one of Minos' horses became skittish and threw its rider. The boy rolled between pounding hooves and managed, through a combination of skill and luck, to roll free, bound to his feet and chase down his horse, remounting like a Greek and swiftly calming the beast, returning it to the turma. When the final move came, and the three turmae thrust their spears into the air, crying out in unison the name of Aeneas, hero of Troy and father of Rome, Fronto let a burst of relieved breath free. He watched as the turmae pulled together into three identical formations, facing Caesar, and their lead riders stepped their horses out forward to accept the judgement of the man responsible for it all.

Fronto didn't listen to their ritual imploring, nor Caesar's gushing of praise for the youth of Rome. He didn't need to hear the results, for he'd been watching, and he could anticipate them better than most. Minos' team had suffered five accidents or hiccups, two of them pretty bad. Theseus' team: two, neither particularly noteworthy. The Minotaur and his men had not put a hoof wrong in the whole display. The teams already knew, too, from the look of them. The pride and satisfaction on the face of every boy in red said they knew they had done everything right, and gold laurels were coming their way. Similarly, the Minos turma were sagging with defeat, knowing they were destined for the bronze. Pleasure was evident on the faces of the Theseus team as they waited for their silvers.

No matter how they might currently feel, though, Fronto knew, every last one of them would feel like a king tonight. Each rider here was the son of a Roman noble household, and each and every one would be celebrated with a party at their house tonight in their honour, as well as receiving praise and gifts from their relatives. Best of all, the older ones would benefit from wearing their victory wreaths in the coming days as the swooning girls of Rome vied for their attentions.

Fronto's eyes were on his boys. Marcus and Lucius, both eight years and separated by mere hours, sat as proud as could be, almost glowing as they received Caesar's compliments and their rewards. Marcus, slightly darker and heavier built, and Lucius, only a little slighter and lighter, both the spitting image of their grandfather, in Fronto's opinion, in his earlier days, when he had still been a worthy man.

Lucilia was so relieved when it all ended and the boys were intact that it made Fronto's heart ease too. His wife positively chimed with energy and positivity, for the first time since her father's death over a month ago.

'Will you be long this afternoon?' she asked him.

Fronto shrugged. 'I shall watch the two main races. The comedy race I'm not bothered about. Then I'll be home. I'll be in plenty of time. Are you sure you don't want to come?'

Lucilia shook her head. 'I'm sure it will be thrilling, but we have a party to prepare for the boys and I want to make sure their gifts have arrived. I know the staff will be doing everything, but will they be doing everything right?'

Fronto smiled at her. 'Go and keep things right, my love. I'll be along in a while. The boys will not be back until mid-afternoon anyway. They'll be larking about with their team mates at the stables for a while and drinking wine like grown-ups. Try not to shout when they stagger home in several hours' time, filthy, stinking of horse manure, and probably having had a skinful.'

She arched a brow. 'They know their limits. They can stick to them. They're still boys.'

Fronto laughed. 'Not this afternoon. This afternoon, they're heroes.'

'Stay and watch all the races,' Lucilia said. 'You'll enjoy the comedy one, and the chances of you tearing Galronus away from them before they're completely over are next to none anyway.'

With a kiss, she departed, Masgava stepping forward from where he'd been standing protectively close by. Fronto saw them go, smiling, then turned back to watch his boys leaving the field, laughing and pushing one another as their whole turma sang and cheered. As he rose, he spotted Faleria and Galronus making their way along the stand.

'They were superb, Marcus,' his sister smiled.

'Quite,' the Remi said. 'The Romans are a people bred for feet, not hooves. Back home we were all but born in the saddle, and yet your boys could have given Remi children a run there. Very sharp. We have a gift for them this evening.'

'Go and enjoy your chariots,' Faleria said.

'You're not coming?' Galronus frowned.

'Lucilia will be fussing around the house preparing for tonight. Without someone to keep her grounded, we may be wading through rose petals and ducking garlands all night. I need to set her a decorating budget.'

Fronto chuckled, and the two men wandered off as Arcadios came over to escort Falaria back to her litter. Chatting and reliving the more exciting moments of the Ludus and the Naumachia, they strolled through town, Aurelius and two servants trailing along discreetly behind them. They stopped for an hour or so in a caupona and had a pleasant meal and a few cups of wine, Aurelius joining them as the two servants did a little shopping for the house. It was the ninth hour before the pair reached the great Circus Maximus. There was something of a festive atmosphere about the city, and after an exciting and successful morning, looking forward to a good social evening, and with the thrill of the races impending, Fronto and Galronus laughed and joked as they used a combination of their clear social standing, their chit for some of the best seats, and their accompanying hard-faced ex-legionary, to edge their way through the crowd for a speedy entrance.

Caesar had secured the very best seats for his familia and close friends. They sat in the front row all around the lead in and lead-out of the curved end of the track. It was neither at the gates of the carceres nor at the finish line where all the excitement happened. That came at the curve, where the riders had to slow, to be extremely careful in order not to overturn or plough into the wall, while at the same time taking the great opportunity to undertake their competition. It was here that all the things happened which made the audience cheer or wince. If there were ever an indication of where the excitement was going to happen it was the doors in the circuit's outer wall right beneath Fronto's seat where the stretcher bearers and debris removal crews lurked, ready to clear the track of the more unfortunate drivers, vehicles and horses.

'Who do you favour in the first race?' Galronus asked, licking his upper teeth as he looked down the list on his tablet.

'It's frowned on for our sort to bet on this sort of race. This is no ordinary competition between famous riders. This is a celebration and a religious rite. All the riders here are volunteers from among the supporters of Caesar or his clients.'

'I know. The best odds are on Lucullus.'

'Oh?'

'Nine to one. Which is surprising. I checked on his form. Turns out he has his own hippodrome at his villa and bought three quadriga this year.'

'That suggests to me that he keeps wrecking quadrigae.'

'He's perfecting his turns. I read all about it. Just trust me, Fronto, Lucullus is where the money lies. We need to get in before too many people realise and the odds change.'

'Put me down for fifty, then.'

'Aren't you worried about being frowned on?' grinned Galronus.

'Shut up. And put me another fifty on Octavian.'

Galronus pulled a face. 'You're out of touch. He's down at three to two. Hardly any profit to be made there. And I'll tell you now that Octavian hasn't been near a chariot in the past month or two. As soon as he put his name down for this I started watching him.'

'Think about it. Octavian is Caesar's great nephew. He's racing today. Whether he wins or loses, the general is likely to be benevolent to those who supported him. Think of it not as throwing away fifty denarii, but as giving fifty denarii to Caesar.'

Galronus nodded. 'Good thinking. I'll put fifty on Octavian too. And I might just drop twenty on that Thracian from Byzantium.'

'The odds for him are the worst in the race. Hardly worth the investment.'

'He's my fallback, to recover some money if it all goes wrong,' Galronus grinned. 'He's a ringer. He got adopted by one of the Cornelii last month, just before the deadline for entry. He raced for years out east.'

Fronto turned and threw out his arms in the motion of an orator appealing to his audience. 'Come and witness the vaunted savage honour of the Gauls.'

'Shut up, Fronto.'

'Well, you're more decadent now than a hot bath full of fat senators eating shrimp off the backs of naked slaves.'

'You say that as though it's a very familiar scene.'

'Now it's your turn to shut up. Go put the bets on before betting closes. There's movement at the carceres, now.'

As Galronus ran off, opening his purse, to find one of the many race-accountants that lurked near the passageway entrances at the top of the stands, Fronto smiled, relaxed, and flagged down one of the concessions, a pasty, bald fellow with a tray of greasy foodstuffs.

'What have you got?'

The man looked at him levelly. 'I have honeyed dormice, flamingo tongues in liquamen, boar's heart pate…'

'Bollocks. That's all going to be offal with fancy names. Do you have sausages?'

The man chuckled. 'Sir knows what sir wants. Yes, I have sausages. I have pork, beef and fowl… but the fowl are fowl in more than name if you get my drift. Or the very popular three-meat-sausage. Not enough fowl to be foul in there, and they come with a very piquant sauce from Sardinia.'

Fronto pursed his lips. 'Two pork, two three-meat, please. And when you see the wine-bearers, send them my way.'

'Certainly, sir.'

The man gave him a thin board of wood with four sausages and a tiny pot of sauce, and Fronto fished out sufficient coins to pay him, then sat back. Moments later, Galronus returned and hooked one of the sausages off the board.

'All done. Here's your chits.'

'Thanks. Look, there's movement.'

They could see through the bars of the carceres now as torches flared. Vehicles were visible, the horses snorting and dancing as the riders fastened their reins and tied their helmet straps tight. A horn blared from somewhere and as the gates were opened, the crowd fell into a tense hush. One hundred and fifty thousand pairs of eyes focused on the eight gates and as, a moment later, the first chariot emerged into the bright sunlight, the crowd roared, many people standing and throwing their arms in the air. Everyone loved the races, even when it was gifted amateurs taking the track. *Especially* when it was amateurs, for the chances of exciting gruesome accidents was that much higher.

'That's Lucullus,' Galronus said, excitement tingeing his voice, as the second chariot emerged from the gate. 'The first one's the Servilian. He's just here to make up the numbers.'

Fronto smiled at his friend's attitude as the Remi named each man to emerge, telling him any strengths or weaknesses and giving his personal opinion, which sometimes involved the word 'arse.'

'Only two left, so we know who they are,' Galronus breathed, his fingers gripping his betting chits so hard they were crumpled into little balls. He slapped his forehead. 'Emerites of Byzantium in the seventh lane. That makes Octavian the outsider. Gods, but that's dangerous.'

Fronto nodded. The outsider had the most work to do to avoid disaster. He had to avoid ploughing into outer wall, or worse even, getting a wheel caught in the narrow ditch between that wall and the track, and somehow to manage to move in across the sand and cut across in front of his opponents at the same time. That Caesar's great nephew had the most difficult starting position could only be deliberate, but had it been Octavian's decision, or the general's?

Certainly his garb had not been the general's idea. Each of the riders had dressed themselves as figures from legend or history, to wow the audience and to give them a race personality. As Caesar's great nephew and a scion of the Julii, descended from Venus and Aeneas, one might have expected something appropriate. As it was, then, his choice had to be a little jarring for the general.

'What's he doing in that get up?' Galronus frowned.

Fronto sighed. I'm guessing that Caesar's refused to take him to Hispania and he's rebelling. That's an Etruscan King, he's being. I reckon it's Servius Tullus. His father was descended from that line, while his mother was of the Julii. It's a fairly damning statement, I'd say. Caesar will not be best pleased.'

'He'd better win then.'

The chariots took a single lap, slowly, in line, waving to the populace, receiving cheers, jeers, and a few marriage proposals, and returned to the starting line where an official kept them in place, making sure no one crossed the mark before the off.

The horn went.

The charioteers slapped their reins down, shouting at their horses.

The vehicles began to rumble into life.

The crowd went wild.

Fronto watched intently. As the racers made their way along the first straight, directly towards Fronto's seat, he tried to weigh up the chances, but Galronus was, as ever, way ahead of him. 'I was right,' he shouted, slapping Fronto on the arm. 'Look at them. Lucullus already has a clear half-chariot lead, and the Thracian is right behind him. I'll be rich.'

'Octavian is doing well,' Fronto added. The young man *was* doing well. For a rider with, as far as Fronto was aware, little to no experience of driving a chariot, Octavian was doing astoundingly well, not only keeping the thing in a straight line, but keeping pace with good drivers. He watched as the lad hurtled towards the curve.

'Oh, shit, no,' he murmured as he watched Octavian's reins twitch.

'He can do it,' Galronus said, leaning forward in his seat.

'No, he can't. A professional would. But not him.'

They watched, tense, as Octavian tried to cut across the track early, on his approach, attempting to force the man to his left into the next vehicle, but his momentum was too much, and instead of posing a threat to the next chariot, he cut in front of them. For a heartbeat he was almost in the lead, but his position was untenable. With three chariots bearing down right on his tail and nowhere to go inwards for the leaders were already pulling ahead there, he was running out of time and space. If he tried to keep this position, he would charge straight at the wall. To the collective moan of the crowd, he gave up his brief lead and pulled outwards again into the wide curve as he raced past Fronto and around the end of the track. He was back in the outside position, but his failed manoeuvre had cost him precious moments, and now he was fighting to keep out of last place.

'He's too inexperienced,' Galronus noted. 'He should have made at least one full circuit, gauging each rider and the space on the track before he tried something like that. Had he waited, it might have worked.'

'Or he might be nothing but meat and kindling,' pointed out Fronto.

The eight racers had all made their first turn, which impressed both of them, for the rate of attrition at the races was extremely high even among professionals, let alone men such as these. Fronto watched, increasingly tense, as the riders made their way down the far straight, weaving and winding, taking advantage of anything they could in an attempt to move up in position. The second turn heralded the first disaster. One of the unknown riders edged his chariot too close to his competitor. Their wheels met, and the chariots bucked and bounced. The man he'd struck managed to control his slewing, dangerous vehicle, and bring it back into line, slipping behind Octavian to secure last place, while the one who'd struck him was out of the race. The vehicle lurched up into the air, the pole cracking and the traces straining. The chariot tipped on its side and the unfortunate driver found himself attached to the reins of four panicked horses separated from their chariot. Miraculously he managed to pass the wreckage of his own vehicle as it cartwheeled through the air, but was then dragged agonisingly along the grit at breakneck speed even as he found the knife at his belt and cut through the reins to free himself. Finally, he rolled away and the nearest team emerged onto the track to recover the limp and bloody driver and to shift the wreckage to the edge.

They managed the third turn, below Fronto, without incident, and Octavian even managed to come out of that turn early, cutting past another of his opponents, moving up from sixth place to fifth. They thundered down the straight once more, approaching the carceres end, and Galronus mused on whether Octavian might try his manoeuvre again, but the young man prudently pulled a little inwards and kept his position. Fronto realised why, as they rounded that end. Had Octavian pushed for a place, he'd have had to try to cut outwards, and there would have been a danger of collision with the wreckage of the last chariot at the track edge. As it was, he hurtled along, looking good.

'D'you know,' Galronus said, tapping his chit, 'that Octavian might just do this. Oh, he'll never win, but if he keeps his head and continues the way he is, he could just take third place, and then these bets will be worth something.'

Fronto nodded, couldn't do much else. Something was happening, and his eyes were still on Octavian. The young man was leaping about in his chariot now, looking this way and that, and mostly down.

'Something's wrong.'

Galronus frowned. 'He's going to…'

But he was going to do nothing. Fronto stared in horror as Octavian's chariot exploded beneath him. The men near him to both left and right veered wildly to avoid being dragged into the disaster, and the remaining six riders raced away along the track, but Octavian was in trouble. The pole had broken, and its shattered end bounced on the track once, twice, thrice, and then dug in. In one of the most spectacular racing accidents Fronto had ever seen, the entire vehicle tipped end over end, and Octavian was hurled towards the four horses pulling it.

The horses were free, though. The pole had shattered, and they were no longer attached to the ruined chariot. The only thing that connected them now was the reins, and Octavian seemed to have let go of them. The horses raced off ahead, still attached to one another, despite being separated from the chariot. The vehicle itself bounced end over end twice more, carving grooves in the track, before clattering to a halt, one wheel trundling off forlornly on its own course. Fronto watched Octavian bounce a couple of times, his momentum carrying him to the edge of the track, where he rolled into the ditch. The team was out immediately, four men throwing ropes and grapples into the wreckage to pull it off the track, two more racing ahead to grab, calm and retrieve the horses, two more with a stretcher running for Octavian.

Fronto looked around. The crowd was either cheering or staring in shock, but no one seemed to be moving. He turned to Galronus. 'Come on.'

'But, the race?'

'Screw the race. Come on.'

In moments, with the Remi at his heel he was ducking into the archway and pounding down dark stairs beneath the stands, the whole place echoing and empty with every eye on the track above. As they ran, following Galronus' directions, for the man knew the circus better than anyone Fronto had ever met, they passed only occasional staff members going about their business, or concession stand owners, taking the chance to stretch their legs during the race. When the two men reached the sealed door marked private, Fronto hammered on it.

After a while the door opened and a much-abused face with a slanting nose appeared beneath piggy eyes and brows that could be used to sweep a floor. 'What?' grunted the man.

'Let us in. I need to see Octavian.'

'Private,' growled monosyllable man.

'I am here for Caesar,' Fronto lied glibly. 'Let me in.'

'Check,' the man grunted, and tried to close the door. Galronus wedged it open with his foot, and Fronto pulled it clear, the two of them barrelling past the surprised slave and hurtling into the recesses beyond.

'This way,' Galronus said, running off to the right.

'How do you know your way around the race enclosures?' Fronto hissed as he ran.

'I spent a lot of time here when we were last in Rome. Best way to learn what's what: talk to the slaves.'

With the slant-nosed-eyebrow-monster in tow shouting warnings angrily, they made their way to a room where slaves scurried this way and that. Fronto and Galronus pulled them out of the way and dipped into the room. Octavian lay on a table, two men in white smocks attending to him, one carefully pulling pieces of gravel from his flesh with a pair of tweezers, the other washing wounds. Octavian was a mess. Bloody and grazed, with a black eye. Yet he was still compos mentis, for he turned as they entered and gave a weak smile. 'I reckon I'd have won. What about you?'

The brute caught up with them then, but at the urging of the medics and Octavian himself, the man retreated, still grunting.

'What happened?' Fronto said.

'I really don't know,' Octavian said, then hissed as more gravel was removed. 'I never hit a bump, never touched another chariot, and I was going straight. There was a horrible cracking sound and the whole thing just exploded under me. No idea what happened. I just had to do what I could. Before the race, Lucullus told me straight: if anything goes wrong, cut through the reins fast and jump free. Get to the edge and through a door before the chariots come round again.'

Fronto nodded. 'But you didn't cut yourself free. I saw it explode and you let go of the reins and throw yourself to safety.'

Octavian gave him an odd smile. 'Everyone told me to tie the reins to myself for safety, but when Lucullus told me to cut the reins when things went wrong, I started to wonder why I tied them in the first place. So I didn't. A good thing, too. Probably saved me.'

'Gods, but that was lucky,' Fronto replied. 'Your great uncle will be beside himself.'

Octavian sighed. 'Even less likely to take me to Hispania now, I suppose.'

Fronto allowed a little chuckle, and motioned to one of the medics. 'He's alright?'

'A bit battered and grazed, but he'll live. Nothing broken. Nothing short of miraculous, in my experience.'

Fronto nodded and turned back to Octavian. 'No. I don't think you'll be going to Hispania. But we're going soon, and it'll all be over quickly.' He grinned. 'I promise you this, Octavian. I told my wife this would be my last campaign. If Caesar decides he still needs to move on Syria next year I'll tell him to give my place to you.'

Octavian smiled warmly. 'I always liked you, Fronto.'

'Keep on liking me. Hispania looms and I'm getting old. I need all the help I can get.'

PART TWO

HISPANIA – CRUCIBLE OF WAR

"Caesar […] had had much business to complete before he took to the road; but this was now disposed of, and he had come post haste to Spain to finish off the war."

- Unknown author, attributed to Caesar: *De Bello Hispaniensi*

CHAPTER NINE

Late November 46 BC

Gaius Didius scanned the battle, blinking in the sea spray. He was determined to finish the rebels here; today. The two fleets had met at the Balearic Islands, where a decisive engagement had taken place. Didius knew that there had been concerns over his ability to successfully conclude Caesar's sea campaign, and he had heard half-mutterings that the command should have gone to Brutus, a man with considerable naval experience, and all that had done was make him determined to prove himself all the more. The two fleets had clashed around the islands several times until they met in open battle. His tactics there had been non-traditional, and the trierarchs had argued with him, but he'd been insistent, basing his attack upon Iberian cavalry tactics he had learned to his cost as a young tribune on the peninsula many years ago. The result had been a resounding success. The unexpected manoeuvres had confounded the enemy commander, and the rebel fleet had been broken soundly. Didius had secretly and silently heaved a sigh of relief as his trierarchs had cheered him on, while the Pompeian commander and what was left of his fleet fled west towards mainland Hispania.

Since then, the trierarchs had been his, obeying without question. They had chased the rebels to the coast, near Lucentum, but the enemy commander was fast, driven by fear, and managed to stay out of reach. Still, Didius had been close enough on their tail to prevent them being able to take safe harbour there. Indeed, he had chased and harried the surviving fleet all along the Hispanic coast, nipping at their heels, so close that never once had the enemy had the chance to put into one of their allied ports. Day and night they had sailed, until this afternoon they had rounded the

Pillars of Hercules and entered the dangerous strait that led out into the great encircling ocean.

There they had found something of a surprise. The wily enemy commander had been making for the bay of Carteia just beyond the northern pillar, for there sat his reserves. As soon as the enemy fleet had entered the bay, signals had been given and the rest of the rebel naval power had mobilised and raced to join them. Didius' trierarchs had moaned in dismay, for now they had faced an enemy not much smaller than the one they had already ousted in the Balearics, and this time, Caesar's fleet was exhausted from the chase. Still, Didius had been determined.

He had reasoned that only the fresh crews on the reserve ships would be fully alert and strong, and they were coming in a small block. The shape of the bay had suggested to Didius that both encircling arms enclosed somewhat shallow water at the edges, with only the centre of the bay as it stretched towards Carteia formed of deep water. Out of time, and faced with a hard fight, he had settled on a somewhat drastic plan.

As the ships they had been chasing slowed and turned, ready for the reserve fleet to come alongside and bolster them, Didius had three of his triremes move close together. Most of the crew left two of them, swimming to the third, and those two, running with only a small complement, made one last great effort at speed. They raced ahead of Didius' fleet, making for the block of fresh reserves coming up to the left. As they reached a good pace, the crews pulled in the oars and abandoned them, spilling pitch around the deck. At the last moment they lit the pitch on both ships and leapt into the water, swimming for their fellow ships coming along behind.

The enemy reserves had been doomed, then. Didius had seen it with an air of satisfaction. They could not move further towards the shore for fear of grounding themselves, and the fleet Didius had chased from the Balearics filled the rest of the open water. The reserves did all they could, slowing and backwatering as the fireships drifted at speed towards them, but their momentum made that troublesome, too. The two blazing vessels struck the reserves even as they began to retreat, setting more and more ships afire, sparks leaping in the sea air and catching on the sails of others. It was a dry, warm afternoon, with the breeze endemic of the straits, and the fire spread through the fleet in moments.

Before the enemy commander could change his plan, Didius and his men, invigorated with such early success, were on them. They had ploughed into their fleeing enemy like lions, and the battle had been vicious, but almost entirely one-sided. The battle had raged for the past half hour, but now it was almost over. Didius peered at the remaining rebel ships. Four triremes remained functioning amid the floating wreckage, including the ship of their admiral. He, it was, that Didius wanted now. Didius had broken the enemy fleet and effectively taken control of the seas around Hispania, but to truly put the wind up the rebels on the peninsula, he would like to capture or kill their naval commander. Plus, of course, it would look rather good in his report to Caesar.

The enemy knew it was over, and those vessels were moving now. One had turned sideways in an attempt to block the waters and provide cover for the other three as they slowly spun and made for the harbour at Carteia. Didius chewed his lip now. It was already a great victory, but he was damned if the man was going to escape. Giving the signal, Didius gestured to the trierarch of his flagship, and the vessel broke off its engagement with a half-sunk enemy ship and began to plough carefully between the various wrecked hulls and screaming, drowning sailors, aiming for the fleeing rebels. Half a dozen of his vessels followed, disengaging from their clear victory and chasing down the survivors.

They were in close pursuit. The fastest of their ships moved into a vanguard position, signalling their intent to Didius, and he silently thanked that trierarch. The powerful trireme out front moved to ramming speed, pulling ahead. The pace was one they could not maintain for long at the best of times, but after two battles and a three day pursuit where the crew slept only for a few hours at a time and in shifts, it was impressive they managed it at all. The trireme struck the sidelong enemy vessel amidships, its ram tearing into the hull, ripping the enemy blockade into two halves. The two ships became entangled, a mess of troubled timber, but the blockage had shrunk considerably, and Didius and his six ships ploughed on, skirting the ruined blockade with ease now, and chasing down the enemy.

They were close, but Didius fretted. His men were simply too tired to give that last extra burst. They were keeping pace with the fleeing commander, but not gaining on him. He set his jaw, determined. Alright, if they couldn't catch them before they made Carteia, he would catch them *at* Carteia before they had the chance to disembark. As they closed, he frowned. He could see Carteia, ancient walls and close-packed buildings huddled near to the shoreline above a small river's estuary, but the enemy did not seem to be making for the harbour. He scanned the coast. The river was narrow and too silted up to be navigable, and much of the coastline was either shallow and sandy, or filled with ridges of submerged rocks identifiable only because the sea broke across them from time to time. He realised then why the enemy were not making for the harbour. The place was fortified. Two ships had been scuttled in the harbour entrance, creating a blockade within artillery range from towers. He smiled. The enemy commander had scuppered himself there. He'd had Carteia protected from enemy assault, but then left himself with nowhere to run, trapped in a narrow bay with an unforgiving shore.

He focused. If that was the case, then why were the enemy still making for the shore? He watched as the three surviving enemy triremes raced for the land. The harbour was no use, they were to the west of the rocky shelves, and all Didius could see further west was the bright aquamarine of shallow water, where the submerged beach was such a gentle slope that it ran far out to sea.

Between the rocks and the sands, there must be a narrow, navigable stretch, where the enemy intended to beach their ships and flee ashore. Well they might manage to beach the ships, but Didius would be on them before they could wade to land.

'Follow those ships. Beach if you have to.'

The trierarch, displaying a similarly determined look, nodded and passed signals to the other ships. The aulete picked up the speed of the tune on his pipes, trying to coax just a little more pace from the oarsmen, but they were already giving all they had. The ships raced for the shore. Miraculously, the enemy seemed to be slowing, just a little, while two of Didius' ships had managed to edge just a little closer. They were going to make it.

The first he knew of the trouble was when his lead ship, a fast vessel determined to be the first to stop the enemy admiral, suddenly slewed sideways and halted, tipping over. He stared as that ship slumped into the water, the crew bellowing in shock as oars snapped and the mast smacked sidelong into the water.

Didius stared. The enemy ships were even now, some short distance ahead, grinding to a halt on the sands, their crews leaping from the rails to land in waist deep water and wade to the shore. His lead ship, however, was done for, slowly settling into the water, though part would continue to jut from the surface, so shallow was the bay. Without the need for Didius to call off the pursuit, the trierarch of his command ship bellowed orders and the vessel turned sharply. Didius realised then just how close to disaster he'd come, for the oarsmen all along the vessel's starboard side cursed, their oar blades dragging in the sand under the water, just below the keel, due to the tilt of the ship. They had almost run aground.

As they veered away from the shore, Didius gripped the rail, cursing, and watched as another of his ships fell foul of what he now realised were carefully placed traps. The enemy, aware that the harbour was blocked, and knowing only one section of nearby shore was suitable for beaching, had submerged chains and wreckage, attached to anchors, all along the shore. They had known where they were, and had slipped easily between them, but Didius and his fleet had been entirely unaware, and had consequently blundered straight into them.

The other ships were turning now, two vessels done for, tangled and sinking in the shallow water. Didius fumed, watching the enemy ships disgorging their crews, from the meanest oarsman to the Pompeian admiral himself, all vaulting into waist deep water and wading ashore. He had failed to catch the bastard.

'Never mind, sir,' a nearby centurion said with feeling. 'He might be running, but he's doing it with his tail between his legs. You've cleared the sea of enemy ships. We control the coast now.'

The man was right. Didius nodded his thanks. They had won a tremendous series of victories over the past few days, culminating with this in the very heart of the enemy fleet's base. He might not have taken their admiral, but the man no longer had a fleet to command.

'Slow in open water and let the survivors swim aboard,' he told the trierarch. The crews of his two foundering ships would need to be saved, and, while Didius and his fleet now ruled the seas, the coast was still solidly held by the enemy. Swimming ashore was no option. Now they would have to find somewhere with a safe harbour where they could secure a bridgehead. Plenty of places on the Iberian coastline. And then they would settle in, patrolling the coast, keeping the enemy land-bound and awaiting the arrival of the army to finish the job.

* * *

Fronto sighed as he sank back into the chair in the general's tent and sipped the wine. It had been a furious journey, but he had to admit that the general, after those debacles in Aegyptus and Africa, seemed to be back to his strategic forte. Labienus and the Pompeys had to be guessing at what was coming, struggling to plan any kind of defence. Didius had sailed months ago for the Balearics, where it was known that the Pompeians had established a powerful naval presence. Caesar had hoped that the new admiral would be able to best the enemy there and make a big noise doing it, drawing the enemy commanders' attention that way. In fact, the reports they'd received suggested that Didius had done better than they could ever have hoped, smashing the fleet and wresting control of the Balearics from the enemy. The man had not stopped there, though. Last reports had him harrying the enemy fleet south along the coast towards the Pillars of Hercules. The Pompey brothers would be watching that area intently, knowing that Caesar now had control of the waters, and any invasion could easily come via the Balearics or even along the coast of Africa.

Additionally, Caesar's pet mercenary captain, Publius Sittius, fresh from destroying Scipio's fleet at Hippo, had infiltrated the Iberian coastline at Saguntum and Carthago Nova and had managed to overthrow the pro-Pompeian commanders, securing the two great port cities in the name of Caesar. Word of their fall must have reached the enemy commanders swiftly, and with the two greatest harbours on the eastern shoreline in Caesarian hands, the danger of Caesar's invasion force arriving by ship via the Balearics was a strong one. Labienus and the Pompeys had probably argued for days about where their forces were best disposed to stand against Caesar.

But both of these were little more than distractions, drawing the enemy's eye. In truth, the bulk of Caesar's forces had been moving for months now. The legions and shiploads of supplies had assembled at Narbo, on the coast south of Gaul and close to the Pyrenees, under the watchful eye of Gaius Trebonius, a man who had served throughout the war in Gaul with distinction. There, Trebonius had begun to gradually move the legions and supply train on into the north-eastern corner of Hispania, down through Tarraco and into the peninsula's heartland. It had been subtle, and slow, far enough from the enemy in Baetica to the south, not to draw too much attention.

Caesar and his officers, along with alae of cavalry, had taken ship at Ostia after the celebrations ended and all had been made ready, and sailed for Narbo. Labienus and the Pompeys would undoubtedly think Caesar still lounging in Rome, while had, in fact, been marshalling his army mere miles from the border of Hispania, with the army already on the move. It was all very neat.

Trebonius had done a tremendous job, but there his involvement had ended. The man had, apparently, been expecting to join the staff upon Caesar's arrival and move into Hispania with them in command of a legion. Caesar had instead commanded his old warhorse to sit out the campaign, remaining in Narbo at the hub of the supply train. Fronto had watched Trebonius' face and added his name to those of Antonius, Brutus and Octavian on his growing list of people who were pissed off at being sidelined by the general. Still, despite his grumbling, Trebonius was clearly still excelling at the job, for as the general and his cavalry and officers rode at speed to catch up with the head of the army, the supplies continued to move neatly.

They had travelled unopposed down the coast and headed inland from Saguntum, receiving reinforcements there from the city secured by Sittius, and joining up with the forces already gathered in Hispania under Quintus Pedius and his generals. Pedius, another of Caesar's great nephews, had shown sensible restraint. While some of the officers had chided him for not having pushed against the Pompeys and Labienus, Pedius had pointed out that the enemy had considerably outnumbered them, had control of most of the powerful cities, had their supplies in place, and had the popular support of most of the southern peninsula. Pedius had thought it prudent not to throw away his men, in his own words 'on some deluded heroic blunder,' but to await the arrival of Caesar and his army, giving them sufficient forces to remove the enemy. Caesar had been impressed and pleased with the decision, and so the two armies had amalgamated.

The journey then had taken them west, leading the Caesarian forces ever closer to the enemy's concentration in Baetica, and this evening the army had settled and encamped in the plains outside Ilugo. Fronto had planned to spend the evening with the Tenth, who formed part of Caesar's legionary column, and whose senior centurion, Atenos, Fronto had not seen since Thapsus. However, as the army had shuffled into positions, it transpired that a small group of deserters from the enemy force had reached Ilugo today on a path to Saguntum, where they had hoped to find Caesar and his army.

Even now, the general was outside once more, seeing those deserters into the care of a prefect who was to find them food and accommodation. They had been interviewed for an hour in front of the men of Caesar's staff, and much had been learned.

In response to the fact that Caesar and his forces seemed to be approaching from all over, northeast, southeast, and directly at the east coast, Sextus Pompey had largely drawn the enemy's forces back into central Baetica, the best to keep the army concentrated ready to face them. If the rebel deserters were to be believed, then the enemy power base was now at Corduba, less than a hundred miles to the west, and every twenty miles or so of road between here and there was settled with enemy pickets, ready to warn of Caesar's approach.

There, the deserters had begun to differ in their information, for they had come from two different enemy units. One group was convinced that Caesar's best target was to strike directly at Sextus Pompey in Corduba and tear the enemy's fortress out from under them. They were convinced that, though Corduba would be a hard nut to crack, it was possible, with a clever enough strategy. They even went so far as to suggest a nighttime assault. The other unit, however, had tried to persuade Caesar to move first on the city of Ulia to the south of Corduba. There, the other brother, Gnaeus Pompey, was busy besieging the town, which had declared for Caesar.

Caesar had received this information with interest, nodding his understanding at each point raised, keeping quiet along with the rest of his officers. When the deserters had completed their report and stepped back, quiet, Caesar had steepled his fingers.

'What of Titus Labienus?'

There had then been some discussion among the deserters. They seemed to have a variety of conflicting reports as to the location of Caesar's old lieutenant, ranging from the far end of Iberia, near Gades, up into the mountains at the peninsula's centre, down to Malaca on the south coast. The upshot, they admitted in the end, was that they did not know. He was somewhere in Baetica. The one thing they all seemed to be able to agree upon was that Labienus was his own man, commanding a powerful cavalry force and not falling under the direct command of the Pompey brothers.

Now, as Fronto finally relaxed and looked forward to a possible catch up with Atenos, Caesar returned to the tent, the deserters seen to.

'Plans need to be made, gentlemen.'

Pedius coughed. 'Of the three enemy commanders, by far the most dangerous is Labienus, and, since we do not know where he is, it will be difficult to plan effectively.'

Caesar nodded as he settled in his own chair. 'Labienus is clever. He knows I'm here. The Pompey brothers can play on their famous name to gain support in the cities, and that's what they're doing. Labienus doesn't have that advantage, and so he has become a ghost, flitting around Iberia with a fast moving cavalry force. By the time we get any report of his presence, be assured he will be gone from there. He will keep on the move and ready to strike. He will wait for us to make our move against the Pompeys and use whatever advantage he can find then. Gods, but I wish the man was still one of this group. What a mind.'

Fronto sipped his wine and put down the cup. 'So whatever we do, we cannot consider Labienus in the plan, just put in place whatever safeguards we can, and be prepared for a nasty surprise.'

'Quite. So the question now is where we make our first move. Both options commend themselves.'

Pedius shuffled and leaned forward. 'Corduba is the de facto capital of Baetica. It is as much a symbol of rebel control as the Pompey name itself, General. I have seen the city myself, and it will be a vicious place to take, but if we can do it, perhaps we can put an end to Sextus Pompey and take control of the seat of rebel power all in one go. You know what damage we would do if we removed their capital and one of the three generals. And while Sextus is the younger of the brothers, in my opinion he is the most strategically minded.'

Caesar took all this in, nodding as he listened. 'Everything you say is entirely correct, of course. Very astute. But the question is whether that outweighs the advantage to be gained at Ulia. Ulia was sending petitions to Rome months ago begging to be aided against the rebels. Of all those who have entreated us, Ulia has stood staunch for our cause despite being all but surrounded by the enemy. To let them fall to Gnaeus Pompey would send a bad signal to any other city that might come over to us, while to ride to their rescue might tip many others to our cause. Additionally, while Gnaeus is undoubtedly the less talented of the brothers, he is still dangerous, and his name is still as powerful. His capture or demise would strike the enemy as much as that of Sextus. You see the dilemma? Ideally we would move in both directions at once.'

'Then why not do so?' Hirtius asked quietly.

Fronto pursed his lips. 'It would be dangerous. We would be dividing our forces and fighting a war on two fronts.'

'Yes,' Galronus said, interjecting to the surprise of all, 'but I fear focusing on one target exclusively is playing an equal risk.'

'Oh?' Caesar asked. 'How so?'

'You have an enemy force in Corduba, an enemy force at Ulia, and at least a third cavalry force somewhere, probably close, under Labienus. If you attack Corduba, you risk being trapped against its walls by Gnaeus Pompey and Labienus. If you attack Ulia, you risk the same there from Labienus and Sextus Pompey. Seven years ago we attacked Alesia. I know we won, but remember how dangerous it was. Having to double fortify against an enemy reserve?'

Caesar frowned. 'An interesting point. Of course, if we move against both, and keep both Pompey's occupied, we still have to worry about Labienus.'

'I didn't say it was a perfect plan, Caesar. Just pointing out a danger.'

Caesar sagged back. 'In truth, I fear the decision has been made for us. We cannot afford to ignore the chance to trap Sextus in Corduba, but we cannot let Ulia fall. We must move on both. I shall continue to lead the main force against Corduba, and we shall send a smaller force to Ulia in an attempt to break the siege there. Who do we have who knows the land hereabouts, Lucius?' he asked Pedius.

The officer tapped his lip. 'I have the man for you. Lucius Vibius Paciaecus. A solid, able commander, who's led vexillations for us since the winter. He's been active in these hills for months, and is known to the Ulians.'

Caesar's smile appeared then. 'Good. Send for this Vibius Paciaecus. We'll give him six cohorts of the best heavy infantry we have. Give him the Fifth. They cut their teeth on Alesia and have been consistently successful since then. They're understrength, so six full cohorts will leave only the engineers and the baggage with our column. Without the baggage, they'll move fast.'

Pedius made a note on the tablet sitting on the table beside him. 'Will six cohorts be enough?'

Caesar pointed across the room. Galronus, standing in the line of Caesar's gesture, frowned. 'General?'

'You will join him and take six alae of the best horse we have. Between you, I am content that you can deal with Gnaeus Pompey and save Ulia.'

Galronus bowed his head, and Caesar leaned back. 'The rest of us will move on Corduba and attempt to wrest it from the younger Pompey.' The general peered at the map on the wall, noting their current location and that of the two cities they were contemplating. 'More or less a hundred miles to each, though the Ulia force will arrive first, unburdened by baggage. It would appear that Ulia and Corduba are less than twenty miles apart. We will keep a constant swarm of scouts in the area, all around us, ranging ten miles, to give us warning should Labienus hove into view, and we will set up a system of couriers to keep the two armies in close contact throughout. I don't want anyone to be taken by surprise.'

* * *

Atenos passed the jug of wine over to Fronto. 'We seem to be lacking a legate.'

Fronto took a sip of the wine and pulled a face. 'Out of whose sweaty arse crack did you bottle this stuff?'

The centurion laughed. 'This shit is the stuff you used to drink with us. I think a few years in the wine trade has made you too snooty, Fronto. Anyway, you're supposed to water it.'

'Especially this stuff,' Fronto grunted. 'You sip it unwatered to check the quality, and *then* you water it. Mind, I'm regretting having done so. I'll be tasting that for a week.'

'Get it drunk, you Roman petal.'

Fronto tried not to be offended and broke into a weary grin. Atenos was so thoroughly Roman, Fronto often thought of him as one, and forgot that the man was, in his history every bit as Gaulish as Galronus. In some ways, Caesar's invasion of Gaul had done much to bring Gaul into Rome rather than the other way around.

'So?' Atenos said

'So what?'

'We've no legate, and you're on the staff. Would be like old times if these two things became connected.'

Fronto chuckled. 'I'm old, Atenos. Probably too old for the sort of thing we used to get up to.'

'Balls. And this might be your last chance. I hear you're planning to hang up your sword. And if this ends the war, there's a good chance the Tenth will be put into garrison for a year or two to make sure that the world stays settled, and then disbanded entirely as no longer necessary.' He leaned closer, conspiratorially. 'It is my distinct impression that this war in Hispania will be the Tenth's last. It would be rather nice if our last battle with Caesar was under you.'

Fronto smiled. It was true. This probably was his last battle. And while he would miss the life, he was getting too creaky for a lot of this, and his vow to Lucilia was no empty one. He had missed too much of the boys growing up. Having watched them at the Ludus Troiae, he was determined that this wouldn't happen again. When the war was over and the summer come, Fronto would be done with the army. And Atenos was right. These legions had largely been raised for war in Gaul and then for the extended civil conflicts that followed. If everything returned to peace, there would be no need to maintain so many expensive legions and most, if not all, would be disbanded. His favoured Tenth, who he had led to so many famous victories, would be done.

'I think I might just tell Caesar that the Tenth is mine, or I go home.'

Atenos clinked the lip of his wine cup against Fronto's. 'That's the spirit. Now if we're going to fight one last campaign together, then we'd best stick to tradition and get drunk together first!'

And they did.

CHAPTER TEN

December 46 BC

Paciaecus shouted to Galronus, who finally heard on the third call, and steered his horse across to join the commander.
'What?'
'It's getting worse. We could blunder straight into Pompey's army at this rate.'
'I thought you knew this area well?'
Paciaecus glared at him. 'I *do* know it well, but in these conditions I couldn't find the back of my own hand. Even a local would get lost today.'
Galronus nodded at the truth of this as he pulled his cloak tighter around him. The rain had started within a day of departing the column at Ilugo. The next day the rains had intensified, turning the dirt roads they followed into light brown streams of sludge, and making the crossing of small rivers troublesome. The third day had seen no improvement, and then this morning the winds had begun; powerful, chilling gales that seemed to cut through all protection and clothes and batter at the soul. The wind was freezing and strong, but it also carried the rain almost horizontally, making it very difficult to see and making every step a miserable one. The horsemen in Galronus' force were unhappy enough, but the infantry, slogging along in such conditions, had it worse. Centurions kept reminding them of the huge pot of gold Caesar had given them in the summer, most of which had been invested immediately or buried away on family properties for safe keeping. That, at least, kept the men going.
'Is that city walls?' Galronus asked, blinking into the squall, but before Paciaecus could answer, he'd already realised it wasn't. That a copse on the crest of a hill could be mistaken for city walls said much about visibility.

'Look on the bright side,' Paciaecus said. 'If we can't see Pompey's army, then they can't see us either.'

'But blind is not the ideal way to fight a war.'

'True.'

There was a long silence between the two, filled with the whistling of wind and the clatter of rain on shield covers, armour and men. Suddenly the commander threw up his hand. 'Halt,' he called, his other hand going to his sword. Galronus, too, gripped his weapon ready as a figure emerged from the gloom ahead, riding towards them. The two men relaxed and backed down as the man waved, signalling that it was one of their outriding scouts and not an enemy horseman.

'What is it?'

'We've found Pompey's forces, sir,' the rider said.

'Tell me.'

'Haven't seen the town yet, sir, or the bulk of the army, but just ahead are sentry points by the road.'

Galronus sucked on his lip. There was no way, even in this, they were going to slip right past a sentry. He looked across at Paciaecus, who had a thoughtful expression. 'Have you moved off this road?' the commander asked.

The rider nodded. 'We've done a thorough check, sir. *Every* road is guarded. Every access to the city has sentry points.'

'And between them?'

'Sir?'

'In the olive groves.'

'They're clear, sir, but the sentry points are not more than a quarter of a mile apart in most places, with a good field of vision.'

'In this?'

The scout smiled. 'I see what you mean, sir. It would have to be one of the more covered approaches.'

Paciaecus straightened. 'Find me one of the olive groves between sentry points that comes close to the town, with the largest gap between Pompeians. We'll wait until dusk. This storm's been going for days now, and I doubt it'll stop before tonight. Once the light dims, if we're careful, we could slip between the sentries and get close to Ulia before we're spotted.'

The army settled in for a while then as the scouts probed Ulia's outskirts, and within the hour, they had reported their findings. With the afternoon falling into evening rapidly, they skirted the edge of Ulia until they reached the scouts' optimal route. There, every man used what he could to tie up scabbards and wrap shields, dampening any sound they caused with movement. As the light faded, with no sign of the storm diminishing, the column moved off into the trees, keeping as tight a formation as possible. Despite riding or marching four abreast, the column was long, some six thousand infantry and cavalry together, and Paciaecus had taken up the rear guard, Galronus the van. His eyes nipping this way and that in the dismal gloom, hand repeatedly going to his face to wipe away the excess water, the Remi constantly tried to make out the shapes of any Pompeian sentries off to either side. More than once he was about to hold up a hand and halt the column, or shout the alarm, when he realised it was just his eyes playing tricks on him. Every gnarled trunk in that olive grove seemed to be an enemy sentry until he focused long enough, blinking away the rain.

They had been travelling for some time when a hissed warning came forward. One of the riders behind him had seen movement in the trees, but it had been momentary and had disappeared before he could identify it. Still, as they moved on in relative silence, no alarm seemed to be raised and no force of Pompeian legionaries swarmed from the flanks. Galronus, satisfied that it had been some wild animal and not a soldier the rider had seen, led them on, thanking the gods for this terrible weather.

His nerves were taut and his eyes tired when finally he spotted through the grey ahead the walls of Ulia, and realised that not only were they now past the sentries, but actually close to the city and therefore close to the enemy army. He made 'be ready' signals to his men, the message passed back, hands going to sword hilts.

The olive grove they traversed was bordered at the far end by a thick hedge, which, even denuded by winter, remained solid, and as Galronus approached a gap in the hedge with trepidation, legionaries stepped from that space, pila up, shields hefted. Behind them, through the gloom, Galronus could just make out lines of tents and men going about their evening's business hurriedly and miserably, dashing to get out of the rain. They had stumbled straight into the enemy.

His mind whirled, his hand going up ready to signal the attack, other on his sword, moving from pommel to grip, ready to draw.

'Where are you going, sir?' one of the legionaries asked, and his respectful, curious tone threw Galronus. He blinked and adjusted swiftly. Of course, they were well within enemy lines now, and the man had no reason to presume they were Caesarian. They were all Romans here, after all. He had to force himself not to smile, and instead formed his face into a furrowed expression of distaste and worry.

'Not to our tents, you lucky bastard,' he said. 'Have you not had orders? We're to effect a nighttime assault on the Corduba Gate while Veranius' men make a lot of noise in the southeast to draw them away. You must have a persuasive tribune to avoid it, soldier.'

The man grinned. 'Some of us are just Fortuna's favourites, sir. Good luck. This gate's been a bastard for days.'

Galronus tipped his head in acknowledgement as the soldiers stepped aside and saluted. Still suppressing his smile, he signalled the column and they moved forth once more. He could hear a slight distant murmur behind him as whispered word of the bluff passed back along the line through his cavalry to the infantry and eventually to Paciaecus, five thousand paces behind him. He hoped that the commander would do nothing stupid, and was grateful for the veteran nature of his riders as they moved in among the tents of the enemy, for each man affected a resigned and worried expression appropriate to a man ordered to attack in the rain at night.

It was impressive. Now well within Pompey's forces, they moved straight through the midst of the enemy camp and approached the powerful gate in Ulia's walls which faced them. They were stopped by a prefect, at a ditch and rampart of stakes facing the walls. Here torches burned and covered artillery sat silent and still in the dusk.

'What's this?' the prefect demanded as Galronus held up a hand and halted the column once more.

Galronus repeated his explanation to the officer, whose brow folded in concern. 'I'd heard nothing. Hold still while I send for confirmation.'

The Remi nodded. He'd been half expecting something like this. The men at the front line were going to be a little more alert. 'We'll marshal in the open while we wait,' Galronus told the man. 'Strung out among the tents we're just in the way.'

The man paused, uncertain for a moment, then nodded as he beckoned a messenger. 'Run to find our section commander and confirm that an assault on the gate has been ordered.'

As the man hurried off, the prefect chewed his lip, and then issued a command that the artillery crews be brought forth and the entire legion put on alert. Galronus, heart pumping, ignored this, face frozen in his mask, and led his men out, directing them to either side of the approach, in the open ground between the siege line and the city. There they massed in two groups. As the first men passed, while the prefect was busy, Galronus hissed his orders to the initial pair of riders, who passed the instructions back as they fell into position. They had to be quick, and he hoped they would have sufficient time before the senior commander denied any knowledge of the attack via messenger.

He watched as his riders finished lining up and the men of the Fifth moved into the open. He thanked Fortuna that the weather had been bad enough that every man had made sure to use his leather shield cover, hiding the design that could mark them out as Caesar's men.

His pulse was racing as he saw, simultaneously, the end of their column, Paciaecus approaching the gap in the fence, and the enemy messenger racing back towards the prefect in a panic. They'd done it.

'Good luck,' Paciaecus said as he rode past in the lee of his soldiers. Galronus nodded as the world erupted. Their ruse had been undone, and the prefect was staring, wide-eyed as the runner told him these men were the enemy. Orders were shouted urgently, horns blown, men running everywhere.

The Caesarian force, though, were ready, Galronus' instructions having filtered back through every man. Now that the entire force of six infantry cohorts were clear of the enemy camp into the open ground, they were racing for the city gate, bellowing Caesar's name to identify themselves to the city's defenders. Even as Paciaecus led his men to the gate, Galronus' riders began to move. Already divided into two units, they turned and raced back into the gap through which they had already passed, and into the Pompeian lines once more. This fresh shock sent waves of panic through the besieging army, who were even now struggling to arm themselves and move into position.

Leaving the other group of fifteen hundred riders to their work, Galronus led his half to the left inside that gap, the space between the fence and the tents. Here the enemy were mustering, and the artillery sat silent as engineers worked to bring them back into life, removing the huge leather covers that had been thrown over the machines to keep them dry, and to prevent their torsion cables becoming saggy with the rain. Galronus grinned.

Behind him, his riders moved onto the offensive. Every time a horseman passed one of the multitude of burning pitch-coated torches that illuminated the camp, he leaned down from the saddle and swept up the blazing staff, wielding it carefully. Others scythed out with their swords, cutting down panicked, unprepared Pompeians left and right in the chaos. Galronus rode forth, leading them as his men cast their golden brands into tents and onto artillery.

In moments, he reached the prefect who'd challenged them and even now was calling to his signallers, sword in hand. The man fell with a cry of agony as Galronus' blade slammed into his raised sword arm, smashing the bone and all but severing the limb. The man went down, wounded, and was thrown this way and that, battered to death by hooves as the Remi rode over him.

All along the enemy siege line facing the city walls, artillery burst into bright flame, their leather covers having kept them tinder-dry throughout the storm. Men emerged from blazing tents screaming, little more than human torches themselves, only to fall in agony among other tents, spreading the inferno. It was chaos and utter destruction. The enemy had no chance to rally or organise, the fire among them, their artillery burning, riders cutting down any man who tried to issue an order. The freedom would not last long, Galronus knew, for even now he could hear the distant calls of other legions moving into life in response to this unexpected disaster.

But Galronus had not intended to lift the siege. That was too much for the men he had with him as yet. He was here to do damage and demoralise. It was mere moments before he reached the next gap in the siege lines, each opening spaced evenly around the city walls to allow the attacking army to move forth en masse. At this gap he swept out his sword once more, cutting down a centurion busily trying to muster a defence. Then he led his men back into the no-mans-land between siege line and walls, and away from the Pompeian camp, doubling back the way they had come, making for the gate they had initially approached. Their way was lit now by the inferno of the enemy lines, tents and siege engines ablaze. He could see that the defenders of Ulia had opened the gates in response to the column's arrival, and the men of the Fifth were almost inside, pouring into the city to bolster its garrison. Even now the two forces of cavalry were emerging from their devastating attack and racing to join the infantry behind the safety of the walls.

As Galronus rode for the gate, he looked back over his cavalry. He was missing very few riders, while the devastation among the enemy was immense. It would take days for Pompey's men to recover, and weeks to rebuild artillery, and even then only beginning after the rain stopped. As he passed beneath the arch of the gate, Galronus grinned at Paciaecus, who threw him a happy salute to a background of raucous cheers from the relieved citizens of Ulia.

Now the city stood a chance.

* * *

Fronto looked back among his men, wishing that Galronus were with him. He was a competent horseman, but no cavalry commander, and the Aedui chieftain leading the auxiliary horsemen was unknown to him. His eyes played across the force, two thousand riders in a mass, more like a Gallic warband than a Roman unit. Of course, that was the point.

Ahead, through the stinking weather, he could just make out the glow that was Corduba, but before it, he could see the Pompeian cavalry. He gritted his teeth, hoping his plan was not as foolish as he was beginning to suspect.

The Pompeian horse were encamped near the bridge that guarded the approach to the city. The defectors who had fled to Caesar had laid out the situation rather bleakly. The enemy camp was strong and crossing the bridge without taking it would be impossible. If they became bogged down besieging that camp they would lose all surprise and Pompey would have time to prepare. They had to somehow take the camp, and swiftly. It had been Caesar who had suggested that the answer would be to draw out the enemy cavalry and destroy them in the open. But how?

Fronto had been the architect of the solution. The enemy cavalry force was estimated at five thousand. They would only move out to deal with an inferior force over whom they felt confident of victory. Thus, Caesar should field perhaps half that number, drawing the enemy to them.

'But how then do we hope to overwhelm them?' Postumius had put in.

'Simple. Our riders won't be light skirmishers, but heavy veterans. We only send less than a thousand light armed Gauls at the front. The other two thousand we form from the Tenth.'

'What?'

'There's a reason the legion is the Tenth Equestris,' he reminded the man. 'Right back in the days of Ariovistus we put the Tenth on horseback and used them to shock the enemy. Let's do it again. The enemy will think they're dealing with a unit of light skirmishers, but once they're committed, they'll realise that we've got half a legion in among them.'

Caesar had smiled then, and agreed it.

It had sounded so plausible.

Now, as they raced towards Pompey's camp, it was seeming more than a little foolish. What if they didn't come out at all? What if there were more than the deserters had estimated? What if…?

His first worry was answered almost immediately. Ahead, he could see neither the camp nor the river yet, but a force of cavalry was bearing down on them through the sheeting rain. He tried to estimate numbers, but it was impossible under these conditions. He just had to hope that their intelligence was accurate and that the Aedui commander was capable and stuck to his orders.

As they rode, still at a steady pace, and not a charge, presenting a tempting target, Fronto looked to his own men. He rode behind a single line of Gauls, a thin screen. Indeed, most of the front line consisted of Gaulish riders, fierce, but lightly armed and armoured and trained to skirmish tactics rather than heavy mounted combat, much like the enemy riders coming at them. The men of the Tenth Equestris, Fronto's legion, had foregone their shields, cloaks or crests, anything that might identify them as legionaries, instead wielding Gallic shields and plain bronze helmets. Behind a screen of true Gallic riders, they would appear much the same.

They were not.

Both units now had to play to their strengths.

The enemy gave a roar, still somewhat distant, the sound almost lost in the battering rain and howling wind, and pressed forward into a charge. They moved into a wedge as they came, spears levelled. Fronto took a deep breath. That, he'd anticipated. He held up his hand and dropped it in signal the moment he judged the enemy riders close enough to be unable to break off their attack.

In response, his own riders began to change formation. A thousand Gauls peeled off to the flanks, half to each side, slowing as they did so. Fronto's four cohorts of mounted legionaries reacted instantly. Each man leapt from his mount, slapping it on the rump and sending it away. As the horses scattered back the way they'd come and out to the flanks, the legionaries ran and dropped into the contra-equitas formation, Gaulish shields, similar in size and shape to their own, locking into a two-storey shield wall as spears and pila were pushed forward, forming a deadly hedge.

The enemy had no time to halt, though the horses tried. It is a standard factor in cavalry action that even trained war horses are largely unwilling to charge such an obstacle, and even though the stunned enemy variously tried to pull back or press on with the charge, the horses largely shied and bucked. The pressure of the force carried a great deal of momentum, however, and the unfortunate riders at the front of the wedge were driven straight into the wall of legionaries by the sheer power of muscle and flesh behind them. The Tenth, prepared, braced and thoroughly experienced at the manoeuver, were momentarily knocked back and scattered, but in heartbeats had pushed back in again, forming solid lines as the spears jabbed out into men and beasts.

While Fronto's legionaries began to cut down and impale the enemy riders, the Aedui noble commanding the Gallic contingent led his riders out and round as planned, bringing them back in from both sides to hit the enemy riders in the rear and the flanks. Here they performed their traditional role, harrying them, picking off whoever they could, keeping them in disarray and driving them continually at Fronto's legionary wall.

Fronto remained on Bucephalus behind the shield wall, watching the action, aware that his plan was succeeding, but that it would take only one breach in his formation for everything to change. He bit his cheek as he watched, his fingers dancing on the pommel of his sword. He had made silent promises not to put himself in excessive danger. He had a wife and children waiting for him in Rome, praying he would survive this one final campaign. And he was getting too old for the fight. He knew it. He felt it in the ache of his bones on cold mornings, in the strain of rising from a low chair, and in the fact that he had a tendency to doze off these days whenever he sat for a time. Everything in him told him his place was here, safe and comfortable.

It surprised even him, then, when his fingers closed on the grip of his sword and pulled it free, and his heels kicked Bucephalus into motion. He was too old for the fight, and he had to be careful.

Screw it.

In moments he was at the edge of the conflict, where legionaries were even now filing out of the third line and extending the contra-equitas wall to prevent the enemy flanking them. Fronto peered at the men they were facing. They were neither Italian, not Gallic. He recognised the garb as Iberian, though. He'd seen such units many years ago in Hispania with Caesar. He also knew what their officers – their nobles – looked like. It took only moments for him to spot the man. In the end it was not the elaborately embossed helmet with the high, black horsehair plume that identified him, but rather the fact that despite the panic on his expression, the man was throwing out a finger at men around him, bellowing desperate orders.

Fronto, lip wrinkling, estimated his chances. There were just three riders between him and the enemy commander. Reaching to his belt, he plucked the pugio dagger from his sheath. It was no throwing weapon, and centurions would beat their men for wasting such a blade in such a manner, but Fronto didn't care. He flung the knife at the first rider. It spun in the air and struck the Spaniard full in the face, hilt-first and with nose-breaking strength. The rider cried out in pain, sword swinging wild as he lolled in the saddle. Fronto pushed past him, leaving the legionaries extending the line to finish him off. He was vaguely aware of a spear plunging into the man even as the rider gripped his bloodied face in pain, but his attention was already on the next man.

Instinct kicked in. Fronto was already tired from the ride and his fresh exertions, but a lifetime of warfare had honed both mind and body to a level where conscious decisions were a luxury rather than a necessity. Even as an unseen rider tried to cut him off, his blade lanced out and took the man in the sword arm. Simultaneously, Fronto jerked Bucephalus with his knees and the great black stallion pushed left, barging another horseman out of the way. The man reeled and fell in the press, sliding from his saddle blanket, lacking the stability of a Roman horned saddle. The one man between Fronto and the officer lunged for him, his curved, leaf-shaped Iberian blade coming down hard. Fronto's left arm shot up, empty-handed, even as he drove his mount in closer. He caught the man's wrist in his grip, preventing the sword's further descent, and slammed his own gladius into the armpit beneath. The man screamed, sword falling from his fingers as Fronto twisted the blade left, then right, then pulled it free amid a flow of blood.

The man was still between him and the officer, and Fronto realised that there was no realistic way to get past with the dying, floundering rider between them. Gritting his teeth, he simply pushed Bucephalus forward, driving the stricken Spaniard and his mount together into the officer. The two riders and horses collided, the officer suddenly realising the danger he was in. Fronto tried as hard as he could to somehow get past the dying man, and finally resigned himself to the fact that this was not going to happen. Instead, even as the commander tried desperately to get away, hampered by the press of his own men, Fronto watched and waited. The moment came, and he struck. As the flailing, blood-soaked rider he had already butchered, lurched back in a spasm, Fronto leaned hard forward in the saddle, throwing himself over Bucephalus' neck. It gave him just enough reach. His sword whispered past the dying man and slammed into the throat of the officer's horse beyond. The beast whinnied in pain and panic, and bucked. The officer, like his men, rode with only a saddle blanket, and he was held fast only by his hands on the reins. As he slipped from the beast's back, yelping, he lost his grip. The last Fronto saw of the enemy officer was as he disappeared with a scream beneath the churning hooves.

In heartbeats, Fronto was carefully backing Bucephalus out of danger, using his sword to bat away occasional desperate opportunist swings of enemy swords or thrusts of spears.

He was weary now, and the danger was increasing by the moment. He was immensely grateful as he managed to make his way behind the nearest line of legionaries and put the contra-equitas wall between him and the enemy.

The ruse and the tactics had worked well. The enemy force was being cut down in droves, and the legionary wall was cunningly moving back a few steps every now and then at a centurion's command to prevent the build-up of enemy dead getting in the way. At the latest slight fall back, Fronto marvelled. So many fallen Iberians and their horses with remarkably few legionaries among them.

The Gauls were savaging the enemy flanks. Taken so by surprise and not given the opportunity to recover or regroup, the enemy had milled and panicked, unable to escape the trap, legionaries killing them in droves to the front, furious whooping Gauls slashing at the rear and both flanks. By Fronto's rough estimation the enemy had begun the conflict outnumbering his force by perhaps three men to two. Now, Fronto's army must outnumber the enemy two-to-one.

Heaving in deep breaths, he watched the battle reach its peak, that moment when one side is so ascendant that the other must break. In this case, the Caesarians had utterly devastated their enemy, and the rout began suddenly, but took only moments to turn from a few panicked horsemen trying to break free of the press, to a mass flood of terrified men.

The Aedui commander was as good as Fronto could have hoped. He knew that to try and hold the fleeing force could result in disaster, and so his men allowed them space to break, though they then moved to the next phase. Instead of attempting to block the way of the fleeing riders, they simply raced alongside, keeping pace with them, like dogs snapping at the heels of a running man. As the enemy fled, so the Gauls lanced and slashed, cutting them down as they rode away, taking at least every other man without facing any danger themselves.

Fronto gave the command to his men. The legionaries were no longer under pressure as the enemy cavalry broke and fled, and as the Gauls continued their butchery, the legionaries began to chase down and collect their mounts, which were largely grazing safely out of the way of the fight, back across the grass. Leaving them to it, Fronto joined the Gauls, cantering across to reach the Aedui chieftain.

'A good fight,' the man announced with a grin, a spatter of blood across the bottom half of his face. Fronto nodded. 'Let's try and stop survivors getting across the bridge.'

Together, the two officers rode off in the wake of the mobile clash, the remaining Spaniards being gradually brought down on the run by the fierce Gauls. The two men raced past a steady stream of fallen horses and men. Fronto was pleased to see off to the right that the enemy camp had been all but emptied. That would no longer present an obstacle to Caesar's army, which marched on around an hour behind them.

His face fell as the conflict before him opened up and through the siling rain and the grey gloom, his eyes fell upon a fresh problem. The camp may no longer present an obstacle, but this might.

Behind the camp the river sealed off the escape route for the fleeing horsemen, for the bridge to Corduba had gone.

CHAPTER ELEVEN

December 46 BC

There was no longer any hope of a surprise assault on Corduba. Sextus Pompey had seen to that with his demolition of the bridge. There were other, more distant, approaches to the city, but nothing as direct as the bridge that had gone, and the wily general had kept eyes on every approach. By the time Caesar's army had arrived at the river, Pompey had withdrawn the scattered garrisons to the city to bolster his defence, drawn in everything of value, and dispatched riders. The horsemen seemed to go in every direction but that of Caesar's army, and though not one had fallen into their hands, no man on Caesar's staff was under any illusion as to where they were bound. Every rider would be heading for either a garrison town or a mobile force, drawing them back. That meant probably the besieging force of Pompey's brother at Ulia, but it likely also meant Labienus and his cavalry. Some among the staff had voiced satisfaction that perhaps this could be settled in one go, Roman-style, in the open field. Postumius had been the one to crush that joyous thought.

He and Hirtius had been working on the numbers. Caesar's army numbered three legions brought from Italia, the Fifth, Sixth and Tenth, along with roughly the same number of cavalry. To this he had added the army already in Hispania, which consisted of more or less equal numbers. Six legions at less than full strength would mean perhaps twenty five thousand men. Another twenty five thousand cavalry and auxilia. It sounded like a force to be reckoned with, and the staff officers had nodded their satisfaction. Then estimates of enemy numbers were voiced. Based on reports, scouting missions and the details from enemy deserters, it was clear that the Pompeys had been recruiting solidly in their time here. Thirteen legions and an equivalent number of auxilia and cavalry. More than double Caesar's numbers.

Postumius had mused on their quality. Of those thirteen, only two had been longstanding in Hispania, a third formed of settled veterans and a fourth that had been brought from Africa. The rest had been formed from deserters, auxilia and desperate levies. Nine legions would be of poor quality and largely untested, against Caesar's veterans. Still, the numbers were telling. Caesar would have to be careful. If the enemy managed to pull their entire force together, they could swamp the Caesarians with ease. Caesar would have to launch precision attacks and win smaller, individual victories, and with the fortifying of Corduba, the chances were that if they besieged the city, long before it fell they would be surrounded by the rest of the rebel forces. Simply: they no longer had the time and leisure to take the enemy capital.

Thus, while the legions busily replaced the bridge, Caesar's engineers filling wicker baskets with stones and using them to create a causeway topped with thick beams, the officers argued tactics. Undoubtedly the other Pompey was already on the way from Ulia, and in short order they would be trapped against Corduba's walls between the two brothers.

'We need to reduce their numbers,' Caesar had sighed, tapping his finger at known positions across the map. 'It would take far too long to bring fresh men from Italia to balance the odds, and I have pushed Rome's elite as far as I can with taxation, so the raising of fresh legions there would be costly. Would that we had the gold and silver mines of Hispania that the Pompeys currently control. I admit that we have underestimated rebel numbers in Hispania, to our peril. However, we still have the better men, the initiative, and the superior strategists. Put your heads together gentlemen. Find me a garrison to destroy that will not land us in the lap of one of our enemy generals.'

To that end, as the bridge was completed and the army led across, scouts had been sent out with spare horses and orders to ride hard and fast across the region, returning with what dispositions they could find. The officers chafed at their inactivity, for the army had been encamped on the Corduba side of the river in three camps close to the new bridge, awaiting fresh intelligence, settled in, staring now at the back end of winter and new year approaching. Fronto, however, had known that the general was up to something. Six centuries of veteran legionaries had been drawn from the legions and had left camp on 'detached duty' for Caesar, a number of couriers had been dispatched, and the general had that twinkle in his eye.

'We could at least use our time trying to take the city,' one of the officers had grunted.

'And be weighed down and pinned with all our supplies unloaded, siege engines and all our gear in place when Gnaeus Pompey arrives? I think not.'

And that had been that.

Information had started to come back quickly. The siege of Ulia had indeed been lifted, Gnaeus Pompey and his army marching north, heading for Corduba. The enemy commanders seemed to have a large number of small garrisons spread around, but one prime target had come to stand out. A day's march southeast lay the town of Ategua. Three of the Pompeys' legions garrisoned the town, including one of his veterans, for Ategua was, after Corduba, their second most important supply site. The scouts had reported that the town was well defended, but its loss would be a crucial blow to the enemy. Losing a quarter of their heavy infantry and a quarter of their entire military supply would go a long way to evening things between the two armies.

The problem was that Gnaeus Pompey's army would be in the road between the two cities, for Ulia lay also in that direction.

'We could probably take his army if we march,' Postumius had murmured.

'And open our back to the other Pompey marching from Corduba to join him,' Fronto replied. 'That was exactly what we've been worrying about. Right now we're in danger of being trapped, and chasing one of them will allow the other to attack us from the rear.'

'Then why are we just sitting here and waiting for them to trap us? To the north the mountains seal us in, to the east lies only our own territory, Gnaeus Pompey comes from the south. Perhaps we should press west and seek Hispalis?'

Hirtius shook his head this time. 'Labienus is likely out there, and then we stretch ourselves, leaving both Pompeys to cut off our supply lines.'

'So we wait to be trapped or we march into the trap ourselves.'

'No,' Caesar said quietly. We draw Pompey here. The closer he is to Corduba, the further he is from Ategua. Remember our campaigns against his father in Illyria? We would draw him out, surprise him and move off in order to gain distance. We shall do the same here.'

'But we'll be trapped between the bridge and Corduba.'

'I have seen to that.'

Thus it was that Fronto stood, tense, watching as Gnaeus Pompey's force fortified their camps across the river. The general had settled his army, more than a match for Caesar's numerically, in a similar fashion on the far side of the bridge; three camps in an arc. In the preceding day, the Caesarian forces had drawn a line of fortifications linking their camps and surrounding the northern end of the bridge. Why, Fronto had been unsure. It appeared as though Caesar intended to hold the bridge at all costs. Even as Pompey's forces had settled across the river, his men had begun to fortify and build similar ramparts beyond the bridge. Already, a number of small skirmishes had broken out across the river, arrows and javelins cast, a little damage done. The men of both sides were itching to do something, though the river sat between them, and an assault on the bridge would commit them to a dangerous course. And so, they continued to fortify and argue at a distance. How long it would be before Sextus Pompey decided to leave Corduba's walls and attempt to crush them against his brother was anyone's guess.

Fronto ground his teeth and finally snapped, marching back through the camp and straight to Caesar's command tent. The praetorians on duty made a spirited attempt to stop him, but Fronto simply shouted to the general, and was finally admitted, noting with sadness the absence of Salvius Cursor and wondering whether he was still breathing back in Rome.

Caesar was poring over the map in his tent, pinching the bridge of his nose.

'Level with me,' Fronto said, folding his arms.

'Marcus?'

'You've got something planned. You're not delaying for no reason, and everyone is tense, speculating. Why are we digging in when we should be leaving? What have you got planned?'

Caesar gave him a wan smile. 'Very well, Fronto. In fact, I have two possible plans in place. Since Corduba was effectively closed to us, I have set my sights on Ategua.'

'This we all know, but it does not explain all this.'

'I have called in a number of debts and favours, Marcus. Even now, a sizeable number of reinforcements will most certainly be on the way from Saguntum and the northeast. I have neither time nor funds to bring forces from Italia, but there are sources closer to hand. I had hoped they would arrive before Gnaeus Pompey, and that we might have enough to plough through him and then march on Ategua. However, I have yet to receive any tidings of them, and Pompey is here, digging in. My first option has failed. Thus I now move to my second plan.'

'Which is?'

'We do what we did to his father. We lull him into the impression that we are digging in, and while he settles himself we get ready to run. We move fast and suddenly and skirt around him, making for Ategua. That way, we can pick up our men from Ulia and invest Ategua before Gnaeus can pull it all together and follow.'

'And we're just going to fly over the top of him?' Fronto's brow folded in suspicion. 'The couriers you took were the ones sent for reinforcements, but the centuries you withdrew… they were engineers, yes?'

Caesar smiled. 'Quite.'

'So while we've been making a big noise here, they've been building a second bridge.'

'Some way to the east, out of sight of the city and Pompey's camp. Wide enough for us to cross at speed.'

'And just like Dyrrachium, we'll burn torches and have men on the ramparts to the last moment while the army moves out.'

'Precisely. But for the continued value of secrecy, I have kept this plan from the staff and the men. Spies abound and while we daily take in stray deserters from the enemy, be sure that they do the same from us. I cannot afford word of such things to leak out.'

Fronto nodded. 'So we need to make this look real; like we're settled in to stay.'

'We do.'

'Then we need to draw some blood. Make Pompey fret and concentrate.'

'What have you in mind?'

'There are constant clashes between us, but sitting here and doing nothing we give Pompey no reason to believe we have a goal; a plan. We need to focus him.'

'How?'

'Have one of the couriers fall into his hands. Or some volunteer officer. Leak to him the news that your reinforcements are coming. Then he will understand why you stay here.' Caesar nodded. 'And,' Fronto added, 'make it clear to him that the bridge is important.'

'How?'

'Try to take it.'

Caesar frowned, but Fronto smiled. 'It sounds dangerous, but bear in mind how narrow the bridge is. Casualties can be kept to a minimum while making it look like a real attempt. We bring forward stakes, barrows and timbers, as though we intend to take the bridge and fortify their end of it.'

'And consequently they will press back.'

'They will deploy everything they have and settle for the long war. That will make it all the harder for them to move swiftly when we depart.'

Caesar smiled.

* * *

'With the greatest respect, if I see you in the press, sir, I will punch you myself.'

Fronto glared at Atenos, but the primus pilus of the Tenth met his gaze with a steely one of his own.

'Alright. But be careful. I want as few casualties as possible.'

Atenos gave him a long-suffering smile and turned to his centurions. 'Carinus, you and I take pride of place. The First and Second Centuries have the most weight and muscle. We're going to drop into testudo the moment there's any resistance and push forward. I want to reach the far side of the bridge straight away. Then, Nonius, you start ferrying over rampart materials behind us. Carinus, the moment we're in real danger, fall your men back, while Quintus brings his up to cover you, and I'll do the same while Statius covers me. We need it to look like we've overextended and had to withdraw. I don't care if you have to push a few barrows and beams into the river to add to the look.'

The officers saluted, and in moments they were moving. The enemy were still busy at their camps, clearly visible across the bridge, busily extending their ramparts to the water's edge where pila and arrows were still being exchanged. The Tenth moved without a signal given. The first two centuries simply burst out of the Caesarian lines and ran for the bridge, only falling into formation as they reached the end of the plank surface.

Atenos and his fellow centurion, leading from the front as always, gripped their shields and pulled them up, covering their front as they now ran onto the makeshift bridge, wary of the fact that there were no rails to either side. One hundred paces long, eight men wide, the bridge stretched across a river deep enough to drown a cavalry unit and fast flowing enough to carry a man to his doom.

As they ran, he kept his eyes on the Pompeian camp ahead, two hundred paces from the end of the bridge. Someone among the enemy had seen the sudden movement and responded, for now men were assembling in centuries and beginning to move to counter the charge. Atenos grinned. They had the advantage of surprise and speed, and were certain now to make the far side before the enemy could reach them. They wouldn't need the testudo after all. The enemy had been slower moving than he'd anticipated.

As they pounded across the bridge, the enemy moved to a run, attempting to reach them, centuries forming and following on, not waiting for a full legion to be ready.

'Three men apiece and then on the defensive, remember,' Atenos bellowed.

He felt, rather than saw, the change in terrain as they reached the far end of the bridge. Rather than the clattering boards, he felt the solid turf of the south bank, and shouted the order to halt. The Tenth pulled up sharp and began to form the shield wall even as their mates bumped into them from behind with the momentum. In moments the Tenth had fanned out into an arc around the south end of the bridge. Shields clattered against one another and the front line edged their blades into the gaps ready, while the second line formed and brought pila up, prepared to stab over the top.

Atenos watched the men coming towards them. They gleamed too much, and their shields were too bright. Freshly painted. New armour and untouched shields. A green, novice legion. He smiled. Well, they wouldn't be untouched for long.

'Brace.'

The Pompeian legionaries hit their shield wall like a tide, and Atenos had to give them their due, for they lacked nothing in courage or strength. Still, their lack of experience began to show immediately. The men of the Tenth, many of whom had served in Gaul, Greece and Africa, held their line like professionals, refusing to give any ground under the pressure of the enemy. Their blades jabbed out between shields when any opportunity arose, each time forcing an enemy legionary back, staggering, either wounded or badly bruised through his chain shirt. There was no concerted effort to the enemy attack, and Atenos had to feel for the centurions he could hear and see among the Pompeian legion. Unlike their men, they would be professional veterans, and their voices were angry as they repeated again and again orders to their men to hold, to move together, to keep their shields up, not to over reach, and so on.

The rate of attrition among the enemy was appalling, while few of Atenos' men suffered. Finally, one of the enemy centurions succeeded in having his men withdraw a step or two, regroup and form up afresh. At his command, they moved forward for a new attempt, but Atenos was ready. Catching Carinus' eye across the line, he bellowed 'tilt!'

In a single, well practised manoeuvre, as the enemy legionaries came at them, each men in the Caesarian shield wall stamped their right leg forward, the turning of their bodies tilting their shields and exposing their right side. This allowed each man plenty of space with his blade, and swords lanced, hacked, chopped and slashed all along the line in the sudden freedom. The enemy attack crumbled once more, every second or third man staggering back wounded or ducking away from a blow.

Damage dealt, every defender pulled back their right leg, closed the shields once more and kept their blades visible only through the gaps. As they breathed, the second line took advantage of the enemy's shock to stab hard with pila, some casting them enthusiastically over into the enemy crowd.

The piles of bodies were beginning to mount, and Atenos realised then that they were in serious danger of winning here. They were only supposed to be making a show of it. If they actually took the bridge and managed to fortify this end, it would make leaving secretly a great deal more difficult. His men were too good, the enemy too green. He had to screw it up somehow.

Even now, planks and stakes were arriving behind them, ready to fortify. Atenos apologised to his gods. There was little he hated more than losing a fight, and doing so on purpose was truly galling, even if there was a solid tactical reason for doing so. He turned and hissed through clenched teeth. 'Allow them a breach this time. Fall back, else we'll have to build a wall here.'

His men, realising that they were doing too well for their own good, grinned.

The enemy regrouped, clambering over the piles of their dead, and pushed for the Caesarian line once more. Atenos let them come. He had half a dozen manoeuvres he could pull yet to wear them down, but that really wasn't the point. Indeed, he could see over the top of the enemy back towards the camp, a veteran legion forming up ready to support the push. Once they got involved, the number of Caesarian casualties would rise phenomenally.

As such, he let his men work. The optios and lead men of each tent party were used to working together, and each man was a veteran, knowing how to make the best of any situation. As the enemy hit their wall, someone in the middle cried out and fell back, as though wounded, his mates pulling him through the second line and into the third. The enemy roared their success and pressed into the gap. Atenos felt pride in his men as he watched them at work. As the flanks pulled back in, edging onto the bridge, the apparent breach in the centre closed once more, denying the enemy, but began to move back, as though caving under the pressure. That was not what they were doing, though, for they moved carefully and slowly back, one step at a time, allowing the extended, curved line to straighten and pull back together, leaving no one stranded beyond the bridge.

Atenos stabbed out at one man desperately trying to leap in among the shields, delivering a blow of which any training officer would be proud, the point jamming into the neck between helmet and chain shirt. As the man fell away, the centurion kept pace with his men, backing away across the bridge one pace at a time. Warnings came forward for any obstruction, and they backstepped carefully over discarded timbers and around barrows and baskets, leaving apparent evidence of their intent to fortify the bridgehead.

Once they were on the bridge and moving, the enemy centurions stopped their own advance, preventing the legion from moving into a fresh attack across the cluttered space. The veteran Pompeian officers were all too aware that any attempt to follow up on their 'victory' would undoubtedly land them in very much the same position as the Tenth had just occupied.

Atenos watched with satisfaction as the enemy jeered and whistled, watching the Caesarian force retreat across the bridge. As they reached the north bank once more, they moved across the grass and retreated behind the ramparts, a bank of earth and wicker fence dotted with timber platforms, all of it higher than a man. They passed through the gate, still backstepping as they went, and Atenos turned to see Fronto grinning at him.

'Bugger me but I thought you were going to try and take them for a while.'

'Nearly did,' laughed Atenos.

* * *

Fronto watched the last unit depart and turned to glance back towards the ramparts. He had two hundred men, more or less. Three understrength centuries. He'd chosen them himself for four factors. Firstly they had to be good horsemen. These were the best riders in the Tenth Equestris, for they needed to mount up and race away swiftly. They needed to be good shots with scorpions, onagers and pila, which they were. They had to be longstanding veterans, because that meant both that they could take orders and that they were lucky enough to ensure survival. And lastly, they had to be mad bastards to a man. Mad enough to volunteer for this.

Two hundred men. And they had all been briefed. They would get no sleep this night, and neither would Fronto. He'd had them being very visible. They had lit more torches than usual, and campfires burned all across the deserted camps, an indication to

Pompey's scouts that the force remained in quarters for the night. The two hundred had spent the last three hours marching around palisades and being visible on the platforms. They had been back and forth to collect debris from the fight at the bridge, making themselves very visible. As far as anyone watching from Pompey's camp would judge, nothing was amiss among the Caesarian forces. Certainly no one would suspect that all bar two hundred had moved out as soon as dusk fell, unburdened by unnecessary kit and moving quietly and fast. They had travelled a mile to the new bridge upstream and had crossed there, arcing out east to pass by the Pompeian force unseen.

Fronto had been timing it carefully, allowing his men their easy ruse, knowing that the break point would come soon. His eyes had been on the eastern dark sky all night, despite having had men watching it for him. They had all been aware that Gnaeus Pompey would have pickets and scouts out, and Caesar's force would have to overcome at least one of them. If it was noticed, that could ruin the entire ruse, and so Fronto had a distraction ready when required.

Still, it took a moment for him to realise what he'd seen as the distant spark glimmered in the black night, a fire arrow sent up as a signal. That meant Caesar had encountered one of Pompey's sentries or pickets and was in danger of discovery. Fronto had to move fast. Everything now was about drawing all of Pompey's attention.

He threw an arm out at the cornicen, who gave two short blasts. The small garrison began to move immediately. New torches burst into life high on the artillery platforms, even as twenty men picked up a mantlet and began to move towards the bridge. Behind them, four men ran, carrying two scorpions between them, two more bringing up boxes of ammunition.

A call went up in the enemy camp almost immediately and figures began to move. Fronto grinned. This would keep them busy. He'd had his artillerists note distances and ranges all afternoon and some of those men who'd been retrieving gear from the bridge had taken the opportunity to mark the range with a coloured stick. There was no need for a command, or for further signals. His men were thoroughly briefed, competent, and knew what they were doing. The men with the covered shelter, holding it up at knee height in the manner of a litter, ran it out onto the bridge, looking as though they intended to reach the enemy camp. Fronto could see Pompeians now hurrying towards the artillery the enemy had put in place only hours earlier. The mantlet reached a position more than halfway across the bridge, marked with a white stick, and was unceremoniously dropped, creating an armoured shelter on the middle of the bridge. In moments the other men had reached it and were putting the scorpions into position, their launching runners lined up with the small slits in the mantlet's forward facing timber wall.

In moments, they were at work, the men selected as the best scorpion crews in the Tenth. The machines were ratchetted back, loaded, aimed through the slit, and released. Fronto watched with a grin as two men with crests standing on the Pompeian rampart disappeared with a squawk. Even as the two officers fell, the crews were already at work, ratchetting, loading, spotting their prey. They would keep working until the signal, and they were good. No one was safe. As the enemy hurried to get their own artillery working, Fronto watched signifers, officers, scouts, musicians, and even a man with a priest's folds across his scalp busy blessing the Pompeian artillery, all disappear in a cloud of blood and a scream. They were picking their targets well.

And every moment allowed Caesar to deal with any pickets he found without drawing undue attention and move off to the south, heading for Ategua.

The very moment the enemy shot began to come, the crews leapt into action. Now that they had the Pompeians' attention, and before they were taken down by enemy artillery, the crews lifted the mantlets and scorpions and moved back twenty paces to the yellow stick marker. Fronto almost laughed as they settled into position again and went back to work. The shots were difficult now for they were at maximum range, but they were his best men. Not bothering to select important targets any more, they now aimed for groups of men, and so still their missiles struck home. The enemy artillery, however, less experienced and well-trained and similarly at maximum range, were falling short of the mantle and flying wide with every launch.

Fronto could almost sense the frustration in the enemy officers, all of whom were now keeping safely out of range. Unable to effectively counter Fronto's nagging artillery strikes from the bridge, the enemy sent out a half century of legionaries at a run, heading for the bridge to take the scorpions out. Fronto listened for the telltale noises and smiled as his own artillery moved to their response. Even as the two scorpions on the bridge continued to launch at the enemy camp, the platforms all along the rampart began to launch, their missiles falling invariably into that small cloud of running soldiers. He watched as the half century was struck repeatedly, leaving a trail of bodies across the grass, until finally the men lost heart, turned and ran back for their own lines, stripped of half their manpower.

For the next half hour he watched the to-ing and fro-ing of enemy attempts to deal with the irritation, and at one point they succeeded in knocking out an artillerist, though he was swiftly replaced, and once they managed to land a fire shot on the mantle, though that was doused with river water in heartbeats. Finally, one of the sentries reported a second flare way off to the east. The signal that Caesar's column was clear. The army had crushed a picket post, leaving no survivors to report to Pompey. Caesar was on his way to Ategua with the legions, and Pompey remained unaware, his gaze fixed firmly on the bridge.

At a silent signal from Fronto, new fires were lit in the camp, others fed fresh fuel, cloaks and shapes were propped up by the fence, resembling men in the dark, and finally the crews at the mantlet withdrew, running back across the bridge.

Fronto waited for a while in the strange silence that followed, watching the enemy camp. Finally, someone decided that the Caesarians were done, and a small unit was dispatched to the bridge to remove the mantlet and scorpions. Fronto grinned, gave a wave, and his artillerists made the enemy regret running out into the open once more. Men died in droves as they ran towards the bridge, and once again they gave up halfway and returned to the camp to watch and glower.

Fronto smiled at the centurion standing nearby.

'I think we've warned them off following for a while. Have everyone fall back to the corral as quietly as they can. Let's put some distance between us and this place before Pompey discovers we've gone.'

He smiled all the way to Bucephalus. Two generations of Pompeys had fallen for the same ruse. Now to hit Ategua.

CHAPTER TWELVE

New Year 45 BC

Galronus peered off into the mist. The skeletal, crabbed fingers of winter trees loomed like faint shadows in the blanket of white. He turned to the native rider beside him, a volunteer from Ulia.

'How far to the furthest fort?'

'Three miles from here, five from camp.'

'And the nearest?'

'They span the road every mile,' the man replied, 'give or take. As per best practice they were positioned on high ground with gentle slopes and a good view.'

Galronus snorted. A good view today meant being able to see as far as your feet. The man gave a wry smile. 'In theory, anyway.'

He nodded again, peering into the mist. Four days they had been here now. Caesar's messenger had reached Ulia during a local festival, when the city's inhabitants had been unveiling a temple rededicated to Venus Genetrix in honour of Caesar, their saviour. Pompey's army had remained invested at Ulia only a few days more before word had come of the general's approach on Corduba and, frustrated, Pompey had abandoned the siege to run and help his brother. Additionally, the rains had stopped and, despite the mid-winter date, the air had warmed a little, leading to thick morning mists that only burned off by afternoon. The citizens had celebrated for three whole days, ostensibly for the festival, but largely out of relief from their sudden freedom. Galronus and Paciaecus and their men had become instant celebrities and honoured guests.

It had been something of a subject for moans and grumbles among the men when they had been forced to abandon the festival and gather their kit once more. Caesar had drawn both Pompeys to

Corduba and neatly sidestepped them, making for a major enemy garrison at Ategua, and wished his army to recombine there. Ategua being only ten miles from Ulia, it had not taken long, and Galronus and the others had arrived half a day before Caesar, giving them adequate time to scout the area. They had identified the best positions for camps and were already beginning to settle in when Caesar and the rest arrived. Given Galronus' activity thus far, Caesar had left the cavalry to it, and while the general worked on fortifying a camp close to the heavily-defended town, and beginning preparations for a siege, Galronus had had his officers pitch camps all around the area, especially concentrated on the road from Corduba. A score of local volunteers, who had joined them in Ulia, had been instrumental in selecting the sites, and in each they had created a cavalry camp for an ala of three hundred riders.

'And we've heard nothing?'

'Nothing since last night, but that's no surprise, sir. We didn't arrange regular reports, since each camp was within sight of one another, especially with camp fires.'

'Lack of foresight,' Galronus chided himself aloud. 'In this stuff we couldn't see our *own* camp fire. Organise riders to make for every fort and check in. From then on, I want hourly reports delivered to the central camp.'

The man nodded and turned his horse, riding off into the mist. Galronus sat alone and uncomfortable in the blanket of cold, damp white. He could just make out his favoured turma of Remi and Aedui riders, kitted for action, as they always were. Trotting across to them, he beckoned to the leader.

'This is making me nervous,' he announced. 'Let's ride the Corduba road and check in.'

As the unit fell into formation and moved onto the road, Galronus stepped his horse out in front and stroked her mane, calming her. She seemed unusually skittish this morning, but then he felt much the same. The mist had that effect.

The very heart of the winter, and as they rode, Galronus found himself increasingly uncomfortable. The air was far from hot, yet was warm enough with the mist to make clothing unpleasantly clammy, and his tunic and trousers clung to him as he rode. He almost jumped as they passed a bushy hedgerow and something wild, startled, scurried away, accompanied by cracking and shuffling noises, the loudest thing he'd heard in this enveloping blanket of white silence. Even his own cavalry, accompanying him, were oddly muted in these conditions.

They came across the first of the outlying Corduba road forts almost by surprise. Though they had already estimated their travel at a mile, the suddenness with which the turf rampart and wattle fence emerged from the mist still startled them. A sentry saw them at the same time as they saw him, just a distance of perhaps twenty paces. Alarmed, he called for them to identify themselves and only relaxed when he knew they were allies. Even in the morning light, they had torches burning along the ramparts in an attempt to improve visibility and help keep the sentries warm.

'What have you heard?' Galronus asked him.

'No activity so far, sir,' the dismounted rider replied. 'We've a picket a few hundred paces up the road, and at first light there had been no sign of trouble further forward. Apollinaris, from the next camp, sent back a deer they'd brought down as a gift for the chief. He said they'd seen nothing but rabbits, birds and the deer.'

'Lucky to see anything at all,' noted Galronus, then thanked the soldier, and they moved on, passing the picket just up the road, holding his cavalry tuba ready to blow an alarm at the first sign of trouble.. Another mile of white-shrouded silence, and they found the second camp with ease, sitting atop a rise right beside the road. The soldier there had similar tales to tell. No sign of trouble and contact with both adjacent forts at first light. They moved on, and once again passed the picket with his horn, looking jumpy in the mist.

A third mile passed, and Galronus was relieved to see the shape of the ramparts emerge from the sea of white, torches flaring intermittently along the fence. His nerves jumped, and he only realised something was wrong as he approached the camp and noted no figure standing at the gate. The hair rose on his neck and his hand went to his sword hilt.

'Watch yourselves,' he said. 'Fan out. Find the picket.'

As three men rode ahead and the others split off into small groups, weapons drawn, searching the impossibly white world around the ramparts, Galronus and five men made their way into the gate. His worst fears were realised in a moment and his sword slid from its sheath. The guard lay on his back a few paces inside, his chain shirt soaked with blood and a bent pilum ruining his discarded shield. As they moved around the camp's interior, a tale of massacre unfolded. The cavalry unit had been destroyed in detail. He could see men lying face down with arrows peppering their back, others clearly butchered while trying to fasten helmet straps. Two men lay dead, covered in sword wounds, at the entrance to the corral, hurrying to retrieve the horses for the unit before the enemy overwhelmed them. They had failed. Even an estimate at the number of bodies he could see in the mist suggested a complete massacre of the unit. Their horses had gone, taken by the attackers, as had the supplies from the small compound in one corner of the camp.

'Sir,' one of the riders said, his voice tight.

'Yes?'

'If they already hit here, where did they go?'

'A very good question. We didn't pass them on the road. They hit this place by complete surprise. The whole unit was butchered before they could arm and mount up. Come with me.'

Alarm racing around his body now, he trotted back out of the gate in time to meet riders converging.

'Picket was taken out by archers,' one announced. 'Never even had time to lift his horn.'

'They came from the Corduba road,' said another, 'but they left across open country, off to the east.'

'Tracks?' Galronus asked. 'How many were there? Horse? Infantry? Are we talking about an advance unit or Pompey's whole army?'

'Only boot prints on the road,' one said. 'Hard to tell numbers.'

'Boots and hooves across the fields,' another added. 'Probably about a cohort. No more than two.'

Galronus nodded. Between five hundred and a thousand infantry. Clearly legionaries with archer support from the evidence in this camp. Pompey's vanguard in all likelihood. They'd hit the place completely unexpected, and then moved off road. Why? The answer struck him as he glanced back. They'd been lucky to put down the picket, for he'd have been watching the road with care. They might not manage the same twice, and if the defenders had time to prepare, the attack could be far worse. They were coming from the fields next time to minimise the chance of an alarm. That was why Galronus and his men had seen no sign of them.

'Form up. We need to warn the next fort.'

Moments later they were moving off once more, this time at speed, hurrying back south along the road and making for the next cavalry installation. Galronus rode with his heart in his mouth. Pompey's army had to be close, and Caesar's garrisons were being taken out systematically in the fog. Had they not ridden out to check on a whim, he was quite certain that Caesar would have quietly finished his lunch to discover Pompey's army a stone's throw from his tent. A thought occurred to him, and he pointed at three of his fastest riders. 'You three, split off. Two of you head to the other camps on the Ulia road and the Ucubi road. Pompey's had long enough since Caesar left Corduba to divide his army, and I reckon they'll hit every approach: one force to each road. The third of you, move off road to the west and ride for Caesar's camp with the news. All of you go careful and avoid any encounter.'

As the three riders hurtled off into the white, Galronus concentrated on the road they travelled back towards the middle fort.

They were too late, and he knew it even before they passed the body of the picket, horn untouched, arrows jutting from his face and neck. He knew it because of the noise. Galronus had grown so accustomed to the muted silence of this foggy world, that the sound of battle seemed a peculiar thing, especially when heard muted, yet completely invisible in the wall of white. As they approached the gate, he could see a struggle ongoing within the fort, men charging this way and that, screaming, pila flying, and a distinct lack of mounted soldiers. Once again, Pompey's cohort had surprised the cavalry before they could mount up.

He was about to order his men to join the fray when something smacked into his arm. In surprise, he lifted his sword arm and stared. An arrow had hit him just above the elbow on the back of his upper arm. By sheer chance it had been a glancing blow and had torn into the flesh and wedged there, having missed bone, muscle and sinew. His men were not all so lucky. Three riders around him fell to the hail of missiles. He growled, turning this way and that. The source of the arrows was still invisible in the white, though from the direction whence the missile had struck him, he could estimate the archers' location, off the road opposite the cavalry fort. Once the enemy infantry had gained the camp's gate and ramparts, the archers had been useless for fear of hitting their own, and had moved off out of the way until Galronus and his men appeared.

With a cry of rage, he directed his men towards the unseen archers. His riders roared and wheeled their mounts as a further volley emerged from the blanket of mist and thudded into men and horses, felling them. Had he more time to consider his moves, Galronus would have cut his losses and run. The men in the fort were done for, and he'd had only thirty riders with him, that number already whittled down by a third.

They charged into the white, and he realised his error only at the last moment. The archers were not unprotected. The horseman to his right, a veteran he remembered from as far back as Alesia, thundered from the mist straight into the infantry, a double line of legionaries formed to defend against horse, a bristling armoured hedge of shields and pila. The man's horse stumbled to a halt in refusal, the rider thrown forward, only held in place by the horned saddle, where one of the spears lanced out and took him in the side.

Two other men fell in the initial discovery, and Galronus himself almost joined them, hauling on his reins at the last moment, immensely grateful that his own mount was exceptionally brave and well-trained. Rather than bucking, it obeyed instantly, and the Remi backed up several steps as pila lanced out towards him, narrowly missing.

An arrow from somewhere behind the infantry clattered off his helmet, slightly dazing him.

They were done for.

'Retreat,' he bellowed. 'Back to camp.'

Turning, he felt more arrows whispering past him in the white, and his heart raced as he retreated into the mist, finding the road blindly and then turning and clattering off along it, heading south. He stopped only when he was sure he was out of arrow range, and then, gritting his teeth, snapped the arrow in his arm, yelping in pain. Then, taking a deep breath, he pulled free the remnants of the shaft, tying a tourniquet of ripped tunic with his free hand and his teeth. By the time he was done, four riders had joined him, all that was now left of the thirty with whom he'd ridden out.

'What now, sir?' one of them asked.

Galronus grunted, gripping and ungripping his hand, feeling the pain in his upper arm. 'Back to Caesar. We ride for the next camp and tell them to fall back on the way, and then we send riders everywhere else, telling everyone to pull back to the main camp.'

'But if they all fall back there will be no outlying force.'

'Anyone out here in the mist is going to get cut to pieces. It's a complete waste. We need everyone together and alert. Pompey's army is here.'

And with that, he kicked his horse into life and the five riders raced for safety.

* * *

Fronto had been quite happy in his tent, leaning back on his bed and drifting into a pleasant dream about the boys back in Rome when the alarm had been blown across the camp, horns blaring, calling everyone to arms. By the time he'd struggled back into his cuirass with the aid of a slave and hurried over to the command tent, where officers and praetorians milled and murmured, word had arrived from more than one source. The first had been Galronus, who Fronto missed, for his urgent report delivered, he'd rushed off to the medical tents to have some minor injury dealt with. After Galronus, though, had come other riders from various outlying camps, each with the same news: Pompeian cohorts had emerged from the mist and cut down the cavalry units with little or no warning. Few riders had escaped at all, and if current estimates were to be believed, they had lost around four thousand cavalry in a single morning, and without any real enemy casualties.

Fronto had cursed, but worse was yet to come. While the Pompeian cohorts had taken out the cavalry camps in the white, the main force had seemingly used the mist as cover to come around from an unexpected direction. Pompey must have set up camp somewhere between Ategua and Ucubi, on the far side of the River Salsum, for a sizeable force had been reported bearing down on Postumius' camp. This was Caesar's main fort south of the river, an infantry installation manned by six cohorts under Postumius, and which held a commanding view of the entire river valley, at least when the mist was gone each afternoon. Without that fort, Caesar would be effectively held to the north of the river.

The general had been furious at this sudden turn of events. The loss of the cavalry was bad enough, but to lose a legion and an important vantage point would be unacceptable. While the entire camp had now gone on the alert, the general would not let that second, smaller fort fall. His gaze had lit upon Fronto and an angry finger jabbed out. 'Marcus, raise the Tenth, the Sixth and the Fifth. Take them all and deny Pompey the fort.'

It had taken no time at all to gather the three legions and march from Caesar's camp. The Salsum was not a large river, just twenty paces across, winding and green, and in preparing the fort to the south they had formed a pontoon bridge of anchored rafts surmounted by planks and boards, so the three legions moved across the flow with ease. On the far bank, the fort was still completely invisible, hidden by the enshrouding world of white, and the only way to identify its location was to examine the ground close by for the marks of passage of many boots and hooves, trodden between the two camps.

Following the tracks, Fronto gradually picked out a distant hum of noise. Despite the blanket of fog that dulled sound, he could just make out enough to identify the muted din of battle. They were too late. Pompey's force had already reached the fort.

As he gave the order to advance at a run, Fronto fumed. This wasn't supposed to happen. The great Pompey had been a tactical genius to rival Caesar, and his end had heralded a marked diminishing in the rebel strategies. The younger Pompeys enjoyed a reputation as competent commanders, but neither had truly distinguished himself as a strategist. How, then, had they managed to turn around from being tricked and outrun at Corduba to being some sort of nightmare army surging out of mists and obliterating Caesar's garrisons?

A mental image of his old friend Labienus swam into focus, and that raised an alarming possibility. Certainly of all the enemy commanders, Caesar's old right hand was the one to watch. Had Labienus finally shown his face, adding his skill to that of the Pompeys?

As they ran, his breath becoming more laboured as the slope began to steepen towards the hilltop fort, he sent out a series of signals to each side. In response, the men of the Tenth at the fore slowed, allowing the Fifth and the Sixth to pull out to each side of them, forming a solid line of three legions rather than a narrow column. Once signals came back that the line was fully formed, Fronto gave another order and the entire army picked up the pace. As he ran, labouring up the slope alongside the Tenth, he became aware of Atenos looking at him. The senior centurion had a curious expression that Fronto suspected was formed from a mix of disapproval at his being at the front, and dry humour at the fact that he was getting too old to run up hills in armour, a fact that was also rapidly becoming apparent to Fronto.

Gradually, the fort emerged as a faint dark shape in the mist, atop the hill, surrounded by a shivering mass that had to be Pompey's assault force. Fronto smiled darkly. Despite Caesar's proximity, it seemed the enemy had no expectation of a relief force being sent. More fool them.

At silent motions from their officers, the three legions closed upon the rear of the Pompeian attackers, keeping quiet, only the sounds of their pounding feet and the clonk and shush of armour and weapons issuing, and that largely dulled by the fog. It was only as they became visible to the enemy that the Caesarians made a noise. As a cry of alarm went up among the jostling foe, Atenos bellowed a terrifying war cry in his native tongue, and the men of the three legions responded with war cries of their own as they slammed to a halt and let go of the pila each man had readied as he ran.

A thousand javelins rose, sweeping up the slope, and fell among the nearest of the enemy, sending a chorus of screams and alarmed cries up from the mass. The relief may have been too late to protect or warn the fort, but the battle was far from over, and Fronto could make out soldiers of Postumius' Twenty Eighth Legion atop the ramparts, desperately trying to hold off a far more numerous force, stabbing down with pila and loosing scorpion bolts into the mass.

Having cast their pila, the men of Caesar's legions broke into a run once more. Fronto roared furiously, and then squawked in surprise as hands closed on him from behind and he found himself unceremoniously hauled back from the front line to a point of safety. Briefly he caught Atenos looking in his direction and formed the opinion that the centurion had arranged to have his men keep Fronto from danger. He spun, trying to identify who had held him back, but it was impossible to tell. Surrendering to the common sense of not placing himself in danger, Fronto allowed the legion to flow past him and into the rear of Pompey's cohorts.

He could sense almost immediately a change in the atmosphere as the confidence and fire of the Pompeians faltered at this unexpected turn of events. As he stood and watched his men press forward, he became aware that the fog was finally starting to burn off. The weak sun glowed as a white shape through the blanket above them, and more and more figures were becoming visible, the hilltop clearing of fog before the plains below.

Pompeians were still trying to take the fort, despite the arrival of Caesar's reinforcements, and figures were clambering up the defences, trying to overcome the legionaries there. Even as Fronto watched, two Pompeians managed to pull themselves across the fence, stabbing out together and taking down one of Postumius' men even as a third attacker was slain with the thrust of a javelin from an adjacent defender. The two victorious Pompeians did not celebrate for long. Fronto could not see what happened to them inside the fort, but moments later five more defenders took the place of the fallen one, and the bodies of the two Pompeians were thrown from the ramparts back into their own force.

Caesar's men, including the ones both inside and outside the fort, had to now roughly match the Pompeians in number, and the battle was becoming hard fought, as the besieging cohorts had begun to turn and fight back against the new arrivals. Fronto found himself almost instinctively falling into the traditional role of a senior officer, and wondered when that instinct had sunk in. When had he stopped being the man at the front, up to the knees in blood, and become the man at the back, ordering reserves into weak positions in the lines?

As he gestured for a century from the Eighth Cohort to move up and support the front lines where they were bowing dangerously back, his eyes played across the enemy and fell upon a sight that surprised him. As the mist continued to clear, he could now see almost to the far end of the fort wall, and there, two figures were visible above the crowd, two men on horseback. Both wore the uniforms of senior officers. One, facing him, was faintly familiar, and it took a few moments to realise who it was: the junior Marcus Porcius Cato, son of the great rebel leader. He had apparently fought at Thapsus and, though his father had died in Africa, the younger had apparently wound up fighting once more in Hispania. Given the eminence of his name, it seemed likely that Cato was the commander of this attack, despite his youth and lack of strategic experience.

Then the other figure turned, and Fronto's breath caught in his throat.

Titus Labienus.

He'd suspected as much, given the sudden upturn in the enemy's tactical decision making. From being run around by Caesar to being a deadly force stabbing unseen out of the fog. Labienus was behind this strategy, Fronto was certain, and yet this was not his attack, for Titus was a cavalry commander by custom, and the force that had swarmed over Caesar's fort had been of infantry cohorts.

He knew Labienus of old, and he had seen that waving of arms, that angry demeanour before. That was Titus Labienus disagreeing with another officer when he knew he was right. Fronto smiled. Cato had led this attack, and the moment Fronto had appeared with the relief, Labienus had told Cato to pull back, calling him off, knowing that their easy victory had just evaporated. But Cato was of no mind to pull back. He could see only victory. The two men continued to argue, and Fronto realised suddenly what a huge opportunity had dropped into his lap. Turning to see that his three legions were even now almost at the fort wall, having utterly battered the Pompeian attackers in this sector, he grinned and waved to a signifer with the Eighth Cohort, his planned reserve. Even having committed three centuries of the Eighth to the fight, there were still three waiting, and the other two legions had a good stock of reserves to help. The signifer caught his gestures and saluted, then began to wave his standard, calling to two other standard bearers. In mere heartbeats, the three reserve centuries from Fronto's legion were on the move, heading his way. As they fell in behind Fronto, who had started to walk along the rear of the army, the three centurions hurried to fall in beside him.

'What is it, sir?'

'Opportunity beckons, gentlemen. See those two officers?'

The three men peered off and located the pair of arguing horsemen in the press.

'Sir?'

'Marcus Porcius Cato and Titus Labienus. Press them and make them run, and this entire attack will falter and fail. Kill or capture either of them, and the enemy suffers a *major* setback; especially Labienus.'

The centurions grinned. 'Come on, lads,' one said, turning to his men. At calls from all three, the reserve centuries began to run. Fronto considered letting them get ahead again, but his jaw firmed and he pushed his own reserves of energy into his muscles and ran with them.

An alarm went up from close to the enemy officers as the two hundred Caesarians bore down on them. Cato threw out a hand and a unit of legionaries as yet uncommitted ran to block the way, undoubtedly Cato's bodyguard. Their centurion threw out his sword, point aimed at Fronto and bellowed at his men. Behind them, the argument between Cato and Labienus became more animated and furious.

'Attack,' cried Fronto, and managed to stay among the frontrunners as they hit the bodyguards. His sword stabbed out and he felt the aching resistance as the point slammed into a chain shirt, forcing the armour inwards. It prevented him impaling the shirt's owner, but there would be ribs broken beneath, for Fronto knew precisely what he was doing. The man's shield, failing to rise to block the blow, swung out to the side and Fronto grabbed at the rim, yanking it and pushing it down, breaking the fingers on the grip inside. The man howled and let go. In three heartbeats Fronto was equipped with a Pompeian shield, which he now used to block a stray sword before delivering the killing blow to his previous victim, a hefty slash to the neck as the man's head tipped to one side and his neck guard opened up space.

The man went down in a spray of blood, and Fronto found himself blocking another blow. Ducking low, he delivered a strike to the man's thigh and then rose, shield up, smashing it into the wounded man, sending him staggering back among his own. For a moment Fronto was free of action and took the opportunity to look around and take stock. His heart skipped as he saw another unit coming this way, and assumed it to be a second bodyguard unit hurrying to aid the first. Then he noted Caesar's Taurus emblem on their shields and realised it was men from the Fifth. The enemy were being solidly beaten back now, two walls of the fort cleared by the relief force, Pompey's men struggling to hold the Caesarians off.

His head came round to their target and his gaze met that of Labienus, glaring at him across the fight. His former colleague simply raised an eyebrow, threw out a last disparaging comment at Cato, then turned and rode hard for the south, disappearing into the mist on the lower slopes below. Silently, Fronto cursed at the missed chance to finally deal with their old friend. As long as Labienus lived, this would not be the last nasty surprise awaiting them.

Cato seemed finally swayed by the need to call off the attack, the more senior officer having fled the scene, his forces on the wane and having been fought back away from most of the fort's defences. The officer bellowed a command, a call to retreat was blown, and the man turned his horse and pounded away into the white on the heels of Labienus.

The enemy broke instantly. This was no ordered retreat, but a complete rout, and Fronto watched in satisfaction as the Pompeians fled down the slope into the mist, many dying even as they tried to run. Cheers were going up within the fort and among the relief forces outside. The first proper fight was theirs.

The bodyguards had been overcome now, and their centurion stood, captive and covered in blood, his arm hanging limp.

Fronto took a deep breath and waved to the nearest cornicen.

'Sound the *Ad Signum*. I don't want any lunatics chasing them into the mist. That way disaster lies. The Fifth and Sixth will take control of the fort, while the Twenty Eighth can join the Tenth and return to the main camp.'

As the orders were given, Fronto gazed off south into the fog.

'Another time, Titus.'

CHAPTER THIRTEEN

Mid January 45 BC

Quintus Pedius turned to the senior tribune of the Sixth, a man with a strangely squat face and all the charisma of a tufa block.

'We do what is asked of us by the general, Tiberius. Work on the siege lines is the command, and so here we are working on the siege lines.'

Sir, we are dangerously close to the city walls, almost certainly within maximum range of their artillery.'

'Which, coincidentally, makes the city walls within maximum range of our siege engines, Tiberius. Handy, eh?' Though he had to admit that the proximity had its dangers. All around, he could see men yawning and struggling, for throughout the night, as they had tried to sleep among the works, the defenders of Ategua had hurled fire brands and rocks from the walls, with occasional successes, for a few tents had burned, and a stack of wicker screens had gone up a treat, illuminating the whole camp for a while.

The tribune shifted from foot to foot and gave Pedius a look that was probably supposed to be loaded with meaning, though, given his peculiar features, he looked more constipated than anything. 'Sir you are the general's great nephew. Dare he expose you to danger here? Could not one of the other legions do this work?'

Pedius sighed. In his experience the senior tribunes were supposed to be competent; a benefit to the legion they served. The junior tribunes were all political wannabes from Rome, desperate to get through two or three years of not doing too much but wearing a fancy uniform in order to climb the career ladder back home, and he knew damn well not to trust a junior tribune with anything more than putting his underwear on the right way round, but the senior tribune was a legate's second in command, a nobleman chosen for the job. Who chose Tiberius remained to be ascertained, but clearly the man needed a kick up the arse.

'Tiberius, we are all servants of the republic, and it is our job to put ourselves in danger. I'm sure you've read my uncle's war diaries, since they've been made available in Rome to the public over the years. He himself has stood in the line and put steel in Belgic flesh. Why should we expect any favours?'

Tiberius grunted a sullen reply and saluted, returning to duty. Quintus Pedius clasped his hands behind his back, standing as he was on a timber platform and overseeing the work all around. He felt a touch of satisfaction at what he could see.

For more than a week now, everything had settled into a strange inactivity in terms of battle. After Cato's push to take Caesar's camp across the river, the enemy had learned their lesson, and no similar large-scale action had taken place. Pompey and Labienus remained in their camp across the river, distant enough to be just within sight, his control of the lands south of the Salsum complete apart from that one Caesarian fort that represented a bridgehead. Labienus was shrewd enough not to attempt a full-scale attack across the river, and so they sat silent, waiting, watching.

Which was not to say they were inactive. The attacks on Caesar's supply lines had begun almost immediately, and foraging in the region was becoming extremely dangerous, for Pompeian forces lurked ready everywhere. The enemy seemed content to pin Caesar north of the river, against the walls of Ategua and let him gradually starve, for that was what would happen as winter rolled on into spring. Indeed, the irregular arrivals of deserters from Pompey's army confirmed that very tactic, just as deserters from Caesar's army had probably informed the enemy of the tightening supply situation.

The arrival of new forces at Caesar's camp had only highlighted the value of Pompey's stratagem. The day after the fight at the fort, a sizeable column had turned up; the very men for whom Caesar had been waiting at Corduba. Gaius Arguetius had brought five double-sized cohorts of strong veterans from Saguntum, a large number of Cantabrian cavalry, whose king, Indo, had fallen to one of the many Pompeian raids on their journey, and who were looking now for revenge, and even freshly arrived Gallic cavalry come from northern Italia. Perhaps the greatest surprise addition, though, had been the army of Bogud, King of Mauretania, a man who had helped Sittius batter the Numidians during the African War. Now free of pressure, the Mauretanian king had brought his forces across the water to aid his ally Caesar further.

The presence of that large relief force brought joy to the men of Caesar's army, bolstering their numbers and bringing them closer to Pompey's level, but it had put extra pressure on the officers. More mouths meant more food, and every day saw less of it arriving. Pompey and Labienus had approached their fresh strategy carefully, and it was going to work. Unless Ategua capitulated soon, and its supplies fell into Caesar's hands, the army would begin to starve.

And so while Pompey sat in his camp and let hunger gradually ravage his opponents, the Caesarian army began the task of taking Ategua. Its fall would save them from starvation and put a massive hole in Pompey's own numbers and supplies.

Five legions were at work around the city, investing it with siege lines ready for the artillery to be brought up. Ategua was a Pompeian city, with precious little sign of support for Caesar, and so there was no great care for the damage its walls might suffer.

'Sir,' called one of the men on another platform, twenty paces away.

'What?'

'The gates are opening.'

Pedius peered at the town. The nearest gate was indeed now peeling back inwards, and the shapes of men appeared in the black maw, a sizeable force, pressed into the space as they burst out like ants from a nest.

'Ad signum,' Pedius bellowed, to which the standard bearers all across the works waved their burdens and the musicians blew the cadence. Men hurried from their work, abandoning barrows and baskets of stones, casting aside saws and mattocks, jamming on their helmets and sweeping up their shields as they ran to their unit standards.

'Damn it,' Pedius fumed. Another day and they'd have had the rampart and ditch complete, which would give them a solid defence against such sallies. The enemy from the town would hardly do enough damage to prevent them finishing, so what could they be…?

He turned, frowning. A hundred paces behind him sat the treeline, marking the line of a seasonal stream currently in full flow. It had served as the water supply for his men the past two days, but it also provided the timber for the siege towers and mantlets being constructed by his engineers ready for the first assault when it was ordered.

His eyes, narrowed, went back to the force issuing from the city gate. There were more fire brands among that mass. They could not hope for a solid victory here, but if they had seen the siege engines being constructed from the walls...

'They're coming for the construction site in the woods,' he bellowed across to the primus pilus who was busy overseeing his men falling in. 'They mean to burn the towers. We need to contain them.'

The centurion looked up at him, then to the approaching force, then back to the woods, then nodded. Pedius watched as the men of the Sixth followed the commands of their centurions with efficiency. He was proud of his command. The Sixth were six year veterans now. Newly raised at the time, they had cut their teeth on the siege of Alesia. This was nothing new to them, and most of the men were veterans from that very campaign.

The enemy were racing down the slope from the hilltop town now, a mass of armed fury. Pedius shook his head. Where was their discipline? These men might be the enemy, but they were legionaries. It only went to show the quality of the legions Pompey had hastily raised in his time here, for the enemy resembled a mob rather than a cohort. As he watched, they divided into two forces, forking out.

'They're splitting,' he shouted. 'Trying to bypass us and get to the work site.'

But the primus pilus was ahead of him, had already seen the change. With just a couple of quick orders, the Sixth altered formation. Four cohorts moved off to the left to intercept one force, four more to the right for the other. Of the remaining two, one settled into a long line at the centre, refusing to leave a gap, while the last withdrew under their commander to the treeline, defending the towers.

Pedius nodded once again. Off to the left, the enemy closed, while the men of the Sixth settled into a triple line, their heaviest and best armoured veterans in the front, forming a shield wall. A gap of a pace followed by the second line, who had collected what pila were available, while the third waited impatiently in reserve. The centurions among them had extended the line and curved it, an action mirrored by the cohorts to the right, so that the entire force formed the shape of a wide, shallow crescent or bowl.

As the enemy closed, at fifty paces, the middle line hefted their pila and, at a horn blast, cast them over the top of the first line. It was a difficult manoeuvre, for hurling the missiles safely over the heads of a line of men five deep was troublesome, but the Sixth were veterans and their manoeuvres well practised. The timing was excellent. The cloud of several hundred javelins sailed out over the front lines close enough to almost brush the crests of the centurions and optios among them. The braced men at the front had to have flinched as the shafts thrummed over their heads just a few feet up. The effect was impressive. The pila ploughed into the front line of the charging enemy almost as they reached the defenders. All across the front of the running mob, men fell, screaming, and chaos ensued as their companions fell over them, tripped on bent shafts, tumbled to the ground or leapt across their fallen friends.

By the time the enemy reached the line of the Sixth they were a scattered mob of panicked, wounded, and half-exhausted shaky men. Pedius smiled to himself as he watched. The line of the Sixth hardly even bent under the pressure, let alone breaking. They simply set to work, butchering. Here and there, Pedius could see small successes for the enemy, where they managed to pull aside men from the Caesarian line and almost cause a breach, but on each occasion the solid legionaries of the Sixth pushed back and filled the gap, reforming the line. That, Pedius mused, was the difference between a well-trained legion that had fought and practised across the world for more than half a decade, and a newly-raised and half-trained levy. No matter the comparative numbers, give him a small force of veterans over a mass of rabble any day. It was Pedius' opinion that the days of the republic's "legions of convenience" were over. There was no room now for the raising and disbanding of units for a particular campaign. They needed to be permanent and well-trained like the consular legions.

The enemy were making no headway, contained perfectly by the professional Sixth, and Pedius smiled. He had been about to give a fresh command, but the primus pilus had apparently anticipated him. Pedius might have the advantage of a good viewpoint, but the senior centurion was no novice to such action. He bellowed out a command, followed by a series of blasts from his whistle, and the entire line of nine cohorts began to change shape, the lines flowing like tidal water, curving gracefully, changing from that shallow bowl shape, gradually into a true crescent. As they moved, they gradually flanked the enemy to each side, driving them from the periphery towards the heart of the fight, merging their two forces into one at the centre, surrounded on three sides by the Caesarian force. As he watched, men were drawn from the rear lines at both flanks, adding their weight to that one cohort at the centre, doubling, then tripling the line.

It was masterful. Now the enemy were in a panic, being flensed from every direction but the rear. Pedius nodded. Better to leave them a way out. With an escape route, men could be broken and made to rout. Trap them completely and you leave them with no option but to fight to the death. He watched them break. First the rear lines of the enemy mob began to scatter, fleeing the mass and running back up the hill towards the town, using their mates as a distraction to cover their flight, but in moments more and more were on the run. Then, gradually, word of the rout reached the warriors at the front, and the fight went out of them. From that moment on, the battle was over, and Pedius just watched as the Sixth massacred running men, harrying them until they had run beyond the incomplete siege works.

As the survivors, not more than half their force, ran up the slope, whistles and cornua blew, standards waved, and the Sixth once more fell into formation within their camp. Pedius wondered whether this was an isolated incident driven by the desire to destroy siege engines visible from the walls, or part of a larger attempt. Had the other working legions faced such a fight?

Shrugging off his musings, he gestured to the primus pilus.

'Fall the men out, apart from sentries. The enemy won't come again any time soon, and the Sixth could do with an hour's rest before we get back to work.' A thought occurred to him. 'And load the enemy dead into barrows. I want them wheeled up to the city gate and dumped in a pile in front of it. Double wine ration and an extra hour's break for any man who volunteers for that duty.'

He smiled. The afternoons tended to get windy at the moment. As soon as the winds picked up and carried in a northerly direction he'd have the pile of enemy dead burned and let the city choke on the smell.

* * *

Galronus hurried out of his tent, belting on his sword. Outside, one of his senior officers sat astride his horse with a bleak expression. 'Tell me everything.'

'They crossed just before dawn, Chief.'

'How many?'

'At a guess, two cohorts, but they've been coming steadily now since first light. It's only a pontoon bridge, but it's doing the job.'

'How many casualties?'

The man shrugged. 'Low double figures, I think. It's the benefit of horses: easy to get out fast. But they're not happy.'

'I can imagine. Caesar's going to want to take this out on someone.'

'Will he deploy the legions to deal with it?'

Galronus shook his head. 'He won't get the chance. This is a matter of pride for the tribes, Druccus. We let this happen. We have to put it right before Caesar can do anything. This is a job for the Germans. Go find Fridumar and tell him I want his entire warband assembled here now.'

As his man rode off to find the commander of the fearsome Ubii, Batavi and Tungri, Galronus fumed. He'd not expected any trouble in that quarter. Thus far all Pompey's activity had been based around the centre, between the two camps, where Caesar's bridge lay, and Postumius' contested fort. The peripheral reaches of the river had been under the watchful eye of small units of cavalry. For well over a week now they had seen nothing but a little activity across the river where Pompey was carrying his lines of defence down to the riverbank. How were they to know what he intended? Some clever bastard among the Pompeian command had lulled them into a false sense of security, and then this morning, before first light, they had brought down rafts and barges to the river side and extended their defences across the river with a pontoon bridge. Before anyone knew it, they had overcome several small cavalry units, sending them running, ferried legionaries across, and begun creating a camp on Caesar's side of the river.

Within the hour, Caesar could have a legionary force ready to fight them out, attempting to take that fort and drive them back across the river, but there were two problems with that. Firstly, it was a guarantee that the mind behind this little move had committed the best of their troops, and so any fight to take the new fort would be a hard one. Secondly, to commit sufficient men to deal with it, Caesar would have to pull critical men away from the siege of Ategua.

No, Galronus was determined. The cavalry had let this happen, and they would put it right. And he had an idea. The Pompeians thought they were facing cavalry, straight and rigid. Their own horse were largely Hispanic. They would not be prepared for the Germans, who Caesar usually kept for special missions. Well this *was* a special mission.

He peered off into the distance. He could see the fort being created even now. They were clever and determined. They had formed a perimeter of sharpened sudis stakes, which they'd managed in just moments while their friends had driven away the cavalry. Now, they were busy within that line, digging a ditch and raising a bank, building a true fort within their temporary fence. Once that was complete, with ramparts and towers, it would be an evil proposition for an attacking force.

He was fretting at the delay and had unpicked the stitching of one of his sleeves by the time Fridumar arrived beside him and announced that his men were assembled. Galronus looked over his shoulder. One and a half thousand horse were sat in the staging ground near the camp gate.

'What's the plan?' the Tungrian chief asked, wiping his nose on his sleeve.

'I wasn't aware you ever stuck to a plan anyway,' Galronus said archly. 'I've never seen any evidence of a plan in your work.'

'To the uninitiated we are an enigma.'

That raised a bark of laughter from Galronus. In the old days, before Rome came, his people had faced almost annual raids from the Germans across the Rhenus. If Rome had achieved anything, they had stopped that, and here he was, relying on men his father had fought back off their lands.

'See that fort they're building?'

'Yes.'

'We need to stop it. They've been fighting cavalry, and will be expecting more of the same. I want you to stop them building and send them packing back across the river.'

Fridumar grinned. The man had an interesting collection of teeth, no two of which seemed to point in the same direction. 'My fuckin' pleasure.'

Galronus gathered his own horsemen, just a small force, and waited for the Tungrian and his tribes to move out, then fell in behind them. He would rather have liked to have kicked a few Pompeian backsides himself, but he'd learned over a decade of serving with these lunatics that it was not a healthy thing to be anywhere close by. Once they committed to action, they tended to kill whatever got in their way, be it friend or foe, and even occasionally their own.

Consequently he kept his men at the rear as they rode for the camp. The Pompeians were hard at work, but as the alarm went up at approaching horse, work halted, and the legionaries grabbed up their weapons and armour and hurried to the fort perimeter. The fence was formed of sudis stakes, essentially a line of giant timber caltrops, sharpened points jutting out. An excellent temporary defence against both infantry and cavalry. Behind the defence, the Pompeian legionaries set up in lines, shields up and pila out, ready to deal with any attack. Back at their pontoon bridge, work on ferrying over supplies was similarly halted, and the men there formed up, blockading their bridge to stop any horsemen attempting to race across it.

Galronus smiled. The Pompeians were ready for cavalry. No horse would charge that fence of stakes, and when they drew up and refused, the legions would cast their pila out, ravaging the force, then set to work defending their fortification with sword and shield. No ordinary cavalry unit would take that place from them.

But then the Germans were no ordinary cavalry.

From the rear of the line, Galronus watched, drawing up his men and gathering in a small crowd to observe the chaos he had unleashed. He was fairly sure that Caesar would be less than impressed that Galronus had committed the Germans, but then they were cavalry, and theoretically part of Galronus' force to command, for all that the general tended to consider them one of his pet units.

Fridumar and his men raced for the stake fence. The men defending it would be starting to wonder what was going on. No cavalry unit in their right mind charged a stake fence like that. Of course neither Fridumar nor any man riding with him could ever be accused of being in their right mind.

He could only imagine the shock among the Pompeians as the Germans did not stop. In fact, it did seem as though the German had a plan of sorts, for his men broke at the last moment into two simultaneous attacks. Roughly half his force ploughed to a sudden halt perhaps ten paces from the fence, leaping from their saddles and rolling, coming up to their feet at a run, bellowing incomprehensible Germanic cries, their horses forgotten, racing for the fence on foot, swords out. At the same time, the other half of the force actually picked up speed.

The Pompeians had no idea how to react. Their centurions yelled conflicting commands, and the defenders variously ducked back, pila raised to cast at the racing horsemen, who could now have no other intention than to jump the fence, or stepped forward to the fence, keeping low, preparing to fight off the dismounted cavalry.

In effect, neither was sufficient. The Germanic riders leapt, their powerful mounts rising and easily arcing over the fence of stakes, to come down amid the ordered lines of defenders. Here and there pila had taken down one of the leaping horses, but not enough to prevent the crazed disaster that then unfolded. The horses ploughed into the mass of legionaries like landing stones from an onager shot, smashing bodies and crushing men. Even as they landed, already Germanic longswords were swinging and chopping, cleaving and cutting. Had this been the only attack to content with, the Pompeians might just have managed to pull together a defence, but there was another horror assailing them yet.

The Tungrians, Ubians and Batavians who had leapt from their horses reached the fence of stakes and simply clambered up across them as though it were little more than a low mount, ignoring the pain of the sharpened points. Here and there a man found himself impaled, but even Galronus, who had seen these men at work before, winced as he watched one Batavian, his thigh impaled in a life-changing wound on one of the pointed timbers, who simply refused to acknowledge that he was done for. Even as he writhed on the sharpened stake, he stabbed and smashed with his sword and shield, snarling and howling, cutting down Pompeians as his blood flowed out in torrents across the fence that transfixed him.

Similar stories were being played out all across the line. German riders were scrambling across the fence with apparently no care for their own personal safety, the sheer bloody desire to carve the heart out of a Pompeian legionary overriding any fear or pain they might feel. Galronus shook his head in awe and amazement as he watched a Batavian busily hacking the head from a legionary, ignoring the fact that the Pompeian's friends were battering at him as he worked. He lifted the head free and howled the name of a god before disappearing beneath a flurry of blows. Even then he reappeared, briefly, holding a severed arm, before he vanished for good.

The riders who'd jumped the fence and waded through the lines of legionaries had managed to force and fight their way free, breaking out into the part-constructed camp behind the legionaries, where they turned and began to butcher the defenders from the rear.

Galronus gave a harsh laugh. They were done for. No matter that they were veterans and with a sudis fence, the legionaries were now trapped between Germans on horseback, carving holes in them, and Germans swarming over the fence and butchering with impunity. There was nowhere to run, even if they wanted to rout, and Galronus watched for a while as the Germans, mostly dismounted now, went about their work. The legionaries who had been at the far side of the camp, as yet untouched, had taken one look at what was happening to their mates, and had legged it, running for the bridge.

Galronus gestured to his men. 'Let's give them a little chase.'

Leaving the Germans to their wanton, chaotic savagery, Galronus led his turma of veteran Belgae in a wide arc, avoiding any potential entanglements, and skirted the camp and the fighting going on there. Beyond the ramparts, they raced for the retreating legionaries, drawing their swords. Even powered by fear, the fleeing men stood no chance of outrunning the horses, and Galronus dealt the first blow, his long sword catching a man across the shoulders, snapping bones beneath his chain shirt and sending him pitching face first into the turf, where one of the other riders simply rode over the top of him. He saw Druccus bring his sword down in a massive overhand chop, the heavy blade striking the bronze helmet of a running man, creasing a deep fold in bronze, bone and brain. Druccus cursed as the legionary fell, shaking and already done for, but the blade was so tightly jammed in his head it was pulled from the rider's grip as the Roman disappeared.

'Bollocks. That sword cost me dear,' he grunted as he accepted a spear from one of his riders, who then drew his own blade. Fleeing legionaries were impaled on the points of spears, cut down by swinging swords, or simply ridden down and ground beneath the hooves.

He only reined in and held up a hand to stop his riders as they neared the pontoon bridge. Other soldiers had created a solid shield wall on the bridge, bristling with javelin points. Even the Germans might baulk at that problem. Attacking across a shaky floating bridge was asking for trouble. Better to stop here. He watched as the last fleeing men, driven by panic, shields and pila thrown away as dead weight, reached the pontoon and pelted across it, the defenders opening up to allow them past.

'Onagers or fire?' Druccus asked.

Galronus frowned as he turned to the man. 'What?'

'Well we want to finish the bridge too, don't we? We either pelt it with heavy rocks until it's kindling and floats away, or we hit it with jars of pitch and fire arrows and burn the bastard.'

Galronus turned and looked back. The Germans were all but done with the camp, busily taking heads from the last few, no sign of a Pompeian survivor running for the bridge. With a grin, the Remi turned back to Druccus. 'I'm feeling unaccountably generous. Let's do both.'

CHAPTER FOURTEEN

February 45 BC

'How long can we maintain this siege?' Postumius murmured unhappily, shifting a little in his seat.

'You have concerns?' Caesar asked, looking up from the map spread across the table.

'Only the same ones we've had for the past ten days. Food. Morale. Other supplies. The constant need to be on the alert for an attack from the other side of the river.'

Caesar shrugged, brushing the worry off. 'We need fear no attack from Pompey or Labienus until matters change. If Labienus were planning to spring some surprise on us, he would have done so by now, and I suspect it is he keeping young Pompey in check and preventing any such attack. They have learned harsh lessons twice now, in attempting to take our fort from your own Twenty Eighth, and attempting to cross the river and establish one of their own, each occasion ably dealt with. Ten days of sullen unwillingness to repeat such failures is indicative of an ongoing stand-off. No, I do not think they will make any attempt against us until the balance changes.'

'And the supplies?'

This time it was Aulus Hirtius who stepped out from the periphery of the room, arms folded. 'Our forces are accepting of the need for half rations at this time. Indeed, the knowledge that a large store of food awaits when Ategua falls only spurs them on, making them more hungry, but for victory as much as grain.'

'Tell them,' Caesar said quietly, addressing Hirtius.

'Sir?'

'The messages.'

The other officers leaned forward expectantly at this hint of something important. Hirtius unfolded his arms and cradled his chin in his palm. 'We are in somewhat careful negotiations with certain interested parties in the city. Despite its importance as a rebel garrison and storehouse, there are those within the walls whose loyalty lies with Caesar. It began four days ago when a lone sling bullet was loosed from the walls and fell at the feet of one of our pickets. It bore the message "'On the day you advance to capture the town I shall lay down my shield." The next day we were given a name, when a message was cast down in a writing tablet. This bore the missive,' he paused and consulted a wax tablet he retrieved from a desk behind him.

'"Lucius Munatius greets Caesar. If you grant me my life, now that I am abandoned by Pompeius, I will guarantee to display the same unwavering courage in support of you as I have shown to him." For two further days we have been in contact. A certain group within the town are planning to open the gates and surrender to us, though it must be carefully organised, as they are townsfolk, and they must defy Pompey's garrison to do so. We must be ready to seize the town immediately and protect those who support us.'

'You will understand,' Caesar put in, 'why this has not been made common knowledge even among the staff.'

They all nodded sagely, more than one pair of eyes slipping to an empty seat in their midst. Publius Sextius Naso's defection had come as a shock to them all. A certain level of desertion from one side to the other had become common, and the problem was afflicting both armies, even tribunes and prefects falling foul of the rot, but for one of Caesar's senior staff to have gone over to Pompey had stunned them all. It had brought home to all the need for tight security over anything important.

'So you see,' Hirtius went on, 'Ategua is ready to fall. The city is almost ours. Starvation is no longer a concern, for when those gates open, the men will eat their fill, and Pompey's strength will have diminished considerably.'

* * *

Fronto was dragged from sleep rudely by a hammering on his door. Scrambling from the bed, still half asleep, he shouted for the visitor to enter. A legionary snapped to attention and saluted.

'The Primus Pilus urgently requests your presence at watchtower fourteen, sir.'

Fronto, frowning and noting that it was still pitch black outside, straightened. 'Help me on with my cuirass,' he said, and hurriedly dressed and armed with the legionary's aid. Emerging from his quarters, he wondered what the time was. There was still no sign of approaching dawn, and he shivered as he waited for the equisio's slave, who hurried across with Bucephalus already saddled and ready. Breath pluming white in the cold air, he pulled himself up into the saddle and cantered off to the front line of the siege works.

All along the rampart with its solid fence, towers and artillery platforms rose, the entire line illuminated by torches and braziers, and as he approached, Fronto could see Atenos standing atop one of the towers with a few of his optios and soldiers, his identity betrayed by a combination of transverse helmet crest and sheer body size. Something important was happening, and Fronto could sense it from the atmosphere around him. Soldiers stood with stern, grim expressions, and there was an aura of distaste across the defences.

Scurrying up the ladders, Fronto emerged onto the platform to an excellent view of the city walls above the Ucubi Gate, where there had clearly been activity, for the flaring of golden light there illuminated a gathering of soldiers atop the parapet. Even as Fronto asked Atenos what was happening, the answer was made clear to him by a call from across no-man's land.

'Marcus Junius Quirina,' intoned a dead, emotionless voice from atop the city walls. 'Traitor.'

A figure was dragged to the battlements, naked but for his loincloth. As he thrashed and struggled, one of the city garrison slowly drew a blade across the man's throat, allowing such a torrent of blood, it was visible even from the siege lines. While the body was still jerking, alive, it was cast from the parapet, allowing the poor bastard the twin joys of a cut throat and a fifty foot fall onto rocks before death took him.

Fronto felt anger rising. Traitors. To the Pompeian garrison, clearly. These, then, were the men of whom Caesar had spoken, men who planned to open the city gates. 'How long has this been going on?' he asked, looking with ire at the small pile of bodies.

'Quarter of an hour,' Atenos replied. 'Nine so far.'

Fronto breathed heavily, white breath frosting in the air. 'This is unacceptable. Death is inevitable in war, but torturous execution is not acceptable. Even Pompey would not allow that to happen to Roman civilians.' A thought struck him. 'Are you recording their names?'

Atenos nodded and gestured to a legionary clerk who was busy scratching Quirina's name onto a tablet. Fronto wracked his brain, thinking back over the conversations they had had in the command tent. Two names had come to light, those of the owner of the sling bullet and of that letter that had been thrown from the walls. 'Tiberius Tullius or Lucius Munatius. Are either of them on your list?'

He waited, tense, as the clerk ran his finger down the list of names. When the clerk reached the end and shook his head, replying 'neither, sir,' Fronto heaved a sigh of relief. Thus far neither of those men who had been in discussion with Caesar had been among the victims. As long as they remained undiscovered, then there was still a chance.

Fronto stood, angry and tense, watching impotently as the horrific acts continued, the clerk logging each name. Shortly thereafter, he became aware of Caesar's presence on the next tower along, standing with Hirtius and watching the display of barbarity. Fronto's jaw firmed and his pulse raced at the sound of Munatius' name accompanying a mostly-naked, blood-soaked corpse as it plummeted from the parapet to the heap below. The man perhaps at the heart of the city's pro-Caesarian group had joined the others. It was not a good sign. The soldiers around them watched with disgust, though they remained blissfully unaware of what this truly meant. If those who would have opened the gates to Caesar had been discovered and executed, then the end of the siege was no longer in sight, and the retrieval of urgently needed supplies was as far away as ever.

The executions went on for almost an hour, and as the final body was cast from the city wall, some officer with a gleaming bronze helmet and crimson plume stepped out front.

'The despot Caesar will not take Ategua,' he shouted. 'Loyal sons of the republic remain in control here.'

Fronto caught a movement out of the corner of his eye as Atenos twitched a finger. He didn't see the source of the arrow initially, but blinked in surprise as the shaft buried itself in the speaker on the wall. The shocked Pompeian officer suddenly clutched his neck and plummeted from the parapet to join his victims below. There was a subdued murmur of satisfaction from the siege lines, and Fronto watched then as the archer who had been moving slowly, almost unseen in the dark, across no-man's-land, hurtled for the Caesarian lines, slinging his bow across his shoulders as he ran. The enemy had not been expecting to counter any action, and it took some time for missiles to begin falling from the walls, none of which came close to the running archer, who returned to the siege lines to a raucous cheer and much slapping of his back.

By the time Fronto was back down at the ground, Caesar and the other officers were gathering.

'Munatius,' was all he said.

Caesar nodded. 'No sign of Tiberius Tullius, though, Marcus. We still have men in the city. We still have a chance. It is perhaps a good thing that Plancus remains in Gaul as governor.'

Fronto suddenly connecting the names. *Munatius Plancus*. 'A cousin?'

Caesar sighed. 'The question now is what effect tonight will have on the others in the city. Either the rest will decide that such a fate is not worth their effort and fall quiet and inactive once more, or they will be incensed by this display and be set all the more upon their course of action. We must simply wait and pray now, I believe.'

* * *

Fronto stood with Atenos on the tower once more, watching the city walls. Two days had passed since the executions, and no further sign had come of a pro-Caesarian resistance within. Despite such, hope prevailed, for this Tullius at least still lived within the city, and the men around the siege lines had been all the more determined to win since the Pompeians' display of cruelty.

The pile of corpses outside the walls had remained in place, attracting scavengers at night and clouds of flies by day, for no one in the city seemed inclined to do anything about them, and on the several occasions men had attempted to leave the siege lines into the open ground and retrieve them for proper burial, they had been attacked and driven back by missile shots from the walls. Indeed, one last attempt had been made at dusk this day, and two legionaries had been injured in the action, one with an arm broken by a sling bullet, the other suffering burns from a cast down fire brand.

Now, on Fronto's orders, as darkness truly fell and the frosty cold settled across the world, a small party of men had gathered at the lines below. Ten of them, carrying jars of pitch and blazing torches. There was no longer any hope of retrieving the bodies, but at least they would attempt to get close enough to the pile to immolate them and render them to ash.

He watched in silence with the centurion as the small cremation party began to run. In order to give them the best chance of reaching the bodies intact, artillery thudded along the lines, trying to keep the walls cleared of men. Fronto watched until the pile of corpses began to blaze and the successful party of legionaries hared back across the open ground, arrows and stones falling all around them. One was hit by something, pausing, falling, yet rising again, aided by a friend, and staggering back safely to the lines.

Fronto had been about to wish Atenos good night and descend the tower ladders when a distant noise had instead drawn his attention, his eyes rising to the gate and walls of Ategua. His sudden joy that the Caesarians within had succeeded in opening the city to them crumbled as he realised that the figures in the gate were no outraged citizens.

As artillery began to loose all along the walls of Ategua, a legionary force emerged through the gate at speed, forming as they ran. A legion's standard rose in their midst and Fronto, peering myopically into the darkness, could just make out the symbols of the First upon it, one of Pompey's veteran legions, and likely the preeminent force within the garrison. They came out like floodwater, crashing down the slope towards the Caesarian siege lines.

'Ad signum,' bellowed Atenos, as whistles and horns blew all along the lines, standards rising for men to muster on. Legionaries burst from their quarters, either tents or hastily constructed timber buildings with thatched roofs, all along the lines, falling in alongside their fellows. Way off to the left, Fronto could hear the call of the Sixth as Pedius similarly fell his men in, and to the right those of the Fifth under Basilus also springing into action.

The enemy meant business, Fronto realised as he peered off at the approaching legionaries. More soldiers from the garrison ran disarmed in just tunics and chain shirts, carrying bundles of brushwood and timber hurdles. Others had ropes looped over their shoulders. Fronto watched them carefully.

'They're forming for a single breach,' he called to the primus pilus. 'They're too concentrated to be attempting a major overthrow of the defences.'

Atenos had apparently come to the same conclusion, and with signals relayed through signifers and musicians, he had the bulk of the Tenth drawn to the centre, opposite the approaching Pompeians. Fronto stood tense, whitened fingers gripping the rail of the tower. The siege engines all along the Caesarian lines were loosing now, though their shots were of little concern to the approaching legionaries, for they were trained for range at the city and each rock or bolt flew well over the attackers and at the walls of Ategua, just as the city's artillery continued to loose at the siege lines, though angling to strike to each side for fear of hitting their own at the centre.

As the missiles flew back and forth, Fronto spotted a second and third force joining the legion, and wondered as to their tactics. The light-equipped archers would have a solid place in such an attack. The fifty or so horsemen were odd, though. Ategua had not been assumed to have much of a cavalry garrison, with no open ground to coral the horses, and fifty was as many as could realistically be expected, but what value such a small unit could be here, he could not guess. Even if they were fed through a breach into the camp behind the siege lines, fifty riders could be dealt with without much trouble.

'Tell the men to watch for arrows,' Fronto bellowed down to the men, and then returned to watching. As the force approached their rampart, those men with bundles of sticks and grapples and so on formed a second line behind the legionary heavy infantry, who slowed and came to a halt some thirty paces from the defences. Sure enough, as Fronto had predicted, the archers continued to come forth, falling in directly behind the men of the First and then beginning to send showers of missiles over the top of the legionaries onto the defenders.

The centurions down below were well prepared and, as the arrows came, the men of the Tenth lifted their shields, presenting them to the falling missiles, protecting themselves from the rain of iron. Scorpion crews along the lines released their own cloud of death, bolts thudding into men all along the line of the First, shots powerful enough to penetrate shield and chain shirts, smashing bones and impaling men. They were not numerous enough to make much of a difference, however, and as the men of the Tenth sheltered from falling death, the enemy lines opened up, allowing the runners to filter between them. The unarmed men cast their burdens under the protection of the constant hail of arrows, bundles of sticks and arms of timber hurdles swiftly filling the ditch before the Caesarian rampart and slamming down to create bridges over the sharpened fence of the siege lines. Ropes came slithering out, grapples hooking into timbers.

Fronto watched, trying not to worry, as two hooks began to tug at the supports of the tower upon which he stood, but Atenos had been ready for such moves, and men with sickles hurried forward, hacking at the ropes until they frayed and broke free.

With the last of the bundles deposited into the ditch and thrown across the fence, the unarmed men retreated behind the legionaries and the archers halted their activity. Along the line Fronto's men snapped arrow shafts from their shields to make them easier to wield, here and there howling men being hauled back from the front line by capsarii, dragged away either for medical attention or to die quietly out of the way, their places filled by men from the Tenth's reserves. A number of unarmed bodies scattered before the ditch showed that despite sheltering from the arrows, the defenders had still managed to pick off a few of the men with ropes and timber.

Now, their work done, the soldiers of the First Legion went to work. Fronto took a deep breath. These were a true legion, not like some of the poor levies they had encountered thus far. Safely removed from the action, he contented himself with what he could do to help. Here and there he gave orders and made suggestions, though Atenos was more than competent and had matters under control anyway. After a while, as he watched the two legions battering at one another along the line of defences, Fronto became aware of movement nearby and glanced around to see that two soldiers had brought up to the tower a crate of weighted darts of Greek style, a barbed head on a short wooden shaft, weighted behind the point with a lead ball.

Smiling grimly, Fronto joined the men in gathering up an armful of the missiles and casting them one after another into the press of men from the First Legion, giving them a hefty throw to pass across the defences and the soldiers of the Tenth and into the enemy. Here and there legionaries fell, screaming as the heavy barbs fell among them, slamming into shoulders with enough force to smash bones, badly denting helmets or, best of all, piercing the flesh of necks, arms and legs, felling soldiers. It had a relatively small effect in the grand scheme, but at the very least the distraction and fear of the falling weapons made the attackers falter and gave the men of the Tenth a small advantage.

The lines were contested for some time as both sides fought hard, the defenders doing what they could from towers and behind the lines, the enemy archers adding their efforts, sending arrows up and over, into whatever target they could safely make out.

The breach came suddenly and unexpectedly. Three adjacent soldiers from the Tenth went down to blows simultaneously, and before their positions could be filled by the reserves, the soldiers of Pompey's First were there, pushing their way in, trying to widen the gap. They forced a wider breach by the moment, and as Atenos bellowed orders attempting to close the line, Fronto watched the enemy. Two dozen of the unarmed men were streaming through with their ropes and burning brands, scattering this way and that, hooking them into platforms and siege engines and into the timber buildings, pulling them down into kindling and rubble even as others set light to parts of the camp with their brands. The reserves of the Tenth hurried this way and that to deal with them, invariably butchering the insurgents, leaving slaves and the wounded to bring buckets of water and douse the flames, limiting the damage.

Atenos watched, tense, and something struck Fronto. He turned to look, and saw those fifty or so cavalry on the move. He turned to Atenos. 'The breach is for their horse. All this is just a distraction. They're trying to send messengers to Pompey. Don't let the cavalry get through.'

The primus pilus frowned, turned, and spotted the horsemen approaching. With further bellowed orders, he had the soldiers of the Tenth moving to halt the incursion. At no small cost in bodies he had the men force the breach closed as the last few of those who had broken through were dealt with. Five horsemen managed to force their way through the closing breach and put heels to flanks in an attempt to break through the camp and race for the river.

The men of the Tenth were ready for them. Three were down before they had passed the lines, a fourth was unhorsed among the tents by guards from the far end of the camp rushing to join the fight, and the last fell as a scorpion bolt from an enterprising artillerist on a platform slammed into the man's horse. The beast fell, crushing the leg of its rider, and with that the hope of the horsemen getting through the lines and racing for Pompey was destroyed.

News of the failure of their plan spread through the Pompeian force in moments, and the attack faltered then. The soldiers of the First, unwilling to sell their lives for the ongoing unnecessary fight began to pull back, men falling in their wake. In a matter of heartbeats they were racing for Ategua's gate once more.

Fronto leaned on the rail of the tower and took several deep breaths. Though he had never during the fight thought that they were in danger of a proper loss, it had been by far the most brutal action since they had arrived here, hard fought by veterans on both sides, and it was only when success had become unlikely that the enemy had abandoned the attack and withdrawn.

Still, Fronto would count it a win. Enemy bodies lay strewn before and across the rampart and ditch, far outnumbering the dead among the Tenth. Moreover, he could even now see his men gathering up captives among those horsemen and unarmed rope men who had broken through the gap, as well as a few legionaries from the fight.

'What do we do with them, sir?' Atenos asked, gesturing to the prisoners being gathered in a small group.

'Wait until first light, then take them out into no-man's land in full view of the walls. Have them executed, but do it quick. A soldier's death. Make it clear to anyone watching from Ategua that this is in answer to their own butchery, but that we are not the savages they are.'

'Will that help our cause, sir?'

'They risked a lot to get horsemen through to Pompey. That suggests that they are in a much worse position than we assumed. In fact, I'm starting to think that those executions we saw were an act of desperation, designed to keep the town in line more than to discourage us. I think they're losing control of Ategua, and the more we can do to dispirit the garrison and support the townsfolk, the better. Keep a close watch on them. I'm going to find a medic to massage my shoulder. Those darts are heavy.'

* * *

'What is the date?' Fronto sighed.

Galronus frowned as he worked it out. He still had some trouble with the Roman calendar. 'Eleventh day before the Kalends, I think.'

'Gods, but I was hoping this would be over by spring. Martius is almost here and we've still not taken one city or fought one true battle. This war looks like dragging on later into the year. Lucilia will kill me herself if I'm not home by the end of summer.'

'Caesar is convinced the city is on the verge of falling,' Galronus replied, shrugging as he dropped into a seat. 'Their attacks are starting to look desperate.'

Fronto nodded as he reached for his wine. That much was certainly true. After that initial foray against the Sixth by one of the recent levy legions in Ategua, the garrison had sat tight, presumably expecting Pompey to come to their aid. Instead, Pompey had settled in to try and starve Caesar's army. The problem was that the city and Pompey's camp could not converse. Finally, the commander in Ategua had decided that their position was becoming perilous and had attempted to send a message to Pompey. That too had failed. The day after that push, another attack had come. It had begun with a salvo of missiles from the city's artillery, attempting to suppress the defenders while the enemy crossed the open ground. They had been remarkably lucky in that two shots of onagers at their absolute maximum range had miraculously struck the same tower, the one that Fronto had been standing atop the day before. The damage had been impressive, the entire tower creaking and cracking and leaning outwards as men jumped from the precarious timber, while others hurried to get away from it in case the whole thing fell on them.

Two legions, one the now-battered veteran First, the other one of the recent half-trained levies, had made another attempt to push through the lines, once again horsemen gathered ready to try and make it through to Pompey's lines. This time, though, in anticipation of the attempt, Atenos had the reserves tightly packed close to the front lines and had used the intervening time to create a secondary barricade against horse incursions. Consequently, this fresh attack came nowhere near breaking the lines as the first had. The enemy contented themselves with managing to fire the tower they had damaged, and then pulled back, dispirited, to the city.

The state of morale in Ategua then became clear over the next couple of days. Deserters began to appear in the lines from the Ategua garrison. On one occasion they had managed to overcome their fellows and open a small postern gate, racing to Caesar's lines as the garrison closed it once more. Other times, men had become quite daring, climbing down poorly-observed stretches of wall on ropes, and some even leaping from the lowest part of the wall, risking broken legs in the process. They uniformly bore the same tidings. The garrison, even the veteran First, were tired of this, and would happily surrender to Caesar, throwing themselves on his clemency, but for their commanders, who kept them in line. Brutal executions and punishments were being meted out for any who spoke against Pompey. Yesterday, things had seemingly reached a new nadir in Ategua, for a woman had thrown herself from the battlements as soldiers tried to grab her. She had made it to the ground and run across no-man's-land with arrows clattering against the ground around her as she fled. She had been brought to Caesar, who had had a tent prepared for her comfort. It transpired that her husband had been one of the leaders of a movement to overthrow the garrison, but before they could put their plot into action they had been discovered and her entire household was put to the sword, including her husband and children. She alone had made it to the wall to escape.

A knock at the door drew their attention, and as Fronto bade the soldier entry, a legionary entered with an eager look.

'Sir, the general has sent for his officers. The gate of Ategua is open.'

Sharing a look with Galronus, which quickly slipped into a grin, Fronto rose, downed the last of his wine, and hurried out into the cold morning with the Remi at his heel. Mounting up, they rode for the siege line, to see that Caesar and his staff were just arriving at one of the entranceways to the rampart, the area gleaming with the standards of many units, praetorians from the general's guard all around them protectively. Fronto and Galronus joined them and looked out up the slope.

Three men were riding out from the city alone, the two on the outside dressed in well-made outfits, each well-groomed, the one in the centre clad in a standard madder-dyed military tunic. None of them were armoured or sported weapons. Indeed there was no sign of a military presence, for the figures who stood around the open gate up the hill were also clearly civilians. Caesar nodded his greeting in silence and then stepped his horse out into the middle of the gateway, his officers gathering behind him, soldiers close but allowing the general his space. A slave hurried out and teased Caesar's crimson cloak into a neat position over his horse's back, and the general straightened, an impressive sight as always.

The three riders rode close, but stopped respectfully two dozen paces from the gate.

'You are the consul, Gaius Julius Caesar?' the central man asked.

'I am.'

The nobleman from Ategua bowed his head. 'I am Tiberius Tullius, and these men represent the city, as the leaders of its ordo.'

Caesar nodded. 'Tullius. The name from the sling bullet that began our hope of a sensible solution. Yet you are no commander, I suspect?'

'I have the honour of having been a centurion in the First, Caesar. However, since a small matter of the legion's pride forced us to overthrow vindictive and cruel officers and take control ourselves for the good of both the garrison and the people of Ategua, I now have the honour of commanding that same legion. Rest assured that no further barbarous acts will be permitted on behalf of the garrison. I now join the ordo here in offering terms to your esteemed self. In return for the universal capitulation of Ategua and the release of all stores to your forces, we ask only that no reprisals are considered against the garrison or the people for acts that have been witnessed in this siege.'

Caesar nodded slowly, and crossed his arms, gripping his reins. 'It would appear that you have visited justice and retribution upon the criminals yourselves. As such you have my word that no one shall be harmed for what has transpired.'

'Thank you, Caesar. Ategua is yours.'

Fronto let out a relieved breath. The siege was over at last. Now, the war looked winnable.

CHAPTER FIFTEEN

March 4th 45 BC

One benefit of the now steady stream of defectors, Galronus mused as he watched the action, was open knowledge of the situation. Of course, despite their recent success the same could be said for the enemy, for there were still desertions *to* Pompey's force as well as from it. And every time anyone above the rank of *miles* came over from one side to the other, the plan of the enemy was laid bare a little more.

Thus, Pompey knew that Caesar now had a force to match his, balanced in numbers and supplies, and the general's goal now was to bring the rebels to battle once and for all, to end this. Conversely, the stream of arrivals from Pompey's camp had clarified the enemy situation. Sextus Pompey continued to sit in Corduba, politicking and attempting to raise more units, filtering in the gold and silver from the north to pay for them. Of the enemy in the field, reports suggested strongly that Gnaeus Pompey was all for meeting Caesar in that cataclysmic battle, but that Labienus had more or less taken strategic control, and the former Caesarian commander knew damn well that while the numbers might be even, Caesar's men were veteran killing machines, while Pompey's were still raw and largely untested. He knew that an engagement was no guarantee of success, and so Labienus had settled on moving the rebel army from one stronghold to another, gradually gathering the troops and leading Caesar further and further from his supply sources until the battle was a much more even proposition.

Having failed to relieve Ategua, Pompey had moved six miles upriver to the twin fortresses of Soricaria and Aspavia in the next step of gathering men. Caesar had followed suit on the opposite bank. The general's frustration at failing to bring Labienus and

Pompey to battle was growing by the hour, for the wily enemy commander constantly moved and camped in positions that would be near-suicidal to attack, keeping Caesar at bay, and so the general had settled for commanding the north bank and keeping Pompey away from his men in Soricaria, denying him extra manpower.

Over the day, as they had travelled southeast, up the Salsum, there had been minor clashes and desertions. Fronto was oddly proud of the fact that thus far the Tenth had lost only a few disaffected legionaries, and no officers, while other legions had endured far worse. Still, Pompey suffered more than anyone. Early the morning after Ategua's fall, an entire cohort of Pompey's men had crossed the river, led by eight veteran centurions wishing to take a new oath to Caesar. Just after the noon break, a cavalry squadron had also crossed to Caesar's side. It was satisfying to ponder on whether Pompey's gathering of new men was even managing to make up for his losses through desertion.

Last night as they had settled into the latest camps, Pompey had sat in his unassailable position and had seventy four pro-Caesarians brought forth into full view and beheaded as a warning to further desertion. Unsurprisingly that had led to a new flurry of men crossing the river to Caesar's standards.

Now, once again, the two forces sat glowering at one another across the Salsum, Caesar blocking the road to Soricaria, Pompey preparing for a last move to Aspavia. Caesar had settled on pushing the enemy into action, planning to deny them not only Soricaria on his side of the river, but also Aspavia on Pompey's. Consequently, he had risked the Twenty Eighth, sending them across the river onto the bank nominally controlled by the enemy. There, the legion had the task of forging new lines of fortification designed to prevent Pompey from reaching Aspavia. If they worked, Pompey would be denied both local garrisons and forced to turn away and move on. The general's gambit had been based on the theory that Pompey would be unwilling to put his men in danger and risk that very battle he had been avoiding.

Galronus was watching now as that gambit failed. Clearly, despite Labienus' strategic sense, Pompey had overruled him, for as the men of the legion worked to block the way to Aspavia, the gates of Pompey's camp had opened and men had poured forth.

First came slingers and archers, who settled into carefully selected positions on the higher ground and began to pour a cloud of missiles down upon the working legionaries.

The Remi commander sat astride his horse, watching tensely. The orders had been clear. The Twenty Eighth had been committed, and the Fifth sat in reserve on the near bank with orders not to commit, but to protect any withdrawal of their fellow legion. The cavalry were similarly not to cross the river and engage without the general's explicit order. Galronus twitched as he watched the men of the Twenty Eighth gradually falling back under the hail of arrows and sling bullets, abandoning the half-constructed ramparts and lurking behind a wall of shields, unable to do anything to counter without opening themselves to the deadly rain. Someone had to do something soon, for even now, Pompey's heavy infantry was emerging and flooding down the hill. The arrows would stop pounding the Twenty Eighth only when there was a danger of hitting their own men, which would give the beleaguered Caesarians a matter of heartbeats to marshal themselves before they were ground against the river by one of Pompey's more veteran legions. Galronus drummed his fingers on the saddle horns, wondering how much trouble he would get into for breaking his orders and leading the cavalry across.

His attention was drawn by a small commotion off to his left, and he turned to the waiting Fifth Legion to see an argument ensuing. A tribune was yelling at two centurions with a puce-coloured face, while the two grizzled veterans blithely ignored him, turned and jogged towards the bridge. Galronus smiled to himself. Tribunes were good and bad, came and went, but the Remi had gained a healthy respect for the centurionate over the years.

The two men paused only at the guards on their end of the bridge, where they rammed their vine sticks into their belts, drew their blades and took shields from two of the guards. With that the two officers began to run across the bridge, heading for the far bank. The troubled legion were perhaps a hundred paces from the crossing, and Galronus almost chuckled as he watched the two centurions pelting towards them as missiles fell like autumn rain.

The two officers, seemingly untouchable, came to a halt in front of the cowering legion, ignoring the missiles falling all around them, shields held over their heads, arrows thudding into the boards, sling shots ricocheting off them. Here and there a missile struck one of the two men in their chain shirt or pteruges, yet failed to even make them flinch. At this distance, Galronus could not hear what the two men were saying, but he could well imagine as one gestured to the shield above him while the other beckoned and pointed at the archers up the hill.

Gradually, courage filtered through the beleaguered defenders, and they began to move, forming solid lines once more with their shields up, straightening and moving forward to take control of their half-formed ramparts. Galronus watched as the Twenty Eighth recovered, their morale rising with every step, and then he winced as the situation changed.

An arrow had plunged through one of the centurions' shields, punching into his arm behind and, as he swore and moved the shield to deal with the wound, he was struck again and again by arrows and stones, thudding into his arms, legs, neck, punching into his chain shirt, clattering off his helmet. The Remi shook his head sadly as the officer folded up slowly in pain, managing one last finger-based gesture of defiance at the enemy, and then crumpled to the ground.

The other centurion paused, looking down at his friend, and Galronus somehow caught the man's expression.

'Shit. Shit, shit, shit.' The Remi turned to his men. 'Follow me.'

The cavalry may have been aware of Caesar's orders, but their immediate commander had given them a command and in a heartbeat the horsemen were racing for the bridge. As Galronus reached the crossing and pelted onwards he could see the Fifth, furious at the loss of their centurion, moving, ready to join the Twenty Eighth on the far side of the river, regardless of orders.

Galronus watched the second centurion across there. He had taken his friend's death personally and turned, pounding up the slope towards the mass of archers, arrows and stones clacking off his shield as he ran. The Remi shook his head. The man was doomed. Even as the missiles stopped, the centurion staggered on up the slope, charging into the waiting arms of Pompey's legions, who were flooding down to meet him. Galronus and his riders would never reach him in time.

Still, they could save the Twenty Eighth and avenge the two officers. He examined the enemy dispositions and turned to Druccus, who was racing along close by.

'I'll lead a charge at the front lines. Take your ala round the side and savage their missiles.'

Druccus grinned nastily and veered off to the right, waving his arm.

Galronus watched as the front lines of the enemy engulfed the lone Caesarian centurion. A few of them fell in the initial clash, but then the Remi caught sight several times of the centurion in the press, slowly succumbing to enemy blows. Damn, but Galronus wasn't going to let them have the brave lunatic's body.

The Gallic cavalry of Caesar's army now had over a decade's experience of working within Roman strategy, being used to harry the enemy or scythe away parts of their flanks. They had taken on more and more Roman attitudes to war. But somewhere deep inside every rider with Galronus lay the heart of a man of the warring tribes, with centuries of inter-tribal warfare in his blood. All it took was an ancient war cry from Galronus, and he felt their blood surge, the tribes' fury overwhelming their Roman discipline. This was not a time for a careful, disciplined clash. This was a time for killing, pure and simple.

The Gauls hit the rebel legion not like a skirmishing unit, but like a runaway cart on a long slope. The front lines of Pompey's men fell in droves, impaled with spears that were then casually cast aside as swords were drawn, or churned under pounding hooves, and then battered, hacked and chopped with long Gallic blades. Galronus intoned the names of the gods of his people as he hewed left and right. Once, he felt the white pain of a sword wound to his thigh, but he ignored it, the red fury upon him. It was quite by chance he found the shape of the centurion, his bull-emblem shield identifying him among the enemy. As Galronus hacked and killed, a second man joining him, he bellowed orders and a third rider slipped from his horse in the chaos, grabbing the centurion's limp body and throwing him over the horse before pulling himself back up into the saddle.

The killing went on. Even with the centurion's body recovered, they fought on, the Gauls' blood up and the desire to chastise Pompey's men in the forefront of their minds. Galronus lost track of how long they had been fighting as his sword arm began to sag with weariness. It was only as he sat back and rose in the saddle that he realised just how far they had pushed the enemy. Beyond the next line of Pompeians, he could see the outlying defences of the enemy camp. They had pushed the rebels all the way back up their hill to their own lines. Of the archers and slingers there was no sign, for Druccus and his ala had hit them hard and sent them in flight back to safety, and even now those cavalry had joined Galronus' pounding the infantry.

They had dealt a nasty blow to the Pompeians here, and had saved the Twenty Eighth from extinction, but they were on the edge of danger themselves now. Galronus could see standards moving beyond those ramparts, large bodies of men gathering, and he could hear whistles and horns. Labienus had seen an opportunity with Caesar's cavalry at his camp's edge. If he struck fast he could wipe out Galronus' force. The Twenty Eighth and the Fifth would be able to maintain control of their ramparts now, but the horse had to withdraw, and fast, before they were surrounded and cut off.

'Form on me,' the Remi bellowed as he fought, sword swinging in wide sweeps. His men were getting separated in the struggle, but he could hear the command being repeated from man to man all across the fight. Still swinging and stabbing, watching men fall, Galronus began to back his horse away from the press, down the slope. As a standard bearer fell in beside him, his stylised boar standard with the red streamer raised and waving in the air, he began to fall back. He was gratified to see that the man with the centurion's body over his horse had similarly managed to extricate himself and was falling back with them, joining Galronus on his descent. By the time he had pulled free of the last of the Pompeian infantry, Druccus had pulled in beside him. In fact, as they withdrew, just in time to avoid being cut off by Labienus, his gaze played across the site of the struggle and he was impressed with what he saw. Few horses were visible in the carnage, but Pompeian legionaries and archers lay in swathes across the slope, stinking and russet-coloured with mud and blood. The cavalry had hit the enemy hard and had fought like gods.

With the bulk of his force intact, Galronus descended the slope and closed on the bridge. While he had been busy, so had the legions. The Fifth had crossed the river now and had joined the Twenty Eighth in manning the siege lines, continuing their construction. A few units of archers had joined them, and mantlets and wicker screens were being brought across to help protect against any repeat attack with missiles. Within hours the lines would be completed, manned and unassailable, and Pompey would be cut off from his other garrison at Aspavia.

On the far side of the river the other legions had moved forward, the Sixth now in reserve where the Fifth had been. As Galronus, weary, with a painful leg, and yet thankful in all, crossed the bridge and reined in on the far side, he spotted Fronto stepping his great black steed out from the gathering of officers.

'You're going to be immensely popular with the general,' Fronto grinned.

* * *

Fronto strolled to the edge of the camp fortifications, enjoying a light play of misty rain on his face, not enough to soak a man, but refreshing after days of dusty, cold dry. A legionary standing on the raised platform was leaning, bored and tired, on his shield, but at the realisation that Fronto had put in an appearance, he was suddenly alert and upright. Fronto simply nodded in response at the man's salute. By rights he should have reprimanded the soldier for slovenly behaviour, but even he had to admit that it was boring. Since yesterday's clash across the river, nothing much had happened, and even then the action had fallen to other units. The Tenth had been placed in a rear position, guarding the western flank, far from the action, allowing them some time to rest after their recent exertions.

All was quiet. His gaze took in the enemy camp on the low hill beyond the river, the Caesarian lines before them blocking enemy passage, the massive Caesarian camp that lay between Soricaria and the bridge, and then the wide spaces of farmland and olive groves against which Fronto's men were set in defence. All that lay to the west was the well-trodden path whence they had come and the road along which periodic supply caravans would ply their way. His gaze rose to the hill in that direction where his pickets occupied a makeshift fortlet formed from an old farm hut, where they could see some distance in every direction. With an hour of weak sunshine past, the watery white disc had already risen far enough from the horizon that shadows had begun to shorten.

'Sir?'

Fronto turned to that sentry who now stood straight, eyes on the horizon.

'Yes, soldier?'

'Sir, I think something's wrong.'

Fronto turned, hands clasped behind him, and strolled over to the man looking out in the same direction. All he could see was the hill with the small hut atop it, half a dozen figures moving about up there. 'What?'

'I see six men up there, sir.'

'So do I,' nodded Fronto.

'There should only be four at any time, sir. There's one tent party up there, half on duty, the other half resting in the hut.'

Fronto shrugged. 'So two men can't sleep.'

'I dunno, sir. I just…'

Fronto frowned. A shiver ran up his spine for a moment. The man was right. Something felt off in some indefinable way. 'Do you know the signals?'

The soldier nodded. 'Yes sir.'

'Signal them with something only our men know.'

The soldier crossed to the signalling beam on the platform, a red-painted timber on a pivot jutting out from the edge, bright in the daylight and which could be ignited to signal in the dark. He began to move the beam in jerky motions, a sequence he repeated three times. On the third iteration, a similar beam began to move atop the hill.

'Well?'

'Someone up there mistook my code for a standard one. They're not our men, sir.'

Fronto felt that shiver again. If his pickets had gone from the hill, they had to have been overcome in the dark, which meant that those men up there, who had to be Pompeians, had been on the hill for more than an hour, maybe a lot longer. The last timed signal from the hill would have been in the middle of the night, and even then that was a standard signal the rebels would know. If they had controlled that signal point for hours, anything could be happening on the far side of that hill.

His mind racing in time with his pulse, Fronto tried to estimate how long it would take Pompey to get a force that far. It would have to move a few miles back downstream and cross, then come back along this bank. It would take hours, but then he'd *had* hours, and in the dark, too, entirely unseen.

Fronto twitched as he turned to the next tower, where a cornicen stood beside another sentry.

'Sound the alarm. Muster the Tenth.'

As the surprised musician began to blow, Fronto looked up that hill. The enemy weren't there in force yet, but they had to be close. He took the steps back down two at a time and hit the ground running, only to see Atenos burst out of a side road between tents.

'Sir?'

'The hill's in Pompey's hands. I reckon his army is close by.'

'Fuck.'

'Well, quite.'

'Shall I fetch your horse, sir?' a legionary asked, one of the equisio's men, but Fronto shook his head. A horse was only so helpful on a steep slope. As a tribune arrived, hastily tying his scarf, Fronto gestured to the nearest gateway.

'Open up.'

The makeshift timber barriers were moved swiftly, and Fronto, accompanied by the tribune and the primus pilus, hurried out into the open ground before the earth rampart, at the base of the hill. As he took position at one side with the two officers, the Tenth began to fall in, coming at a run and settling into ordered lines in their centuries. Atop the hill, the Pompeian interlopers had noted the legion's activity, and now alarms were being raised up there, and not for the benefit of the Tenth.

'What's the plan, sir?' Atenos asked, eyeing the hill.

'Hard to decide,' Fronto replied, 'without knowing what's happening on the other side. We can't let them hold the top, though.'

'A wide line, then,' the centurion mused, 'rushing to take the peak, but also crossing the side slopes. That way if the enemy is also spread wide we meet them as equals, and if they're in a column we envelop them.'

Fronto nodded. 'Which is our fastest cohort?'

'The Sixth. The First and Second are the heaviest armoured for frontlines, the Ninth and Tenth are full of heavy pioneers. Fifth and Sixth I tend to use as runners.'

'Then deploy them in the centre, so they can gain the high ground as fast as possible. The First and Second on the flanks, then the Ninth and Tenth and so on. Move as soon as they're in place.'

Atenos saluted and hurried off to his position at the head of the First Cohort. Fronto gestured to the tribune, who ran off to find his horse and his fellow officers. Fronto stretched and rolled his shoulders. He wasn't going to sit this one out. In a matter of moments, barring the two centuries left to man the camp's ramparts, the entire legion was mustered, and at Atenos' signal horns blew and the entire force moved off, making for the slope.

Fronto crossed the muster ground in their wake and fell in at the rear of the Sixth Cohort, where an optio was busy snapping at his men, telling them to pick up the pace as he clouted them around the backside with his staff. The man looked at Fronto in surprise as the legate fell in alongside him.

'Sir?'

'Just don't hit me by accident,' Fronto grinned, earning a surprised and slightly worried smile from the junior officer. The legion moved in perfect unison, their pace dictated by their officers, the tempo of the advance tailored with whistled signals so that the line advanced together despite the differences in slope and terrain. By the time Fronto had decided that he had been damn right to declare this his last campaign, and had made a solemn promise in the sight of mighty Jove never again to climb a hill taller than him, the centurions had given the order to add a half pace to their speed of march. Fronto blinked in surprise, for he'd assumed them to be almost in position. Certainly, he'd seemed to be climbing so long he half expected the moon to come up soon, and the slope had become steadily worse. Now, he looked up and sighed. They had gone halfway.

His calves screaming at him, Fronto staggered on behind his men, gratified to hear the cursing and groans from the legionaries in front of him. Most were several decades younger than him, drilled and exercised on a daily basis. That they were also struggling was something of a relief, and made him feel a little bit less of a relic. Indeed, the optio was having to force them on all the more as the slope increased.

After another eternity, he looked up, and was relieved to see the crest of the hill within reach. His heart fell as the centurions now called for double time. The entire legion, most of them using language their mothers would have hated, broke into a steady run, which became gradually easier as the slope petered out and they emerged onto the top of the wide hill. Fronto felt the gradient ease and put in private and silent heartfelt thanks to Salus and Aesculapius that his knees had held up to the task. His relief was short-lived, though, as a roar burst from the front ranks of the Tenth.

For a moment he had no idea why they were bellowing, but then the noise made it clear, as clangs and clonks, screams and howls rent the air. They had crested the hill at the very same time as the Pompeian force, meeting at the crest and falling straight into combat.

As the pace slowed and the two armies clashed, pushing into one another, contesting for the heights, Fronto thanked the gods again, this time that his tired sentry had somehow spotted the discrepancy that had saved them. Had they been but a hundred heartbeats later, the unexpected enemy force would have taken the crest, and the Caesarians would have been fighting uphill to seize it from them.

Now, he was regretting the lack of a horse, for he could not see what was happening at the front. Off to the left, a small outcropping of rock rose from the dusty hill, the sentry post in the ruinous hut atop it, and a tribune was already clambering up it, having dismounted, half a dozen soldiers and a musician gathered around him. Fronto jogged, puffing, along the slope behind the legion's rear line and, reaching the rocks, pulled his way up to the walled post. His determination to be involved was fading by the moment as he shook with the aftereffects of the climb. He accepted a hand from the tribune to step up to the highest point, and there he turned to look upon the battle.

It had been a very close thing. Indeed, Fronto's single legion was slightly outnumbered by the Pompeians, but their formation and their timing had allowed them to contain the larger force, and now a combination of greater experience and being better rested was already showing. The Caesarians had been quietly in camp half an hour ago, while the rebels had spent half the night marching to circumvent their foe, climbing the hill at the end in a desperate rush to beat the Tenth to it. At the very last moment their attempt to gain high ground close to Soricaria and above the Tenth had failed. Their weariness and inexperience was showing, as the Tenth slowly, but inexorably, pushed them from the peak.

'Off to the left,' he said loudly, drawing his sword and pointing down the slope. There, the enemy had come in greater force in the hope of drawing a defensive line from the hill across to the river. 'Move reserves from the rear of the Ninth and Seventh cohorts down to protect the flank.'

The tribune nodded his understanding as the cornicen nearby blew a cadence and the aquilifer waved the eagle left, standard bearers picking up the call and relaying it to their units. In moments the rear ranks were pulling away from the top of the hill where they were already besting the enemy, moving along the rear and falling in, plugging gaps in the First Cohort as they opened up. Fronto peered down the hill in the hope of spotting Atenos in the press, but there was no sign of the centurion.

Fronto watched, his gaze keen, his attention roving all across the fight, but apart from the one weakness he had already countered, he could see no position on the hillside that needed attention. Indeed, from the very moment they had met the enemy, he could now see that it had been a foregone conclusion. The enemy were still tired from their march, and had been relying on securing the heights before Caesar's legions were even aware of their presence. They had not been prepared to fight to secure the summit without a rest. Fronto suspected, too, that his men were in the mood for revenge. The story of the two crazed, heroic centurions who had led the recovery of the Twenty Eighth had circulated every camp during the night, and the pair had become instant folk heroes to the army. The chance to make Pompey's men pay for their deaths was too good to miss.

The overall combination made the fight a straightforward one.

Already the Pompeians were off the peak and being fought back down the slope. The retreat was to prove disastrous. As the men of the Tenth pushed harder and with increased ferocity with every passing moment, the enemy were stumbling on the slope as they backed down it, and repeatedly Fronto could see men take a tumble, rolling after tripping on some unseen hazard and bringing down a score of their fellows in the process. The ordered retreat became a nervous run in mere heartbeats, and it took only an extra fierce push from the Tenth to turn even that into a full panicked rout.

The rebel force broke suddenly, already halfway back down the slope. In moments they were running, shields being cast aside to facilitate an easier flight. A distant horn call drew Fronto's attention, and he realised that a small unit, brightly gleaming with many standards, had crested the peak of another hill off across the flat land, the enemy officers putting out the call for their legions to muster on the standards, calling them to the relative safety of that hill.

Fronto turned to the tribune. 'Put the call out for our men to stop at the base of the slope.'

'Sir? It's turning into a massacre. We could kill so many here.'

'But the longer we let the men melee, the harder they'll be to stop. When the enemy get to that hill, we'll be in the same position they were here. We'll have to fight to dislodge them. Don't let the men get too excited and chase them over there. Look. They have reserves coming already.'

And they had. As Fronto's gaze had slid from that hill where the rebel officers sat, back down to the fight below, he'd spotted the glittering column of another legion marching in to join the battered Pompeians.

'We've taken the hill. That's enough for now.'

But it looked like the western flank was not to be the quiet assignment it had seemed. Pompey wanted Soricaria, and he was determined to try. Well Fronto would be ready next time.

CHAPTER SIXTEEN

March 6th 45 BC

Quintus Pompeius Niger was a determined man. Determined to survive. Determined to win. Determined to prove himself to the general and to his men. Determined that Pompey would not take the hill. His gaze took in the enemy force sweeping down that slope to which they had retreated at the closing of yesterday's fighting.

Since then Legate Fronto had sent the Tenth forward, extending defences and fortifications into the plain beyond, denying Pompey that same peak and sealing off access to Soricaria. Yet despite their poor chances of success, Pompey's force was coming again, the cavalry out front, seemingly moving to attempt an overwhelming of the fortifications and to break the Tenth and clear the way to Soricaria. Pompey was determined. But Niger was more so.

He remembered Caesar the first time the general had been in Hispania all those years ago, when Niger had been but a boy, his father a member of the ordo of Italica, one of the peninsula's greatest cities. Caesar had visited, had entertained Niger's father in the Quaestor's palace. Niger had grown to manhood in a household that continued to revere the general, enthralled with tales of his exploits in Gaul. It had vexed him, therefore, when he reached the appropriate age for a military tribuneship that the military of the region, which was being raised and increased constantly, was now under the command of Pompey, and dedicated to seeing Caesar fail.

Thus it had been that he had taken the first opportunity to abandon his own legion and cross the river to swear allegiance to Caesar. He had been welcomed with open arms by the general, and Niger had been more than a little impressed to hear Caesar expound upon the excellent qualities of Niger's father. His loyalty to the general was considered all the more important given his distant blood relation to those very Pompeys who he now fought. He had been neatly transferred into a position as a junior tribune in the Tenth, replacing one of the five extant, who had suffered an injury and was now out of commission.

His name, of course, had given the men under his command reason for pause. They were uncertain. A Pompey, no matter how distantly related, was to be watched carefully.

He was determined to prove himself.

His gaze now played across the cohort for which he was responsible. Oh, he was under no illusion of his command's scope, which was largely limited to relaying Legate Fronto's commands to the centurions, and it was the lower officers who truly commanded in battle. Still, he took his responsibility seriously. A plume and a cuirass might be a sinecure to some, but not to Niger.

The enemy cavalry came first, flooding across the plain. Niger moved forward, sword drawn. In the years he had waited, part of Pompey's legions, watching the reports of Caesar's victories in Africa, then his triumphs in Rome, Niger had been far from idle. He had trained with the men, unlike most tribunes. He had learned the art of the blade better than most, training alongside the rank and file, discovering the value of the gladius in the press of a shield wall, but also with a private tutor, an ex-gladiator, who had taught him the art of the duel, as well as a number of dirty tricks. Niger was not afraid to stand in the lines with the men and face the enemy.

Pompey's tacticians were fools. The cavalry swept towards the ramparts, but the Tenth had already positioned the fences of sudis stakes that formed an almost uncrossable barrier for such horsemen, and the cavalry wheeled impotently as they reached the defences. Oh they drew blood, for sure, javelins cast across the fortifications pinning a number of Niger's men, but their thrown weapons discharged, they were largely useless once more, and consequently withdrew swiftly, pulling back to the flanks and disappearing behind the approaching legions, where two of Pompey's eagles were in evidence.

Niger watched now as those infantry stomped across the rough ground, bearing down on the defences. A command was given somewhere back in the Caesarian lines, and the tribune picked up the call and passed it to the centurions. As the enemy closed to pila range, so the Tenth pre-empted the clash. Scorpions, loaded and cranked in preparation, released their deadly hail into the approaching crowd, while a unit of auxiliary bowmen positioned behind the waiting Tenth sent forth a cloud of arrows that fell among the approaching legions.

He watched with a nod as the flurry of missiles tore huge holes in the enemy lines. It surprised him not a jot, for he knew both those eagles, indeed had trained and served with one until his flight across the river to the arms of the Caesarians. He knew their mettle. He knew that they were new and untested, for all their training. He watched as men began to panic under the missile hail, and he watched as their centurions slowly managed to pull their men back into shape.

The enemy's answering hail of pila was not bad, all things considered, but the Tenth, as Niger was coming to learn, were afraid of nothing, and knew every trick in the book from their long service and many battles. Soldiers ducked aside, locked shields, and managed to largely avoid the pila, a few screaming as the weapons struck, others forced to discard shields heavy with javelin weight. But in half a dozen heartbeats the injured and the disarmed were back among the reserves, being tended or rearmed as men settled in to take their place at the front. It was done so smoothly and instinctively that there had seemed to be no need for commands from their centurions.

Everything stopped.

The enemy, having cast their pila, locked their shields and stood still, thirty paces from the Caesarian lines. Niger could hear the creak of bows being held at their tensest, ready to loose behind the Tenth, and the ratchet of scorpions being readied for a second shot. Other than that, nothing moved. The Pompeians seemed unwilling to contest over those defences, and there was no reason for the Caesarians to commit beyond their lines. Something was happening over on the far flank, towards the river, a small contest between light armed Caesarian auxiliaries and those enemy horse who had wheeled after their initial assault, but it was a skirmish for now, and not enough to bring the two armies to meeting in full.

Tension rippled across the field as every man waited, though Niger could feel, hear, see the difference between the two forces.

His own men waited with a stolid patience, knowing they had the advantage, that all they had to do was hold good defences against an attacking unit. The two Pompeian legions, however, radiated a nervous tension, for their reason for inaction was a general unwillingness to commit to a fight their officers were far from convinced they could win.

A figure stepped out from the legions opposite, the shield wall closing behind him. A centurion. His sword was still sheathed, his vitis stick brandished like a weapon, an oval shield on his left arm. Niger frowned in recognition. Antistius Turpio. He felt his skin prickle. Turpio was no headstrong fool. One of the most renowned veterans among the Hispanic legions, he'd been the only man Niger had wavered when facing across the training ground. What was he up to?

'Who will fight me?' Turpio bellowed out across the Caesarian lines.

This was greeted with a strange silence, which Turpio allowed to rule for a few moments before he filled it once more. 'Did you lose your only two heroes across the river the other day?'

Niger felt the legionaries all around him bristle at that. Turpio was goading them. Why? What could he gain? The answer flitted into his mind easily. Turpio wanted to put down a chosen man from the Tenth for the heart it would give. The Tenth would baulk at the loss of such a man, while the Pompeian forces might just gain the courage they needed to storm the fortifications.

The tribune glanced to his right. Fronto was visible some way along the lines above the men, on horseback, yet dangerously close to the front line for a man of his rank. Niger knew Fronto's reputation. A few years ago, he felt certain, the legate would have stepped forward to answer the challenge himself. Now, though, the man was a grey-hair, for all his wit and skill.

'Chicken livers, all,' Turpio sneered.

'Fuck it,' snapped a legionary somewhere off along the line, stepping out, but the primus pilus' hand shot out.

'Stow that curse, Pansa. You overextend every damn time, and that centurion will have you in the mud in a heartbeat.'

Fronto stepped his horse forward, and Niger actually worried that the legate intended to deal with this himself, despite his age. As Fronto dismounted and handed his reins to a legionary, so

Atenos, the chief centurion, stepped forward, the two officers squaring up. A quiet, but very heartfelt exchange began between the two.

With a deep breath, Niger unclasped the brooch holding his cloak in place, letting it drop to the ground as he grasped the shield of a standard bearer nearby, a small, round board, before stepping out between the front lines, pushing legionaries aside.

'I see you, Antistius Turpio,' he called as he walked forward towards the waiting centurion.

The discussion between the two officers ended as Fronto and Atenos both turned to look in the direction of the young tribune. Niger felt his heart pound as the primus pilus shook his head and his finger together, opening his mouth to tell the tribune to stand down. Yet Fronto, brow wrinkled, squinting in Niger's direction, put a hand on the centurion's shoulder and shook his head. The two senior officers straightened, arms folded, watching, as Niger closed on Turpio.

The sound of tense expectant silence rolled across both armies.

'I was looking for a contest,' the Pompeian said dismissively.

'Look for a handy grave, Turpio,' Niger replied.

For a moment, then, Niger did wonder whether he'd bitten off more than he could chew, as Turpio stepped to meet him, sword up. There was nothing but confidence and certainty in his eyes. Niger knew he was good. But so was Turpio. So good that he'd challenged Caesar's army.

The centurion let Niger close, content to allow the tribune the first strike. That strike came swift, as Niger broke into a run. The centurion's blade and shield both came up to meet Niger's, but at the last moment, the tribune changed his strike. His shield swept round from left to right, arm fully extended, the hide edging smacking away the waiting sword even as Niger's blade darted out like a viper beneath his own armpit, unexpected. There was a reason he had chosen such a small shield rather than the legionary ones available. Manoeuvrability. Speed.

Niger was convinced that any other man would have at least taken a winding blow to the torso from such a surprising attack. That Turpio was already moving and out of the way, spinning and opening up a space so that Niger's blade met only air, said much about the man's skill. The centurion was a superb swordsman.

Indeed, his answering blow came from Niger's right hand side, almost behind him as the man pivoted and spun. But Niger was more than a legionary, and his cat-like reflexes had been enhanced by the gladiator's instruction. The tribune danced into the space Turpio had left, whirling, his own small shield once more turning the centurion's blade.

On the fight went, Turpio moving with such speed, every blow coming unexpected, nimble, every move leaving him out of Niger's reach or with his shield in place. Similarly, Niger moved like a gladiator, ducking, leaping, bending and pirouetting, his own sword dancing out constantly, ever close, never quite drawing blood, his own shield catching Turpio's blade whenever he was not already out of the way.

It was only on the tenth time they separated to draw breath and size up one another that the two combatants realised that their armies had begun to chant their names, like the audience at an arena. Niger felt his pulse race, his skin prickle. He moved in once more, sword whispering past Turpio's neck, shield knocking the man's blade away as the tribune swirled around his opponent. His arm came up and over, his sword stabbing down behind him on instinct only to meet Turpio's blade once more.

The fight went on, hammering and clanging, jumping and ducking. Neither man had yet drawn blood, and many a fighter would already be exhausted, but the economy of movement of a trained swordsman preserved their energy.

Niger only realised that something had changed as the two men parted once more, panting. The chanting had stopped. There was still a din, but it was no longer formed from their names. Both combatants looked about them. The legions were beginning to move. Niger's keen eyes swiftly picked out the reason. That small cavalry skirmish off to the flank had turned into something rather more dangerous, but the fight had clearly gone Caesar's way, for the Pompeian cavalry were racing away, back along the riverbank. As they moved, the auxiliary unit protecting that flank, faced with the approach of the victorious Caesarians, broke. The enemy's flank melted away into a rout. In a heartbeat, the panic had spread to the green legion, who no longer enjoyed any protection towards the river, and knew that they could be flanked.

It took a matter of heartbeats before the entire Pompeian force was moving, routing, bellowing cries as they fell back. Their centurions were crying their voices hoarse, pulling the units back together even as they ran, slowly turning the rout into an ordered retreat.

Turpio took a deep breath and nodded his head at Niger. He said nothing, but the gesture alone spoke volumes. Niger returned the nod, and the two men turned, the centurion jogging off to recover his men, the tribune slipping back between the ranks into his position to the cheers of his men.

Less to prove now, he decided, as hands patted at his shoulders when he passed, and he caught sight of Legate Fronto, mounted once more, nodding his satisfaction to the tribune.

The enemy would not come again today and, in their absence, the Tenth would bolster and extend the fortifications, forever denying them Soricaria. The battle for the hill was finally over.

* * *

March 12th 45 BC

Fronto stretched as he looked at the town ahead. They had to be closing on Pompey now, for his tactics had changed. After the man's failure to take Soricaria and Aspavia, denied both by Caesar, he had withdrawn very suddenly, taking a leaf from Caesar's book, racing away at first light, southwest. The Caesarian forces had tarried for a single day to make sure they took, disarmed and looted the Pompeian strongholds before giving chase. For days thereafter, they had followed the rebel army, always a day behind, thirty miles across the rolling olive tree-covered hills of the region.

Pompey had made Ucubi ahead of Caesar, taking his garrison, stripping the town of stores, and then burning the place to the ground, denying any succour for the army following him. Fronto had arrived at Ucubi to find Pompey's name a curse among the homeless and penniless survivors. A similar tale was told at every town with a wall on their route, each stripped of men and resources and then systematically burned.

At the end of the last day of travel, the scouts had come back with fresh news, though. Ahead lay the town of Ventipo, and for the first time since the clashes at Soricaria, they had found a town still standing, and not mere charred ruins. Moreover, the walls were manned beneath Pompeian banners. A garrison awaited them. There had been chatter about this among the officers as the army began to assemble on the plain before the town. Why had Pompey changed his tactics now? Or more likely, why had *Labienus* changed his tactics, for such surprises were invariably the work of Caesar's former lieutenant? A possible answer had come from a breathless messenger that night as they settled in, preparing to take the city. The rider had come from one of the numerous small garrisons Caesar had installed in their wake, and his message was a worrying one. Forces had been observed leaving Corduba and marching southwest, seemingly aiming to intercept the rebel army and bolster Pompey's numbers. That rather than burning towns, Pompey was now garrisoning them, smacked of delaying tactics, trying to slow Caesar long enough for two armies to combine.

As such, Caesar's response had been plain and simple. Ventipo had to fall in one day and the army be on the move immediately, out into the plain of Munda beyond, where the rebel army seemed to be gathering ready to face them.

The army had made what they could of a single night's rest after the days of marching and before assaulting the town, soldiers drinking with reasonable restraint, gambling, or simply sleeping. Then, at dawn, Fronto had called for Atenos and his tribunes. One of the scouts had identified the weakest spot in Ventipo's defences. On the northern side of the town, one of its venerable gateways had been altered at some point, its grand double arch being reduced to a single open carriageway, the other arch bricked up. Whoever had been responsible for the changes, however, had clearly used cheap contractors, for the mortar between the bricks was crumbling, according to the scouts' reports, and at night they could hear defender's voices through that failing brick almost as easily as through the timber gate blocking the other arch.

Fronto had taken this news to Caesar, requesting that the Tenth be allowed to press this advantage, since they were camped on the northern side anyway. Caesar had been entirely accommodating, welcoming any suggestion that might allow them to move on and bring Pompey to battle with all speed, and without leaving enemy garrisons intact behind them to disrupt supplies.

Thus it was that while Fronto had called his officers together, the engineers had located a heavy tree nearby, cut it, stripped it of branches and formed a good, solid ram with ease and speed. Fronto's plan was simple. Five cohorts would keep the wall defenders busy, using the scaling ladders and shelters, while three more would make a concerted attack on the single timber gate, using that ram. Once the fighting was underway, however, and the enemy fully deployed, the two cohorts in reserve would move forward as if to bolster the extant forces, but at the last moment they would move against the bricked up archway, taking the ram from their fellows at the gate. With luck the enemy would not have identified their own weak spot, and without the Tenth seemingly concentrating there, they would not waste time strengthening it.

Atenos would take the timber gate, he said. It would look odd to the defenders if the First Cohort and the senior centurion were kept in the reserve, and so for the look of things, he would be seen to be assaulting the gate. The tribunes were given positions across the legion, ready to coordinate the sudden changes required.

Now, as they stood watching the city walls across the flat, cold, dusty ground, Fronto tried hard to focus on the crumbling gate wall, wishing his eyesight was better, and acknowledging with regret that this was at least nothing to do with age, and that his eyesight had never been that sharp. Thundering hooves attracted his attention and he turned to see the rider skittering to a halt before him and saluting.

'With Caesar's respect, sir, the Tenth may give the first call.'

Fronto nodded and the man turned and rode off once more. The legate looked at the walls and sent up a brief prayer to Fortuna and to Mars and Minerva. Every god of luck and war would have an eye on this place today.

He turned to the eagle bearer and the small stand of musicians. 'Give the signal to attack.'

In half a heartbeat horns were blowing and standards dipping. With a roar, the men of the Tenth moved off, hungry for victory. Fronto drummed his fingers on his saddle horn as he watched. Eight cohorts moved in, two on the left flank, three on the right, and three at the centre under the standards of the senior cohorts, making directly for the gate. Men, sweating and cursing, carried the great bole of the battering ram between them in two lines of thirty men, the enormous weapon borne aloft on carefully secured ropes. A horn blew somewhere in the city, and a series of artillery pieces along the ramparts began to loose as the Tenth came into range. It took only moments before the legion's own siege weapons were opening up in response, their range greater due to their very nature. While the Pompeian machines threw iron bolts and fist sized rocks into the approaching force, the enormous catapults under Fronto's command hurled rocks the size of sheep at those walls. His artillerists were the best in the Caesarian army, with a decade of practice under their belts. Rather than strike the bulk of the walls where it might take days to open a breach, or at the crumbling gate wall, which would betray their intent too early, the heavy stones were uniformly lobbed at the parapet. Here they sometimes missed, sweeping across the defenders to demolish buildings within the town, but when they struck, the damage was catastrophic, the battlements being smashed to pieces, the men on the walls pulverised. Within the first two volleys, Fronto saw two of the Pompeian artillery pieces demolished into kindling amid screams and clouds of blood-mist.

The exchanges went on as the Tenth approached, eight cohorts moving in perfect unison, two more standing at the rear, out of range of the artillery, seemingly a standard reserve. Here and there, he saw, with some regret, part of his front lines buckle and cave under the hail of missiles from the wall. Centurions' whistles blew as men shuffled and hurried to fill gaps, shields up for protection as capsarii and orderlies scurried to get the wounded out of the way and back to the waiting reserves and the medical tents beyond.

The enemy hail was thinning, though, if slowly, as the artillery points along the walls were carefully targeted, while stones continued to smash the parapet to pieces, killing the men along it.

'I can't see what's happening,' Fronto grumbled to the small knot of men beside him.

'Sir?'

'Oh I can see the legion moving, but I can't see details. I'm going forward.'

'Sir? The enemy artillery. They'll target you.'

'Then that will take the heat off the men at the front, won't it.'

A tribune shook his head. 'Sir, you'll be exposed.'

Fronto looked around, reached down and tapped a man on the shoulder. The soldier turned, his eyes filling with surprise as he hastily saluted. 'Give me your shield.'

'Sir.' The man carefully handed his shield up to the officer on the horse.

Fronto turned back to the tribune. 'Not exposed now.'

As the junior officer blustered out a number of worried reasons why the legate should not leave the rear lines, Fronto ignored him and walked Bucephalus out forward. As he moved closer to the marching legion before him, he had a momentary flutter of uncertainty. As the walls swam into better focus, he saw artillery crews turning their weapons to train them on the senior officer now moving into range. Fronto smiled. At the least, he could, as he'd noted, take the heat off his men.

The Tenth's artillery continued to target the weapons on the walls, and the first engine to lock on to Fronto suddenly exploded into flying shards of timber and broken beams, killing most of its crew in the blink of an eye. The true danger in which he'd placed himself was brought home a moment later as a rock the size of a fist thumped into the ground a few feet from him, the impact so powerful that it was instantly half-buried in the dirt. It occurred to him as he turned and moved away from the impact that even the shield he carried would be as effective as a pot of butter in stopping something like that. If such a rock came at him on target, at best he was going to end up in the medical tent having broken bones probed. Most likely he'd be smashed to pieces.

That was when he settled upon zigging and zagging. He would move forward at an oblique angle for a random number of heartbeats, and then turn back sharply and repeat the procedure. In doing so he slowed his pursuit of the legion, but it almost made him laugh to see the artillerists on the walls constantly trying to move their weapons, retraining them on where Fronto could next be found, only for him to turn once more.

Stones and bolts continued to fall within worrying reach, but none were close enough to make him truly panic, and every rock and shaft that failed to strike him represented a man of the Tenth who would reach the walls intact.

Finally, as he neared the action, he heard whistles blowing, and realised the plan was being carried out. Looking over his shoulder he could see the remaining two cohorts moving forward as if to aid their fellows. The ram was still thudding into the timber gate, but from the rear it was clear that the Tenth had rearranged themselves so that the great trunk could easily be extracted from the press and moved to another unit.

Fronto angled his approach more directly now. As he closed on the rear of the attack, he could see his newest tribune geeing the men on, sword waving, and smiled. Usually men with something to prove were dangerous to have in positions of importance, but Niger had taken his moment back at Soricaria and had displayed courage and, in Fronto's impressed opinion, no small amount of sword skill. Niger was on foot, unlike most of the tribunes, and as he closed on them, Fronto followed suit, slipping from Bucephalus' back and slapping the great black stallion on the rump, sending him racing for the rear lines out of danger.

Niger turned in surprise to find Fronto behind him. The man saluted so automatically that he almost concussed himself with the hilt of his own sword. Fronto grinned. 'Let's get that gate open.'

Behind them, the two cohorts had broken into a run at new signals, and were forming from wide lines into a more narrow column as they hurtled towards the walls. Fronto almost argued when four men suddenly appeared around him and formed a small testudo roof with their shields, but as the first missile bounced off them just above Fronto's head, he acknowledged the sense of it.

More signals were given, and the cohorts shifted with perfect choreographed precision. Fronto simply stood with Niger under his shelter of shields as the units of the Tenth re-formed around him, then moved aside along with his escort as the great tree-ram was moved from the cohorts at the gate to the ones at the blocked arch.

In mere moments, the trunk was swinging back and forth, smashing against the crumbling brickwork. Fronto almost laughed as he heard the distant, muffled, but clearly identifiable sounds of the defenders panicking and changing their strategy to try and bolster a point they had thought safe. They were too late now to do anything, though. Fronto saw the wall shaking and the mortar exploding in dusty clouds. The ram would do its work long before any kind of secondary defence could be raised inside.

'Look at the bricks,' Fronto shouted to the men. 'Look at them. In every damn brick, picture the pay clerk who stiffed you out of half a day's pay. Picture every camp-follower who gave you the crotch-itch. Picture every miserable bastard you lost a dice game to.' He grinned. 'Picture Pompey's fat arse.'

With a roar, the men of the Tenth struck with renewed vigour. Fronto cheered with them all as he saw the bricks collapse inwards, the wall less than useless now. Changing angle, the ram was struck again and again, the breach widening, and then, with a whistle from a centurion, the trunk was unceremoniously dropped, and grapples were attached to the lip of the hole, ropes pulled taught and then heaved upon. With a crack and a horrible groan, the brick wall gave, the whole lot tumbling outwards, injuring a few unlucky men at the front. Blinking away the dust, Fronto realised he could see the houses of Ventipo through the arch now, clear and undefended. Men were desperately falling in to defend the gap, but they stood no chance. Ventipo was doomed, and with its fall, they would be clear to move into the plain and fall upon Pompey and his army at last.

Beside him, he sensed Tribune Niger almost vibrating. He grinned.

'Go on.'

The tribune flashed him a grateful smile, roared like a victorious gladiator, and leapt into the breach with his men.

Fronto took a deep breath, wondering what Atenos would say, and then thought '*Screw it*,' and followed the others into the hole.

Marius' Mules XIV: The Last Battle

CHAPTER SEVENTEEN

March 16th 45 BC

Fronto squinted into the golden inferno as the sun began its final dip beneath the western horizon, shedding a gilded gleam across the rebel army. Caesar was busy expounding on the terrain, presumably for the benefit of the more recently commissioned officers, since anyone who'd fought in a campaign or two before would be able to pick up on the advantages and disadvantages themselves. Indeed, beside him, Galronus and Atenos were nodding half-heartedly at the general's monologue while they examined the ground for themselves.

The legions had covered some fifteen miles the day after Ventipo's fall, scouts ranging ahead and confirming the location of the rebel army awaiting them. Arriving within view of Pompey's force, the general had given the order to make camp and the legions were even now settling for their evening meal, tension crackling among them in the knowledge that nothing now stood between them and finally ending the civil war that had claimed so many of their mates.

Caesar's camp sat on rolling easy ground to the east of a seasonal stream, which was still swift with the winter's floods from the mountains of the south. Beyond the river lay a wide, easy plain with just the gentlest of gradients, gradually climbing to a slope upon which sat the rebel army, sheltered before the ramparts of the city of Munda.

'Good terrain for cavalry over there,' Galronus noted.

'But committing the cavalry without good infantry support would be suicidal,' Fronto replied. 'The moment you moved across the river, Pompey's entire force would have you.'

'And the infantry will be hampered by the stream,' said Atenos in a frustrated tone.

'It's not a wide stream,' Hirtius noted from nearby.

'But the near bank is a quagmire of marshes and bogs. The legions will be slow and laborious even reaching the river, and it will tire their muscles before the battle. I don't like this battlefield.'

Fronto nodded. 'It's not the best. Labienus chose this ground. It's good for his cavalry, has the walls to his back, he's got the high ground, and the swampy river makes our infantry's approach trouble.'

'We could decamp and find better ground?' Pedius murmured.

'But there is no reason for Pompey to follow,' Fronto sighed. 'He has the best position here, you can bet Munda is crammed with supplies to keep him going, and all the indications are that every garrison in Baetica is being mobilised to join him. The longer we delay the harder it will be to beat him. The ground is shit, but we have to fight here. We have to finish it now, while we can.'

'How will the enemy respond if we press them, I wonder?' Pedius mused.

'That,' Caesar said, finishing his appraisal of the terrain and turning to them, 'is the important question. Pompey has thus far shown little interest in offering an easy fight, preferring to dominate the high ground. He has done as much in every engagement so far. I doubt Pompey will be keen to bring his forces down into the plain to face us in a fair fight. He will want us to assail his position.'

'Which will further tire the men,' Pedius sighed. 'First the marshes, and then a struggle uphill to the enemy lines.'

'But,' Fronto added, 'Labienus and his cavalry will be largely useless lurking behind the defences on the hill. He knows that his best chance of taking the initiative would be to hit us on the plain, fast and hard just as we struggle across the stream. If he can get Pompey's infantry down there with him, they can kick us hard as we make good ground.'

'So what we're saying,' Pedius said, 'is that we cannot predict what the enemy will do. It all depends who wins the argument in their headquarters. Either Labienus will lead a strike at us on the plain, or Pompey will have them all settled in on the hill. So we cannot prepare for either eventuality.'

'Or rather, we must prepare for both,' Caesar said. 'They have, if our intelligence is accurate, thirteen legions, six thousand or so light infantry and around the same number of horse. That puts their numbers at somewhere between seventy and eighty thousand. We have eight legions now, some eight thousand cavalry and just five thousand auxiliaries, totalling just over fifty thousand. Pompey outnumbers us significantly, but we know from experience that his legions are still largely new and green, while ours are uniformly experienced veterans.'

The general began to point across the field. 'Galronus and King Bogud will have the command of the cavalry, who have the edge in numbers over Labienus. We cannot be certain of our best position until we see how the enemy deploy, but I want our cavalry ready to counter theirs. Labienus will want to use his horse to best effect, so I need our cavalry to stop them. As long as Labienus cannot find a way in, this will come down to the legions, and when that happens, we have the advantage. Pompey has thus far been putting his weaker legions in front, using them to wear us down, but not tomorrow. We will field our strongest legions in force at the front and break them early. Tomorrow, we cross the marsh, we form with the Tenth and Sixth beside me on the right, and the Third and Fifth on the left under Pedius, who will take that wing. The rest of the legions will hold the centre. It is my belief that the Tenth and Sixth will be able to best any force Pompey throws at us, and so they will be the ones to break the enemy, though Pedius' wing will be almost equally strong and will attempt the same. The cavalry will cross after the infantry, by which time, Pompey and Labienus will have deployed and so the horse commanders, to whom I grant autonomy in this engagement, will deploy their forces as they see fit to contain Labienus.'

'It works,' Fronto said. 'In principle.'

'We shall by necessity be slow in crossing,' Caesar noted. 'With luck that will bring the enemy down to the plain. But if not, we shall take the fight to them. Terrain or no terrain, by sunset tomorrow this war will be over.'

* * *

'They're not coming,' Tribune Quintus Pompeius Niger murmured, sheltering his eyes with his hand and peering off into the dawn-lit distance.

'There's time yet,' Fronto noted, riding alongside at the rear of the Tenth. The legion had slowed as they reached the low ground near the stream, men plodding wearily through the sucking mire, cursing and complaining. Such was the difficulty that even the centurions, who would usually be barking at their men to hold their tongues, let the grievances run amok, adding their own curses to the refrain. Fronto felt Bucephalus starting to suffer with the marshy ground now. The army was going to be weary when it reached the fields beyond, and Fronto eyed the rise with distaste.

The scouts had informed the officers before dawn that Pompey's army had mobilised into battle formation by the third watch, and were waiting on the hill as the sun rose in their eyes. Even with Fronto's eyesight, he could determine their battle lines. The legions were amassed in a solid block, with auxilia to the sides, and then cavalry on the flanks.

With difficulty the Tenth, alongside the other Caesarian legions, made the far bank and with some relief began to squelch and slosh up onto good solid ground at last. Still the enemy remained atop the hill, watching from a distance. Though the slope would present them with its own difficulties, he was, in his own way, relieved that apparently Pompey had won the argument. Had the enemy flooded down and met the Caesarians plodding out of the river ditch, it would have been damn hard work. With a series of calls, the army re-formed on the western bank, the legions re-dressing their lines, while the auxilia took positions towards the rear. Given the disposition of the enemy, Fronto had expected the cavalry to divide, placing half their number on each flank, facing those of Pompey. Instead, he frowned as just two turmae of horse took position on the right, outside the Tenth, while the vast number formed on the left. It was only as they moved closer across the field and more of the enemy's details came into view that Fronto realised why.

Off at the far flank, way over to the left, the enemy cavalry was stronger, and the banners visible suggested the presence of Labienus and his Gallic riders there. The wily bastard had concentrated his strength preparing to do something sneaky, but it seemed that Galronus and Bogud, the strange Mauritanian, had spotted the ruse and moved already to counter it.

A rider reined in and saluted. 'New orders from the general, sir. Form deeper and shrink the line. Caesar wishes to limit operations to the centre of the field.'

Fronto nodded but paused before passing on the order to the musicians, inwardly marshalling his arguments. Caesar might think the Tenth invincible, and damn it they were the closest thing, but pulling them away from the edge of the field with such a small cavalry screen increased dramatically the chance of being flanked. He turned to Niger.

Ride out to the front. Find Atenos and tell him to ignore the orders the horns are about to give. Tell him he didn't hear the call.'

'Sir?'

'I'm not being flanked because Caesar's worrying about the terrain. You didn't hear the call. Responsibility rests with me.'

Niger rode off, looking unhappy, and Fronto plodded on behind the Tenth as the mass of Caesar's army crossed the plain. His gaze took in the forces on the hill ahead, and he recognised what was happening up there, the realisation bringing a smile to his face. The rebel lines were undulating, bowing in places, backed by a cacophony of calls. Fronto knew those cadences, standard legion ones that ordered the men to hold their ranks. The men up there, many still untested by true battle, were itching to run down the slope and charge the Caesarians. Labienus was probably urging them on, in fact, while Pompey was constantly having the orders to hold position relayed in order to keep them atop the slope.

Fronto's grin ratcheted up a notch as an idea occurred. He trotted forward until he was close to one of the optios, stomping along at the back and driving any slackers on. The optio saluted.

'Sir?'

'Pass the word. Without calls or signals, I want the legion to come to a stop every twenty paces. Just a momentary pause and then the centurions can order them on again until further notice.'

Frowning, the optio saluted again and then spoke to his men. Fronto watched the command ripple out across the Tenth from the rear, and noted no few centurions' faces turning to him in surprise. Still, the command spread silently, and suddenly the Tenth staggered to a halt. A moment later, centurions were blowing whistles and bellowing at their men. The legion moved once more. Fronto's gaze rose to the force atop the hill. As he'd predicted, the front lines there were rippling as eager men were held back by their officers.

A few moments later, the Tenth paused once more and the centurions shouted them on into action. This time, atop the hill there was activity. Though calls to hold firm were blown like mad, whole centuries of Pompey's men were stepping out across their defences, eager to take on the Tenth, for now every green recruit on that hill was under the impression that the Tenth were reluctant to attack.

The third pause was expertly carried out, for now the men at the front had realised what they were doing, and made it look as realistic as possible. One or two even decided to break ranks and make to flee before they were ordered back into line by their centurions. Horns blew with desperate urgency up the slope, but Pompey's legions were moving. They had not committed to a charge, for even they were not ready to utterly disobey their commanders, but they had moved forward some twenty paces from their initial position. It might not seem like much to the raw recruits of those legions, but Fronto knew what a difference it made. A few moments ago, the Tenth were facing the entire slope, and would be fighting up the last of it against a front line who held the brow of the hill, and who enjoyed the additional support of a two foot rampart, all that could be managed on the rocky hill in the time they had. Now, however, the enemy were deployed on the slope itself, forward of their meagre defences.

Fronto felt the terrain change now, as the army began to climb that slope. Still, the Pompeians atop it shoved and shouted, expecting an easy fight.

'Pila at fifteen paces,' Atenos bellowed from the front. 'Watch for their volley first.'

Sure enough, as they neared the enemy lines, Pompey's men braced and released their javelins. Atenos knew what he was about. The enemy could afford to release at thirty paces, for they had gravity on their side. The Tenth were throwing uphill, and their range had to be reduced appropriately. All along the slope, pila came out from the rebel lines like a black cloud against the blue sky. Centurions along the line bellowed, and the Tenth braced as best they could, pausing for only moments to take the strike. It was impressive, and to the layman, it might even appear that the rebels had brutalised the Caesarians. Fronto knew better. He'd seen good volleys and bad, both cast and received. Despite terrain, these were not well thrown, and it was only quantity and the weight of gravity that made it formidable. All along the line, men of the Tenth cried out and fell, but the drills were familiar to every man on the slope, and hardly had the javelins stopped vibrating with impact before the injured were pulled back into the press and gradually filtered through to the rear, where medical staff could deal with them. Pila were pulled free of shields and, where this was not possible, the shields were abandoned, and replaced with others, passed forward by their mates in the rear lines. In a matter of heartbeats the front line of the Tenth was intact and, with the centurions' whistles, marched on once more.

The speed of the legion's recovery and their implacable nature had to be unnerving the rebels now, who had probably never faced such a threat. Fronto tried not to laugh as Atenos took up the task of adding to the enemy's quaking bowels. The primus pilus began to shout, and the entire legion echoed his words.

'Rip their throats!'
'RIP THEIR THROATS!'
'Pompey's whores!'
'POMPEY'S WHORES!'
'Shit in their mouths!'
'SHIT IN THEIR MOUTHS!'
'Pompey's girls!'
'POMPEY'S GIRLS!'

The chanting went on in time with the thud of five thousand boots, and Fronto chuckled as he watched small pockets along the rebel front trying to pull back behind their little rampart, only to find they couldn't as the whole army had shuffled forward with them.

Finally, the command to halt went out, and the entire front line of the Tenth braced and cast their pila with a blood-curdling roar. The effect of this volley was vastly different. The Caesarians were throwing uphill, so their arc was low, and the javelins thudded into the front lines, rather than coming down like rain. Fronto watched men all along the lines fall, and no one in the enemy legions seemed to be ready for it. There was no flood of reserves filling the holes in the line, but more a bumbling shuffle as they attempted to re-dress the front. Indeed, they had done nothing to ready themselves when the order to charge was given and the Tenth suddenly surged up the last fifteen paces of slope, slamming into the rebel lines.

Fronto took a deep breath. It had begun.

* * *

Galronus peered ahead. He rode out on the left flank with the Mauritanian king, where he could get a good view of what was happening. Whistles were blowing in the enemy lines, and horns trumpeting, while the cavalry on the flank largely waited, scuffling occasionally, but sitting back and letting the infantry battle it out for now.

'What are they doing?' Bogud asked him in his thick African accent.

Galronus concentrated. Labienus and his horse remained in position, their discipline holding well even as the legions fell apart. They held the flank implacable and immovable. Next to them, at the southern edge of the enemy infantry, he could see the legions thinning from the rear. Now those calls he was hearing made sense. Glad that he had learned the legions' calls over the years, he turned to the king.

'Sounds like Fronto's causing him trouble. Pompey's pulling a legion from here to help at the far flank.'

'That gives us an advantage.'

'It does. They strengthen their left and weaken their right.'

'You know this Labienus. What do we do?'

Galronus sucked on his teeth. 'We have to keep him out of the main fight, but also break the weak spot where they've thinned.' He smiled. 'What do you want, Majesty, battering the cavalry or flattening the infantry?'

Bogud grinned. 'There is nothing I like more than riding across screaming enemies.'

'Good. Take your horse and put the infantry flank to flight. I'll keep Labienus busy.'

Bogud gave him a friendly wave and then turned and galloped off, shouting to his officers. Galronus watched him go with mixed feelings. The Mauritanian cavalry had a good reputation, but he had yet to see them in action. Would they be capable of routing legions? He wasn't sure. But then, he also would not trust an untried force against Labienus, who fielded men the Romans called Gauls, men of fierce tribes, tried and tested over a decade of war.

'Druccus?'

The Lingonian chieftain turned, spotting Galronus, and rode for him, as the Remi spun and called also to Fridumar, commander of the Germanic contingent. As the two officers converged on him, Galronus gestured up the slope.

'Their infantry flank has been thinned. Bogud is taking his Mauritani to break them, but that means we need to keep Labienus out of the fight. The moment he commits, wherever he presses the whole fight might change. At the moment he's sitting and watching, waiting to see where he can do the most damage. He doesn't want to commit against us, because he knows we'll be a struggle and that prevents him from breaking the infantry elsewhere. So we're going to force his hand. We're going to make him fight us. He's used to fighting us all. He knows our tactics, even yours, Fridumar. He knows how to counter them all, how to take on each of our units. He's put his tribes out front because they're the strongest and most experienced. We need to give them something they don't know how to deal with.'

'But you said it yourself,' Fridumar frowned. 'He knows how to deal with all of us.'

'Not at once.'

'What?' said Druccus.

'He's faced the Aedui and Lingones and the Arverni among us. The Helvii and the Santones, and every tribe of your lands and peoples. He's fought us, too. The Remi and Bellovaci, the Suessiones and Mediomatrici, all the men of the Belgae. Then he's fought the Germans of Fridumar, from the Tungri and the Ubii, the Treveri and the Suevi. But we're all different. The tribes of the south prefer to slowly cut away lines of the enemy in sweeps. My own people like to punch a hole in the enemy line and hack at them from the inside. We all know how Fridumar's lot work,' he added with rolling eyes that made the German chieftain grin.

'What can I say?' Fridumar laughed. 'I like to take heads.'

'But Labienus knows us all,' Druccus reminded him.

'But he's never had to deal with it all at once. Here we have all the forces together. Druccus, when we give the call, I want each of your standards to fall in beside one of mine, and the same goes for you, Fridumar. Between the first and second whistles, they all move, and so by the time the second goes, our army is all mixed up, whether you be Boii from across the Rhenus, Helvii from Rome's old lands or Remi from the north. Then we attack together. No separation of our forces. Labienus won't know how to counter it.'

'It could work,' Druccus mused.

'It'll make him shit himself,' Fridumar laughed.

'Pass the word to your men. We go as soon as we can. We need to keep Labienus off balance so he can't stop Bogud.'

As the two men hurried off, Galronus quickly repeated the plan to one of his chieftains with orders to pass it to the others, and then sat watching, thinking. Off to the right, Bogud was gathering his riders and the Third were peeling back a little, shortening their line to make extra room for the Mauritanians to charge. The Remi took a deep breath and looked up. He frowned. A bird was circling low, over the cavalry. That alone made little sense. One of the first things a warrior learns about battle is that the sky will clear of wildlife when the clash begins, and when it returns it will only be the carrion feeders over the swathes of the dead. Yet above the riders, Galronus could see the singular bird, impossible; incongruous.

It swooped again, a small bird with a white chest and black and white wings spotted in a regular pattern, its species clear from the red patch on its belly. He held his breath. A woodpecker was the chosen bird of Icovellauna. He could remember from his earliest days leaving offerings at her shrine at Durocortorum with his aunt, one of the goddess's most devoted servants. It had been a woodpecker that had decided him on leading the warband to Caesar's side all those years ago. A woodpecker had no place in the sky above a field like this.

As he watched, the woodpecker finally came out of a swoop and darted off west in a straight line. His wide eyes followed it as it disappeared into the distance above the enemy lines, first a bird, then little more than a dot, and then nothing but blue sky. Galronus' eyes slipped downwards from that place, and somehow it came as no surprise to find himself staring at a shape standing out among the waiting cavalry, surrounded by standards.

Titus Labienus.

A command from the gods themselves.

His heart fluttered. The gods granted such things, but they could demand a price, and sometimes the price was high. His aunt had paid such a price. On the interpretation of a sign, she had set out to raise a statue by the great river Mosela. She had done so, and that statue had brought her a husband from among the Treveri, who had given her a young chieftain, but with his arrival she had passed from this life on the birth bed. The gods gave. The gods took. Icovellauna was offering him Labienus, but what would she take?

His memory shot back to a dozen nights this past two months shared with Fronto and good wine. Talk of what was to happen in Hispania and of what was to come after. This would be the last battle for Fronto, and probably for Caesar. Atenos felt certain that would make it the last battle for the Tenth, and therefore for him. And for Galronus of the Remi, prince of that people, but also senator of Rome, betrothed to a patrician? He'd not yet thought on whether this would be his last battle, but suddenly the notion that it may not be his decision arose. That perhaps he would be selling his life for that of Labienus. He closed his eyes and found his mind full of images of Faleria. He shivered at the thought of never seeing her again.

When he opened them, he was decided. He would pray, beg that he walked away from this field and saw Fronto's sister again. That this would be his last battle, but not his last day. But the gods had offered him Labienus, the man who had driven half the campaign against Caesar, and who had slipped their clutches at every turn across the whole world.

He had to try.

A call told him that his men were ready. He looked around. Bogud's standards were on the move now, pressing towards the enemy, leading a charge against Pompey's legions. Galronus looked across the cavalry and nodded to the trumpeter, who gave a single, powerful blast. Like a choppy sea, the mass of cavalry on the flank began to move, currents of men and horses pulling this way and that, and as Galronus watched, he saw their standards converge. Despite their many differences, the standards of the three peoples shared much in their design and content, and that, he realised, was something that they had always had, but which Rome had seen and capitalised on.

They moved so swiftly into position that he realised with a start that they were ready and awaiting the signal. He gave another nod to the musician and then rode forward. Riders gave him looks of surprise and worry as he forged a path between them to the front lines. Only there was he going to reach Labienus, and oddly, though he had a doom-filled premonition of the day, since the goddess had offered him Labienus, he also bore a certain sense of invincibility. He might end this day sightless and still somewhere on the field, but not while Titus Labienus still breathed, and that meant that no man could fell him until then.

Armoured with divine certainty, Galronus moved to the front lines of his people, settling in at a trot alongside the others. Across a narrow stretch of open ground kept deliberately there by both sides, the rebel cavalry awaited.

Galronus gave a roar, thrust his sword up and forward, and the cavalry bellowed their war cries, horns resounding, and surged forward into a charge. His horse pounding, the Remi brought down his sword and, noting that he had adequate space to his right, held it out ready to swing. A heartbeat later the two sides met with an almighty crash.

Had he more leisure to watch his tactics at work, Galronus would have marvelled. As units of Remi and Bellovaci and their Belgic allies smashed into the enemy lines here and there, pushing in deep, the riders of the Gaulish tribes instead struck fast and turned, sliding away before they could be repelled, ducking around their allies and then falling in somewhere else along the line and repeating the process, like dolphins leaping in and out of the water. And while this was happening, the Germanic riders were scattering like the seeds from a fallen pomegranate, some leaping from their horses and disappearing beneath the bellies of their enemy's steeds to rip them open under their riders, others simply pushing in and hacking around them with weapons in both hands.

The rebel horse failed to achieve an adequate defence. They tried, and tried admirably, but their inability to cope with such a varied and unpredictable attack was evident, and they were being cut down rapidly.

Galronus, of course, saw little of this, for his gaze was set upon that collection of standards dead ahead. The Remi's sword swung and hacked, chopped and sliced, carving a path through the enemy horsemen, heedless of danger. He saw Labienus here and there through the press, and caught the moment the enemy commander realised what he was dealing with. Orders were given out and relayed by enemy musicians. The riders were called back into formation, but other calls were made, too. Labienus seemed confident. The man knew now what Caesar was up to, and had decided how to deal with it. Galronus found himself praying with every sword stroke, through the mizzle of red and the screams of agony that surrounded him, that he could get to Labienus before the enemy recovered. He knew that his tactic had worked for now, but he also knew that it was a one-shot thing, and that when Labienus managed to deal with it, the bastard would gain the upper hand somehow. By then, Bogud had to have broken through, and Galronus had to have reached the enemy commander.

All around him he sensed the change in the fighting. The Gauls of the enemy cavalry were dancing their horses around now wildly, even as they fought, and the beasts were turning the tide against the dismounted Germans, trampling them and kicking them, breaking bones. Coming to know what to expect from the Caesarians, they were now raising their shields to protect them from the skirmishing riders of Druccus, who had cast what javelins they had and were now coming down to sword fighting. Things were slowly moving into a solid, traditional struggle.

Something clanged off Galronus' helmet and for a moment he went both deaf and blind, vomit rising up his gorge. He threw up over a rider as his eyes began to focus once more. His head hurt. But he was still alive and still in the saddle. He was also almost alone, just he and half a dozen of his men, cut off by the surrounding enemy.

Then, ahead, he saw Labienus once more, and realised how close the enemy commander was. And in that moment, the former Caesarian lieutenant turned and their eyes met. Galronus felt the recognition in Labienus' gaze, and then the man was lost to sight once more.

No. Labienus had to fall. If he lived, this would not be the last battle after all.

Gritting his teeth and ignoring the pain in his head, Galronus pushed his way on.

CHAPTER EIGHTEEN

March 17th 45 BC

Blows were landing left and right, each turned by Galronus' chain shirt, his shield or his blade, but it was becoming more difficult, and he was taking more damage with every heartbeat now. His shield, an extended wood and hide hexagon with a bronze rim and a large boss, painted with the ancient symbols of the Remi along with Jupiter's thunderbolts, was now little more than a chipped and shredded handful of broken boards and twisted bronze, centring on a dented dome around his fist. Still, it took blows. His sword had acquired nicks all along the blade, though it was hard to tell through the mess that covered it. His chain shirt would be beyond salvage, and would simply be discarded, for the shoulder doubling had come away in pieces, hanging down his back, twisted and torn holes were in evidence, and one sleeve had almost come away. He knew he'd been scratched in half a dozen places, but he knew equally that none of them, miraculously, would be lethal. The gods were with him.

To his right, one of the Aedui with him screamed and fell forward over his horse's mane, blood welling up through the neck of his chain shirt from some unseen wound. He lolled to one side, dead, yet still mounted thanks to the stability of the Roman saddle. As Galronus hammered at a snarling horseman with his sword, he watched that dead, swaying figure carried off into the press by its panicked horse.

Four men were still with him, and he could hear the rest of his cavalry close behind, pushing to catch him up. He'd lost sight of the banners now, had no idea where Labienus was, other than somewhere ahead. A sword came out of nowhere, and he caught it with what was left of his shield, feeling his knuckles vibrate and ache under the blow. The dent it left in the boss was now pressing on his knuckles and making the shield more or less a waste of time. Even as he parried another blow with his sword and used his knees to drive his horse forward into the mass, he finally cast aside the remnants of his shield. He was left with a defenceless side for only a moment before an Arvernian off to his left took a spear to the back and straightened in agony in his saddle. Galronus swept out his left hand and grabbed the sword that fell from the rider's fingers, gripping it tight and flipping it round to block yet another blow. It occurred oddly to him, too late to notice, that he wasn't sure whether the dying horseman had been one of his or one of Labienus'. Strange how this civil war had not only pitted Roman against Roman but, because of their now long service to Rome, it was also pitting tribes against their own.

He was more than a little surprised when his sword cut down a rider and suddenly he could see an open space. For a heartbeat he thought he had carved a path right through Labienus' cavalry and emerged behind them, and wondered where the commander and his standards had gone, but it took only moments and a straying of the eyes to determine what had happened.

He had been turned around in the press. While he'd thought he was pushing on west into the enemy, he had gradually, accidentally, curved to the right, and the space he had emerged into, strewn with thrashing horses and screaming near-corpses, was actually a breach in the enemy lines. Behind him, the Third Legion were surging forward into the gap. Ahead, he could see Pompey's reserves shuffling in to try and plug the hole, but the cause was clear. The weak point in the enemy lines had been hit so hard by Bogud and his Mauritanian cavalry that they had broken through swiftly, leaving swathes of rebel dead, and breaking out into the rear. In fact, as Galronus peered off in that direction, he could see a new fight rising on the field.

Bogud and his horsemen had emerged into the space behind the enemy. A few of his men had peeled off in small units to take down signallers, musicians, standards, and small pockets of officers and messengers, attempting to limit the ability of commanders to control their army, but a sizeable force had made straight for the enemy camp behind the Pompeian lines. Galronus should have realised what would happen. Bogud's men may be fierce, but they were not a disciplined fighting force such as Rome preferred to field. In fact, they were little more than a band of desert raiders tied together by loyalty to a king. The moment they had achieved their breach, as they'd been ordered, the next thing that had leapt to their mind had been plunder, regardless of the fact that the battle was still going on behind them. The Mauritanians were racing for Pompey's camp with a mind for loot.

Ordinarily, Galronus would curse them for such a failing, which could easily lead to disaster for the Caesarians, but clearly the gods were still at work, gifting Galronus the chance of victory.

Labienus had seen the Mauretanians break through and race for the camp and, in a moment of hard decision making, had split his own force, leaving half his cavalry to hold Galronus' riders, and taking the other half back across the field to chase down Bogud. For a moment, the Remi saw Labienus and his standards racing across the open ground back towards their camp and the rampaging Mauretani.

The man was a Roman commander of the old school and, despite Fronto's examples, a Roman commander did not commit to fighting in the front lines. His place was at the rear, where he could see the ebb and flow of the battle and issue orders appropriately. Consequently, while Labienus' riders, several thousand strong, were racing on the heels of Bogud's Africans, the commander himself, along with a small bodyguard, two standards and a musician, trailed along behind, looking this way and that, seeing what they could do to regain control of the battle.

It was an opportunity. Galronus could see the commander clearly, and there were but a dozen men around him. He had to get there before the Pompeian reserves fully blocked the gap, but he needed men with him. He was near exhausted, and couldn't consider taking on several men at once, let alone a dozen.

'Is that him?' asked a voice at his shoulder.

Galronus turned to see Druccus sitting astride his horse, sheathed in gore, and with one eye welded shut with blood and viscera. Behind Druccus were a score of his riders, each wounded and coated with crimson, but each armed and with a fearsome expression.

'That's him.'

'Then what are we waiting for?'

In a matter of moments, Galronus was galloping. He knew, could sense, Druccus and the others were with him, and he could hear the roar as the Third flooded in to try and hold the breach. Ahead, another roar announced the arrival of one of Pompey's legions, hurrying to plug that gap. Galronus angled his mount, trying to hit that weak spot where the newly-arriving legionaries met the struggling horsemen Labienus had left on the flank. He hit the wall of men and riders like a cormorant plunging into the sea, his small party of horsemen at his back. His gaze was locked on the retreating figure of Labienus and his standards, following his riders, who in turn chased Bogud's Mauritanians.

He was heedless of obstructions, now. His horse ploughed into the infantry, trampling them as he charged. He felt the glancing blows as he passed, and knew that his horse was suffering with strikes here and there, and yet he still knew that he would break through them, for the gods had offered him Labienus, and he would not fall until the Roman had. As he smashed through, he was aware that he had lost men in the charge, but Druccus was still with him, and a few other riders behind. His horse was whinnying in pain at numerous small wounds, yet still it pressed on with his direction.

Suddenly, he was in the open. He had perhaps half a dozen horsemen with him as he raced for that banner up the slope. Labienus had more, and they would be untouched as yet by combat. But Galronus' men were fierce riders of the tribes with everything to fight for and their blood up, hungry for victory. For all that most of Labienus' cavalry were men of the tribes, the commander was a Roman at heart, and those men surrounding him as he followed the clash wore red tunics and shiny breastplates, Roman noblemen, not seasoned warriors. But most of all, the gods had already decreed what was to happen. It was no contest.

Kicking his horse's weary and injured flanks, Galronus bore down on the small party of Roman officers and bodyguards, the thunder of hooves in his ears telling him his men were still with him. He was aware of a surge of noise from behind, a new intensity to the sound of the battle, but for Galronus of the Remi, Munda had become more than a battle against the rebels. It had become personal.

Labienus had been a friend. He had been, of all Caesar's officers, the one who had shown a true understanding of the people of the tribes. He had held the Belgae in high esteem and had decried their destruction. He had, over those years in the Gallic War, taken those tribes to his standard, and had become a leader among them, favouring their horsemen over Rome's legions. He had been the man to lead the riders of the tribes for Caesar.

And then he had betrayed the general. And in betraying the general and Rome, he had taken the Belgae and the men of Gaul and had turned them against their own. The tribes had been Caesar's men, but Labienus had turned them away and made them fight for him and his rebel allies. It was because of Labienus that Galronus had now spent three years fighting his own countrymen.

And Pompey was a figurehead just for his name. He could rally a certain resistance to Caesar, but there was no doubt in anyone's mind that since the fall of the man's great father, and then Scipio and Cato, it was Labienus who drove this war for the rebels. It was his strategies that kept it going. Pompey or no Pompey, without Labienus the war would end.

The Romans had finally become aware of the riders bearing down on them, and had turned, leaving their own horsemen to deal with Bogud's Mauritani.

'The commander is mine,' Galronus shouted.

'We'll clear the way,' Druccus replied, and the eight of them gripped their swords ready, kicking their mounts into an even faster charge, using up the last of the horses' energy. That Galronus' own horse could still plough on was a small miracle in itself, given the bloody stripes all over her.

The shiny Roman riders had gathered in front of Labienus and his signallers. Their musician was now blowing out a desperate call, while the standard bearers waved their burdens back and forth. The Roman noblemen set their faces into grim expressions, their swords out, left hand on the reins. Their blades were short, traditional gladii.

Galronus eased off at the last moment, letting his pace slacken. Druccus and his men managed to pull ahead, and two of the riders slipped in front of their Remi leader. They hit the Roman guards like a crashing wave, and Galronus smiled a rictus of war as the two men who'd got ahead of him hit their targets at just the right angle to force them aside, clearing a path for their commander. Suddenly, as the fight began, Galronus was face to face with Titus Labienus, eyeing him with a cold expression.

The cavalry commander lifted his sword, horse dancing this way and that, nervously.

'Prince Galronus,' was all Labienus managed to say before the Remi swung his horse left at the last moment, his long, Gallic sword slashing out wide. To Labienus' credit, he leaned back in the saddle and hammered out with his own sword, managing to avoid the blow and turn it away. Galronus could not help but notice that the Roman's blade was a long example, a sword of the tribes, not a shorter, Roman weapon.

Labienus' answering blow as he spun his horse back, was a powerful overarm chop, aimed for Galronus' right shoulder. The Remi managed to turn in the saddle, bringing the second sword in his left hand across even as he leaned back. Labienus' powerful downward strike hammered into the raised sword, smashing it back painfully against Galronus' shoulder and almost knocking it from his shocked fingers. The Remi hissed in pain, but managed somehow to retain his grip.

He wheeled his horse once more.

'For Caesar,' was all he said, through gritted teeth, as he swung both swords at once.

Labienus saw them coming, but there was little he could do. He managed to slam his own blade in the way of one and tried to lurch away from the other, but like the closing of a pair of shears, he was trapped. The blade in Galronus' right hand clanged off that of Labienus, sliding away with a shudder-inducing rasp, but his other sword smashed into the commander's left arm and even above the din of battle, he heard the bone break.

Labienus bellowed his pain, still attempting to maintain control. He tried to back his horse up, but his left arm was useless, the fingers falling free of the reins. He swung with his right arm, but the blow lacked both strength and accuracy as the Roman, teeth gritted, struggled to master the pain of his shattered humerus.

Galronus swatted away the strike and swung again, his second blow smashing into Labienus' side. Fury and desperation had lent him unexpected strength, and the sword slammed into the Roman's cuirass hard, leaving a deep, long dent in the bronze. Even as

Galronus danced away to make room, he knew that the dent was too deep for Labienus to survive. That blow had broken bones and torn the body beneath the bronze. Indeed, blood began to sheet down from inside the cuirass, flowing across the leather pteruges at Labienus's waist.

'…Caesar,' was all the man managed to hiss in agony as he lolled back.

Galronus struck again, this time from high, the blade slamming down into Labienus' neck, almost separating his head. The Roman howled as he fell back. Still Galronus did not let up, another blow to the man's chest further denting the cuirass and sliding down it to hack off a piece of the saddle horn. No longer secured, the dying Roman slid from the saddle and fell to the churned and muddy ground, jerking wildly, sword fallen away.

Galronus watched the man die. Somehow, after everything they had all been through, he felt he could never be certain Labienus was gone unless he'd seen it with his own eyes. He watched the jerking end, watched the blood pouring. Watched the face take on a grey tint, and the eyes fall still, staring up, sightless, into the sky.

It was only when he could say for certain the man was gone that Galronus looked up. Labienus' riders had chased Bogud's cavalry into the great camp where, undoubtedly, a new fight was breaking out. Druccus lay nearby, fallen and sporting a massive gash to the side, a pool of blood around him growing rapidly. Two of the riders who'd accompanied him were still in the saddle, both badly wounded and exhausted, but every Roman lay dead. Galronus almost let out a cry of shock as his horse suddenly crumpled beneath him, and he realised as the beast collapsed and he leapt free only just in time to avoid being trapped beneath it, that his mount had taken more wounds from Labienus' guards during this last fight. The horse was done.

He rose to his feet, shaking.

Labienus was dead.

It was almost over.

* * *

Fronto watched the men of the Tenth heaving the enemy back. Their initial success had since met with resistance as Pompey had brought reserves across from the far flank. As the Tenth felt the weight of extra forces pressing against them, Fronto had hoped that Pedius and Galronus were faring better, that the source of those reserves had left a gap for his friends to exploit.

Still, despite the pressure and the constant stream of injured soldiers filtering back through the lines to the medical section, it was clear that they were still the better force. As Fronto stepped Bucephalus forward, he continually avoided trampling the bodies of the fallen as he followed the rear of the Tenth, but now, among those bodies were the corpses of the enemy, for they had once more begun to push the rebel legions back up the slope.

With a roar, his men heaved forth again, and as Fronto followed, he struggled. This was, he was sure, the last battle. As long as they managed to break these legions and kill the commanders, the war would be over. He would retire. Rome, and Lucilia awaited. It was so close.

But what was life without this? He had devoted his whole career to this, eschewing the positions expected of a man of his status. He could hardly contemplate an aedileship now. Or some stuffy political role as a praetor. He didn't want to be a governor. He didn't want the responsibility of an entire province, and he had no real need for the gold he would be expected to skim from the top of the taxes. He most certainly didn't want to be a senator. In fact, the only thing, other than war, for which he was suited, was sitting in a bar and getting drunk, and he wasn't at all convinced that Lucilia would consider that a career choice. Would he be one of those old soldiers who, bereft of a battlefield for their talents, just sat by a fire telling the stories of their youthful days as he faded into a shadow of a man?

No. He had the boys. He had friends. There were always possibilities.

But still, if this *was* the last battle…

He was not at all sure what he planned to do as he urged Bucephalus forward, other than that he needed to do more than just follow along at the back. He had led the defence of Bibrax, he'd stood in the line with Caesar as the Belgae came howling. He'd shed blood hunting Ambiorix and roared defiance at Vercingetorix over the ramparts of Alesia. He'd faced Pompey at Pharsalus and struggled in the burning city of Alexandria. He was damned if he was going to let the war end without unsheathing his blade.

As he reached the lines of legionaries, he swung down from the saddle, cursing as his knee threatened to give way with the impact. Steadying himself, he handed the reins to one of the various couriers, orderlies and ancillary staff at the rear, and then moved forward on foot, bellowing for people to move aside. Men were lurching out of his way, then, as he pressed forward, a ripple of warning spreading through the Tenth ahead of him. He realised how far they'd pushed the enemy as he crossed the low rampart behind which Pompey's army had waited for them.

As he crossed it, the sudden height the rampart offered him revealed an excellent view of the battle. He was just eight rows back from the fighting now, and he could see the struggle going on, like two teams at a tug-of-war, the line surging back and forth with every fresh kill. And there, two thirds of the way back through the enemy force, he could see the banners and standards that marked out Pompey's location. He grinned. Maybe he could finish this by ending the younger Pompey. Fresh determination filling him, he pressed on into the mass.

A few moments later he was joined by a tall figure in a gleaming breastplate as Pompeius Niger appeared beside him, his own sword out.

'Should you be this far forward, sir?' the tribune asked in concern.

'Bollocks,' was all Fronto said, eyes ahead, still pushing forward. Niger shrugged and fell in beside him.

'I saw Antistius Turpio a few moments ago,' shouted Niger.

'Who?' Fronto frowned as they pushed on.

'Centurion I faced at Soricaria,' the tribune reminded him.

'Ah yes,' Fronto nodded, remembering the strange, almost heroic duel. 'Try not to get yourself killed. The Tenth needs good officers.'

Although for how much longer, he couldn't say.

He became aware that they had reached the front of the fighting only when the legionary in front of him screamed and fell back, fountaining blood, and Fronto realised that the next man in the line hefted the shield design of one of Pompey's legions. Niger was suddenly busy, bellowing threats as he veered off in the direction of a red crest that betrayed his own quarry, eager to pick up their duel where they had left off.

Fronto saw the man coming at him and, aware that he had no shield, turned to his left, opening up a gap as the man lunged. The sword scraped across Fronto's cuirass, leaving a gleaming line through the images of two winged victories and a medusa head. As the man overextended, Fronto leaned in and stabbed past his angled shield, driving his blade into the unprotected flesh below his arm.

The soldier bellowed and fell back. The blow had been awkward and not deep enough to kill instantly, but he'd cut flesh and drawn blood and if the wound wasn't mortal, then it was certainly enough to put the man out of the fight. As the legionary fell back, Fronto stepped forward, ready to face the next man, but the Pompeian legionary behind was looking the other way. Fronto frowned, but his ears registered a new sound. An air of panic among the enemy.

As he stabbed at the inattentive legionary and pushed forward once more, he listened, catching snippets. He blinked in surprise as he heard what appeared to be the news that Labienus and his cavalry had fled the field back to their camp. That did not sound like Labienus to Fronto. Caesar's army had gained the upper hand, certainly, but the battle was far from a foregone conclusion yet. Pompey still had larger numbers and the higher ground, his troops were better rested. Why would Labienus leave the fight and run back to the camp? It made no sense.

But it mattered not whether what he was hearing was true, nor, even if it was, why it was so. What mattered was that the enemy believed it. A collective bray of panic roared through the enemy legions at the news that their cavalry had fled the field. That meant the flank had fallen and that Caesar's army would be surging forth to fold in on their southern edge, trapping them on two sides.

In that moment, Pompey's army broke.

In heartbeats, the panic became a howling din of terror, and rebel legionaries were abandoning even a fighting withdrawal in favour of simple flight. The rawness and inexperience of Pompey's huge force was telling, as men who could still have fought a disciplined retreat to the town simply cast away their shields and ran for their lives.

Fronto tried to stab out at a man, but the legionary was gone before the blow landed. All along the fight, the enemy were routing, the men of Caesar's legions pushing on with renewed vim. Here and there, pockets of rebels continued to fight. Cohorts of Pompey's legions drawn from experienced units tried desperately to hold their ground while rebel centurions and senior officers raced this way and that shouting, trying to halt the rout and to rally the panicked legions, and all to no avail. There was no hope now of stopping the flight.

His gaze darting this way and that, Fronto spotted the banners of Pompey. The man was still in the field, bellowing orders at his officers. He could see Tribune Niger shouting in fury as the centurion he had been facing once more disappeared into the press, unwilling to throw away his life even for a duel of such importance to the two men. Turpio was making for Pompey's banners, but there was no hope of reaching them, for at that moment the enemy general clearly decided that the battle was lost. Pompey gave one last glare of distaste at the site of his failure, and then turned and rode away, the banners and standards going with him.

Fronto hissed in frustration. There was little chance of catching them, for they were on horseback and already at the rear of the field. Pompey was going to get away. Breathing heavily and rolling weary shoulders, Fronto looked this way and that. Pompey escaping meant that it wasn't over. It couldn't be over until the two Pompeys and Labienus were removed. But at the same time, he could see how total their victory had been here. Caesar's legions were now swarming over the hill and towards Pompey's camp and the city of Munda beyond. The enemy forces were melting away, some of them making for Munda and the perceived safety of its walls, though the majority were shedding armour and weapons as they ran and fleeing into the open country. It had taken Pompey two years to amass a force large enough to face Caesar, and it had only been the African campaign and their time in Rome that had granted the young commander such an opportunity. He would not get another.

There was, quite simply, no way this army was going to be pulled together and fielded once again. It was done. And now that Caesar was here in Hispania with his legions and finally, seemingly, unopposed, there would be no chance for the rebels to build a new force. The war was all but over, and this should be the last battle after all. Now, they had to hunt down the three commanders and make sure they were dealt with before they could rally anyone, and they could not run far. With the exception of the trouble in Syria at the far end of the world, nowhere in the republic would now give succour to Labienus and the Pompeys.

He watched with an air of satisfaction as the legions of Caesar cheered among the fallen ramparts of Pompey's rebellion.

* * *

'It was the Remi commander, sir,' one of the centurions explained.

Fronto, still shaking from his exertions, once more astride Bucephalus, looked across at Caesar, who was nodding slowly. He turned to look back at the ground. Titus Labienus lay twisted and bloody, his flesh a deathly grey. It had not taken long, as the army routed Pompey's forces, chasing them from the field, for someone to report to the general that one of the three enemy commanders had fallen. Caesar and Fronto had been together on the right flank when the news arrived, and had ridden side by side to the site.

Fronto looked at the body with conflict in his heart. Labienus had had to die. Of all the commanders remaining among the rebels, it was Labienus that would never have stopped. As long as Caesar lived, Labienus would oppose him, alone if need be. As such, he had to die. There had been no hope for capture and clemency here. And yet as Fronto looked down into those sightless eyes, it was extremely difficult not to recall the good man he remembered from the north. The man who had lamented the destruction wrought among the Belgae, who had been able to see a better future even as it failed to manifest. He had been the enemy for years now, yet, no matter how misguided or wrong Labienus' decisions had been, every man here knew that the commander had only ever worked from the noblest of motives. He'd believed he was right, and that what he was doing was right and for the good of the republic. No amount of blood could obscure the purest of motives.

Caesar was clearly experiencing the same strange struggle. Finally, the general breathed in and out, slowly, heavily, and straightened. 'Find Galronus of the Remi and ask him to seek me in my tent. I wish to thank and congratulate him personally.'

'He might have fallen, sir,' the centurion said. 'There are so many cavalry down.'

Caesar shook his head. 'No. He lives. Find him and have him come to me. And organise a burial detail. Titus Labienus was our enemy, but he was the best of men. He will be buried here, where he fell, and a mound raised, with a monument to mark the site. See to it.'

The centurion saluted.

Fronto sat silent as Caesar expounded on the importance of their victory, and he hadn't realised just how tense and worried he had been until he finally caught sight of Galronus, staggering wearily towards them, leaning on a fellow unhorsed cavalryman.

'Well thank fuck for that.'

PART THREE

HISPANIA – LAST STANDS

"For this was the last war that he carried through successfully, *and this the last victory that he won.*"

- Cassius Dio: *Roman History*

CHAPTER NINETEEN

Late March 45 BC

'The Fates conspire to keep us from going home,' Fronto grunted irritably as he reined in with the other officers, close enough to converse with Galronus but far enough away from Caesar not to cause that dreaded raised eyebrow of his.

'This is one of the things about Roman war,' Galronus said in a knowledgable tone. 'When the tribes fight each other, there's a clear victor and a clear loser. One lot get dragged away and left for the crows and the other goes home with the loot. It's like an argument. One has to turn and march away or it goes on forever. Roman war is different. You always have problems to settle afterwards. Like stamping on an ant nest. The nest is gone, but then you have ants everywhere.'

This simply raised another grunt from Fronto. He'd much rather have done this particular bit of 'mopping up' on his own, yet Caesar had insisted on coming along and bringing the Sixth for good measure, as if the Tenth should not be enough.

After the battle, the rebel survivors had fled in clusters in many directions. It was said that Gnaeus Pompey had run for Carteia, where his forces still maintained their naval base, impotent though it was, given than Caesar controlled the waters all around it. Others had fled to the city of Munda beyond the battlefield, which shut its gates and manned its walls defiantly. More still had run for the rebel heartlands in either Hispalis or Gades or Corduba.

A few cohorts had immediately been dispatched in pursuit of Pompey, but the rest of the army had concentrated on the immediate issues. Caesar had gathered the officers as the legions encamped around the city, and had stated his intention to grant not a whit of clemency to the survivors. Throughout this war he had repeatedly granted mercy to his enemies and released them, only to find them a year later raising new armies against him. Munda would be the last battle. No man would be permitted to live long enough to raise another army. Both Pompeys would be hunted down, along with any officer of any importance. Any soldier or civilian who had put their faith in the rebels would be stripped of their riches and positions and sold into slavery. This was the decree. Some times in his life, Fronto might have argued against such a Draconian stance. Once upon a time he would have lain down his sword and walked away. But this war had gone on long enough. If a statement had to be made to end it, then let it be so.

Still, even Fronto had baulked at the sight of the siege lines Caesar had built around Munda. No ditch was dug, no earth mound raised, no fence or palisade hacked from the trees of the region. The rampart that surrounded Munda was five feet high, but formed from the stinking, bloated corpses of the rebel soldiers dragged from the battlefield, each arrayed so that their accusing gaze fell upon the survivors in the city they surrounded. The fence atop the grisly rampart was formed from spears, swords, armour and shields taken from the dead, and atop each spear, jammed into the mound of corpses, sat a rebel head, decaying in the spring sunshine as their hollowed eyes stared at the city.

It had come as no surprise that the city remained silent, no jeers or slogans chanted. Every soul within knew their inescapable fate, and should they forget, they needed only to look out from the walls.

The escape had been daring, therefore. The second night of their grisly vigil around Munda, the legions had mobilised with a cry at a sally by a half-cohort of infantry. The soldiers had been dealt with efficiently and harshly, yet it had turned out to be nothing more than a distraction. While Caesar's officers had concentrated on this struggle, a band of horsemen had fled the far side of the city, racing to escape through the Caesarian lines. Two thirds of the fleeing riders had been killed or captured, but such was the surprise that a number had escaped into the countryside. Interrogation of prisoners – prior to their very public torture, execution and display – had revealed that the escapees had included two of Pompey's staff officers, Valerius and Scapula, who were making for Corduba.

Caesar had been adamant the next morning. The two officers had to be made examples of. Valerius had been the commander of Pompey's push at Soricaria, and Scapula had not only been the commander of Munda city, but had been one of Pompey's most crucial generals during the recruitment and deployment of the rebel legions. More than most, these two must be held to account.

Thus it was that Fronto had found the Tenth and the Sixth marching north for Corduba along with Caesar and Hirtius, leaving Pedius to oversee the final fall of Munda.

'It would appear that we are anticipated,' Caesar mused from the low rise facing the bridge that led to the city, only hastily constructed by Caesar's men a few short months ago. Fronto nodded. A small military camp sat at the far side of the bridge, occupying the space where Fronto had been settled back in the winter, while the watching officers stood on the site of Pompey's camp.

'There are not enough to hold off two legions,' Hirtius muttered. 'What could they hope to achieve?'

The scouts were riding back towards them now, and as the men reined in, saluting Caesar, their report, drawn from locals, clarified all.

Corduba was in turmoil. Sextus Pompey had received the news of Munda with dread, and had fled Corduba in the middle of the night with just a small band of bodyguards and a bag of gold. His intended destination and current whereabouts were unknown. With his flight, the pro-Caesarians in the city had risen against the garrison, and currently Corduba was in a strange stand-off, with periodic fighting in the streets between the two parties. As such, no one had been able to open the gates to the survivors of Munda, and Valerius and Scapula had found themselves trapped against the walls of the city with Caesar's army on their heels. Corduba awaited, but Scapula and Valerius held the bridge with their small, ragtag army of refugees.

'Take the bridge,' Caesar said casually. 'And take the two commanders alive. I want them crucified in sight of the walls.'

Fronto's lip curled. Crucifixion was an illegal sentence for a citizen like the two officers, and it rankled to even consider such a thing, but he fought down his distaste. Had the rebels not crucified

Caesarian men in Africa? And every atrocity they committed now was another nail in the coffin of the rebellion against Rome.

Fronto glanced across at Caninius Rebilus, current legate of the Sixth. Caninius shrugged. 'Feel free,' he said.

Fronto nodded and rode forward to where Atenos waited with the six tribunes of the Tenth.

'Caesar wants the bridge and the camp taken and the two commanders captured.'

Atenos saluted and in moments the officers were moving among the Tenth, bellowing orders, blowing whistles, cornua blaring, standards waving. The enemy had already mobilised, but Fronto could only shake his head at the pointlessness of it all. Barely a cohort of men manned that bridge, a number of them wounded, few with full equipment, a number of dismounted cavalry and auxiliaries among the citizen soldiers. They had no artillery, few supplies, and no hope at all.

The First Cohort of the Tenth formed on Atenos at the centre of the field, directly in front of the bridge. As they moved into formation, awaiting the signal, Fronto's engineers brought forth the scorpions. Their three day journey from Munda had been by necessity a speed march, and so Fronto had been forced to leave behind the supply wagons that would eventually catch up, as well as the main heavy artillery, which was still being used to threaten Munda. But every cohort carried a scorpion, and the small bolt throwers were easily portable by horse, so the legion had brought all ten with them.

The weapons were arrayed in a wide arc around the southern approach to the bridge, each with a team of artillerists, each protected by a century of men. As they were positioned, angled and loaded, ratcheted back, and the stack of ammunition prepared, some enterprising soldier among the rebels, who knew the danger to come, led a sally against one of the weapons. He and his twelve men died before they had crossed half the ground from the bridge, fallen to a volley of pila from the century protecting the weapon. There were no more brave and foolhardy sallies from the bridge.

Then the killing began. It was not a battle. It was a massacre. The men on the bridge lifted their shields and sheltered as they could, but the scorpions were powerful and relentless. The first volley saw five men pierced through and thrown from the bridge into the swift waters of the River Baetis, to disappear beneath the surface, dragged down by their ragged armour. No one moved from their position on the bridge as the scorpions reloaded. A second volley ended the life of seven men on the bridge, two of whom remained where they fell, trembling to stillness, the other five claimed by the muddy water.

The third volley took three, for the range was increasing now, the nearest targets all fallen. At a command from Atenos, the scorpion crews picked up their weapons and carried them halfway to the bridge, moving into a ready range for the next group of defenders. Their legionary protection moved with them, and Atenos led the First Cohort twenty paces closer as the Caesarian noose tightened on the bridge.

Someone in the enemy camp seemed to have little care for his men, for a moment later a fresh group of battered and tired soldiers emerged from their pitiful rampart and ran onto the bridge, bolstering the doomed force there. The scorpions were almost in place when someone decided that dying in a desperate rush was better than cowering and waiting for the inevitable. Another sally emerged from the bridge, racing at the left hand arc of bolt throwers. Again they were met by volleys of pila, though this time they had come in more force, and succeeded in closing on the weapons having lost around half their number. As they howled their fury, though, the defending centuries of legionaries simply reformed in front of the artillery, presenting a fierce shieldwall that made short work of the desperate fugitives. Swords stabbed and hacked, and the poorly-armed and exhausted rebels were cut down to a man, having killed one of Fronto's men and sent another back to the combat medics cursing and clutching his arm. No third assault came, and the scorpions were settled into position once more, loaded, aimed and released.

Men all across the bridge fell with cries of agony, and Fronto watched impassively as the defenders were systematically butchered where they cowered, the bridge gradually cleared. It was no great and heroic end for the men, but Fronto was under no illusion as to Caesar's intentions, and dying by scorpion bolt on that bridge had to be a quicker and more noble end than anything that might befall them if they came into Caesar's hands. Better to die in a hopeless struggle on a makeshift artillery range than wait on a crucifix for the slow agony to claim you.

Atenos finally gave the signal as the scorpions once more cleared everyone within range. Only the far third of the bridge remained manned, and the men there seemed ill inclined to cross the surface any closer to the deadly artillery. The scorpions fell silent, their crews stepping back as the First Cohort began to move, closing on the end of the bridge.

'Something's happening in the enemy camp,' Galronus said, nudging Fronto and pointing beyond the action.

Fronto's gaze rose from the bridge and its carpet of bodies and crimson pools, to the low ramparts, reused from Caesar's own camp so many months earlier. The enemy had fortified a small area of that camp as their own. They had no tents and no supplies, and no materials to create a corral. Their rampart was formed from debris, their horses tethered to graze outside the defences, their tents nothing more than ragged sheets forming roofs with mismatched poles. Still, Galronus had been sharp eyed to spot the fresh activity.

The officers had assumed the entire enemy force now committed to the bridge, for the camp had seemed to be empty, and a telltale crimson plume confirmed that at least one of the officers was guiding the defence at the far bank. The camp may be devoid of soldiers, but a small group of unarmoured figures in ragged tunics seemed to be gathering all the debris they could find from the camp, even pulling down those makeshift shelters, piling the entire collection of bric-a-brac into a heap in the centre of the camp.

'What in Hades are they doing?' Fronto murmured.

'A beacon?' Caninius posited. 'Maybe they're signalling some unseen unit? Or it's a signal to their allies in the city. It certainly *looks* like a beacon.'

Caesar rubbed his chin reflectively. 'I cannot believe that there is any force nearby sizeable enough to be of aid to them. Intelligence suggests that the garrisons that were marching to join Pompey at Munda have melted away into the countryside, and any other survivors of the battle would surely have joined Scapula and Valerius for mutual protection. I cannot see what value any kind of warning could be to the city. Yet I concur that it does appear to be a signal beacon.' The general turned to Galronus. 'Have scouts ride out three miles in every direction and confirm that we are indeed alone here.'

Galronus nodded and hurried off to find his riders, while the officers turned back to the fight. As they watched Atenos and his veteran First Cohort approach the bridge, Caninius turned to Fronto with a raised eyebrow. 'Wouldn't Valerius be a relation of yours?'

Fronto sighed. He'd almost been waiting for someone to make the connection. 'So distantly even that beacon wouldn't shine the light on it. We've been Falerii, not Valerii, for four generations since my great great grandfather abandoned his patrician roots to become Tribune of the Plebs. And those Valerii who do acknowledge our existence tend to look down their noses at us.'

Caninius gave him a sly smile. The bastard knew all about it of course, but poking fun at slipped nobility was almost a pastime among the senatorial class. The legate straightened. 'Valerius won't let himself be taken, you know?'

'You're familiar with him?'

'We served as praetors together back in Rome, before all this. He's not a bad man, but I tell you now, he's a bloody-minded one, and as you said, his nobility is at the heart of his being. He'll not let himself be made an example of.'

'Don't suppose you know Scapula too?'

'By reputation. He's a bit of a showy bastard. Renowned for throwing huge parties for small victories, that sort of thing.'

Fronto nodded absently as he turned back to the action. Atenos was leading his men across the bridge now, marching with determination, shields up, swords out. The enemy moved from their various positions where they'd been cowering from missile shots and formed the best shield wall they could with their varied battered and oddly-shaped boards, legionary shields slammed against hexagonal or oval cavalry ones, small round shields from signifers, and any number of shields from random Hispanic auxiliaries. Spears and swords of all sorts were pushed out. The two forces met with a roar and a clang of metal, and the screaming began. Fronto watched his cohort with little difficulty tear their way through the ragged rebel force, pushing the wounded and dead into the water to make way for their advance. Bodies were cast aside without breaking their pace, and in two dozen heartbeats they had reached the far bank, filtering out into a wall forty men wide and ten deep. There they halted for a moment, re-forming and preparing as the last straggling survivors huddled into what might be only generously termed a shield wall.

Fronto could see that officer now, his red plume proud, his cuirass gleaming, as he moved up and down behind the block of his men, nudging them into line and barking something inaudible at them. Atenos blew his whistle, the rebels braced themselves, and the Tenth broke into a charge. Fronto watched with a lump forming in his throat. They were the enemy, and they needed to fall, but it was rare a man got to watch a hopeless last stand performed by what were clearly inordinately brave men. The Tenth hit their foe hard and in moments the rebel line crumbled and collapsed. Atenos' triple whistle blast released his men to open melee and in moments the few enemy survivors were being surrounded and cut down efficiently and mercilessly. The centurion himself, with four men at his back, stepped across the line of fallen rebels, closing on the man with the red plume. Fronto held his breath.

The officer did not run. He watched Atenos stomping towards him and his sword came up. As Atenos stepped inexorably, the officer loosened the straps of his cuirass, letting it fall away. Fronto nodded, realising what was coming. Caesar was about to be robbed of one of his examples.

'Valerius?' he mused, leaning towards Caninius as they watched.

'Yes. Going like a proper Roman.'

The two men watched, solemn, as Atenos moved faster. He had to know what was happening, and likely Atenos would respect it, but he was under orders from Caesar to take the leaders alive. He was too late. In moments, Valerius had turned the blade, placing the point over his heart, and then, with his face turned upwards, imploring the gods to witness him, fell forward. The hand on the sword pommel struck the ground and the blade was slammed between ribs, through heart and organs. Valerius died as Atenos arrived, standing over the corpse.

Fronto and Caninius both turned to Caesar, whose expression was unreadable. The general seemed to change his mind several times, then finally drew a deep breath and straightened, decision made. 'Have Valerius' body retrieved and cremated. Have the urn delivered to his family in Rome.'

Fronto sagged with relief. A noble death for a noble man deserved to be treated with respect. Plus, of course, the act of magnanimity would do Caesar's reputation no harm in Rome.

'What of his counterpart, though,' Fronto muttered.

'I think that question is about to be answered,' Caninius replied, pointing across the river. Fronto squinted, trying to see the detail of what was happening in the camp. A figure had emerged from one of those makeshift shelters. It seemed to be wearing a toga. Of course, a ragtag band of refugees who couldn't even rustle up sufficient weapons was unlikely to have carried a pristine toga, and so the garment was likely one of those many shelters used as tents, wrapped as neatly as possible and draped over the man's arm. It had to be the other commander, especially in light of Rebilus' description of the man.

'What *is* going on?' Caesar breathed in surprise.

Beyond Scapula, a dozen slaves or attendants of some kind in lowly tunics followed him. Two carried burning torches, the other a long knife.

'A spectacle, I'd say,' Caninius sighed.

'Will he light the beacon?' Hirtius frowned. 'Who will he signal?'

'Can you see around him?' Caninius said, eyes rolling.

'No.' Fronto had enough trouble making out the figures.

'He's got carpets down and tapestries. There's tables of food. It's like a bloody banquet over there. That's probably what the slaves are for: to serve the food and wine.'

'He's mad,' Fronto shook his head.

Then Scapula climbed up onto a high stool and threw out one arm in the manner of an orator addressing the crowd. The gesture was so familiar, and so oddly out of place, that every figure on both sides of the river stopped moving and fell silent.

Scapula now spun to face the city behind him and spread out both arms.

'People of Corduba, hear me, for I am the last vestige of the republic. With me dies the Rome you know. All that comes is a monarchy. The reign of a new tyrant. A new Tarquinius the Proud. For you should be certain that when you open these gates to Caesar you invite a king into the palaces of Rome. Caesar has made sport of the bodies of the noble defenders of the republic, displaying their heads at Munda. Such is to come here, and such is the fate of all who oppose this blight-filled monarchy.'

'Someone shut him up,' Caninius hissed, but Caesar simply shrugged.

'It is nothing new. I have listened to these tales time and again. Let him rant.'

And he did so, even as scorpions were moved into range, loaded and cranked, trained on the toga-clad orator on his stool.

'I shall not let the despot display my corpse for his nefarious political agenda,' Scapula continued. 'People of Corduba, resist the dictator. Sell your life dearly.'

The man turned, gesturing to his attendants.

'Felix.'

The man with the blade approached. Across the river, Atenos raised and lowered a hand. A scorpion released, but failed to take Scapula, for the man at that moment dropped down from his stool and the bolt whispered harmlessly through the air above his head. Fronto watched, wincing, as the slave slowly and neatly pulled the sharp knife across Scapula's throat. As the nobleman stepped back, still standing, he turned slowly, arms held out to the sides as blood sheeted down the white garment, stark even at this distance. The act and its result would be as clearly visible from the walls of Corduba as it was from the officers' position.

Once he had turned fully twice, displaying his suicide to all among the gathered legions and in the city, Scapula tried to walk across to what Fronto now realised was no signal beacon, but a funeral pyre. He staggered, close to death, and Felix hurried over and helped him. Weaving, swaying and shuffling, Scapula finally reached the pile of kindling-dry detritus and managed to collapse onto it. Showing what seemed to Fronto to be remarkable fortitude even as the last strains of strength faded from his body, the rebel commander pulled himself up onto the pyre, climbing, white as snow now, leaving a crimson trail across the wood.

In an almost theatrical moment of drama, the man achieved the highest point and raised one arm as if in triumph before collapsing in a heap, immobile. The other two attendants stepped forward and ignited the pyre. Fronto, Caesar and Caninius watched as Scapula's body was consumed by the roaring flames.

'Well that, I would say, is that,' Caninius sighed.

'Except that Corduba remains solidly closed,' Fronto noted, pointing at the distant city.

'We shall have to see what the next few hours bring,' Caesar sighed. 'Scapula's little episode could sway things either way. We know that the city continues to struggle between the two parties.'

'Your orders, General?'

'Have the legions clear out all that,' Caesar said in a tone of distaste, sweeping his arm at the display across the river. 'Have the bodies buried somewhere nearby, and set camp over there in front of the city. We have a few days' grace. Let's spend them outside Corduba, waiting to see what happens.'

* * *

Fronto had been having a peculiar dream. He had been in his house in Rome, playing with the boys, when a bull had burst in through the atrium, snorting and stomping across the delicate mosaic floor towards him. Then, as the great and fearsome beast had cornered them, and Fronto held out his hands preparing to sell his life to save the boys, the bull had opened its mouth and in a pleasant, sing-song voice, asked him what wine he would like.

He was still utterly confused as he blinked into wakefulness at the voice of the soldier outside his tent.

'What is it?' he asked blearily. A lifetime of habit had taken over and, though he as yet had no idea why he'd been called, he was already slipping into his leather subarmalis and reaching for his boots.

'Sir, Corduba is on fire.'

Fronto blinked, still trying to rid himself of the image of the pleasantly helpful bull. In moments he had slipped into his boots and pulled his sub laces tight, fastening the belt around it. Slinging his sword baldric over his shoulder, he grabbed his helmet and emerged from the tent, turning to the city.

The soldier had somewhat overstated the situation. He'd half expected to witness a major inferno with a golden sky topped with roiling black smoke. In fact, Corduba sat glowering behind its walls in the dark, while three fiery glows arose somewhere inside, columns of smoke curling into the night. Still, fire in a city was always dangerous. It happened at least annually in Rome, and usually resulted in half a hill having to be rezoned and reconstructed.

As he reached the north gate of the camp, where Caesar already awaited, for the man was notorious for his minimal sleep and habit of working through the night, already one of the equisio's men was hurrying across with the officers' horses. Caninius was also on his way, a slave handing him his sword belt as he jogged.

'Gods, is someone emulating Scapula,' the legate said, falling in beside Fronto.

'Got to be the work of rebels. Sacrifice Corduba rather than letting it be taken. Bloody idiots.'

'Listen,' the general said quietly.

Both men beside him stopped talking and cupped their hands to their ears. Over the general noise of the camp and the rumble of the great river behind them, they could hear the distinct sound of conflict. Corduba was under arms, with fighting in the streets. Cries and shouts, clangs and explosions, and even as they watched, a fourth column of golden fire suddenly burst into life.

'If they aren't stopped soon, those fires are going to spread.'

Caesar nodded. 'The gates are opening. Get those fires under control and stop the killing.'

Fronto looked to Rebilus, who nodded. 'You deal with the fires, I'll deal with the rebels,' the legate said.

By the time Fronto was mounted, two cohorts of the Tenth had already fallen in, and he could hear the calls as the others similarly piled out of their tents, arming hastily. Atenos staggered to a bleary halt beside him.

'Two cohorts?' Fronto noted.

'Ready to go sir.'

'Good. Caninius is dealing with the rebels. I want one cohort gathering buckets. If they have nothing else, fill their helmets with water. The other cohort needs to grab ropes and grapples. We're going to pull down buildings to form fire breaks while we extinguish the flames. We can't let Corduba burn.'

* * *

By the time Fronto staggered wearily back into the camp, he was soot-stained and sweaty, scorched in places, and green blotches swam in front of his eyes. For two hours the Tenth had toiled across Corduba. Four more cohorts had joined them as soon as they were assembled, and they had moved across the city with speed and efficiency, pulling down whole city blocks and leaving only swathes of rubble to catch the sparks drifting on the wind. Families stood in the streets, wailing as all their worldly goods either burned up in the inferno, or were pulled to pieces by legionaries.

Here and there they came up against scuffles between the warring parties, but uniformly, before they could come to grief, men of Rebilus' Sixth were there, putting down the rabid rebels. Caesar had been at his most heroic that night, in Fronto's opinion. Better than any time when he had stood in battle, the general had commanded the respect of all. Amid the flames and the violence, he had moved about the city streets accompanied by Hirtius, two clerks and half a dozen of his praetorians with horses loaded with sacks of coin.

He had given coins to every dispossessed citizen, commiserating with them, and stating quietly the unfortunate need to damage some homes to save the city. As he moved, his clerks took the details of every building burned or pulled down, and of their owners. The homeless were directed to the camp before the river and given the spare tents for the night. Every sad citizen of Corduba ended that day under shelter, his or her name in a ledger, and with the general's promise of full recompense for their loss.

As Fronto turned towards his tent now, tired and dirty, and promising himself a good bath in the morning, he had found the general standing with the other officers and wandered over.

'It would seem we have taken the rebel capital,' he sighed with relief.

Caesar nodded. 'The job is not over yet, though. Munda will fall to Pedius, but for us, I think Hispalis awaits. And then Gades. We cannot leave Hispania and sail for Rome until all the enemy leaders are dealt with and all their strongholds returned to the republic.'

Fronto sighed and nodded as he staggered off towards his tent. Never this spring had Rome seemed further away, despite having fought their last battle. As he removed his sword and dropped it to the floor, he wondered whether the bear had brought the wine yet.

He was asleep almost before his head hit the pillow.

CHAPTER TWENTY

Kalends of April 45 BC

Fronto stood on the battlements of Hispalis and reflected upon the seemingly easy time they had enjoyed since the fall of Corduba, and upon the tasks still to be undertaken. Leaving the rebel capital under Caesarian control, the legions had then marched west along the Baetis valley, past Munda, which was still invested and holding out to the last. They had finally arrived in the closing days of March at Hispalis, where the great river had widened into a huge, navigable waterway, plied by copious shipping. The city was much of a size with Corduba, a massive trade centre sprawled along the river's eastern bank across the wide, flat, fertile plains. Fronto had half expected a gathering of enemy garrisons. Had he been a Pompeian commander out here in western Baetica which had been the enemy heartland, having heard of events at Munda, he would have gathered every garrison remaining and put together a final force.

As it happened, they had arrived to find Hispalis in much the same position as Corduba had suffered, riven by struggles between factions supporting the defeated rebels and pro-Caesarian officers. In an attempt to let the city solve its own issues without military intervention, Caesar had encamped the two legions away from the walls to the east, in the least threatening manner he could, and waited for a deputation.

The presence of the general and his legions had had the desired effect. The Caesarians in the city had taken great heart from the arrival of the army, and had managed to overcome their opponents in the city, both politically and militarily. Fronto had watched as a ragtag band of rebels, not more than a score strong, had ridden from the city to the north as though Cerberus himself were snapping at their heels. Caesar had half-heartedly ordered a cavalry turma to give chase, but all knew they had precious little chance of catching the rebels.

An hour later, a deputation had arrived and offered the hospitality and full support of the city to their cause. Caesar had graciously accepted and had entered Hispalis to cheers, rose petals and adulation. Fronto and Caninius had accompanied the general, alongside Hirtius and a number of tribunes and officers, followed by two centuries of the Sixth who were to stay here and serve as the garrison of Hispalis until the region was fully clear and settled.

That night had been one of banquets and sycophancy, with politicians and councillors falling over themselves to appear loyal to the general. The city's ordo had been split between the two factions, and a number of pro-Pompeians were produced for Caesar to pronounce judgement upon. Despite his earlier vow, Caesar had resorted once more to his characteristic mercy. These men, he had reasoned, were civilians and Roman citizens. Caesar too had had friends who had taken sides against him, including Pompey himself, and so he would not prosecute a man for his beliefs. That they had not taken arms against him was enough. They would all be free to return to their lives with no ill effects. The same would not be said about the one of their number, a certain Philo, who had led the flight of the riders from the town, refusing to accept Caesar. Philo would be found, and a sentence of death was pronounced upon him.

To Fronto's mind, any local who knew the area was likely to be able to disappear without trace, and Philo was almost certainly safe. Still, his property had been taken, and his name besmirched. The ordo had been insistent that Caesar have the best accommodation in the city until he decided to move on, but the general had settled instead upon remaining in the camp beyond the walls, with the Tenth and most of the Sixth. They would be here only a few days and then move to Gades, and Caesar had no intention of getting comfortable in a position where he would be at the mercy of politicians with their requests and entreaties. Caninius, he said, was in line for a consulship, so he could deal with the political aspects.

Fronto had been happy to camp with the Tenth once more, but when Caesar had generously donated coin to buy increased wine rations for the two legions during their sojourn, the legate had accompanied Atenos on a visit into the city to select a good, reasonably priced wine there. They had spent much of the afternoon in the warehouses of the city's excellent wine merchants and, though Fronto could have wished that Catháin was present with his encyclopaedic knowledge and business acumen, he was still content that by sundown he had made a number of good deals.

Even now, as the last light disappeared in the western skies and the torches and lamps began to illuminate the city with their golden glow, men of Caninius' Sixth garrison centuries were busy escorting cart loads of amphorae out through the gate and across the gentle grassland to the camp of the legions.

He turned to Atenos. 'Job done?'

'Job done. Do we return to camp or make the most of the fact that we're not expected?'

Fronto exchanged a sly grin and a raised eyebrow with the primus pilus of the Tenth. Caesar had taken to regular briefings first thing in the morning and before retiring at night, and the majority of the subjects covered were always tedious logistical issues. Fronto had already acquired a reputation for sleeping through them, and had little wish to add to it.

'A jar or two would probably not go amiss. The general will excuse us. He knows what we're up to. There were several likely looking places back near that last but one merchant, close to the north gate.'

The two men left the legionaries to their work, transporting the wine back to camp, and descended the steps from the wall, ambling happily through the evening-purple streets of Hispalis, heading northwest.

'I've been giving thought to my retirement,' Atenos said as they strode through the city.

'Oh?'

'You and I both know that Caesar cannot legitimately maintain these legions once the threat is gone. The senate won't stand for it. He has to play the political game now. Even Syria will have to be settled with words. If he wants to avoid a whole fresh fall-out with Rome he has to finish this here and stand down the army. The Tenth will be settled. I already hear rumours that Caesar is considering Narbo for them.'

'Narbo is nice. I've always liked the place. Not too far from my villa at Tarraco, either.'

'And the place still retains some vestiges of my people.'

Fronto nodded. He often forgot how Gallic Atenos really was, for he appeared so Roman. Much like Galronus, who waited for them back at the camp.

'Anyway,' the centurion continued, 'I don't know what to do. I've never tried anything but war. Even before the legions, when I worked selling my sword in the east. That's the question, Fronto. Do I go where the war is and begin again? Or do I try and worm my way through Rome's military? The legions may be stood down, but there are private armies, as you know, and the next time Parthia or the Suebi decide to cause trouble, whoever's consul at the time will raise new legions.'

Fronto just walked on in silence, and so Atenos continued. 'Or do I try to settle down. To tell the truth, I think I'm more nervous about trying to live in peace than I ever have been about fighting. But I have a good amount of savings, and more coming to me when the legion is settled. I'll be quite wealthy. What do you think?'

Fronto tried to imagine the hulking Gallic centurion operating a dress shop, or mopping up his tavern after closing to customers, or even just sitting on a veranda with a walking stick and a glass of wine. None of it looked right. A thought occurred to him and he smiled.

'Have you thought about going into the gladiator business?'

Atenos frowned. 'I'm no slave. And that's...'

'I meant owning, selling and training. Be a lanista? If you have the money, you could buy a big place somewhere, get it fitted out, and stock it with staff and burly slaves. I've seen you training the Tenth. With a few ex champions helping, you could make a go of something like that. And every city wants gladiators. If you get settled in Narbo, there'd be a call for them there, or even back in Tarraco. And as for Rome...'

His voice trailed away as the two men stepped from a shady alleyway into the open space inside the north gate. He and Atenos had spotted it at the same moment, and both men, placing their hands on each other's arms, had stepped swiftly back into the shadows.

The city's north gate was open, and, while there could be any number of legitimate explanations for that, the scene inside made it clear. Several dozen figures in chain armour and with blue shields suggesting some sort of auxiliary unit, were moving about the square, checking doors and looking into side streets. Another group stood in the gateway itself, where several people were dismounting. The bodies of men in red tunics with the shields of the Sixth lay in small piles around the square. Fronto heard bootsteps from an unexpected direction, and his gaze rose upwards. More blue-clad men were scurrying along the walls from the gate in both directions.

'Shit. They're back.'

'Who?' murmured Atenos as the two men slunk further into the dark street away from the scene of brutality.

'The rebels. That Philo, probably. He's found reinforcements and come back for Hispalis. We have to get out of here. If he's already dealt with the garrison, they'll start to hunt for officers next.'

'Shit.'

With that, the two men turned and pounded away along the street. Passing the way they had come, Fronto remembered seeing a livery stable. Now, upon their return, a slave was busily sweeping the street in the archway, prior to closing for the evening. Tugging at Atenos, Fronto turned into the glowing archway, racing past a startled slave, and into the stable itself. Ignoring the shouting staff, he and Atenos made for two stalls, pulled the doors open and swiftly threw bridle and reins around the horses' heads and fastened them.

The stable's owner had been found as they worked, and came running, only to stagger to a halt as Fronto threw a small pouch at him, which slapped heavily into his chest. 'That should cover it,' he said as the two men pulled themselves up onto bare backs, and then flicked the reins and smacked the flanks, racing out past the owner and his slaves, all of whom now began to kick up a fresh clamour. Out into the city they rode, and then clattered along the dark streets until they turned out into the space inside the east gate.

Fronto felt his heart race. The men of the Sixth had already left now with their wagons of wine, trundling back over the turf to the camp, oblivious to what was happening in the city behind them.

Even as they rounded the corner, Fronto could see blue figures descending from the wall, others busily knifing Caesar's legionaries and dragging their gurgling corpses back into darkened doorways.

As he took all this in, he saw the gates slammed shut and the bar dropped across them.

'Damn it,' he hissed.

'South gate,' Atenos said, wheeling his horse. Fronto, nodding, followed suit. If Philo and his rebels had taken the north gate and infiltrated the city from there, the last place they would reach would be the south gate, and they were trying to be subtle, not raising the alarm, seizing the city without anyone becoming aware. That meant they would all be moving quietly, on foot, which would give the two riders the edge.

He and Atenos raced along the wide streets of the city now, keeping to the fast routes, regardless of subtlety. The last thing they wanted was to be trapped inside a city controlled by their enemy. As they rode, Fronto occasionally caught glimpses of the city walls in the distance along side streets, and each time he was sure he could see crouched figures scurrying along them. They didn't know how long men had been in the city. The rebels could even already be at the far gate.

Rounding a final corner, they hauled on the reins. The struggle for the south gate had begun. Philo's rebels were swiftly overcoming the men of the Sixth. It was no great surprise, really. They'd not truly been expecting trouble, and had assigned only two understrength centuries as garrison. One hundred and twenty men across an entire city, and at least thirty of them were out there in the countryside, escorting wagons of wine to the camp. After all, what madman would try and storm a city with a few fugitives, when two legions were encamped close by?

The answer, clearly, was: Philo.

The gate was still open, but men were dying in the shadow of the arch and even as the two riders watched, half the great double gate was slammed shut.

'Come on.'

Kicking his horse into speed, Fronto raced across the flagstones of the square, drawing his sword. A blue-clad figure with a spear rushed across to stop him, thrusting the weapon. Fronto's sword smashed through the haft, snapping it in two as he raced past, and Atenos' sword felled the man. Some rebel leader was shouting a warning now, pointing at the two riders, and rebels who had finished dealing with their targets turned and ran at them. Fronto pounded on towards the gate, but felt hope evaporate as the great timber leaf swung closed.

They were trapped in Hispalis.

Atenos had clearly realised the hopelessness now, and turned with him, putting their backs to the soldiers in the square. As they retreated, Fronto caught movement out of the corner of his eye, and spotted four archers stepping out into the open and fishing at their sides for arrows. As they nocked them and stretched the bows, Fronto and Atenos raced away from the gate and back into the heart of the city.

As the arrows clattered into empty streets behind them, the two men hurtled into side alleys, rounding several corners until they were comfortable they could not easily be followed, then reined in.

'What now?' Fronto huffed.

'The port? A ship?'

The legate shook his head. 'The port would be as important to secure as any gate. They'll already have it under control. The city is sealed, man.'

'Then we have to either fight back or go to ground.'

'Two against hundreds are rather poor odds.'

Atenos gave a wolfish smile. 'There are still others in the city. The men of the ordo who claimed for Caesar. They'll be targets for Philo now, which makes them allies for us.'

* * *

Dawn's light stabbed through the shutters, startling Fronto into wakefulness. He blinked, blearily, sleep encrusting his eyes. The night had already been well advanced when they'd finally slept, and even then they'd slept poorly. It was all well and good trusting in Marcus Mattienus Firmus, wealthy plutocrat and member of the ordo, but in a city riven with factions and currently enjoying danger from both within and without, Fronto had still kept one eye on the man.

They'd found him where Fronto had last seen him, in the warehouse of a wine merchant. Firmus had been a vocal opponent of Philo in the city, and would now be marked for death, as the Lusitanians, for that was the nature of the blue-clad soldiers, busily went through the city like a steel-edged plague, killing anyone known to favour the Caesarians and hanging their bodies in squares.

Firmus had brought them to this place, his cousin's house, in desperation. His cousin was currently in Africa on business, and his house empty. The man was rich, just like Firmus, and his house looked out upon the monumental heart of the city, enjoying two whole storeys of opulence.

As Fronto rose wearily, stretching and listening carefully, he noted both Atenos and Firmus at the shuttered window, their shadows moving back and forth across the beams of silver light.

'What's happening?'

Atenos turned. 'I tried not to wake you. Our friends are arguing.'

'Oh?'

Firmus took up the explanation. 'Philo is out there amid the dangling corpses of our colleagues. He has with him Caecilius, the man who brought the Lusitanians to his banner. Philo is insistent that they hold Hispalis until the surviving rebel forces come. He maintains that since both Pompeys still live, the rebels will rally on Hispalis and restart the war. Caecilius seems to be of a different opinion. Caesar has already begun to besiege the city. He has ships blocking the river in both directions and the cohorts all around Hispalis. Caecilius is rather angry. It seems he came with Philo on the assumption there would be a large force of rebels waiting to help them. He says that the idea of his Lusitanians holding the city against two legions is ludicrous.'

'He's right, of course,' Fronto said, rubbing his eyes. 'He cannot possibly survive this. We have to throw the gates open.'

'Just listen,' Atenos insisted.

Fronto joined them at the window.

'No,' said the darker of the two figures. We go, and we go today.'

'Caecilius, we only need to hold for a few days. Besides, we're under siege. How do you expect to leave? Caesar's hardly going to be merciful after you massacred his men.'

'*You* massacred his men. You just used *mine* to do it. Your sister always warned me you were trouble, Philo. Now you've got us trapped.'

Fronto couldn't help but smile. He'd panicked that they were trapped in an enemy city. It was heartening to know that that enemy in turn felt trapped too.

'You can say what you like, Philo, but we are leaving. I will find a way. I have no intention of my men and I dying here for a cause that's already dead.'

Fronto watched, fascinated, as the two men moved closer, squaring up. Philo reached to his side and pulled a sword free from his belt. Caecilius held his arms out wide, conciliatory. 'Come now, Philo,' he said. 'We may disagree, but we share a banner. There is no need for threats. Are we not brothers through your beautiful sister?' As Philo lowered the blade, Caecilius crossed the last step and enfolded him in an embrace. Fronto frowned, and was not at all surprised when, as the two parted once more, Philo was looking down at a dagger protruding from his gut. Across the square, two of Philo's men shouted and took a single step before they began to sprout arrows and topple to the ground.

'This is your last mistake, brother,' Caecilius said as his victim gasped, and dropped to his knees, gripping the knife hilt.

Ignoring the dying man, the commander turned to two of his officers standing nearby. 'Philo has how many men of his own?'

The officer eyed the two dead men across the square. 'One hundred and nine now. He lost a few taking the city.'

'Pass his orders to them. We flee the city at sunset. We will fire three ships and sail them into the blockade, then Philo's men will take the first ship through the wreckage, and we will follow in the second.'

'Sir? That's dangerous. Caesar has to be watching everywhere, and as soon as fireships appear, he'll know what we're doing.'

Caeciliis fixed his man with a level look. 'That is why *we* will be leaving the north gate at a gallop while all this happens. My idiot brother-in-law's men are the distraction. They will all die, either in the flames or trying to get downriver, where Caesar will undoubtedly have other men. But while he concentrates on this, we will run for home, back to Lusitania and safety. Philo can undo what he has done even in death.'

The men turned and began to move away across the square.

'All we have to do then,' Firmus sighed, 'is sit tight and wait. Philo's men will die on the river, Caecilius' men will flee to the north, and the gates will be opened to Caesar again.'

Fronto shook his head.

'Not quite. I don't like loose ends, and this Caecilius and his Lusitanians are clever and dangerous. I don't think we want to let them get away where they can do things like this again.'

'But how will we stop them?' Atenos asked. 'He's clever, and he's right. Caesar cannot expect two separate foes in the city and will devote all his efforts to the ships.'

'Then we need to warn him.'

Thanking Firmus for his help, and advising him to stay firmly hidden in this place until the city was free of rebels, when he could throw it open to Caesar once more, the two men left all their armour and uniform, barring their tunic, belt and sword, hurried away and out of the house via a slave entrance in the rear of their complex beyond the garden. The city was still undert the control of the enemy. They were not present in huge numbers now, though, and having done their work purging the town of Caesarians, they were not prevalent in the streets, mostly gathered on the walls, at the gates and in the port.

By dint of avoiding any place they might expect to run into rebels, Fronto and Atenos, indistinguishable at first glance from the general public barring their swords, moved through the city carefully. Each time they found a built up place, they checked for blue tunics and armour, moving away elsewhere if they spotted them. It was not long before they found the street Fronto was looking for and, with a few coins, purchased what he needed.

Then, preparing themselves mentally, they moved in a meandering, slow manner towards the east gate, keeping up their careful movements. It was an hour before they first found what they needed, and an hour more before they found it again. The first time, they saw two of the blue-clad Lusitanians entering a tavern, and followed cautiously. Poking their heads in they had quickly recoiled and slipped away at the sight of a dozen more Lusitanians inside. The second time, when they followed the pair into the bar, there were only locals inside. Better still, Fronto could almost cut the air with a knife such was the sense of dislike and resentment that echoed from every face at sight of the Lusitanians.

The two men crossed to a table, sat down and one clicked his fingers at the innkeeper. Fronto and Atenos nodded at one another and followed, drawing their swords.

The other denizens watched this development with interest, and their looks must have warned the two Lusitanians, for they turned then, beginning to rise from their seats. They never made it upright as Fronto and Atenos struck the two men on the head simultaneously with sword pommels. As the soldiers slumped, Fronto grinned at the barman.

'Don't mind us.'

As they slipped the two unconscious men out of their armour and uniforms, Fronto continued in a conversational tone. 'I think they're a troublesome lot. I wouldn't let these two be found by their friends. If others come, you might want to deny ever seeing them. Two doors down there's a pig breeder. I hear they are superb for disposing of bodies. And keep any change they might carry, and their swords, too, to pay for the trouble.'

In moments, Fronto and Atenos, arms piled high with gear, slipped through the back and out into the inn's yard, where they swiftly changed into the Lusitanian tunics and re-equipped as rebels, sheathing their own swords at their sides.

'Trust you to find a bloody midget,' the big Gaul growled as he tried with some difficulty to haul the tight tunic over his huge frame. Fronto gave him a hand, and had to admit, once he was dressed, that the big man looked like an overinflated waterskin.

'Don't breathe too deeply, or it'll burst open.'

With another steadying moment, they made their way back out into the city, abandoning their subtlety of earlier, and now striding down the streets as if they owned the place, the way the rest of them seemed wont to do. Occasionally, they met other soldiers, and simply nodded a greeting as they passed, praying nobody recognised the equipment and protested. In half an hour they were at the city wall, two towers north of the east gate.

With little trouble they found a set of stairs and climbed to the wall walk. There, they passed another Lusitanian, who didn't even look at them, and moved into the shadow at the side of a tower, partially hidden from view. Relieved that they had got this far safely, Fronto drew from his purse the mirror they had bought in town, and scanned the siege lines outside the city. It did not take him long to pick out one of the scouts in a picket position. Leaning his arm out of the shade and angling the mirror as best he could, he flicked the shiny surface up and down, reflecting a beam of sunlight so that it danced up and down across that figure in the Caesarian lines. It took three attempts before an answering flash came their way. Quickly, aware they could be discovered at any time, Fronto relayed Caecilius' plan to the sentry, confirming his own identity in the process. Finally, the sentry signalled that he understood all, and hurried away back towards the camp.

Fronto drew a heavy breath, putting away the mirror, and he and Atenos emerged from the shadow, almost bumping into a man who looked them up and down, and then walked off with a grunt. Fronto silently thanked Fortuna, for a moment longer and he might have been caught signalling.

The two men skittered back down the steps and off into the streets. This time, they found two tunics busy drying on washing lines in back alleys and snatched them before hurrying away. In a dim corner somewhere they abandoned the blue uniforms and slipped into the garb of poor locals. The last thing either of them wanted was to be swept up with the Lusitanians' flight and be forced to leave the city with them

As they emerged into the city streets once more, they moved quietly, meekly and slowly through the tangled alleys, drawing as little attention as possible. Arriving at the north gate, they found a scruffy, low drinking hole with a view of the gate, and they slipped inside, buying poor, cheap wine and sipping it throughout the afternoon in silence, watching events outside.

They had no idea what was happening at the port, though there was every reason to believe Caecilius' plan was proceding readily. At the gate, they watched, as the light began to fade, the Lusitanians gathering, several of their number having found every horse they could.

As the light failed and the world slid into a purple hue, Caecilius himself arrived, briefing his men, some four hundred of them, in a voice quiet enough that Fronto caught none of it. They watched from the bar, along with a number of interested locals. The evening set in, and then, suddenly, the world burst into activity. Some signal had been given, and Fronto heard something about 'ships' and 'fire', and the Lusitanians were moving.

Each man had a horse now, and they were gathered just inside the city gate. At a barked command, the gate was thrown open, and hauled wide, the men responsible then pulling themselves up onto horseback and joining their fellows. The cohort's-worth of blue-clad riders began their flight, kicking their horses to speed and racing out of the archway, leaving the gate open behind them, caring not what happened to the city.

As soon as the last man was through and gone, Fronto and Atenos were up and running. Across the square they pelted, drawing the interested, worried looks of locals. Reaching the gates, they each put a shoulder to them and began to heave them closed. Atenos, with his bulk and muscles, managed easily, and then settled for glaring at Fronto, willing him to move faster until the second leaf slid shut. Between them they lifted the bar into place, and then, puffing and sweating, ran up to the wall top to watch.

It had begun before they got there. While Caesar's legions had moved south to deal with the fireships and the flight of the rebels there, Galronus had brought two thousand of Caesar's veteran Gauls and Germans to lurk in wait for the Lusitanians. Caecilius had led his men through what looked like a weak point in the siege line, straight into the waiting arms of the Caesarian cavalry. The two officers watched as the blue-garbed rebels were systematically butchered. They continued to observe as fifty or sixty broke off and raced back for the relative safety of the city, only to find the gates shut to them.

Fronto smiled in grim satisfaction as he watched the Gallic cavalry butcher every last Lusitanian. One of the last to die was Caecilius, who contrived to throw a bitter glare up at Fronto above the gate, who replied with a happy grin. It was over in a hundred heartbeats, and as the cavalry moved around finishing off the wounded, Galronus rode out of their number with a couple of his men, approaching the wall and looking up.

'Fronto? That you?'

'It is. Atenos, too.'

'Thank you for the warning,' the Remi said, bowing his head. 'It never ceases to amaze me the lengths you'll go to to avoid Caesar's briefings.'

'I had better things to do.'

Galronus laughed. 'As it happens, your little adventure meant you missed something important.'

'Oh?'

Galronus straightened in the saddle. 'We've had a messenger from Carteia. It seems they've captured Gnaeus Pompey.'

CHAPTER TWENTY ONE

Mid April 45 BC

Gnaeus Pompey was a determined man. His cell for the past week had been a small prison close to the port of Carteia, usually used to hold those accused of piracy or smuggling until they were dragged through the courts in the city's forum. As such it was very secure, comprised of solid stone blocks with a concrete roof, having been designed to hold dangerous men. The door was thick timber strengthened with iron bands, pivot-sunk into thick stones above and below, with two padlocked bolts on the outside and a small hatch near the base where food could be roughly shovelled, which it was, twice a day. The only light came from a small window, a foot square and strengthened with a grille of iron bars, as though any prisoner could hope to fit through it anyway.

It had been that window that had been his sole source of hope since his incarceration. He knew that Hispania still seethed. That not every town's ordo was prepared to roll over and show its soft belly to the despot's sword. Pompey was his father's son. Unlike Sextus, who preferred to skulk and put walls between him and danger, Gnaeus was the scion of Pompey the Great, and he would never stop. Sextus had fled Corduba, they said, and his brother knew that was the last anyone would really hear of him. He would not concern himself with rallying the republic against the continued threat of Caesar. And with Labienus dead, alongside the other solid officers they'd had at Munda, everything would now come down to Gnaeus Pompey. As long as he lived, Caesar could never rest, of that he was determined.

He had run with his surviving men to Carteia, knowing little was to be gained at Corduba in Sextus' trembling hands. No, Carteia had been their naval base and one of their strongest centres of power, and despite Caesar's continued wars in the peninsula, he had yet to take Carteia. From the sources of intelligence, Gnaeus had gloomily concluded that only Asta, Gades, Munda and Urso held out for the republic, and Caesar was already marching on Asta, while his navy had begun to blockade Gades, which would fall in days. Munda was under siege, and once it fell, Urso would be the last town in the entire peninsula to hold out against Caesar. Apart from Carteia.

Or so he had thought.

Then, as he had begun to send out missives to draw what naval power they could still rely upon, and entreaties to allies in Africa, to his eternal bitterness, Carteia had turned on him. A pro-Caesarian faction he had never suspected existed had risen from nowhere and had secured military strength, taking control of the port and walls, and the next thing Gnaeus had known, he had woken one morning with a sword tip at his throat.

A week, but he'd not given up. The city may have thrown in its lot with the despot, but his own supporters remained devout. Every few hours a new scrap of parchment or wood was dropped through the window vowing that Pompey would not end his days thus. That there was change in the wind, and something would happen. Then, last night, a final scrap had come through. All it had said was 'Three rings. Be ready.'

Since then, he'd ignored the food passed through the door, and spent every moment crouched by the window, listening for a bell. He'd not slept, but that did not bother him. He would run on his nerves and his hunger for victory and revenge. That would sustain him when sleep would not.

In the end, he really did not need the warning of three bells. The sun had been up for perhaps an hour, still a bright, cold thing shining between roofs, when it began. He heard the telltale sounds. Somewhere across the city an alarm went up, a horn blaring and suddenly silenced. Then crashes and shouts in the distance. Finally someone got around to ringing a bell three times, but by then Pompey was already standing by the door to his cell, tensed and prepared. He heard it happening. He heard the shouts of the two guards who stood outside his cell day and night. He heard their weapons readied. Then he heard the fighting, the screaming, the curses. The silence.

The hatch opened at the base of his door.

'Domine?'

Pompey crouched. 'Yes. I'm here. The keys to the locks are held by the ordo, not the guards.'

'We have no need of keys, sir. Step back.'

He did so, frowning in interest as he heard scraping around the bolts. Peering into the crack at the door's edge, he saw wire looped around the two bolts, and similarly, a thick rope was fed through the hatch at the base, looped through the hinges of the shutter. He saw them strain tight, and then heard whinnying. The slap of a hand on a horse's rump and a neigh. The creaking of both iron and timber. More slaps, more neighing, more creaking.

When the door gave, it did so in an explosion of wood and torn metal, ripped from the jamb and dragged across the flags outside by the two horses attached to it. The doorway glowed with bright light, and outside stood several grizzled men in the madder-dyed russet tunics of legionaries. Beside them was a small hand cart upon which lay Pompey's tunic and boots, cuirass and helmet, and his sword.

'Victory is by no means certain, sir,' the nearest soldier advised him. 'The despot's men still outnumber us, we have word of Caesarian troops in the hills under Lento, and their fleet under Didius sailing for us from Gades. The prefect who set this off died on the walls as the bell rang. Command is yours once more.'

Pompey nodded. 'Estimates of manpower?'

'In the city, we can muster maybe a hundred. There are twice that arrayed against us. We have been victorious so far by dint of surprise alone. When they regroup, we'll find ourselves in trouble.'

Pompey chewed his lip. 'The forces outside the town?'

'Unknown but they must number more than a cohort.'

'Carteia is lost to us, then.'

The soldier nodded bitterly.

'But as long as we live,' Pompey said, straightening, 'there are things we can do. Caesar is not universally popular, and men can be bought. We still have friends in Lusitania, and the gold mines can be seized. If we do this, we will have coin sufficient to raise new legions or hire mercenaries. With coin I can send offers to allies and to those in Rome who still distrust Caesar. We must leave Carteia, and somehow skirt Didius and his fleet. We cannot meet them yet, but we must go by sea. We cannot trust anyone on land. We seize the port and all ships in it and sail west. Once we are past Gades, the great encircling ocean is ours and we can move up into Lusitania, beyond Caesar's grasp. There we can begin to rebuild.'

The soldier gave him a satisfied look. 'We already have a half century of men down at the port, attempting to take control.'

'Are there still plenty of ships there?'

'Twenty two,' the soldier replied. 'And they are crewed by loyalists, who have resisted the city's betrayal. If we can make it to the ships we can escape the city.'

'Good.' Pompey stripped down to his loincloth in the street, the acrid stink of shit and urine filling the air. He'd had nothing but a bucket for facilities for a week now. By the third day he'd dreamed of a bum-sponge. As he began to pull on his fresh tunic and boots, donning the armour, he looked this way and that, his eyes having finally adjusted to the brightness.

From here he could see down into the port, on the edge of which the prison stood. To his experienced eye, their chances of securing the port were fifty-fifty at best. He could make out at least four fights going on, each of which could yet go either way. More of his men were busy at the port's heart, raiding a pile of supplies on the dockside, while a party of men who were clearly not part of his force were approaching along the sloping road down from the forum. When they arrived, every man would have to fight to survive. As yet the ship crews remained on their vessels, uncommitted. If he were to be charitable, he might admit that their reluctance was sensible. If they committed to the fight in the port, they might lose too many men to effectively sail, and many of their rowers, thanks to short manpower, were slaves who needed to be controlled and supervised. Yet, there was also the fact that a sensible man would probably watch and wait now, to see who won, before committing to either side.

Well, that would be him.

Finally armed and ready, Pompey drew his sword. 'Signal the men. I want every soldier we have down at those ships. We need to sail.'

One of the soldiers produced a short cavalry horn and blew three shrill blasts followed by one long wail, then dropped the instrument and followed as they hauled themselves up onto horses and headed down towards the port.

As they cantered, Pompey used his sword to point at the twin lighthouses that marked the end of the two arms of the harbour. 'There is a ballista at the end of each. They need to be neutralised before we sail, or we will lose ships as we pass by.'

The soldier nodded. 'We have men on it, sir.'

Indeed, at that moment, he could see more fighting breaking out at the ends of the two harbour walls. 'We'll pick up survivors as we pass.'

As they reached the harbour side, Pompey reined in and simply let the horse go. A shout drew his attention, and he turned to see a fresh group of the enemy emerge from some warehouse substructure nearby. His men stopped rifling through the stores and formed up, turning to face the fresh threat.

'Sir, you need to get on a ship.'

Pompey nodded, but still he stood, watching as the two small forces closed. He realised his mistake only at the last moment. As the soldiers, armed with javelins and shields, bore down on his exhausted legionaries, they spotted the escaped general and gave a shout. Ignoring the men waiting for them, half a dozen of the enemy soldiers thudded to a sudden halt and launched their javelins up into the air. They were not careful, aimed shots, but there were six, and the distance was not great.

Pompey leapt away from the cloud of deadly missiles, but as he tumbled through the air, he felt the flesh of his left calf tear and yelled in agony. The javelin that had pierced him had ripped a chunk from the back of his leg, and a square of flesh there flapped open and shut as the blood poured free. The crimson missile clattered off along the dockside as Pompey rolled and staggered and lurched to his feet. He looked around, eyes wild now. The soldier he already considered his second in command, the man who had broken him out of jail, stood transfixed, pinned to a crate with a javelin, blood pouring from his open mouth.

The other, the man with the horn, was trying to marshal what men they had and urge them over to the boarding plank of a ship. The men who were facing the javelineers were fully engaged now, hammering at the new arrivals. They were winning, at least.

'Sir. We have to go.'

Pompey turned, hissing at the pain as his leg almost gave under him, and saw the musician waving him towards a ship. He looked around. More and more enemy units seemed to be crawling out of the woodwork, making for the port. The man was right. If they didn't leave now, they'd soon be overcome.

Limping, cursing, he reached a boarding ramp and staggered up it, almost toppling off into the water at one point. Then, finally, he was lurching aboard, and sailors were gripping his shoulders, helping him, half-carrying him over to a wooden chair bolted to the deck, usually occupied by the piper who kept the rowers in time. There, he slumped with relief as a capsarius hurried over with his bag, preparing to at least clean and bind the wound.

As the man worked, Pompey hissing with pain repeatedly, the commander watched, unable to do much more. The last of his men hurried down to the port, overcoming the javelineers and then hurrying for any ship close by. Already, vessels were pulling out into the water, turning, making for the gap between the reaching arms of the harbour wall.

He felt the lurching of the deck as his own ship departed, though at the time his eyes were solidly closed, partially through the exhaustion starting to catch up with him, and partially because he continually winced with pain at each prod and tug of the medic dealing with his leg. When he finally opened them fully, as the capsarius stood and stepped back, pronouncing that he had done what he could, the ship was two thirds of the way across the harbour and making for the open sea.

To his dismay, it seemed that his men had secured only one of the ballista port defences, for the other was merrily loosing into the fleeing ships. One trireme had been holed and was already beginning to dip below the water still inside the harbour. Another had made it through the opening, but was foundering and arcing east, its mast leaning at a ruinous angle.

Pompey clenched his teeth as they closed on the gap. The troops that had moved to take that ballista had not only failed to do so, but had in fact entirely disappeared. Consequently, the artillery remained active, being angled against ships and loaded, but also Caesarian archers had mustered at the wall edge and were loosing into the passing vessels.

'To starboard,' he bellowed at the trierarch, eying the ship in front of them, which was being raked with cloud after cloud of arrows as it passed, men dropping like flies as they sprouted shafts. Despite the damage to the crew, the ship managed to slip through to open sea, the last victim being the vessel's trierarch, who toppled into the water with a cry.

The pilot of Pompey's vessel did what he could, but there was no space to move starboard, away from the archers, because of the other ships hurrying to reach the sea. Gritting his teeth, he watched as they closed, unable to avoid the death-run. He had no chance to lurch out of the way this time, for his leg was numb, and he could not stand as the missiles began to fly. An arrow tore a small chunk from his shoulder, ripping away the leather pteruges, and then disappeared into the water with a plop.

Pompey roared with pain and fury as the fire of the wound raced through his veins. As the ship slid at speed past the crowd of archers, darting for the open blue of the bay ahead, the rebel general could see the faces of his would-be killers, the hunger in the eyes of men desperate to be the one to kill the general. Then they were past, through the harbour wall and into the open water, the impotent fury of the archers left behind. His shoulder pulsated with pain and blood ran down his arm. He was injured. Again. But they had made it out into the bay. From here, unless Didius was around the corner, they could cross to the African side and hope to slip past the Caesarian admiral without engaging him.

Then, the rebuilding could begin.

* * *

A fight had broken out between two of the water gathering parties, a barrel lying on its side and tipping its precious contents out onto the sand as men punched one another, shouting recriminations. Pompey stood at the rail and watched, a half-smile pulling at his lip. There was no real damage being done, just men taking out tension and frustration on one another. Better like this than on board and with a blade, after all.

The punch up raged until the fire started to go out of it and the men got tired, then faded into snarky name calling as the two groups separated. Of course, normally an officer would have stepped in long before now, had their names entered onto a clerk's tablet for latrine duties or worse, and had men dragging the combatants apart. Not so now. A grand total of three centurions led his men, far too few to keep control of so many troops, but he'd not had the leisure to appoint new centurions yet. Soon, perhaps.

'They've found us.'

He turned in surprise and, seeing the lookout waving at him, stumped his way to the opposite rail, where he stumbled with a hiss, gripping the timber to prevent collapse. 'The man is like a bad rash, all over and very hard to get rid of. How did he find us?'

'Maybe he got all the way to Carteia and turned around.'

Pompey nodded. If he had, then by gods the man had been fast. His twenty ships had slipped away from Carteia and turned east as though making back for the heart of the republic, an attempt to lay a false trail among those who were watching from the port. They had then, around the headland and out of sight, changed course, straight across to the coast of Mauretania. He had briefly considered attempting to gather support there, but with the knowledge that Bogud, the Mauritanian king, had been among the enemy at Munda, he maintained his original plan. They'd sailed along the coast and then, finally, they had crossed the straits once more at the wider point. Once they'd sailed past Gades, giving it a wide berth, logic said that they had to have missed Didius and his fleet, and they'd heaved a sigh of relief. Now, four days after their flight from Carteia, they had eased up considerably, knowing they were almost at the point where they would turn north and make for Lusitania proper. With a sense of freedom, they had pulled the small fleet into the coast and anchored there this morning, sending parties ashore to forage and hunt, to bring aboard fresh water from two local streams and supplies for the voyage, supplementing the meagre quantities they had secured at Carteia.

The last thing they had expected was Didius' fleet.

Yet the lookout was right. The swarm of ships that were even now hurtling around the next headland bore the sails of Caesar's fleet, and they were on the hunt, as was clear from their speed and formation. How they had determined that Pompey had doubled back west and had turned and raced to catch them, he could not fathom, but the fact remained they were here.

Moreover, they would be well-supplied, well armed for war, and stocked with soldiers.

Conversely, Pompey's fleet was a quarter of the size, manned by stretched skeleton crews, barely armed, and poorly supplied. If it came down to a fight, there was no question as to the end result.

'What are your orders, sir?' the trierarch asked, a touch of nervous energy in his voice.

Pompey ground his teeth. No. He'd escaped. They thought they'd finished him and his cause – his father's cause – the *republic's* cause – at Munda, but he'd escaped. They thought they had trapped him in Carteia, but he'd managed to get away, prepared to start all over again. Now, Didius thought he had him. No. He didn't. He couldn't. The cause was not lost. The war would never be over.

'We cannot beat him.'

The look on the trierarch's face was in full agreement. He looked relieved. 'Sir?'

'Have every empty ship thrown at him. Send the slaves in. Slow him down.'

'Sir?'

'Didius is a sailor. He has ships. He won't be able to pursue and finish us on land. Get every loyal man who can walk off the ships. Arm them all. We move into the hills and disappear. Give the order and pass it to the other ships. I will be on the shore, marshalling the men there.'

He'd sounded so positive and prepared, he wondered whether it sent mixed messages when he then took a single step and the agony in his wounded leg sent him crumpling to the deck. Teeth clenched in determination, he pushed himself with great effort back to his feet, grabbing the rail to steady himself. Passing a worried looking soldier, he snatched the pilum from the man's grip and used it as a staff to step with more ease across the deck to the ramp. Behind him the trierarch started to bellow orders.

Pompey took his eyes off the world around him for a while then, staggering with pain in each pace down the ramp to the beach. Every step was an oath.

He was the son of Pompey the pirate killer. He would not fail.

He was the scion of a great republican family. He would not see Rome die.

He was better than his cowering brother. He would rise once more.

Oaths drove him across the sand and while he was stamping with determination, he was still grateful when a soldier appeared with a pony they had unhitched from the water barrel sled. He mounted with difficulty then realised the soldier, an optio from his kit, was watching him expectantly.

'We move for the hills. I know this land. We will lose our pursuit and find allies in the Lusitani. Every man on this beach needs to move now. Get into the treeline and be ready, armed. We move as soon as all the crew who can be saved are on land. Go, now.'

The optio saluted and hurried off, shouting and pointing, waving his arms. Pompey let him go. It was always best to let the centurionate and their chosen men deal with the actual carrying out of orders. Pompey turned instead and looked out to sea.

His fleet were all moving now. Twenty vessels. They would never have escaped by sea. Didius and his killer ships were almost on them already. Pompey sent a prayer to Pluto that he be kind to the heroic sailors and, yes, even to the slaves. Some of them were the worst of men, but others were probably debtors and foreign captives, and they were now being made to give their lives for the cause. Every one of the twenty ships was crewed by but half a dozen free men and three oar banks of slaves. Every one of them was a dead man already.

Didius was, Pompey realised, very good at what he did. Even as the Caesarian fleet sped across the water, the admiral passed orders and the fleet changed form. He had looked to each of Pompey's ships and had sized them up in a heartbeat. Those which could be easily taken and salvaged were targeted by Caesarian ships with heavy marine occupancy, often quadriremes. The lesser ships, the ones already partly damaged, crewed by the least men or aimlessly drifting, were not considered worth the effort.

In a heartbeat fire bolts and ballistae were at work from the prows of Didius' ships, tearing into those ships the commander considered unimportant. They struck mercilessly, burning, holing, sinking. Pompey, a man who had not once in his life given a thought to his own slaves, suddenly found his eye watering with a single tear for all those men he had condemned, each one shackled to a bench that was either burning or being submerged, engulfed in an inferno or sinking beneath the waves.

As most of his ships disappeared into gold or blue, a few were overcome and became the scene of fierce fighting. Pompey finally tore his eyes from the scene and turned back to the beach. Those men who had been brought ashore from the ships were almost all safe now, back across the sand and among the trees.

He had already cast back his prodigious memory to a map he'd seen of the region. He was now plotting his route, a journey that would take him to the burgeoning settlement of Ebora, a rat-hole of a town founded on some native shit-pit but which was something of a nexus for the gold trains of the region. He had already figured the first three stops on his route, and was confident that with Didius controlling only ships and marines, he would not be able to follow, or at least, not for long.

'Sir,' called the optio, now standing at the treeline ahead.

Pompey nodded in his direction, turned, took one look at his fleet that was variously burning as it settled into the water, or being taken captive and manned by new, Caesarian, troops, and walked off into the trees.

* * *

Gaius Didius turned to the man beside him. 'It would appear that Pompey is truly scraping the bottom of the barrel looking for forces now. These ships are part crewed at best and rowed by slaves. How long does the man think he's going to hold his rebellion like this?'

'Maybe he has nothing to lose sir?' the man replied.

'Rubbish. Alright, Caesar has pronounced a death sentence on all the enemy leaders, but we all know that Caesar is a pushover for a contrite speech. If Pompey decided to lay it on thick and plead for mercy, Caesar would grant it. Hirtius reckons he still feels guilty that the man's father was beheaded. Wasn't responsible for it himself, but the general would have liked to have had the great Pompey submit, bow and accept his failure. He'd do the same for the boy, if he begged. But if he fights, yes, he'll just die.'

'Several hundred managed to get away to the trees, sir.'

'Yes.' That part irritated Didius. He'd managed to anticipate Pompey's moves rather nicely. He'd reasoned that if the man went east, there was nowhere safe for him to go. Similarly, Africa and Mauritania were now closed to the rebels. As such, Pompey could only reasonably go west, up into territory he'd been dealing with over the past few years. He would feel safe there. Consequently, Didius had gone towards Carteia only far enough to meet up with Lucius Caesennius Lento, the man Caesar had sent to the city by land to secure Pompey. Lento and his force, fast moving light infantry and Hispanic cavalry, had met them at Baelo, and the plan had formed there. Didius had hoped to destroy Pompey at sea, but there was always a land backup now.

'Signal Lento,' he told the man beside him. 'This is no longer just a sea pursuit.'

The man saluted and stepped across to the rail, raising his flags and facing the shore, northeast, away from where the rebels had disappeared into the treeline. With a flicker of signals, he fell still, waiting. After a few moments there came a series of flashes from the hills off to the west. Caesennius Lento was in pursuit.

'What now sir?'

Didius took in the destruction all around them. Ships were now jutting from the water, sinking into the blue, while others roared in flames and yet more were being sailed back to his own lines to join the Caesarians. Months ago, he had chased the Pompeian fleet into Carteia. He'd won two impressive sea battles, and yet he'd still not been able to stop their commander fleeing onto the land and escaping. Caesar had been appropriately thankful and handed out plenty of praise, and yet none of it had mattered to Didius. That he had not completed his goals at Carteia still rankled. Since then, he had spent months securing ports, blockading them, building the fleet and patrolling from Gades to Carthago Nova. Now, once again, he had had Pompey's fleet in his grasp, he had chased them down and thought to bring them to destructive battle off the south coast of the peninsula. Instead, he had accidentally come across them gathering water and supplies, the ships at anchor, the bulk of his men on shore. His naval victory had been about as memorable as the time he had entered a swimming competition at the Piscina Publica only to find out that he'd accidentally entered the childrens' level, facing competition more than a decade his junior.

And now once again, his prey had fled inland, escaping his grasp. And now Lento was going to gain Caesar's ear for having been the man to capture or kill one of the three great rebel leaders.

'Fuck it.'

'Sir?'

Didius turned to the signaller. 'Once the fleet is secured, I want all marines and excess crew on that beach. Lento is moving to take Pompey, but the villain won't escape again. We're going to follow him. With luck, we'll get him before Lento.'

CHAPTER TWENTY TWO

Mid April 45 BC

D idius hauled on the reins of his horse and came to a halt on the top of a ridge, skittering gravel beneath with small patches of dry vegetation dotted about, nothing more than a knee-high bush. The view was excellent. The hill path below the ridge streamed with marines, still adjusting to the solid ground after weeks of shipboard life. A thousand men, split into three cohorts, enough to find and finish Pompey. His gaze took in the signal from the bare hilltop perhaps two miles to the north. Lento and his cohorts.

Pompey would be feeling the pinch now. He had moved north from the beach at the greatest speed he could manage, but it had not taken Didius long to finish off the enemy fleet and land his own force. Since then, every time they had reached a high peak, his signallers had picked out Lento and his scouts, the two forces remaining in close contact as they moved in on the fleeing rebels like pincers from the south and the east.

His gaze now moved to the high ground ahead. He couldn't make out the details of what was happening there, but there was definite movement, figures like ants on a nest, swarming over the peak. Pompey and his men were there, and Didius' scouts had been very informative. Too much so for their own good, in fact. As a naval force there had been few horses aboard the ships, and all of them had been employed by Didius and a few men chosen for their eyesight and hunting skills as scouts. Still, for all his efforts, they were poor compared with the native scouts usually employed by a Roman army and, while they had managed to provide a great deal of information, that was because they had come far too close and almost been caught and killed. The latest had lurched back to the column, badly injured.

Pompey was also wounded, or so it seemed. More than one injury, and debilitating, too, since he had now resorted to being carried on some sort of stretcher. Perhaps two hundred men accompanied the rebel general, all of them also tired and injured, yet determined and resistant. They had reached this place and now, it seemed, were digging in. Didius had mused on the situation as they rode. Had Pompey resigned himself to a last stand? A defiant showing in the face of insurmountable odds? Had he managed to signal someone and was holing up and waiting for reinforcements to reach him? Was he perhaps under the impression that he could still win? It was said, after all, that the Lusitanians continued to harbour support for the rebels and to resent Caesar's control. It mattered not. The plan had to be the same. They had to take him down, and they had to do it here and now.

Didius did not know Pompey, other than by reputation. They said he was a pale shadow of his father, a tactician of limited scope. Thus far, however, the general had proved surprisingly wily since his escape from Carteia, and only luck and educated guesswork had allowed them to catch up with him. Pompey's instincts were clearly still good, for in this world of green and grey peaks and valleys, the rebel general had chosen his position well.

A horseshoe of hill a quarter of a mile across, surrounding a single peak at the centre, was itself surrounded by a wide valley. Pompey had deployed half his force around that U-shaped ridge, while he himself, and his other hundred men had retreated to the heart of his domain, fortifying at the peak in the middle. Unless the man could pull something magically out of his sleeve, the result was still a foregone conclusion in Didius' opinion, though he had to admit that he would lose a lot of men by the time he'd got to Pompey. Taking a slow, calm breath, he turned to the tribune he'd brought with him.

'Deliver the plan to the centurions. We travel slowly, for Lento is perhaps an hour behind us, and we should hit him at the same time. Pompey must know we're on his trail, but he might not yet be aware of Lento. We hit him from north and south at the same time and spread out as we arrive. I want our men approaching in an arc from west to east. Send a rider to find Lento and tell him this, advising him to do the same from the north, so that we can be sure of trapping them and not letting the villain escape. Once we're all there, give the signal and the men can take the hill from every side. Once we control the outer ring, we can gradually close in on the central one.'

The tribune nodded his understanding, saluted, and rode back down the slope to the moving column of marines. Didius watched that distant hillside for a moment longer and then dropped back down to join his men.

For two more hours the three marine cohorts traipsed across the hillsides of southern Lusitania, always heading for that peak. As they climbed one forested slope, a scout ahead gave the signal. They were on Pompey at last. Following his gestures, the centurions began to lead their men out now, along the slope rather than up it, fanning out to create a cordon over a mile long, thin but wide. When they were in position, Didius looking left and right along a bristling, armoured line, the lookouts confirmed that Lento was in position, and the signal was given. The cohorts began to march up the hill, tightening the noose around Pompey's position. Didius drew his sword as he urged his horse up after them. He would not be expected to bloody it, of course, but it always looked good for a commander to appear to be in the thick of it, and if the opportunity presented itself, he would love to be the one to finish it.

The cohorts crested the hill, flowing around that scout like a river around a rock, and then swarmed down the slope into the wide valley, their commander following on his steed, close to the men at all times. As he moved over the crest, he could see the rebels now and was impressed. Beaten in the greatest battle of recent months, limping away, these men had struggled at Carteia, fought for control of it, freed their general and then fled by ship. They had sailed west, fought another engagement and then fled once more across the hills to get here. Yet, rather than collapse in exhaustion, they were even now raising a fence and digging a ditch up there as best they could.

The marines flooded down into the valley and then began to climb that horseshoe hill, moving through the sparse, dry forest as they bore down on the defenders. The fighting started before Didius could see it. He could hear the shouts and the clangs and thumps, whistles and screams. As he emerged from the treeline towards the peak, he took in the scene with a moment of shock.

His men had arrived at a jog, climbing the last stretch of the slope only to meet a prepared and determined force. As they had emerged from cover, the enemy had unleashed their pila in a mass volley, and the effect had been gruesomely impressive. Didius arrived to see his front lines staggering back, stumbling to the dust, pinned and impaled. Marines fell to the ground, clutching at mortal wounds, and that single initial volley had cost Didius a quarter of his force. He could not see Lento's men but the chances were that they were suffering something much the same.

His centurions roared and blew their whistles, urging the faltering charge on.

The cohorts regrouped from their initial disaster, stomping up between the bodies of their fallen companions, racing for that makeshift rampart. Didius watched, heart in his throat. He had seen this as a foregone conclusion, but his certainty had already been shaken. Now, it was diminished once more as he saw his men struggling to take that rampart from the defenders. The rebels had to be exhausted and hungry, but they were also the strongest of Pompey's veterans. Indeed, in a swathe of destruction, Didius watched his attack falter again, marines falling all along the line. He felt his pulse pounding, and threw a prayer of thanks to the gods as his centurions once more urged their marines on and this third time saw some success. Through sheer numbers, they had finally managed to break breaches in the rebel lines and had penetrated the defences in places. The officers were hard at work now, directing the killing, securing those breaches to make sure there was no need for a fourth assault.

Then, in a sudden move, some enemy signal was given, and the rebel soldiers were gone. Disengaging from the fight they simply ran back away from the ridge. The retreat was so sudden, speedy and well-coordinated that the marines dithered too long to effectively pursue them. The centurions brought their men back into lines once more. As Didius now rode up to that hill crest, he could see what the enemy were up to. Lento had similarly taken the outer ring of hills to the north, his standards visible there. The enemy, though, had all pulled back and were even now climbing that central hill, where they pushed through the line of their fellows and into the position of reserves, heaving in relieved breaths.

Didius could see the figure that had to be Pompey on the hill now, at the peak in the centre, throwing out commands. 'Finish it,' he shouted to the officers on the hill. Remaining where he was, on that ridge with a good view, Didius, surrounded by a half century of guards, watched the fight. His men flowed down that inner hillside, across the narrow gap, and then up towards the peak where Pompey's legionaries waited. He saw the two sides crash together, and knew finally, with some relief, that it really was, now, a foregone conclusion. His men would overcome the enemy, despite heavy losses, and Pompey was doomed. It would end here.

His gaze rose to the crest once more, and he frowned. Pompey was not there.

Shaking his head, he looked this way and that. The figure he'd seen at the centre had gone, and as his gaze raked the hillside, he could see no sign of the man. He felt a chill shudder through him. No, he *couldn't* let the bastard slip away again. Pompey was certainly not visible from here. He had to be off to the northwest, then. Didius closed his eyes and rubbed his chin. That way lay the open arms of the horseshoe. If Pompey could slip through the lines of the Caesarians, he would disappear, and it would be much harder to track a small group than it had been this ragged band.

Didius looked around. The ten scouts he'd managed to find horses for had once more gathered, and he gestured to them. He needed fast men now. 'Come with me.'

With that, he kicked his horse and began to canter off along the ridge, heading west, around that central hill. With the ten men following close, he rode for the open end of the horseshoe, his gaze always on that peak where the fighting raged. Nowhere was there any sign of Pompey. He couldn't have slipped through anywhere Didius had been watching, so it had to be somewhere in this direction. He was galloping now, heedless of the dangerous ground. Ahead, the hillside dipped away into that low ground at the opening of the U, and his gaze tore through the vegetation, trying to find any trace of Pompey.

With his men at his heel, he raced down the slope, turning and angling back towards that central hill. His eyes scoured it, and he could see his men some two thirds of the way up, struggling to overcome Pompey's defenders. They were winning, slowly. Still no sign…

A flicker of movement caught his eye. As he turned to focus on it, the cause had gone, whatever it was. In truth, it could have been almost anything. A bird of prey, one of the large, indigenous wild cats, even a falling branch. Yet somehow, in his bones, Didius knew it was Pompey.

Turning, waving the riders on with him, he made for the low ground, a small ravine at the base of that central hill. As they closed on it, the sounds of distant combat audible on the hill above, Didius and his riders slowed, swords at the ready, and began to make their way into the ravine. The enemy came at them suddenly, leaping from the rocks to either side. Four of Didius' horsemen were down before they managed to pull ahead, yanked from their saddles. On the ground they struggled with Pompey's desperate soldiers, swords and knives out, curses abounding, blades flashing and blood flowing. The rest of Didius' men dismounted now as three legionaries edged towards them, swords ready.

Leaving his men to deal with them, the admiral took the two remaining riders, stepping around the fighting, heading for a gloomy black opening in the rock that they were clearly defending. As they approached, Didius dismounted and the three of them, on foot, stalked towards the cave.

One of Pompey's legionaries managed to dispatch a Caesarian scout and ran after them. Didius turned at the last moment and managed to throw his own blade in the way, before one of the pair with him dived on the legionary, cutting him down, dropping him to the dusty ground, where he kneeled on the man and hammered his sword hilt into the soldier's head again and again.

Leaving him to it, Didius and his companion stepped into the dark.

'Beg Caesar for clemency,' he said to the motionless gloom. There was no reply, then finally one piece of blackness detached itself from the rest, and a faintly human shape moved closer. 'Caesar never regretted anything more than the way your father went,' he tried again. 'He has vowed to end this and to see all the leaders of your rebellion dead, but one entreaty from you, and he would be merciful. Surely you know this?'

'Rebellion?'

Pompey moved out of the darkness now, into the gloomy light of the cave entrance where Didius stood. He was leaning on a stick for support, his leg ruined, and his arm hung useless by his side. Still, despite his clear pain and the failure of his last stand, there was a strangely triumphant gleam in the young general's eye.

'Your rebellion is over.'

'Only the despot would consider this a rebellion,' Pompey spat. 'Caesar defied the just decisions of the senate of Rome. He did the unthinkable. He led an army on Rome, breaking so many laws he could have paved his journey with them. He threatened violence to the true senate of Rome, and forced them to flee for their lives. Senators, Didius! Forced to leave Rome itself, for Caesar's army was coming to the capital in defiance of our oldest statutes. And because the senate of Rome stood against him, Caesar declared them enemies of the state and replaced them with men who would support him. Those true senators and their supporters were forced to flee to the periphery of the republic, to take arms against him. We fought to the end. We still do. But not in some rebellion, you blind fool. The rebel is the man you serve. We are the republic. We are Rome. And when you kill us, you kill Rome. What you do next will change the world, Gaius Didius. I give not a fig for my life. Take it, but I will never bend the knee to your criminal master. I will die a son of the republic, and my conscience will be clear.'

Didius nodded. He'd heard such sentiments before, of course. This was the rallying cry of the rebels. But he'd never had it put to him so succinctly and with such heart. It took some inner strength to straighten and nod once more.

'I hear you, but I also know that Caesar has taken an ailing republic and saved it. He will step down when this crisis is over, and what he will leave will be a stronger Rome.'

'What he will leave will be a *throne*,' Pompey hissed, and staggered a painful step closer. Amazingly, given his condition, he let that walking stick fall away and lifted a blade. 'If you want me, you must take me by force.'

Didius breathed again and stepped forward to meet the man. The scout beside him moved to intercept, but Didius waved the man away. He might not be the best swordsman in the republic, but Pompey was done for. The rebel general made a desperate lunge and Didius sidestepped it with ease as Pompey staggered forward and fell to his knees with a cry of pain. The man was no longer wearing a cuirass, his wounds making it difficult, and Didius' blow, a single stab down with his gladius, slammed into the man's back, grating between ribs and then sliding with a sigh through the offal within, coming to a halt against the inside of Pompey's breastbone.

The general gave just a whimper and then jerked a few times and fell still.

The scout stepped forward now. 'Sir, what do we do with the body?'

'Caesar's orders. Remove the head.'

His lip twitched as he said it. Had the general really meant it? Caesar had been furious when this man's father's head had been delivered to him. But that was the standing order if any senior commander of the rebel army was found. The head was to be delivered to Caesar, and he'd not made any clear exceptions for Pompey.

'Take his head and a small force of riders. Deliver it to Hispalis. Caesar was last known to be there.'

He turned and strode from the cave, breathing heavily and trying not to listen to the gory sawing sounds behind him. It was done. The second of the three rebel leaders dead. Only Sextus left, and the man had disappeared. It appeared that the war was finally over.

* * *

Two days later.

The beach was quiet, the sun already sinking into the west, and Didius waved his acknowledgement to the optio who was calling him over to the camp fire for food. He sagged, tired. After the fight at the hill of Lauro, his scouts had joined Lento and taken Pompey's head back east to deliver to Caesar. Didius had read the butcher's bill with a heavy heart, having lost more than half his men. Still, they had killed Pompey, and most of his force, a few of the survivors of Lauro slipping away into the Lusitanian hills. Wearily, Didius and his column had begun the long trek back to the coast and the fleet.

Back on the beach, he had given the orders. The majority of the fleet had been dispatched that morning, sent back to Gades for the general. Didius himself had remained at the beach with two centuries of men and the crews of two ships that had been damaged during the engagement and which were being repaired in situ. They would be complete in a couple of days, and they would then follow the fleet and return to Gades. In the meantime, he had kept with him the more wounded and exhausted to give them a rest after their victory before going back to work.

There was a jubilant atmosphere. The war was over. Whether Sextus Pompey could be found or not, only a couple of towns in the whole peninsula now held out, and then Caesar would have control of Hispania and they could all return to Rome...

Some small, dark part of his soul then asked him whether that was a good thing, and he fought down the uncertainty. Pompey's words had rung in his ears whenever the silence fell since that moment in the cave. Didius resolved to look deep into Caesar's eyes when he returned to the general. He would know, somehow, when he peered into those two orbs, whether the general was what Didius had always claimed: the saviour of the republic, or what Pompey had earnestly believed: that he was its last dying breath.

'Sestertius for your thoughts, sir?' a centurion asked, falling in beside him.

'Just wishing I was home. Still, soon we all will be. How are things?'

'Quiet, sir. I've got four lads on watch, but we've seen nothing more than gulls in a day and a half.'

Didius nodded. 'Get along to dinner, Centurion. I'll join you all presently.'

As the man stomped away across the sand, Didius, stretching and enjoying the evening air, stopped at a pile of freshly-cut timbers and leaned against them, scrubbing his face with his hands. It was quite by chance that he happened to be looking across at the far end of the beach when the trouble began. As his gaze fell upon the man on watch on a low hillock beyond the beached shape of the *Demeter's Arrow*, the figure suddenly disappeared behind the rise. Not a sound, but Didius' breath stilled, his pulse racing. His gaze snapped round to the other end of the beach. The man there had gone too. Similarly, there was no sign of the two men up towards the line of vegetation above the beach.

'To arms,' he bellowed, even as the enemy appeared. Figures were pouring across the sand now from both ends of the beach, carrying pots and torches, blazing in the evening gloom. As the camp exploded into activity, there was nothing they could do to stop that attack, for already pots of pitch had been hurled at the two beached ships, fiery torches cast after them, catching the dry timbers and roaring across them. In mere heartbeats the two vessels were roaring infernos of golden fire.

The two centuries were doing their best to form up, but they had been taken entirely by surprise, and half their equipment was still either in their tents or on those very ships now burning away. As Didius hurried back towards the camp at the centre, drawing his sword, he turned his gaze to the men attacking them. Most of them wore just ordinary tunics, armed with long knives or axes or staves. Locals, he surmised. Lusitanians. For a moment he wondered what could have roused the locals so against him, but then he began to see familiar shapes among them. The survivors of that hilltop at Lauro. It appeared they did not yet consider the war over, and in their hike on Didius' tail all the way back to the coast, they had picked up friends.

He gritted his teeth. He'd beaten this lot once, under a great general. He'd damn well do the same now, with their ragtag band of Lusitanian rebels.

As the centurions gathered their men into units, Didius gestured to them. 'Falco, take that lot over by the Demeter. Statilius, take the others. Flaccus, you're with me. We're the reserve.'

In response to his command, the force separated. The two centurions each took their centuries, hurrying over to deal with the two ragged forces that had fired the ships. The remaining men, the ships' crews, remained with Trierarch Flaccus and Didius at the campsite, watching their fellows fighting at the ships.

Damn it, but that was irritating. They'd burned the ships. Now Didius and the others would have to slog the hundred and fifty miles back to Gades by land, slowly and carefully, unless they could secure from another port. And if the Lusitanians could be so easily roused against them here, then the same could happen again.

Still, he said to himself, at least they had the best of it. The Lusitanians were unarmoured and lightly armed, and even tired and injured, Didius' marines were more than a match for them.

Even now, they were overcoming the two groups of attackers, having taken a few casualties.

A cry drew his attention, and Didius' head snapped around.

A fresh flood of figures was now pouring from the trees, across the sand, making for the shambling group of tired sailors. Much the same as the ones at the ships, they were largely tunic'd locals with makeshift weapons, a small core of the survivors of Lauro among them. They matched the sailors in number, and as Didius started bellowing orders to form into a line, he tried to estimate their chances. There were few professional soldiers among the attackers, but then there were few among Didius' reserves, too. Those men were poorly-equipped, but so were Didius'. The rest of the enemy were untrained locals with a bitch against Caesar, probably the usual over taxes and rights, fuelled by Pompeian propaganda, but then Didius' men were sailors not soldiers. And while the locals would not be as strong as his sailors, they also had not spent all day chopping down trees and sawing wood.

It was too close for comfort.

Bracing, he held his place as the line of worried looking sailors formed to either side, two deep, many wielding either a small knife or some sort of tool, a mattock or axe. A quick glance over his shoulder told him he might be in trouble. The two centuries were still locked in their own fights near the ships, and Didius realised now what they were doing. The two enemy groups there were holding the marines to the fight so they could not come to the aid of those men remaining in the camp.

Turning back, he knew that all he could do now was pray and fight, and so that was precisely what he did. A trio of hasty prayers to Mars, Minerva and Neptune, vowing altars if he made it back to Gades, and then the struggle began. A filthy, tired, yet furious-looking Pompeian legionary, still wearing his chain shirt and carrying a war blade, leapt at him.

Didius managed to turn the blow, wishing he was armoured or had a shield, and somehow stepped past the man, turning to the next attacker. A man in a blue tunic, travel-stained, his beard ragged, his hair wild, came at Didius with a cleaver, and he managed to miss the swipe, then knock the attacker aside, smashing his sword into that arm wielding the blade. Before the man could recover, Didius had delivered two blows, to his gut and then to his weapon arm. The man fell away, but another took his place, a long dagger slashing into the flesh of a sailor, who screamed and disappeared in a cloud of spraying blood and kicked up sand.

Didius was on his killer in moments, hacking and stabbing like a madman.

He was no great warrior, sadly, and he knew it. He realised his mistake only as it came back to strike at him. He'd sidestepped that first soldier and assumed someone else would deal with him. But as he'd dealt with cleaver man and then the knife wielder, that soldier had simply stopped behind him, turned, and struck from behind.

Didius felt the legionary's blade sink in. It was a professional kill, a masterful attack, aimed well as the man was under no pressure and had been presented with Didius' back. The blade entered his side below the armpit, piercing vital organs and severing critical blood vessels. As the sword was pulled free, Didius felt a strange cold hollowness as evening air flowed into the wound for just a moment until it turned warm again, torrents of his lifeblood sheeting out and down his side.

He spun, gasping, staggering, to face his killer. His hand twitched. He tried to bring it up, but realised he'd dropped his sword. He tried to speak, but all he could manage was grunts and gurgles. He could do nothing now to stop the second blow as that sword, coated with blood – *his* blood – was pulled back and then slammed into his chest.

Didius felt the indescribable pain, but somehow the sense of confusion and dismay was stronger than the agony, and it was almost a relief when the sword was pulled free again and he collapsed to his knees. He saw the man's legs only as the legionary moved off to kill another.

Didius toppled slowly forward to the sand. His watering eyes took in the scene even as his sight began to fade. They were lost. The enemy had simply overrun them, presumably in revenge for Lauro and Pompey's death. It was a fair exchange, he supposed in a strange way. His death for Pompey's. He could see the last of his men being finished off, and then the burning remnants of his ruined ships.

His fading gaze settled on one heartening sight. Between the two blazing hulks he could just make out a small boat, a pinnace, which had miraculously survived the fire. He could just see half a dozen of his men desperately rowing out to sea, and he willed them on. It would be a long and fraught journey for them to get back to safe lands, but they had made a start, and no one on this beach would catch them now. Those men would carry word of what happened here to Caesar.

Didius' eyes closed, scratchy and filled with the sand in which he lay.

A last breath escaped his lips.

At least he'd finally caught Pompey first.

CHAPTER TWENTY THREE

Late April 45 BC

Fronto heaved in a weary breath as he reined in Bucephalus beside Galronus, the two men looking down across the all too familiar valley. Fronto immediately found himself eying the gentle slope that led from the walls of Munda all the way down to the stream and its marshy banks, ignoring the legions now camped there and replaying in his head the battle, wondering how things might have been done differently.

'Just Munda now, then? Galronus murmured.

'And Urso,' Fronto reminded him.

Behind them, the Tenth began to filter across the low rolling hills, and Fronto sagged. Two more cities. Caesar and his forces had left Hispalis with a small garrison, and had moved south, meeting up with Rebilus and several other legions, then marching on the rebel stronghold of Asta, sitting proud on a plateau and looking out at Gades across the great salt basin in between. Whether it had been the clear faltering of the rebel cause, a sudden change of heart, or the arrival of a powerful army on their doorstep, the ordo of Asta had thrown open their gates, offering full support for Caesar's cause and celebrating their 'liberation'.

Leaving Asta with a small garrison they had moved on to find the great port city of Gades already under their control thanks to the tireless efforts of Gaius Didius. It had come, therefore, as something of a shock to learn of his demise at the hands of a few Lusitanian animals. With only Munda and Urso remaining in enemy hands, Caesar had settled into Gades and waited there, administering the province and attempting to bring a level of peace to it.

Two legions had been dispatched into Lusitania to keep order there and prevent repeats of what had happened to Didius. The head of Gnaeus Pompey had been brought east, displayed to the people of Hispalis, and then sent south to Caesar. Satisfied that all was proceding well, and the war almost done, Caesar had dispatched what legions he could now spare to invest the remaining cities. Fabius Maximus already besieged Munda with three legions, and had been doing so since the battle, but now legions were sent to invest Urso too, ready to bring the very last rebel towns under control. Fronto and the Tenth, along with a detachment of cavalry, had made their way to Munda to join that siege and move things along.

Fabius' army had utilised Pompey's camp from the battle, and had driven siege lines from it all around the city, settling his legions into position all around it. The city would need to be taken by storm at some point in Fronto's opinion. If it had held out this long, they had no intention of surrendering. Besides, everyone inside had to be well aware of their fate if they did. Caesar had made it quite clear with that display of heads and bodies outside. Of course, that grisly rampart had been removed after a few days of display. No besieging army wants to sit among decomposing bodies. And Munda, of course, had been one of Pompey's main supply bases. It would likely be able to hold out for a year yet.

Fronto stopped trying to rethink the battle and pondered instead the city and its ramparts, then the Caesarian lines outside.

'No weak points,' he noted with a sigh.'

'Ladders and towers?' Galronus questioned.

'If it were that easy Fabius would have done it. Munda's on a hill. Towers would lean out away because of the slope. Ladders would have to be unreasonably long, and are no guarantee of gaining the walls without rams and towers. Rams would be trouble, and I remember the ground around here. It's hard as nails. Undermining the walls would be the work of months if it's possible at all, which I doubt. No. No conventional siege tactics are going to take Munda. Our only hope for a swift end here is something unusual and ingenious. Caesar was irked that it's taken Fabius so long, but I can see why.'

'He's very little cavalry,' Galronus muttered. 'I can see maybe two hundred gathered in two separate camps.'

'There's not so much use for cavalry here,' Fronto replied. 'Not when he's got...' He paused. 'How many men do you reckon Fabius has here?'

There was a long pause, filled only with the sound of the Tenth and their Gallic cavalry companions rumbling and traipsing over the dry ground. Finally, Galronus shrugged. 'Better part of fifteen thousand. Three legions. You can actually see the standards. The Third, the Fifth, and the Twenty Eighth.'

'And that doesn't strike you as odd?'

Galronus shook his head. 'No, why? That's three legions.'

'That's three *full* legions,' Fronto said. 'The numbers on paper. We've been fighting here for months and lost a lot of men at Munda, and these legions were understrength to begin with. So why are they so well manned?'

Galronus was frowning now.

'Come on,' Fronto said, kicking Bucephalus into motion. 'Let's go talk to Fabius.'

Leaving Atenos to see the Tenth down into the siege lines and find a place to camp, the two officers rode off ahead. Fronto was pleased when a picket stepped out and demanded their identity. At least Fabius was conscious of the potential for rebel troubles still. Once in the Caesarian camp, they were met by a tribune from the Third, who escorted them in a business-like manner to the praetorium, where a large tent marked the general's headquarters.

As the two men dismounted, the tribune rapped on the door frame and disappeared inside for a moment, reappearing and gesturing for the pair to enter. Fronto and Galronus stepped inside wearily.

Quintus Fabius Maximus was busy dictating to a slave scribe, and held up a hand then waved it, dismissing the man before gesturing for the other two to come closer, and pointing at seats.

'Good to see you, Fronto. You too,' he added, nodding at Galronus. 'In fact, only this morning I penned a letter to Caesar explaining that Munda can only realistically be stormed if I have two more legions. I presume you've brought at least the Tenth?'

Fronto nodded. 'And solid cavalry.'

Fabius dismissed that with a wave as unimportant to a besieging force. 'Maybe, just maybe, with the Tenth on side we can afford to assault the place.'

'Quintus,' Fronto said, leaning forward, 'how are your numbers so strong? The Tenth can muster just over three thousand at the moment, and we're one of the stronger legions. How are yours at full strength?'

Fabius gave himan odd smile. 'Deserters.'

'What?'

'You'd be surprised how many of the enemy have little faith in their cause now. We took in more than two thousand survivors from the battle who drifted in over the next week or two with their hands raised. And after a month of this, another two thousand fled Munda one night and came over to our side.'

Fronto pursed his lips. 'So of the fifteen thousand you command here, somewhere between a quarter and a third are the enemy?'

'*Former* enemy,' Fabius corrected him. 'I had them all take a new oath before the eagles. Gods, Fronto, but we need the manpower.'

'I quite agree, but taking in men from Munda is a little dubious at best.'

Fabius nodded. 'On one level I agree. But it's what we've been doing ever since we arrived in Hispania, taking in deserters. On of your own tribunes is a former Pompeian if I remember rightly.'

'But that was earlier on. All the enemy left now are die-hard Pompeians.'

'Or those who know they have lost. Fronto, I'm not an idiot. I didn't arm them all, give them an eagle and let them take their place as a new legion. I had them split up into centuries and distributed among the three legions already here. They are settled piecemeal.'

Fronto shrugged. 'Alright. What's your plan?'

Fabius gave a hollow laugh. 'Gather sufficient numbers that when I throw them at Munda, some of them get in. We've tried everything, Fronto. The place is a hard nut to crack. This is not like some Gallic oppidum.'

Fronto caught the glare Galronus threw the man then, and privately agreed with his friend. His memory of some of the oppida they had faced was of bitter, hard fights. 'We need to find a sneaky way in,' he said. 'Have you any men on the inside?'

'No. We know a few names of the defenders from those who came over to us, but that's all.'

'I want to have a word with them. Once I've settled in, can you arrange for the more senior ones to come visit me at my command tent.'

Fabius rolled his eyes. 'I'm on top of things, Fronto. This is not your command.'

'I'm not trying to undermine you Fabius, or take over. I just want to help get this finished as soon as we can.'

'Alright. I'll have a dozen or so of their centurionate sent to visit you.'

'And in the meantime, Fabius, if you're not watching those men you took in, you need to be doing so.'

'Really, Fronto, I...'

'Did you know that Gaius Didius is dead?'

That stopped the commander mid-sentence. 'No.'

'He let his guard down, thought he was safe after he'd taken out Pompey's last force in Lusitania, then they mobbed him on the beach and killed him and all his men. And these were mostly angry locals. Half a dozen survivors got away in a boat. Don't make the same mistake. Have the deserters watched.'

Fabius chewed on his lip, but finally nodded. 'Alright, Fronto. I hope you're wrong.'

'So do I. But it's better to be prepared for trouble and not find it than the other way around.'

'True. Alright. Settle your men in on the southern side and get some rest. There's a makeshift bath block down near the stream if you need it, and I'll have adequate supplies sent over to you. We've got four hours or so until sunset. I tend to have small gatherings of the senior officers once it gets dark. We can discuss anything then.'

Fronto nodded, and he and Galronus stepped back outside. Mounting once more, they walked their horses back through the camp of the Third towards the edge of the lines. As they rode, Fronto tried to identify any centuries of Pompeian deserters, but it was impossible to tell. Their shields had been repainted, apparently, removing their former legion designs, and now they were indistinguishable from Fabius' men.

They met up with the Tenth as the legion was moving into position. Atenos and the six tribunes were in deep discussion, and Fronto and Galronus reined in beside them.

'We have the south, where the lines are thinnest. Have the men settle in from the edge of the Third over there, and all the way round to the Urso road, around the rear of the Twenty Eighth. Get the command tent up as soon as you can. We're going to have some Pompeian guests over for a chat.'

* * *

There was a knock at Fronto's command tent door, and at a call, the legionary pulled the door open and two of Fronto's best men stepped in and took position at the edge of the tent. Fronto nodded at them as the former Pompeian deserters were led in. Along with Atenos, Galronus, Fronto and the six tribunes, there were now eleven blades in the tent in case of trouble, and the primus pilus had made sure the visitors were disarmed before entry.

Fronto looked at the grizzled centurions as they fell in in two lines, legs the regulation distance apart, vine sticks under armpits, chins high. Twelve of them. There was a strange sound to one side, and Fronto turned to see Quintus Pompeius Niger leaning forward in his seat, his face angry. Fronto followed his gaze and realised why as his eyes lit upon the figure of Antistius Turpio, the centurion he had fought in single combat at Soricaria, and then failed to reach in the battle on this very spot.

Noting the man's presence, Fronto felt more certain than ever that he couldn't trust these men. Turpio, in his opinion, was a die-hard, more likely to cut his own throat than surrender to the enemy.

'Tell me about Munda,' Fronto said.

'Sir?' one of the centurions replied.

'There is a weak point. Every city has a weak point. You were in there for weeks. If you want this to end, tell me where the weak point is. Give us a place to attack. Give us a target.'

He fell silent. The former Pompeian centurions looked at one another, but Fronto could only feel the bristling hatred crackling in the air between Niger and Turpio. Niger, of course, was also a former Pompeian, but not in his heart, and the tribune had proved himself again and again throughout the campaign.

'The west,' one of them said finally, earning swift looks from the others. Fronto swept his gaze across the centurions, noting their expressions. Few centurions were politicians, and it was hard for them to keep the truth from their faces at the best of times. Fronto nodded slowly.

'Before I settled in here, I spent half an hour riding slowly around the lines, looking at Munda. I have been besieging cities since most of you were bouncing on your daddy's knee. I saw no sign of weakness to the west, or anywhere else.'

The centurion who had spoken straightened. 'It is not obvious, legate. Maybe twenty paces away from the Urso gate, a seasonal stream once existed, and the wall occasionally sags above the ground there, as it is softer and less stable. It's not visible, as it's always repaired and rebuilt, but above that creek the wall will be more vulnerable than elsewhere. Well placed onager stones could take it down.'

Fronto nodded slowly. 'Interesting. A weakness we cannot see. I shall take this under advisement. Thank you. You may return to your units.'

The centurions saluted and filed out of the tent, followed by Fronto's legionaries. He waited some time for them to be far from the tent, and then turned to the others. 'What do you make of it?'

'How are we to prove the truth of such a weakness other than committing to it? Atenos murmured.

'They lie,' Niger said flatly.

'That's because you'll never trust your friend out there,' another tribune snorted.

Fronto took a deep breath. 'Niger is right. They were lying. Did you see the way they looked at each other. If only one of them was willing to volunteer information that they should all know, I would have expected some reaction. If they were truly all on our side, they would have been leaping to agree or discuss the matter. In fact, their faces were kept very deliberately neutral throughout. This was planned and carefully executed. Galronus and I looked the city over earlier. Care to tell them about the place they're talking about?'

The Remi shrugged. 'Where he's talking about there are no artillery pieces on the walls, and little in the way of manpower. Fabius' men assumed the lack there was them concentrating their force at the gate, but this suggests otherwise.'

Fronto nodded. 'They have created a tempting place to attack. There's only one reason to do that. They are well prepared and it's a trap. Niger is right. They are lying. Every man who stood here just now still fights for Pompey. They have taken a false oath to get within our lines, and they're biding their time to let us get used to them. Once they are such a regular sight we don't notice them any more, something very nasty is going to happen.'

Niger straightened. 'We need to be ready. I think…'

Fronto gave a wicked chuckle. 'Have no fear, Pompeius Niger. I'll make sure you're posted near Turpio.' He leaned back. 'Tonight, when I speak to the other legates and tribunes, I think I'm going to have to be very persuasive. In the meantime, I want every centurion and optio in our legion warned about our suspicions. Not the men. I don't want the enemy to get wind of it, and a legionary with a wineskin can be very talkative. But the centurionate know how to keep things secret.'

* * *

Pompeius Niger had slept with one eye open. In fact he'd always been a light sleeper, but for three days, since they had arrived at Munda, he'd felt a tension unlike anything he was used to. It didn't help that Fabius and his officers remained sceptical of the danger. Niger had spoken to Fronto on that matter, but in the legate's opinion, that helped. As he pointed out, they knew that something was up with the Pompeian units, and he had persuaded Fabius to be prepared. But until anything happened, as long as they were ready, a healthy disbelief among most of the legions helped lull the Pompeians into a false sense of security.

Indeed, all in order to keep those enemy unaware that their true purpose was known, Fronto had begun fake preparations for a major push against the supposed weak spot. All around the Caesarian siege lines, Pompeian units were resting, taking part in the usual duties and in camp life, but all around, they were being watched. And just in case, Fronto had made sure to put some of his own men in position near each and every one, against the possibility that Fabius' men were so disbelieving that they were not prepared.

Niger had lurched awake a dozen times a night since that meeting, every time something clonked, rattled or scraped outside. Every time a low voice drifted across the nighttime air. Every time an owl hooted, even. His sword stood propped against the stool beside his bed and he had taken to sleeping in his tunic and boots, with his leather subarmalis and his belt on that same chair. Over the three days of practice, he had taken getting ready down to something that took twenty heartbeats.

This noise was new. It was a crunch. It was close. As quietly as possible, he slipped from his cot and padded across to the tent door. With economy of movement, he edged the flap aside and peered out in the direction of the noise. A shadowy figure was creeping through the dark between the tents, having come so close to Niger's that he'd trodden on one of the many twigs the tribune had placed there to catch the unwary sneak.

To the average legionary, it would probably appear to be one of their mates creeping to the latrine and trying not to wake them. Not to Niger. Not now. In moments he was back in his tent, pulling his sub on, lacing it at the side, and then fastening the belt. He eschewed the helmet for its habit of restricting sound and vision. Then he was outside once more. He had lost sight of the figure, but knew what direction it had been moving in, and so paced away after it. As he moved out into a wide space between tents, he glanced this way and that, and his fears were confirmed. He could see more and more movement in the section of the camp occupied by Turpio's century.

Turning, a suspicion settling upon him, he looked back at the city beyond the siege lines. At first glance it looked exactly the same as it had every night. Then he noticed the difference. Between every third pair of torches on the walls, another one burned, raised slightly above the level of the others. A very subtle signal. There was now no doubt whatsoever in his mind.

Straightening, he cupped his hands to his mouth and shouted.
'Tarpeia.'

A signal chosen by Fronto. Tarpeia had been the treacherous Vestal who had sold out Rome to the Sabines. It was short, easy to remember, and very, very apt.

Before he'd repeated the call a second, and then a third time, the Caesarians were on the move, and not long after, the men of Fabius' legions, who had never really believed in the danger. It took only moments for the men of the treacherous century ahead to realise that they had been discovered. There was a momentary lull as, Niger suspected, the Pompeians tried to decide whether to lie down again and protest innocence, or throw their caution to the wind and simply attack anyway.

The latter won out and, as Niger's men came barrelling along the lines between tents, shields up and swords out, the Pompeians, discovered before they were ready, desperately scrabbled to arm and equip. With one last cry of 'Tarpeia' for good measure, Niger ripped his blade free and ran.

The Pompeians were moving fast. They had been semi-prepared, waiting for the signal, but had through necessity kept their movements small and hidden to prevent attracting too much attention.

A distant roar made Niger turn, and he saw back along that wide space between tents, past the rampart at the front and up the slope, the gate of Munda had opened. Clearly it was a well-planned attack. Having insinuated themselves into Caesar's forces, the deserters would wait for the signal and then attack the Caesarian army from within their own lines, while the garrison of Munda would sally and take advantage of the chaos to tear great holes in Fabius' force.

It was not going to happen that way now. Not since the Tenth had arrived and the Caesarian force had been ready for it. Four men fell in at Niger's heel, and then a centurion joined them from another line between tents, bringing five more. Others were converging on the camp, moving in small numbers, tent-parties mostly. They had been posted in small, unobtrusive groups all around the enemy. Just as the Pompeians were spread out in small numbers so as to appear almost invisible, so Fronto's men had done the same to them. One century of Pompeians was facing three centuries of men flooding at them from all sides.

The enemy had managed to muster half a dozen fully armed and armoured soldiers, who had dropped into a shield wall, blocking the way between tents in front of Niger. As the Caesarians bore down on the line, the entire siege camp now up in arms with a din of action, the centurion beside Niger directed several of his men to a new course. As they moved to meet the shield wall, others peeled off, disappearing into the tents to either side and then emerging from underneath the leather panels, past the shield wall and inside the Pompeian camp. Niger and his men hit that line of men hard, knocking several back, and the tribune dispatched the first with relative ease, ducking a clumsy thrust and, while in a crouch, slamming his own blade up into the man's inner thigh, next to his groin. Blood gushed in torrents from the well aimed blow, and Niger's fist glistened wetly in the moonlight as he pulled his hand free, shoved the screaming legionary out of the way and piled on into the camp. In his wake, the impressed centurion and his men dealt with the Pompeian resistance, but Niger was focused. Fronto had given him this specific position for one reason and one reason alone and, as he burst into the centre where men were still arming in a panic and throwing each other equipment, his gaze fell on the figure of Turpio at the centre, busily waving his vitis at his men and using it to stab out, giving orders.

'Turpio!'

The centurion paused in the midst of bellowing orders at a soldier, turning, vine stick held out. His eyes lit upon the tribune, and he gave a single nod. A legionary came running at Niger from beyond the centurion, blade out, yelling imprecations, but Turpio simply shoved the man aside, out of the way. The surprised Pompeian frowned in confusion at his centurion, but shrugged and ran off to fight someone else.

There was no preamble. Turpio spoke not a word as he broke into a run. This was no honour duel now, but a fight to the death between a loyal Caesarian officer and a traitor. Niger had just his sword, but as he stepped resolutely forth to meet the running centurion, his gaze lit on a sword standing proud of a body, and he pulled it free, hefting it in his left hand.

Turpio hit him from the side, angling at the last moment, his sword slashing even as the vitis came down in a separate blow. Niger leaned precariously back, the sword tip whispering past his chest, and thrust up the weapon in his off-hand, catching the descending vine stick. He spun as he straightened, his counter-strikes coming instantly and with the placement of a professional.

His sword touched Turpio's pteruges as the man leapt away, but his left hand blade landed a heavy blow on the centurion's vine stick. He noted in that split second a wince as the shockwave from the blow carried up the vitis and into the centurion's hand and arm, and that, he knew, would be his way in.

The two men spun apart and then launched at one another again, a flurry of blows, each expertly dealt, each expertly parried and dodged, and then, as they remained locked in combat, the blows came thick and fast, Niger giving ground under the barrage of swords and sticks. Yet even as he backed away, he kept one eye warily on the hand gripping the vitis. Each blow from that stout length of vine was a good strike, but Niger, aware of the problem, could tell that already the blows from it were lighter, weaker than before. And though even Turpio probably wasn't aware he was doing it, Niger could see the slight flicker in the centurion's eyes every time he felt a tremor through his left wrist.

He felt Turpio's energy waning with the constant onslaught, while he had preserved his, blocking and sidestepping neatly, and as the centurion's latest blow went slightly wide with expended effort, Niger went on the offensive once more. In a heartbeat they were retracing their steps, Turpio now forced back under the flurry of strikes, but Niger was doing more than trying to tire his opponent, and he was maintaining his energy, not attempting any powerful blow to break through the centurion's defences. What he was doing was concentrating on that weakening hand.

The turning point came as they neared where they'd started, and Turpio held his vitis out wide to block the latest of Niger's swings. At the last moment, the tribune pulled in his right hand, and both blades slammed against the vitis. The sheer force of the double blow sent the stick sailing away through the air out of suddenly numb fingers.

Turpio snarled in frustration and came back with renewed vigour, his sword nicking Niger's arm and drawing blood, but even as they once more battled across the corpse-littered ground, the tribune giving way as he went, the dynamic had changed. With only one weapon, Turpio was now facing two sword blows each time. He was fast, and he was good, but even he could not manage to block two blows repeatedly and still find time to deliver one of his own. As his exhaustion and his frustration began to tell, now Niger began to use all his force, the reserves of strength he had built up by economy of movement throughout. His spinning and lancing blades came fast and unexpectedly from all sorts of angles, and Turpio's expression became panicked as he struggled to stop them.

Suddenly, it was over. One of Niger's strikes had caught the centurion's blade, but instead of being turned by it, the man's arm now too weak to push hard, it slid down the steel to the hilt, where it jumped from the guard and took the tops from Turpio's knuckles.

The centurion bellowed in pain, lurching back, trying hard to maintain a hold on his sword with the agonising feeling in his hand. By the time his grip had strengthened enough for another swing, Turpio had lost.

He looked down at his arm as the blade fell from it. As he'd lifted the sword, Niger had struck. He'd not had the angle for the man's armpit, but the blade had cut deep into the bicep, severing the artery within. Blood gushed free and poured down the man's arm, splashing his side.

Turpio frowned at the wound, as if not knowing what it meant. Niger knew. It meant death. Only a good surgeon was going to stop that flow, and the Pompeians had no medical staff here. Turpio was going to be dead by the count of fifty and nothing would stop it now. Niger took a breath and stepped back, lowering his arms.

Turpio lifted his gaze from his own arm to the tribune and focused glazing eyes on him. He gave a single nod, and fell to the ground.

Niger, heaving in breaths now, turned.

The fight in the camp had finished some time ago, the Pompeians outnumbered three to one, and the Caesarians from two different legions who had destroyed the enemy in their midst had spent the latter part of the fight watching this duel.

'Remove the bodies,' he said in a tired voice. 'Then get some sleep. Next, we take Munda.'

As the men scattered, he turned. The sally that had poured forth from the city had taken one look at what was happening in Caesar's lines and had changed their mind, retreating and slamming the gates, though not before the Caesarian archers and artillery had killed a hundred or so of them.

Munda teetered.

Marius' Mules XIV: The Last Battle

CHAPTER TWENTY FOUR

Late April 45 BC

Fronto crouched in the dark, peering out at the city gate, huddling beside the walls. His eyes, white in the darkness, played across the landscape outside the town and then back towards the Caesarian siege lines. What had seemed like such a good idea in a warm, bright tent a couple of days ago now looked awfully dangerous and unlikely.

The signal would be given any time now. Currently the camps encircling Munda looked the same as they had done every night since that attempted betrayal, though that was as much an illusion as the traitors' oath had been. In reality, Fronto knew, the camps would be crawling with people getting prepared, last moment things being put into place.

His gaze moved to the forty eight men of the understrength century of the Tenth legion who waited with him, and then out, past the gate to the shadowy, nebulous shapes of the other diminished century under Atenos. Less than a hundred men altogether. Not a lot upon which to rest the end of a war.

The plan had been simple enough. When the traitors in their midst had risen, the town's garrison had been ready to sally forth and attempt to cut Caesar's army to pieces. The tension in the following days in Munda must have been unbearable, for it had been clear that there were people within who would happily surrender the town just to get it over with, and there had been fights inside. Yet still, Munda held. The notion was to repeat the near disaster.

If the garrison could be made to think that the rebels had survived to make a second attempt, perhaps they could be persuaded to sally forth once more. And the last time they had done it, the only reason the city had prevailed had been because they had retreated and closed the gates before the Caesarian forces could catch them. Not a second time. This time, if Munda disgorged its military, Fronto would make sure those gates stayed under Caesarian control long enough for the city to fall.

It had taken three hours to get into position. Every man here had been prepared carefully. Every one wore a tunic that had been dyed black. Every man had rubbed damp soot onto their blade to prevent shine, similarly marking their faces. No one wore gleaming and noisy armour. They had even moved with their blades out, leaving the scabbards back in camp. The only noise any of them had made during their journey across the open ground had been the soft pad of their boots on the earth.

The lads back in camp, as part of their show, had made plenty of noise and drawn lots of attention with faked arguments in camp, tugging at the eyes of the city's watchers as black figures scuttled through the dark, moving carefully. The shadowy force used the abandoned and broken remnants of earlier assaults as cover, nipping from charred timber carcass to charred timber carcass until they pulled themselves flat against the wall of Munda beside their mates, directly underneath the garrison, who would have to lean out over the parapet to see so close to the wall's base.

Three hours and much distraction it had taken, but now the black-clad force was in place, hidden and remarkably close to the gate. Now it was all down to how convincing Niger and the rest of the Tenth could be, and how desperate and gullible the rebels had become.

Along with the others Fronto waited, tense, continually forcing himself not to fidget, to drum his fingers on his arm and so on. When one of the legionaries had given a stifled cough half an hour ago, every man had tensed, ready for the worst, which had never come.

He had begun to worry that he might miss the signal, but when it came, he realised that there'd been no chance of that. He grinned as he peered out across the dark, debris-strewn no-man's-land towards the Caesarian lines. For days now, since the uprising, they had made sure to have the survivors of the rebel plot clearly visible, being punished and contained by the Tenth in full view of the walls. Several hundred rebels had been captured and the garrison of Munda were well aware of both that and of where they were being kept.

Only tonight, just after dark, those rebel prisoners had been moved quietly away, into the camp of the Fifth, and men of the Tenth had taken their place, pretending to be the prisoners. Now, just when everything seemed calm, those fake rebels had risen against their captors. It was incredibly convincing, Fronto had to admit. It began slowly and quietly, just a little motion, then a few screams, then the increasing din of combat. Finally, desperate-sounding calls went up from the musicians of the Tenth, and as the fake revolt truly kicked off, the Caesarian lines folded in on themselves in chaos, those men on watch at the ramparts running back into the camp to help stop the rising.

The men by the city walls tensed.

Nothing happened.

Fronto pinched the bridge of his nose and asked a favour of several gods.

Above, atop the wall, men were shouting and pointing out at the Caesarian lines. There were arguments. Still nothing really happened.

When the gates finally opened, Fronto had been on the brink of ordering his men back to camp. He and the others each pressed themselves back against the dark wall, barely visible in the black. The mob that emerged cared little for looking about themselves and considering what might be lurking in the dark. Their gaze was firmly fixed on what looked like a crumbling weak spot in the siege lines. Right now there was virtually no one there to stop them ploughing into the Tenth's camp.

Fronto watched, trying not to grin. The sheer volume of men hurtling out of the gate had to represent the bulk of the city's garrison. He waited until the last of them ran out, the entire mob pounding, with little in the way of organisation, across the dark ground towards the Caesarian lines. Once they were at least twenty paces from the gate, he gave the signal. A single arm wave.

Ninety six men ran at the gate from the two sides. The enemy above, atop the walls, continued to watch the progress of their own sally, hopeful, completely unaware of the danger swarming towards them below. The men of the two centuries hit the gate at the same time. The twin leaves of timber were each being held by two soldiers, ready to shut them if the sally went wrong. The look of utter shock on their faces was almost amusing as Fronto and Atenos and their black-clad men burst through the archway and attacked in eerie silence. Dark shapes mobbed the few men holding the city gate.

Fronto, close to the head of the attack, leapt at one of the men gripping the timber. The soldier had managed to pull his blade just an inch from the mouth of his sheath when Fronto's own sword slashed into his neck, crushing the windpipe and gullet even as it cut into flesh. The man never even had the luxury of screaming, just a panicked hissing gurgle emerging from his ruined throat.

Similar scenes were playing out across the gateway. Men were dying with every heartbeat as the black legionaries poured across the defences. Atenos stopped inside the walls, blood running from his blade, pointing at the doorways into the gate towers. One of them had been closed by a quick-thinking defender, but the other remained open. Men of the Tenth hurtled for that door, barging in as someone tried to close it. The alarm was now going up atop the wall, horns blaring.

Fronto left the primus pilus to direct his men. With a couple of men ahead and several behind, he ran for one of the stairways that climbed to the wall, and pounded up them two at a time, heaving in breaths and promising himself for the thousandth time that year that when he got home he'd get Masgava on to designing a fitness regime once more.

Atop the wall, he took it all in over a matter of heartbeats. At the expense of any other approach to the city, the defenders on the wall were all running towards this gate to try and halt the breach. Along with the odd stragglers now emerging from the city itself, arming as they ran for the walls, they would be sufficient to overcome Fronto's force. Looking out across the dark, he prepared to make the decision.

If the force that had sallied had quickly turned around and were running back for the city, Fronto and his men would have to shut the gates until they could be dealt with by the besieging army, and he would then have to hold the gates against all comers from inside.

He watched carefully, trying to judge the outcome of what he was seeing. As his professional eye took it in, and he predicted what would happen, he heaved a sigh of relief. Niger and the Tenth had done their job perfectly. They had left a hole big enough to entice the entire rebel attack, and the sallying force had fallen for it completely. The rebels had charged into the Caesarian camp only to discover that the whole thing had been a ruse, that there was no rebel uprising happening there, that in fact the Tenth legion were armed and ready, waiting for them. But the moment realisation had dawned on them, and they had let out panicked cries and turned to run back to the city, the Tenth and their fellow legions had closed the trap, cohorts supported by Gallic cavalry racing to cut them off and seal them inside their enemy's camp. There was no hope of them returning to Munda's gate now, and even as Fronto watched he could tell that the enemy force was shrinking rapidly as they were overcome.

Of course, there would be many more in the city, and now the alarm had been raised, they were racing to stop Fronto. He looked down over the parapet inside to see Atenos looking up at him, questioning.

'Keep them open. Our lads are coming.'

The centurion nodded, and began to gesture once more, throwing out pointing fingers. Carts were overturned, blocking streets approaching the gate, barrels and timbers moved into place. The men at the gate itself hefted the twin bars used to seal it, carried them outside and cast them into a shallow ditch, preventing the gates being shut tight. While in the arch, they lifted the torches from their sconces to each side and began to wave them back at their own lines, signalling that the gate was fully under their control.

Men of Munda were now reaching them from the city streets, fighting to regain control of the gate, but Atenos and his men were still erecting their barricade and paused long enough to put down any man trying to stop them. One gate tower remained under the control of the garrison, its doors sealed, though it was no problem for the Caesarians. Eventually they would have to come out, and until then they could do nothing of value.

The main danger right now was coming along the walls, but already men of the Tenth, still blackened but now liberally spattered with blood, were forming a wall against them using shields taken from the fallen defenders. They had only to hold long enough.

Fronto watched as the barricade rose inside, shielding Atenos and his men from the increasing number of men emerging from the city streets. Not everyone was arrayed against them, though, for as he watched, tiles and bricks were hurled down from rooftops and upper storeys, smashing into the garrison as they ran through the streets below. The soldiers might rush to hold Caesar out, but it seemed that the general was less unpopular with some of the citizens.

A new noise arose outside, and Fronto turned to look out into the darkness. All was changing out there now. What was left of the rebels' sallying force was now being overwhelmed somewhere in the heart of the camp, lost for good. The threat, such as it was, being nullified, the legions of Fabius Maximus were on the move, rolling towards the open gate like a tide of brutality. Fronto nodded his satisfaction. They would not have to hold for long.

Rebels were reaching the men of the Tenth on the ramparts now, hammering at their shield walls, trying to break through and seize their own gate, but their level of desperation was clear as they threw themselves into the fight, heedless of the danger. For every blow they delivered to Fronto's men, three of their own were thrown back, bleeding and crying out in agony. He saw the line falter for a moment as one of his legionaries howled, dropping his shield and clutching his face as he toppled from the wall, and leapt forward to fill the space, fighting down the irritation and slight disappointment as another of the soldiers from the blackened Tenth slipped in before him, grabbing the shield and plugging the gap.

He straightened and turned, looking about the scene once more. The legions of Caesar's army were flooding towards the gate and at this point the enemy could not possibly hope to hold them out any longer. Of course, they did not know that. The poor bastards down in the street couldn't know yet that a sizeable part of their garrison had been butchered to a man out in the darkness, while three legions now moved in to take the city. All they knew was that a small group of enemies had seized the gate and it had to be retaken.

As such, the fighting down at Atenos' barricade was fierce. Fronto watched as more and more rebels hurried from the city streets, but in mere moments everything changed. With a roar, men of the Third Legion poured through the city gate into the space behind Atenos' barricade, and the carts were pushed back upright and wheeled to the side, barrels, crates and sacks cast away to allow access to the city now. The enemy, moments earlier leaping at the defences to get to the Caesarians, were now running the other way in panic. Back among the streets, from his advantageous viewpoint, Fronto could see that men were emerging from buildings and side streets, learning what had happened and were flinging away their weapons and shields, stripping down to tunics alone in an attempt to blend into the civilian populace and avoid capture or potential execution at the hands of the victors.

Nothing could stop it now. Munda had fallen. The last but one stronghold of rebel Hispania was theirs.

***

May 45 BC

Munda was a hard fight. I lost three centurions in the battle and another during the siege that followed. Between these last two cities we took so many prisoners we could have repopulated Tarraco if we wanted. ~~The siege lines were~~ *Tell the boys that their father was the man to end it all. That it was me who led the assault on the gate of Munda and held the walls until the city fell. It was magnificent.* ~~We had to put up a temporary rampart in~~ *I expect Caesar will take all the credit in due course, but it was Fabius Maximus, Atenos and myself who took Munda. I will tell you all about it when I am home, and that time is fast approaching now, my love. All that remains is to sort out a few political issues, settle some veterans and try to find the renegade Sextus Pompey who has crawled under a rock somewhere. It is all over, Lucilia. The war is over. I can come home. Tell the boys I'm coming home. And then I ~~promise~~ I tell you now that I won't be going on any new cam*

Fronto paused, lifting his pen and looking back over his words. Sighing and grinding his teeth, he grasped the parchment and crumpled it into a ball, throwing it to the ground where it rolled to a halt amid half a dozen similar cast-offs. He'd never been much good at letters, and Lucilia had told him so on more than one occasion. No matter what he tried they always came off looking like military reports that gradually dissolved into drivelling promises. It wasn't that he didn't know what he wanted to say, or even that he couldn't say it, it just sat in his mind as he picked up the paper and then sort of turned into troop dispositions and warbling wetness as it reached the pen.

He sighed and rose, stretching and reaching for the wine jar. He'd write the letter in the morning. For now there was an informal meeting of officers to go to at Fabius' tent. The message, delivered by a grinning centurion, had made it clear that the word 'informal' was the priority. As such, Fronto had foregone armour and uniform, settling for a comfy tunic and a cloak against the evening chill. He'd even taken the last of his good Falernian to share with the other officers, though if Fabius referred to himself in the third person one more time, Fronto might just sacrifice the wine and throw the jar at him.

As he emerged from his tent, he peered off to the north and pondered on the past couple of weeks while he walked through the camp. All around, the legions rested for the evening, cooking meals over the myriad camp fires, drinking a double wine ration and telling each other exaggerated stories of their own heroism and of the women they had known during the campaign. Many of the officers still would not cross the camp without a small entourage, but Fronto was happier on his own, especially among the Tenth, and men respectfully greeted him as he passed. He acknowledged each in turn, his gaze always returning to the city nearby. The city of Urso, the last stronghold of the rebels, theirs. Munda had fallen in that one night, fourteen thousand prisoners and enemy dead to stand witness to the victory. They had stayed only a few days, installing a small garrison, and had then moved on to the last fight.

They had reached Urso, just ten miles from Munda, with ease, and had then sagged, sighed and settled in for another long haul. Urso had a much smaller garrison, was less well protected by walls and by nature, and harboured fewer supplies. Knowing the disadvantages they were at, however, the garrison had done what they could to tip the scales against the Caesarian army. The nearest usable water source lay eight miles from the walls, the town reliant upon wells, and the garrison had made sure that the Caesarians had no ready access by filling in and destroying any wells nearby. Moreover, they had felled every source of timber for some five or six miles and either hoarded it in the city or burned it outside to remove the raw materials needed for a siege.

The four legions had resigned themselves to a difficult time, then. They had begun to create siege lines around the city and created a huge supply chain all the way back to Munda, bringing food, water, timber and other raw materials all the way to Urso.

Whether it was their determination and the inescapable conclusion that Urso was doomed no matter what they did, or whether it was terror at the number of men besieging them, or possibly just the weariness of the protracted war, things had changed. Something had driven the final nail into the crucifixion of the rebel cause the day the huge cisterns spaced around the siege camps had been filled with water from the wagons. The gates of Urso had opened, and a local oil merchant had come out to negotiate the surrender of that last town. It seemed that no one above the rank of centurion remained in command of Urso or its forces. The senior officers and the members of the ordo who had declared against Caesar had been pressed to surrender by the citizens of Urso and in the end, facing inevitable loss, they had, to a man, opened their own veins. The centurions had swiftly acceded to the wishes of the townspeople and agreed to lay down their arms.

Simply grateful that the war could be ended without another protracted siege, Fabius Maximus and the other legates had listened to the terms the merchant offered on behalf of the town and had agreed to them. The military therein would be disarmed and retired with no punishment. The people of Urso would be allowed to continue about their life undisturbed, paying only a small reparation for their part in the war, which would in the end help pay for the settlement of the veterans.

That had been this morning. Since then the army had gradually taken control of the town, and Fabius had composed reports for the general, which had been sent off with a courier just after noon. The rebels were done. The war was over. No town in the peninsula now held out against Caesar. The land was just tired and desired nothing more than to return to peace and attempt to rebuild.

Fronto took a last look at Urso on the brow of the hill, at the camp of the disarmed garrison now under watch by men of Caesar's legions, and slipped into the command tent.

'Gods but are you always this late, Fronto? Caesar warned me you were never on time.'

A chorus of chuckles suggested that the wine had been open for a while already. Fronto glowered at his peers. 'I was under the impression this was an informal gathering. I can always piss off back to my own tent. I've a letter to write.'

There were nods at that. Every man here had spent time writing to their loved ones since the fall of Urso. Fronto found an empty seat and sank into it. Before he could do anything about his drink, Fabius' slave hurried over with a fin, brightly-coloured glass goblet and took the jug from the legate, pouring a glass and then cutting it with a generous amount of water. Fronto narrowed his eyes, determining that if the slave were to be so generous with the water, he might have to pour his own from now on.

'I've had word from the general,' Fabius said. 'I was just telling everyone.'

'Do your messengers have wings now?'

'What?'

'You only sent your report this afternoon and Gades is eighty miles or more from here.'

Fabius rolled his eyes. 'It's not a *reply*, Fronto. Caesar's courier was bound for Munda, but passed through here on the way and happened upon us. The general is finished with Gades and has moved to Hispalis. There he intends to spend two months settling the affairs of Hispania before returning to Rome. Sadly that means that my reports will reach an empty palace in Gades and have to be forwarded on. But still, two more months and then home.'

Fronto sagged. 'I was just telling my wife I would be home soon.'

Fabius nodded wearily. 'I think we're all looking forward to going home, but Caesar is rather insistent that we stay on and return with him. It would not look good if the moment the fighting was done all his officers buggered off into retirement. He wants us to be visible all over the peninsula for a couple of months to remind everyone that the republic is back in control, and when he returns to Rome he wants to do it with his officers and entourage. Imagine how it's going to go down in Rome, Fronto. The war being over. Caesar coming home. It'll be big. The biggest thing in Rome in decades.'

'I have never been to Rome,' Tribune Niger murmured quietly. 'I think I shall enjoy that.'

'Nowhere like it,' Fabius replied. 'Greatest city in the world.'

'Smells like a horse with diarrhoea in the summer and like frozen vomit in the winter. Full of squawking noblewomen and senators who can bore you to death without even opening their mouths. You'll love it.'

Fabius gave him an odd look and Fronto hissed through his teeth and scrubbed his eyes with the heels of his hands before picking up his glass and taking a mouthful. 'I've walked away from the legions a few times, Quintus, and I've always come back. I've only ever felt at home on the battlefield but, you know what? I think these last few years have ended that for me. I'm finally ready. I'm prepared to try my hand at gardening. Or fishing. Or just sitting on the veranda with my boys and telling them stories. I'm ready to go home, if Rome could be said to be home.'

'Will you stay in Rome, then?' Niger asked him. 'I understand you have land in Hispania.'

Fronto nodded. 'I've a villa near Tarraco. I like it there, but I think I want the boys to experience Rome for a year or two. It'll do them good. Teach them how corrupt and shitty a city can get, at least, make them appreciate the provinces. Then, yes, Tarraco.'

He looked across at Atenos, whose expression was unreadable, but certainly not content. 'And many of my friends from the Tenth will be settled nearby at Narbo.'

Atenos caught his eye, frowning, but saying nothing.

'Well whatever the future holds, at least we should have seen the last of blood,' Fabius sighed, gesturing to the slave who crossed the tent and refilled his glass.

'We'll all drink to that.'

* * *

Sextus Pompey climbed the ramp of the merchant ship and turned to look back. The city of Carthago Nova sat noisy and filled with life, encircled by high, grey hills, the arms reaching out to the waterline. The ship rocked gently even here in the harbour.

Behind him his small guard of nine men helped bring his pack horses aboard. The ship's owner, a trader out of Agrigentum, was barely looking at him. The man might be slightly more animated if he knew that the rich man he'd agreed to transport back to Sicilia on his return journey was Sextus Pompey, the sole surviving architect of the resistance to Caesar. The last republican in the republic, in Sextus' opinion. He was going by the name of Marcus Oppimius Marsala for the moment, a rich equestrian with a thriving business, a corporation controlling several quarries of marble and other valuable stones. Ostensibly he was visiting Sicilia to arrange new contracts for his goods. His heavy saddle bags and chests on the cart contained samples of his wares. Indeed, if one opened any of them, one would find just such. Marble, tufa, sandstone and more. One would have to dig to find the layer of rough sacks and then, beneath it the wealth of gold and silver brought from Corduba before it fell.

For Sextus Pompey had absolutely no intention of simply lying down and handing power and control to Caesar. His father had been the greatest general in Roman history and had stood between Caesar and despotism. His brother had been foolhardy, listening to that lunatic Labienus and marching out to fight Caesar, when making the general sweat to take cities had been the clear solution.

And what had they to show for it? Labienus suckling the teat of Hades in the soil of Munda and Gnaeus' head rotting on a spear tip at Hispalis.

He could see Philo, his secretary, giving him a strange look and turned his back on the man. Philo was worried. There was nowhere in the republic they could go, the secretary had said in one of his most outspoken moments. Nowhere that the name of Pompey continued to carry any weight.

Sextus knew different. He had friends here and there, and he had a large sum of money. He would disappear for a time, living a quiet and lucrative life with a small entourage, building a new web of contacts and allies. Oh, there was no one left willing to stand against Caesar now. But within a year the general would think everything had settled and all was peace. His legions would be stood down and retired. His focus would be on Rome, his Aegyptian bitch of a lover and his half-breed runt of a son, on the gold of that ancient land, on the trouble in Syria and on the ever-present threat of Parthia. His gaze would ever look east.

And then Pompey would rise once more. When Caesar thought he was safe, he would almost certainly continue his empire building, pissing off the wrong people, and then, when the despot had almost forgotten he existed, Sextus would return to Hispania and begin again, raising new armies and preparing for war, for Caesar may have suppressed the peninsula, but he'd not conquered it. Once his grip had loosened sufficiently, Hispania would again seethe with resentment, ready for a new uprising.

The ship lurched as the sailors pulled in the ropes.

Philo was waving him over. Sextus Pompey was a far too recognisable face, even with his burgeoning beard, and Philo had worried all the way from Corduba that someone would recognise them, take all the gold, imprison them and deliver them to Caesar. Once they were out to sea, they should be safe. And landing in Sicilia they would swiftly be among friends.

Yes, he decided as the ship slid between the arms of the harbour, slipping out into the sea and away from the high grey peaks, yes, the world had not seen the last of Sextus Pompey.

And the next time, he would do it right.

CHAPTER TWENTY FIVE

June 45 BC

'I am considering issuing commemorative coinage,' Caesar mused as his body slave massaged the day's tension from his shoulders.

Fronto glanced across at Galronus, but the Remi's expression was unreadable.

'For a tree?'

'Sorry?' Caesar opened his eyes and turned to Fronto.

'You're commemorating a *tree*? Did something hit you in the head today?'

They both turned to look at the tree. As palm trees went, it was not a spectacular specimen. It was straggly, partially denuded and looked thirsty and brown, but… it was a tree.

'What the tree *represents*, Fronto. The new shoot. We will have to issue new coinage, anyway, of course. I will run any decisions by the vigintivirate in Rome, but with appropriate permissions that I am sure I can secure, we could have them minted directly in Hispania, since the silver will come from here anyway. It seems appropriate to celebrate the return of the peninsula to the republic with Hispanic silver minted on Hispanic soil. The tree is an excellent analogy for what has happened here.'

'It's an excellent analogy for firewood,' Fronto murmured.

The tree was starting to annoy him now. A week ago it had been funny, but the humour in it had waned with experience. They only had Caesar's word for it that the tree marked his position during the siege, and the general hadn't even been involved in the fighting anyway, being a bystander at best.

The general had been staying and working in the forum of Hispalis for the past half month when he'd visited the army's camp outside the city and discovered the tree – the army was, of course, camped a polite distance from the walls, in the same place it had been when Hispalis was under siege.

The story was already spreading throughout the army, and the province beyond. A tree that Caesar had used as his command position during the siege of Hispalis, and which had appeared to be dead, had given off a new green shoot immediately following the fall of the rebel stronghold. It was a major omen, apparently. Priests and augurs were overjoyed, reading great things into it, for Caesar, for the republic, for Hispania. Caesar was already seeing it as the omen of a new, fresh Hispania, loyal and powerful under his aegis.

Fronto was seeing it differently. His pragmatic mind told him that Caesar had selected the tree as his supposed command point because of the shoot. He seemed to remember Caesar's tent being considerably further to the north, and he was sure Caesar simply stood out the front of his tent. And the general had had about as much to do with the taking of Hispalis as he'd had to do with suckling Romulus and Remus. Fronto knew, because he'd been there. And he'd seen palm trees, too. That green shoot was half a year old in his opinion. Whoever had started this rumour about the magical tree had overlooked a number of fairly simple facts. But that was the thing about priests and augurs. They never let the facts get in the way of a good story. And Caesar was, of course, using it to his advantage. The general had never been more popular, and this tale was probably already crossing the sea to be passed from breathless peasant to breathless peasant across the republic.

Another slave approached Fronto, bowing his head and offering a towel and a massage. Fronto shook his head, waving him away and calling for the wine boy instead, then grumbling as he had to wait for Galronus to have his wine poured first. When had things changed so much that Gauls were served wine before Romans?

'Perhaps it could even be seen as a validation of everything we have done,' Caesar added, then groaned gently as the slave began to pound his shoulder.

'So you're going to use it as an excuse to conquer some more?' Fronto grumbled, watching the wine boy and Galronus impatiently.

Caesar threw him a sharp look. 'I forget sometimes how outspoken you can be, Fronto.' He sighed. 'But in essence you're not far from the mark.'

'If you don't stand the legions down and agree to let go the dictatorship, you're going to make a lot of enemies in Rome. You're immensely popular right now, but there are still those who think you aim for a crown. Don't feed their rumours.'

Caesar shook his head. 'I don't mean to do it like that. Not like a king. But I have plans, for the republic. Until Rome no one could have matched the empire of Alexander.'

'Not this again,' Fronto grunted, rolling his eyes and holding out his glass as the wine boy finally reached him. Many years ago, when they'd first been in Hispania together, Caesar had picked up a minor obsession with the Macedonian king and his exploits. He'd vowed to better them. It had not been mentioned in so long that Fronto had almost forgotten about it.

'It is a matter of pride in the republic, Fronto, not personal glory.'

'Of *course* not. How could *that* be,'

Another acidic glance from the general.

'The simple fact is, Fronto, that with the addition of Gaul to the republic, we are close to being able to challenge Alexander. Rome will be the greatest empire the world has ever known, and I will help to make that happen.'

'You know an empire has an emperor, don't you?'

'Fronto, I am talking about expansion. About a republic that spans the world, unopposed. Now that things are settled across the west, only the east remains to be dealt with. Syria is in foment, and needs to be settled.'

'Not by swords. Not with blood.'

'However it can be. It needs to happen. But we are almost ready to accept Aegyptus into our great republic. Its days as an empire of its own are long gone, and its time as a client state are more or less ended. The young Ptolemy pup has no destiny of rule, and Cleopatra sees the future of her people as part of Rome. Within my lifetime, and I have a good decade of activity in me yet, Fronto, I will see Aegyptus as a province of Rome. Soon, I hope. And If I can secure the governorship of that new province, basing myself in Alexandria, I can turn my attention towards Rome's other great enemy of old.'

'The camel? The pyramid? The dung beetle?'

'Fronto, I swear you are deliberately trying to rile me.'

'Sorry. I'm tired.'

'Centuries ago, the Gauls sacked our holy places. They invaded Rome itself. For hundreds of years, the people of Rome lived with the shadow of the savage Gaul over them. Now they are free of it. Those savage Gauls who sacked Rome wear togas and drink wine.'

Fronto threw a look at Galronus with a wicked grin. The Remi, clad in a Roman tunic and holding a glass of wine, narrowed his eyes dangerously.

'The other ancient enemy,' Caesar went on, 'is Parthia. Alexander managed to conquer them, but his premature death and the collapse of his empire without an heir saw it separate once more and rise again into a dangerous power. From a Roman Aegyptus, if Syria is settled, we can campaign against Parthia and bring that ancient land into the republic. Then we will have outdone Alexander, and our borders will sport no dangerous ancient enemy. Admit it, Fronto, that this is something to value.'

'Convenient that it also gives you the opportunity to start again as you did in Gaul.'

'It has value.'

'Parthia is a field of death. Everyone who attacks Parthia loses. Alexander, dead of fever… *in Parthia*. Crassus. Lost in battle and, if the rumours are true, executed by having molten gold poured into his avaricious mouth… *in Parthia*. Is further conquest truly that important?'

'You would have me retire? Fronto, I know you and your friends refer to me as the old man, but I am fifty five summers, no more. I've only a few years on you. Crassus was seven years older than I when he invaded Parthia. Pompey was two years older than I am now when he led the opposition against us. Are *you* ready to lay down your sword?'

Fronto shifted uncomfortably in his seat. His wine seemed to have evaporated rather fast. He waved the slave over and was further annoyed that the boy once again went first to Galronus, who was still glaring at him over the Gaul comments.

'You know what, Caesar? I am. I'm ready. I promised Lucilia that this would be my last campaign. I missed my boys growing up so far, and I don't want to miss the rest. And I'm getting creaky.'

'You will move into politics?'

Fronto snorted. 'Hardly. If I were going to do that I'd have climbed the cursus like a good little patrician long ago. No. I intend to retire. Properly retire.'

Caesar gave a light chuckle. 'If anyone had asked me back in Cremona when we first prepared to move against the Helvetii, when you were wearing that gods-awful cloak your sister made you, what Fronto would be like in fourteen years' time after fighting across half the world, the last phrase that would have leapt to my mind was *family man*.'

'Well I changed. You will, too, now you have a son.'

The general's face took on a troubled look and Fronto regretted bringing it up, for the mood changed in an instant. Caesar could adopt Caesarion into his family, but the public outrage might just bring him down. It would be killing the general inside to finally have a true son and heir, but not to be able to acknowledge him as such without putting any reputation and inheritance in jeopardy.

'It's time we went home,' he said, finally. 'Lusitania is calm as long as we have men there. There are no rumbles of rebellion, your enemies are dead, and Sextus vanished but hunted and with no hope of starting again. We've seen every important person from every important colony in Hispania this past month. You've made it clear that everything is over, and Hispania is sorted. Are you going to drag this out because of a tree?'

'We are almost done, Marcus. Almost. But there are a few small matters to attend to yet.'

Fronto heard a slight shuffle and looked up to see Galronus darting his eyes meaningfully to the exit. 'I think it's time I turned in. I'm sure I'll have a busy day tomorrow standing around and looking important behind you.'

Caesar chuckled again. 'Very well. Good night both. Briefing at the Third Hour.'

As the two men left Caesar's tent and padded out into the warm evening air, Fronto saw a familiar figure approaching. Quintus Pedius gave them an easy smile. 'The general in a good mood?'

Fronto snorted. 'Planning his next conquest.'

'Hasn't he enough women yet?' Pedius grinned wickedly, and the comment made even the dour-faced Galronus smile.

'Try and persuade him it's time to go back to Rome,' Fronto advised.

'I've been trying to do that for a week now. I think he's become addicted to being adored.'

'I've known your great uncle most of my life. That is nothing new, believe me.'

With a laugh, Pedius strode on to the general's tent, while Fronto and Galronus angled back towards where the Tenth were camped nearby. 'You wanted out?'

Galronus shrugged. 'His attitude was beginning to annoy me. Say what you like about Labienus, he valued my people and saw greatness in them. I always thought Caesar did, but it sounds now as though he only values my people if they are Romans.'

'Ignore it. The world moves on. At least your people thrive. Of all the tribes, the Remi were the only one to side with us from the beginning. They're the oinly tribe to have come through the last decade largely untouched. In fact, I think Caesar's patronage has made your people rich.'

Galronus just brushed that aside. He stopped, then, and Fronto walked on a couple of paces before realising and turning, in the dark, to his friend. 'What?'

'I want to marry Faleria.'

'You've already planned that. It's all been agreed.'

'This year, I mean. When we get back to Rome.'

'That can be arranged, of course.'

'And then I want to leave Rome.'

Fronto frowned. 'If you can stick around for a year or two with us, then I intend to return to Tarraco and the rural life too.'

'No, Marcus, I want to go home.'

Fronto frowned in confusion for a moment, then blinked. 'Back to Remi lands? Why?'

His friend gave him a scathing look. 'Because it's my home. You want to go home, can you not understand why I do?'

'But you're a senator now. Caesar wants you in Rome for the value that gives you. And Faleria has never been north of Massilia. Massilia is nice. You could live there.'

'Massilia is not home. If Faleria loves me, she'll come with me.'

Fronto sagged. She would. He knew his sister, and he knew what she thought of their friend. He was privately of the opinion that his sister would follow Galronus across the Styx to Hades if he asked. 'You'll be hundreds of miles from the circus and the racing. You'd hate that.'

'If the Remi are to be what Caesar says, then it is time we started to enjoy a few of the benefits of Rome. After a decade of fighting her wars for her, I'd say we deserve it. Marcus, the money I've accrued these past few years will make me one of the richest men in the north. And that's what rich Romans do, no? Build public works for the people. We need an aqueduct at home, but we also need a circus. I can build one. I'm not dragging your sister away from Rome, Marcus. I'm taking Rome home with me.'

Fronto was shaking his head. 'But there's half a thousand miles between Tarraco and Remi lands.'

'We'll visit. And you can too. You can bring your boys.'

Fronto nodded, unhappily. Somehow the evening had soured for him now. The two men traipsed back to their tents, and shunned sleep for a while, gathering in Fronto's quarters. They drank and they talked of things past and things present but not, very deliberately, of things future. When finally Fronto sagged into inebriated slumber, his wine cup clonking to the floor and rolling around, Galronus gave an odd smile, picked up a blanket from the cupboard, draped it across his friend, and left.

* * *

The new arrivals were heralded without a fanfare, just by two riders with spears who reined in, announcing their master to the guard at the camp. Fronto, bleary and wiping his watery eyes repeatedly, joined Pedius as the officer strode across the camp towards the gate, outside which a column of horsemen and carts was approaching, kicking up huge clouds of dust.

'What's all this?' Pedius murmured, gesturing at the gate.

'Who knows. Not military, though, and not local I'd say. No soldiers, just mercenary guards, and they have the look of men from home, not from Hispania.'

Pedius nodded. 'Let's go find out.'

Whoever it was, their credentials had seen them through the camp's lines, for the men at the gateway had stepped readily aside, and the two riders, still armed, had walked their horses in and to one side to make way for the rest of the column.

'I feel we should be on horses,' Pedius said. 'I hate looking up at people like this.'

'You could sit on my shoulders.'

A snort greeted this as the two men fell in side by side, soldiers gathering behind and around them protectively. The column was dusty, suggesting they had been riding across the heartland of Hispania for several days and without a great deal of luxury of a night. Despite Fronto's insistence that it was no officer due to the lack of regular soldiers, as the riders reined in inside the gate and the carts were brought in, two more mercenaries stepped aside to reveal a grey, dusty figure on a white horse wearing extremely expensive-looking, though tastefuly not over-ornate, armour and a white cloak. Of course, all of it was grey and dirty, as was the man's head, short, curly hair and a four-day growth of beard all the same monochrome tone as his face.

'Pedius,' the figure said in a familiar tone, a white smile cracking the grey. 'Fronto.'

Fronto frowned. He fancied he knew just about every officer currently serving in the west, and yet this young man he did not recognise. He was old enough to be a tribune. Maybe he was one of the junior tribunes of another legion, just assigned.

'Do I know you?' Pedius asked quietly, echoing Fronto's thoughts.

'You damn well should, cousin.'

The figure slipped lithely from the horse and landed badly, his knee giving way a little. He straightened. 'Sorry. Not been quite the same since the accident, though I'm told it will disappear entirely in time.'

Fronto stared. 'Octavian?'

Caesar's nephew grinned. 'In the flesh. And the dust, sadly. I know, I know, there are good mansios along every road in the whole peninsula, but that's only any good if you're following one of the main routes. It seems our great uncle's campaign has tied up every available trireme in every port in the west. The only way I could find passage was to sail with a wine merchant to Narbo, then take a series of old roads across the centre of this place until I came to somewhere with a name I'd heard of. I'd never have made it if I hadn't hired a couple of natives at a glorified village called

Bilbilis. This place could benefit from a major overhaul of the road system.'

The young man seemed unable to pause in his monologue, even for breath.

'We bought camping gear at Tarraco. Oh, that's where your villa is, isn't it, Fronto? Very pleasant. Reminds me of the Baiae coast. Anyway, I lashed out on some excellent equipment, which was far from cheap, given how many guards and slaves I have with me, and we camped each night, somewhere close to the road. We saw bandits at one point. I was quite thrilled. I had my sword out ready, but one of the guards explained that they wouldn't come anywhere near travellers as well armed as we were, so they left us alone. We crossed a lot of rivers, too. The place needs more bridges. More roads and more bridges.'

'Breathe,' suggested Fronto.

'Everywhere we went we heard of the exploits you fellows have been involved in. And it seems from what I understand that I've missed everything. Which, of course, was my mother's entire purpose. I have demanded, cajoled, begged and insisted all through my convalescence. Any other man my age with an eye on the Cursus Honorum would be serving as a tribune somewhere, but Mother was able to use my injuries as ammunition in keeping me home. I had thought she'd relented and that it was because I was all but well again that she agreed to my departure, but I have since come to the conclusion that she must have had some letter from my great uncle informing her that the war was over, and so now she felt safe in allowing me to come. How much glory am I likely to accrue now?'

'Breathe,' Fronto said again.

'And yet the armies have not been stood down, I see. And if the legions are still active, then there is a reason for the legions to be active. And that means there is still a place for me and a chance to actually earn some pride. Tell me, Pedius, Fronto, where is the action still to be found?'

'Breathe, for gods' sake,' Fronto grumbled. 'You're going to pass out for lack of air if you don't stop talking.'

'There are a few places we still man,' Pedius said, answering the question.

'Ah yes,' Octavian said with a smile. 'I had heard there were two regions that remained troublesome. A place called Cantabria which has yet to learn of Roman steel, and the region of Lusitania that had the gall to butcher an admiral. Are you still putting down resistance there? I could settle for treading on a few Lusitanian rebels before the winter sets in.'

Fronto took a deep breath himself now. 'Your timing is poor, Octavian. We've just about done. In a month or so Caesar plans to return to Rome. The trouble in Lusitania is almost finished, and starting a war in Cantabria would undo a lot of the strides we've made for peace.'

The young man looked crestfallen, and yet brightened immediately. 'Then I shall have to make good use of what time I have. I know my great uncle is eager to try me in a military role. I'm sure he will give me command of some unit in Lusitania for a few weeds to prove myself.'

Pedius rolled his eyes. 'Octavian, you're fresh out of a boy's tunic. There are rules to all of this. Nobody commands straight away. You get given a junior tribuneship first, so that you can get used to the life, the ranks, the system. A tribune is a glorified coat rack at best. He holds the legate's cloak for him, makes sure there's wine in his tent and runs messages when needed. They're not trusted with anything more strategic than breakfast, and for a good reason. They are new. Fresh. They need to learn.'

Octavian narrowed his eyes at his older cousin, a man who had already made something of a name for himself. 'Really? What is the optimum distance for a pila volley, Pedius?'

'Twenty paces. Any longer and range influences the throw, any shorter and the legionaries don't have time to draw their swords afterwards and be ready.'

'You see?' Octavian said, thrusting a hand at Pedius. 'Wrong.'

'No it isn't. That's straight out of the manual.'

'And that's why it's wrong. Manuals tell you where to start, not where to finish, Quintus. Believe me, I've read every page there is on the art of war, from Greeks masters and Roman.'

'Alright,' Pedius snapped, irritably, 'what is the optimum range for a pila volley, then?'

Octavian smiled an irritating, knowing smile. 'There isn't one.'

'What?'

'There isn't *one*. There are *many*, Quintus.'

'Stop talking in riddles.'

'Think about it. That's what I'm saying. The manual tells you your starting point, but you'll never know the answer until you need it. What's the terrain? Pila have better range downhill. Are there any obstacles? Are you using your best throwers or just whoever happens to be at the front? How far have the men marched that day? Have they been carrying their furca pole with their throwing arm? How nimble are the enemy? Can they dance out of the way or are they stuck in position.'

Fronto found himself chuckling. 'He's got you, Pedius. He's right, and you know it.'

'You always were a clever little arse,' Pedius said, rolling his eyes. 'But arrogance is a dangerous trait, cousin. Keep it in check.'

Octavian bowed his head. 'Of course, Quintus. Sorry. I've travelled hundreds of miles with people whose idea of deep conversation is the size of a woman's chest. I've been looking forward to using my sword, *and* my mind.'

'I'll go and tell the general that you're on the way.'

Octavian nodded. 'Is uncle well?'

'Don't call him uncle. Not in the field. He's a general here. Or consul. Or imperator. If you're talking with the senior officers you can get away with "the old man", but uncle just is not going to go down well. Besides, there is no nepotism here. I've achieved what I have through merit, and men like Fabius Maximus and Fronto here still tend to come ahead of me in the pecking order.'

'Got it,' Octavian said with a smile. 'General it is. Let's go see the general.'

'Get yourself cleaned up first,' Pedius advised.

'Ah, no, I don't think so, cousin. If I swan in looking like a primped senator unc… the general is hardly likely to consider me for any active military role. I've ridden like a cavalryman and slept like a soldier all the way from Tarraco, and I think I'll stay that way to attend Caesar.'

'Suit yourself,' Pedius shrugged, marching off towards the headquarters tent, located at Caesar's now famous palm tree.

Fronto frowned at that thought. He wasn't a particularly superstitious man. Oh, he respected the gods, and avoided temples because they were always bad luck for him, but he wasn't a man to run for an interpreter of omens every time a chicken coughed or a leaf hit him on the head. Yet ignoring Caesar's grand notions of the palm tree representing Hispania, it suddenly occurred to Fronto how apt the small green shoot from the old tree on a field of battle was as an analogy for the young man standing beside him. If ever there was an off-shoot from Caesar's tree…

'Don't get in Pedius' way,' Fronto advised.

'Oh?'

'He has no aspirations for inheritance, I think.' He narrowed his eyes at Octavian. 'He simply wants to make his own name, and he's doing a good job of it. He's worked hard to get where he is, and he's campaigned solidly. Don't piss him off by, in your own words, swanning in here and using him as a stepping stone.'

Octavian turned a frown on him. 'Not my intention. Similarly, I want to make my own way. I like Quintus. Of my cousins, he's by far the best. He's a good soldier and a good commander, but I've known him all my life, and he has the imagination and flexibility of a brick.'

Fronto nodded. 'Try not to let him hear you say that. He might get a touch offended.'

'Fronto, I know how to handle people. And I really do not fear Pedius getting in my way. Caesar has vouchsafed his intentions for his will to my mother, and if Pedius features in it, he does so peripherally at best. If I were going to remove an obstacle to my inheritance, Fronto, it would be a certain swarthy babe sitting in my own house in Rome, not Pedius.'

Octavian smiled, and there was something about that smile that made Fronto shiver. He watched the young man go, and then turned and stomped off through the camp to his own legion, then found Galronus in his tent.

'Problem?' the Remi said, busily pulling on a fresh tunic.

'Octavian has come from Rome.'

'I'm not at all surprised. In fact I'm surprised it's taken him this long.'

'The thing is,' Fronto said, making sure the curtain was closed behind him, 'that I think Octavian might have been the man behind everything that was happening in Rome before we came to Hispania.'

'What?'

'Think about it. The issue of Caesar's will is not settled. I heard him in Rome, arguing with Atia. She was insistent that Caesar had promised his inheritance to Octavian, but now there's Cleopatra's boy, and there's Pedius, and there's Pinarius and there's Sextus Caesar, or there was until recently. They're all his son or nephews. And look what's happened to them.'

Galronus shook his head. 'Alright, Pinarius nearly fell in the forum, but that wasn't Octavian. Sextus died in a revolt in Syria. Hard to see how Octavian could involve himself in that. And Pedius and Caesarion are untouched.'

'Are they? Pedius was out of reach, because he was here commanding armies. And Caesarion nearly died from poison in the house's garden in Rome.'

'That was an accident.'

'Probably.'

'And Octavian himself nearly died at the races.'

'Yes,' Fronto said, 'but don't you think it was awfully convenient that he hadn't tied the reins and he was able to jump free?'

'You're reaching, Fronto.'

'Am I? And Caesar's chariot. Paetus was trying to do away with Caesar, by the looks of it, and Octavian was around when Paetus died. In fact he was in control of the building.'

'But Paetus' death is unconnected. He's no heir. He was Caesar's enemy.'

'But Caesar has to be protected. Don't you see? Until he's signed a new will naming Octavian, if the general dies, all his goods are left to a man whose corpse lies out in Syria. Octavian will probably get nothing. I think he's been trying to narrow the field, but to look after the source of his inheritance, all at the same time. And I think he faked his own accident. Salvius Cursor was onto something, and then accidentally ate bad mushrooms? Octavian poisoned Salvius because the man was onto him. And that's why he had his 'accident', to take the heat off.'

'You sound like a nutcase.'

Fronto folded his arms. 'Alright. You think it's so farfetched, let's test the theory. If I'm right, Octavian's come to Hispania in the hope that his uncle will name him in a new will, and possibly to nobble Pedius. How about we make Pedius a nice tempting target.'

'What?'

'We drop a hint that Caesar is considering Pedius as his heir thanks to his sterling work in Hispania. If we play it right, Octavian might make another move.'

Galronus sighed. 'I hope you're wrong, Fronto. I like Octavian.'

'So do I, but I won't underestimate him.'

CHAPTER TWENTY SIX

It had taken some doing, Galronus mused as he waited, lurking in the shadow of one of the command tents. Fronto had truly got the bit between his teeth over this stupid Octavian thing, and had refused to let go of the notion, while Galronus had continued to find the whole idea rather farfetched.

Following his arrival, Octavian had presented himself to Caesar and the pair had enjoyed a heartfelt reunion, the general seeming to have the weight of years lifted from his shoulders at the presence of his great nephew, the young man full of both questions and praise. Galronus had been entirely prepared to ignore Fronto's suspicions until the banquet that evening to celebrate the young man's joining them.

Fronto claimed to have nothing to do with it, but it seemed suspiciously timed to Galronus that over the evening's conversation, Pedius had brought up the subject of the region of Lusitania. It being the one place in Hispania where there were still occasional troubles and where the notion of uprising still seemed to exist, Pedius suggested that the currently-assigned tribunes were handling the place badly, and that Lusitania should have been settled by now. He went on to suggest that perhaps the right officer placed in charge there, with the right combination of political nous and military skill, could settle the place properly.

Galronus had watched Caesar mull the idea over and see the value in it. They had a month left in Hispania at most, and it would be better to return to Rome with a clean record of success. The Remi had seen Caesar's eyes fall on Fronto for a moment, then move on. Fronto was his military warhorse, but no one had ever suggested he possessed even an ounce of political nous. The general's gaze had then passed over Octavian without settling and had fallen back on Pedius. He had agreed with the plan, and had assigned Pedius the job on the spot.

Until that moment, Galronus had seen nothing in Octavian that suggested he harboured anything but familial respect for his cousin. But the moment the general dismissed the young man as a possibility with just a glance and assigned the potential for glory to his cousin, the Remi had caught a flash of something that looked startlingly like hatred in the young man's eyes. It was there for but a moment before it was glossed over with that easy-going smile once more. But in that single moment, Galronus decided that Octavian was, after all, quite capable of everything Fronto suggested. And as to how clever the young man was, he displayed that readily over the next hour. While agreeing with the assignment of Pedius and being impressively self-effacing, the young Octavian managed to talk Caesar into assigning him as Pedius' second for the campaign.

That was how they'd ended up out here, camped four miles from Lauro where Pompey's forces had finally been defeated by Didius, vexillations from several legions and a small cavalry contingent given to Pedius and Octavian while Caesar oversaw the final preparations in Hispalis. They had toured the southern reaches of Lusitania, meeting with the ordos of various towns and smoothing over the recent troubles, listening to pleas and agreeing new terms and treaties, bringing the cities back into alignment with the republic. They had identified trouble spots and hit them hard, routing out rebels wherever they were to be found. Fronto had been assigned to the staff, along with Galronus, for the general wanted a steady military hand there to assist the two commanders, but Fronto had been impressed with the way both of Caesar's great nephews handled the region.

But completely without Fronto needing to interfere further, Galronus had watched a rift growing between the cousins. Each occasion that Pedius achieved success, Octavian congratulated him and celebrated, but now, knowing where to look in the young man's eyes, Galronus had seen the flinty glares Octavian threw his cousin when he was unaware. And not all of it was Octavian's doing. As the second in command, over the weeks there had been occasions when Octavian had found himself in prime position, and had been prepared to deal with matters on both military and political levels. And almost every time, Pedius had stepped in and taken control. The situation had been growing more and more tense as they worked. Lusitania was being settled rapidly, but a whole new war looked like breaking out between the two cousins instead.

Fronto and Galronus had been keeping an eye on Octavian and his staff throughout, half expecting another 'accident' to occur. Nothing had happened yet, but the army was almost done. Soon they would return to Hispalis and then: home. If anything was going to happen, it would have to happen soon.

It was quite by chance that Galronus was standing out in the darkness some way from the heart of the camp, contentedly urinating into a ditch, when he saw the figure. A shadowy shape had slipped from between two tents across the dark ground and moved out into the countryside. Not only had the simple suspiciousness of it drawn Galronus' attention, but more importantly, the two tents from between which the figure had emerged were part of Octavian's gathering. Galronus had finished swiftly, tucked himself away, and stood, silent and still, almost invisible in the darkness, watching that shape.

It did not move too far from camp. There was no military danger here, the ground hard and rocky, and the stop just for the night, and so neither rampart nor ditch had been driven around the camp, but pickets and sentries were positioned at intervals. The figure did not stray far enough from the tents to come close to the cordon of watching soldiers.

The shape stopped by an area of overgrown bushes, and there faffed and fiddled with something, the details of the activity not visible in the darkness at such a distance, but as the figure moved away once more, back the way it had come, it was carrying a small bag.

Galronus watched until the figure slipped back between those tents once more and then hurried over to where the figure had been working. He searched the ground as best he could in the gloom, finding nothing. He turned his attention to searching among the leaves and flowers and it was only as he was becoming frustrated at finding nothing that he realised what he was smelling. A sweet aroma faintly resembling an apricot.

Oleander. He examined the flowers to confirm his suspicions, and then stepped back. He was standing before a wide swathe of flowering oleander. His memory immediately presented him with an image of Caesar's garden in Rome, almost exactly a year ago. Arriving at the house with Fronto and Caesar to find the household in a minor panic because Caesarion had tried eating oleander in the garden and had almost died. It had been Octavian who had explained it all to them. The connection was simply too worrying to ignore.

Galronus had run off then to Fronto's tent and found the legate fast asleep. Fronto had risen sharply and dressed as Galronus explained what he had seen. There seemed no other possibility than this nefarious activity be aimed at Pedius, and so they had agreed. Galronus would keep watch on the army's commander, and Fronto would do the same on the young second in command.

Galronus had arrived at Pedius' tent to find everything apparently normal. To be certain, he had approached one of the soldiers on guard, a bored-looking legionary who had snapped sharply to attention at the arrival of an officer. Galronus had settled the man at ease and exchanged quiet conversation with him, just checking in, doing 'the rounds'. As they spoke, he listened carefully and picked out the muffled sounds of snoring from within. Two individuals, which would account for Pedius and his slave. Satisfied that nothing had yet happened, Galronus had slipped behind the tent and waited.

The night was warm, and here in the heart of the camp, the darkness was no longer held back by the campfires that had burned down to embers an hour ago. Thus the figure was already right in front of him when he saw it. While there was no way to confirm that it was the same person he'd seen out by the oleander, it seemed highly unlikely to be anyone else. It was a slave, clearly. The figure wore just a plain dark tunic, belted at the waist, sandals, and a necklace at his throat which should hold the tag naming his owner, but was empty. One of the slave's hands was gripping something small. The other held a knife. Galronus watched, tense, as the slave approached the back of Pedius' tent, waited for the guard there to patrol, walking away, and then slipped in behind him. The figure ducked to the bottom of the tent and used the knife to snick one of the ties holding it down, allowing sufficient space for someone to crawl underneath, which he then proceeded to attempt.

Galronus clenched his teeth, wondering what would happen if he was caught breaking into an officer's tent. It would certainly look odd. He watched the figure slipping beneath the leather and leapt into action. Jumping the few paces between tents, he threw himself on the slave's legs and began to pull.

There was a muffled curse and the slave lashed out, kicking at him, catching him in the shoulder. Galronus grunted and moved to the side, still pulling. The knife suddenly whispered out under the tent and narrowly missed Galronus' fingers. Unarmed and desperate, the Remi let go of one leg, lifted his right hand, bunching into a fist, and then slammed it down in a powerful punch behind the slave's knee. There was a howl from the other side of the leather wall, and then other voices.

Muffled, from inside, he heard 'Who's there?', followed by the guard out front asking if something was wrong. Much to Galronus' relief, rather than returning to his post, the man who'd wandered away went to join his fellow at the front, assuming something to be happening there. The undamaged leg kicked out once more, this time catching Galronus on the forehead, hard. Dazed and in pain, the Remi let go and rolled away. As he clutched his head, trying to blink away the dizziness, he was vaguely aware of the slave, his chances of entering the tent without discovery blown, slipping back out from the leather and rising, limping away as fast as he could.

Galronus, cursing quietly, rose unsteadily, still shaking his head to clear it. He slipped away between the tents just as the guards appeared, searching around outside Pedius' quarters. Ignoring what was happening behind him, Galronus staggered away after the faint shape of the slave, the man slowed by the pain in his knee.

As his head cleared, the Remi rounded a tent and saw the shadowy figure in the open ground. He broke into a run and then leapt, throwing his arms around the slave and bringing him down to the turf with a grunt and an expellation of air. Winded, the slave struggled for a moment, trying to pull himself free and run once more, but Galronus was recovering fast and he held on to the struggling man. Unable to kick now, the slave flailed with his knife, trying to cut the man holding him but unable to do so effectively, lying face down. Galronus was impressed, though. Few slaves would know how to use a blade in a fight, and this one held it as though he meant it. Indeed, he quickly changed his grip on it, so that he could use it more effectively as he struggled to free himself.

Galronus let go with his left arm and grabbed at the flailing blade, managing to close his fingers around the slave's wrist. Aware of a huge commotion behind them now, where Pedius' guards had clearly found the cut tent cord, Galronus slammed the man's arm against the ground again and again until the knife fell away. The two men struggled again, then, rolling over and over, battering and grabbing, each silent, trying not to draw the attention of the guards.

Finally, Galronus succeeded in getting his hand on the hilt of his own pugio and pulled it from the sheath. The slave managed through sheer desperation to deliver a heavy blow, knocking Galronus back, and the Remi rolled away, cursing. As he recovered and rose to his feet, he saw the slave similarly rising. The man had managed to retrieve his own knife.

'Stop there,' snapped an angry voice behind Galronus, and the Remi turned to see the two men who'd been guarding Pedius' tent, fully armed and armoured, approaching the pair of them. Galronus lowered the knife. He might have some explaining to do, but he was one of the four most senior officers in the camp, and the guards were not about to try anything with him.

The slave's eyes darted from Galronus to the men behind him and then back. He then looked around, clearly weighing up his chances of flight, but already other armed figures were closing in on them. There was no way out.

Calmly, without a hint of panic or regret, the slave lifted the knife and drew it in a hard line across his throat. Blood spurted in great gouts from the wound as the man hissed, the knife and a small bag dropping from his fingers as he lurched two steps and then crumpled to the ground.

'Sir?' one of the guards said.
'Is Quintus Pedius alright?'
'Yes sir. A little confused and tired, sir. Who was that?'
'A criminal. But a dead one.'
'What should we do with him, sir?'
'Leave him with me. Back to your posts, all of you.'

* * *

'Wake Octavian.'

The guard frowned. 'Sir?'

'Do as I say.'

With a worried salute, the guard knocked on the tent post, waited for the muffled voice from within, and then slipped inside. A few moments later he reappeared. 'The tribune is preparing to see you, sir.'

'Waiting won't be necessary.'

The guard opened his mouth to disagree, but Fronto pushed past him and stepped into the tent. Octavian was in his night tunic, having just slipped out of bed and risen. He turned in surprise, holding a belt, ready to wrap it around his middle, and frowned.

'Fronto?'

'Sit.'

Still with a furrowed brow, Octavian did so, perching on the edge of his bed. 'This is a strange time to pay a visit, Fronto.'

'I don't know how you were planning to explain this one away,' Fronto said in a flat tone as he sank into the seat near the door.

'What?'

'Your slave with the oleander met with an unfortunate accident.'

On cue, Galronus stepped through the tent door, and threw the bloody corpse onto the floor in the middle of the room, folding his arms and standing in front of the tent door.

'Aristes. My word. What happened to him?'

'Don't be coy, Octavian,' Fronto snapped. 'I know you're clever, but like many clever men, you make the mistake of thinking the rest of us are stupid. We're not. I'm on to you, Octavian.'

'I have no idea to what you are referring, Fronto. If Aristes has done something you should have brought him to me. I would have had him punished appropriately. I do not suffer insolence or disobedience from my slaves.'

Fronto snorted. 'Oleander.' He lifted the pouch taken from the slave and upended it, pouring the fine rain of crushed petals onto the floor. 'Presumably it was going to be slipped into the foodstuffs the commander would have for breakfast. Or maybe suffused in his wine. Some way in which it would appear that he had some sort of digestive trouble after eating. He would brush it off as a temporary illness, and by the time he realised it was something more, and sent for help, it would be too late for him. Another obstacle out of your way, eh?'

'Fronto, have you been drinking? Your imagination seems to be running away with you.'

Fronto stabbed a finger out at Octavian.

'You can dissemble all you like, but we know. I can't actually prove anything on your part, for this, or for Caesarion, or Paetus, or Salvius Cursor, or anyone else, but I know it was you.'

'Really, Fronto, you're sounding paranoid.'

The finger wagged. 'Quiet. And bear in mind that Salvius Cursor is still alive. If he ever wakes up, I wonder what he'll have to tell us.'

Was there just a flicker of uncertainty in Octavian's eye, then? Fear even? The young man shrugged it off. 'You are exploring the realm of fiction, Fronto.'

'No I'm not. You've been streamlining your inheritance, but it stops now.'

'Fronto…'

'No. I'm not done talking.' He leaned forward. 'I remember you from years back. A clever young bastard, you were. So clearly cut from the same cloth as your great uncle. Even back then he saw you as a successor to everything he'd achieved. Now even more so. All this was so unnecessary. The general would never give his inheritance to anyone else. Oh, I expect he'll throw a bone to your cousins, and he'll make sure his Aegyptian boy is set up for life, but it was always going to be you who followed him.'

'Listen…'

'No. *You* listen now. I always liked you. I still do. You're clever and you have your head on right. You know what you're doing. Gods, but you might even be more Caesar than Caesar himself. You'll go on to great things, and because I like you, and because you're the right one for the job, I'm not going to do anything about this. Everything you've done, everything you've been involved in, none of it will ever come to light, because if it did, it would ruin Caesar every bit as much as it would ruin you.'

Finally, Octavian was silent, just looking Fronto in the eye. No fear, no regret, no joy either. Just silent and impassive.

'So this all goes away. But it stops here. No more. If anyone else falls ill, you'd better hope it's just a natural malady, because if I ever have even the slightest suspicion that these tricks have begun again, I will come for you, Octavian, and you know me. You don't want that.'

'I imagine,' Octavian said, levelly, 'these unfortunate accidents will now have ended, for I have prayed at the altars of Fortuna, of Venus and of Jupiter for my cousins' health and wellbeing.'

'I'll bet your have. And while I'm hoping that Salvius Cursor recovers, if he does, I will have to keep him contained, because if you think having *me* coming for you would be bad, I've got nothing on that bad tempered, bloodthirsty lunatic.'

'Was there anything else, Fronto?'

'No. Just that. Play along with your cousin for a few more days and then we'll be back to Hispalis and then Rome. Be good, and keep your slaves in their place.'

Octavian gave a thin-lipped smile as Fronto rose and joined Galronus in the doorway.

'We'll be watching you.'

Octavian smiled wider. 'Would you mind taking that with you?' he said, pointing at the body on the ground.

'Your slave, your problem.'

With that the two of them left the tent. As they strolled back towards the command tents of the Tenth, Galronus rubbed his aching head. 'There's still no proof, you realise. I'm convinced, now, but trying to convince anyone else would be hard. If he tries again, there's still really nothing we can do.'

'I'm hoping the threat makes him see sense. The stupid thing is that Caesar's driven him to it. Octavian is far too clever to start bumping off the opposition when he's in the strongest position anyway, but Caesar's been eroding that position of late. Bringing Cleopatra and his baby son to Rome and to his house represents a threat to Octavian's future. Then there was assigning Sextus to govern Syria and Pedius to command in Hispania, while not taking Octavian anywhere. And worst of all, having promised a new will that included Octavian some years ago, he's still not actually done it, and so the question of his inheritance remains unsettled. All he had to do was make a new will last year and Octavian's future would be secured, and he wouldn't have been driven to all this.'

'You know the rumours the rebels spread that Caesar would refuse to lay down his powers, and that he has his eyes set on a crown?'

Fronto nodded. 'Yes.'

'I've never quite believed it, but I tell you now, if Caesar doesn't seek a crown, I think that boy might.'

'And it might not be out of reach, either.'

Both men shivered.

'Come on,' Fronto said. 'We've just a few more days and then we're off home to see the girls.' He tried not to think on Galronus' intention to move north then. Some things were not worth considering yet. He took a deep breath. 'I don't think sleep is coming my way. Let's get drunk.'

With a carefree laugh, the two officers strode home through the warm evening air.

EPILOGUE

August 45 BC, Narbo

Gaius Trebonius leaned forward in his chair and poured the wine into two pewter cups, taking one and sitting back. 'Send your man away.'

Marcus Antonius, lips pursed, flicked a hand out at his slave. 'Leave us.'

He waited for the slave to exit, closing the door behind them, and picked up the second cup. In the brief moment the door had been open, the din had insisted itself, all the myriad noises of the busy port, where troops moved this way and that, preparing to take ship, while hundreds of their fellows moved goods on and off vessels, sending the supplies in their constant flow to the general's army in Hispania.

'This will all end, soon,' Antonius noted between sips. 'I had a letter from Caesar. He's on his way back to Rome. The army is being disbanded. The Tenth are coming here, and you've to organise their settlement.'

Trebonius nodded. 'I also had a letter. Narbo is going to be busy. How are you, Marcus Antonius?'

Surprised by the question, one of Antonius' eyebrows rose quizzically. 'I'm fine.'

'Are you? Are you really?'

'What does that mean, Trebonius?'

'Well you've spent the year with less authority than ever. I mean, Caesar pushed you into the reserves after Pharsalus, using you like a puppet in Rome, dancing his dance as he pulled the strings, keeping the Roman audience in its place. That must have mightily pissed you off, I'm sure. But then to remove even that and to leave you... what ? Retired?'

'Hardly. I am between campaigns.'

'Are you really?'

'You're needling me, Trebonius.'

'No. I'm making you face harsh truths, Marcus Antonius. You have been set aside by Caesar now. He used you for what he needed and then when you were inconvenient, he simply cast you off. That's what he does. I led three legions for him in Britannia, remember. I went to the aid of Cicero in that Ambiorix disaster. I led the siege of Massilia, and I was given command of Hispania until things became important to Caesar there. That the Pompeys managed to seize control there and form a power base was seen as my failure. So here I am, hero of Britannia, of the Belgae, of Massilia, playing glorified quartermaster here in Narbo. A year of babysitting sailors and merchants. Just as you were set aside by Caesar, so now am I.'

'You have my sympathy. Perhaps if you'd not let Pompey take your province from you, you wouldn't be here.'

Trebonius shot him a poisonous look. 'We're not alone, Antonius.'

'What does that mean?' the other man spat, draining his cup and holding it out for a refil.

'Others feel they have been undervalued,' Trebonius replied evenly, lifting the jar and filling Antonius' cup. 'Brutus, for example. And others. We are not nobodies to be used and abused, Marcus Antonius. We are all that remains of the true muscle and sinew of the republican senate.'

'This is starting to sound very clandestine, Trebonius. I came here because your message suggested there might be a way for me to secure a new command. All you've talked about so far is how Caesar has taken my old one from me.'

'And that, Antonius, is the point.'

'There is no point here, Trebonius. Just a lot of grumbles and hot air. I have had a year to think, and though I hate to admit it, there is something to what Caesar had said. I do have a tendency to be hot-headed and to throw myself into things without due care and attention. I still think he was wrong and that he could have used my talents in Hispania, but I do, at least, understand his reasoning, and I am a forgiving man… *most* of the time. I will brush this one under the mat, and when I see him in Rome, I will negotiate with the general. Within the year I will be back in prime position. You need to do the same. You don't want to sit here and count grain sacks? Then go to Caesar and find a way to prove yourself again.'

Trebonius snarled, throwing his wine cup across the room.

'I shouldn't *need* to prove myself, Antonius. I have done so time and again throughout my career. I have been overlooked for the last time. Something must be done.'

Antonius' eyes narrowed as he gulped down his second cup of unwatered wine. 'This is sounding more and more like some sort of plot.'

'If Caesar cannot be made to see the value in the people who have put him on the pedestal he now enjoys, perhaps it's time the pedestal were removed?'

'A fall from such a lofty place could kill a man,' Antonius said, his voice flat.

'Yes, it could. Easily.'

'If you are suggesting what I think you are suggesting, Trebonius, shut your mouth tight now and say no more.'

'I am not alone, Antonius. There are others. And this is not just about us being passed over for command. There are real fears in Rome, Marcus Antonius. Fears about what Caesar intends to do. About Aegyptus and his woman. There is even talk that some in the senate will vote him his dictatorship for life. You realise what that means? He would be a king in all but name.'

Antonius glared at him. 'Stop talking right now, Trebonius.'

'You know I'm right.'

'And you know that he's my friend. Any more talk like this and I might just have to gut you here and now.'

Trebonius fell silent and leaned back. 'This is your final word on the matter?'

Antonius straightened. 'Somehow I've lost my appetite and the wine has gone sour. You were always a good man, Trebonius. A good commander and a good Roman. In memory of that I will forget entirely every word you have said today, and I shall walk away from here remembering only that you have always been one of Caesar's staunchest supporters. But I tell you this now. Drop this idea and tell any of your foolish friends to do the same. I will wreak bloody havoc on anyone who sets themself against the general. Remember that.'

Rising from the chair, Marcus Antonius gave a stiff bow, turned and walked out of the room.

Trebonius watched him go, waited for some time, mulling over the man's words, and then finally reached for his pen and the sheet of parchment.

> *'To Gaius Cassius Longinus from Gaius Trebonius.*
> *The horseman is a no.'*

He leaned back in his chair.

Shame. Antonius would have been useful to have on their side, but at least it seemed he would keep his mouth shut, so there would be no need to take further action there. With a deep breath, he picked up the pen again.

> *'Speak to Decimus Brutus next.'*

The end.

HISTORICAL NOTE

The campaign in Spain in 45 BC marks the end of Julius Caesar's military endeavours, though, of course, not his story. For the historian the problems left by this year are some of the most troublesome of the man's life.

Caesar's war diaries are the reason I began working on Marius' Mules some 18 years ago. They represent some of the best accounts of military campaigning in history. Even accounts from the 19th and 20th centuries are at best as good as Caesar's Gallic War diary.

For some background, while these seem to be unique in ancient history, it now seems as though any Roman governor was expected to keep an account of their activity and to log it with the administration in Rome. As such, while these have come down to us as a breathtaking and unique account, they are probably just one example of many that are lost. There were probably accounts of the wars of Corbulo and Crassus and others, now long gone. In that respect it is easy to see a progression in the quality of the works. From 58 to 51 BC Caesar was an exploratory governor, expanding the republic and making a name for himself. It is generally recognised that Caesar probably wrote his accounts of these campaigns himself, and they are the clearest and best in all ancient history. Similarly, when the civil war begins, and Caesar still has to make his name, he appears to have written the account of his wars against Pompey from 49 to 48 BC, with unparalleled accounts of critical battles and campaigns.

When Pompey dies, we see a change in the work. We still have the accounts, but they are clearly not written by the same hand as that which covered 58-48. Caesar is now important enough to not bother keeping his own records. What we then see from 48 onwards is a steady descent in quality. The Alexandrian War, probably written by Caesar's sidekick Hirtius, is poor by comparison. The African War (likely written by someone new again) is, frankly, awful. It is overly-complex, concentrates too much on unimportant minutiae and ignores major events almost entirely. It makes no attempt to provide a motive for anything (which Caesar was very good with in his early books) and so we are left largely guessing why some strange tactical decisions were made. Frankly, I *hated* trying to create a sensible tale from the African War.

Enter the Spanish War. Again, this appears to have been written by someone new. I am going to charitably say someone barely literate and with little command of language. If *The Gallic War* is Tolkien, and the *African War* Game of Thrones, then the *De Bello Hispaniensi* is that last season of Game of Thrones that makes little sense and jumps the shark repeatedly.

A prime example is the fact that Caesar arrives at Cordoba, at the river (Baetis=Guadalquivir), to find he cannot cross it. So he makes cages of stones and forms his own bridge. He then fortifies the north bank as Pompey arrives on the south. The enemy general then camps opposite Caesar and we have the first fight over a bridge. We are then told in the text that "Observing that his opponents were by no means willing to do this, Caesar led his forces across the river and ordered large fires to be lit at night, so as to entice them into the plain just as he had drawn them away from Ulia."

We are, I think, left wondering how he so swiftly and subtly crosses the river again when crossing was so impossible that he had to build his own bridge, which he is now abandoning?

Such is the basis of this book. I have done my level best to keep to the text of our source material, both this, the most badly-written book in the ancient world, and various others such as Plutarch and Cassius Dio. But the simple fact is that working word for word from the Hispanic War would result in unreadable garbage, and so I have made leaps in intuition. I have assigned motive to moves that without such would seem idiotic. Marius' Mules XIV is borne from trying to make sense of a literary miasma.

So, my caveat having been made, where do we start?

There is a strange lull after the African War, when Caesar returns to Rome for a few months before pursuing the campaign once more. I find that the MM series has fans in three general areas. Some want simply a military campaign. Some want a depiction of Caesar. Some want the fun stuff. Few want all three, but it is my job to try and provide them anyway. As such, I suppose I could have made this book purely about the Spanish War (though I may have needed a therapist). But the more I read about Caesar's time in Rome the more I knew it was important in the grand scheme. The triumphs are HUGELY important in the ongoing story, and this is the year that everything begins to change. The foundations are being laid for a plot that will change the world, and even now, even before the last battle of Pompey, already some of Caesar's allies are drifting away, becoming disillusioned, and with the death of Caesar's current willed heir in Syria, a huge question opens up as to his inheritance. As such, I could not avoid telling these tales and using them to move us one step closer to the last book.

Because that is what is coming: the *last* book. I would imagine that anyone reading this has also read books 1-13, and so you have an inkling of what is to come. The series has always been planned to finish with book 15, from the very start. As such, there is one book to go, and anyone who has even the most basic knowledge of Caesar's history knows what is to come in the final volume. The book you have just read, then, might be considered part one of a two-part end-of-series finale. Threads had to be weaved in here in advance of book 15 and I imagine you've seen it happen.

So to Octavian. My plot by Octavian to secure his succession is fictional. Having said that, Caesar's heir at the time, Sextus, did die in Syria in some stupid plot, and for a time, Caesar's will was essentially worthless. In 45 BC, the great man's inheritance would pass to a corpse in the Syrian sand. Anyone who has studied Augustus (as Octavian would later be known) may form any number of opinions about the man. He might be a great hero, remaking Rome, or he might be an autocrat twisting the republic to grant him ultimate power. Whether he's a hero or a villain, one thing that is clear is that he was dangerously clever. He seems to have been a very miscellaneous child in looks, who has still come down to us as the quintessential heroic handsome Roman, courtesy of unprecedented levels of propaganda. Truly, Octavian was more than just bright. He was driven. There is some uncertainty of how and when he joined his great uncle in Spain, but the stories we are left with are that he travelled as some sort of military hero despite not having arrived until the war was over. Such is his level of self-promotion. A winner can say what he likes.

So Sextus had died. The story of Caesar's chariot breaking during his triumph is straight from sources. The others are my own invention. But if one is to break the problem down, consider this:

Caesar had one natural son, but he was illegitimate and divisive. He had four great nephews, but only one of those was through the male line of the family: Sextus. Caesar never seems to have made an attempt to include Caesarion in his inheritance. For years, at this point, Sextus was his heir, as the only male line inheritor. When Sextus died, Octavian had no better claim than Pedius or Pinarius. Indeed, he seems to have been younger than all his cousins. Pedius had been one of Caesar's lieutenants in Spain, Sextus had commanded Syria, and Pinarius was the scion of a great patrician house. Why, then, did Octavian come out of this as Caesar's heir?

Slight spoiler here, as this will come in book 15, but Caesar's new will named three heirs. Pinarius and Pedius each were given one eighth of Caesar's estate, with Octavian granted the other three quarters. Moreover, the two cousins immediately relinquished all claim to their inheritance, letting Octavian have the lot. One might be led to wonder what Octavian had said or done to his cousins that they so readily agreed. A great nobleman and a tried and tested war hero both giving over their inheritance to their pup of a cousin seems odd, no? In the future, Octavian would 'put the screws' on people time and again, and it is not out of the bounds of reason that he had cut his teeth on internecine politics at this point.

The story with the palm tree, by the way, is lifted from two sources, though I have moved it to Seville. The tree is supposed to have been Caesar's position at Munda, but since the general never returns to Munda after the battle, it was rather difficult to reconcile the two events, and so I moved it to Hispalis (Seville). Cassius Dio and Suetonius both recount the tree. Neither were within a century of Caesar!

My portrayal of Octavian I stand by. He was brilliant. Immensely clever. Charismatic. Ambitious. Men like this are the most dangerous on Earth...

Munda is the last battle, for which the book is named. There are smaller sieges and clashes in the aftermath, but they do not involve Caesar, and none of them really classify as a battle. Munda, then is the Pharsalus of the Hispanic War. It is yet another battle in Caesar's life that could have gone either way. It is another reminder that the reason Caesar's legions were so untouchable was that they had at this point been involved in constant warfare for 13 years. This, then, was always going to be another question of numbers vs. experience. Gnaeus Pompey had more men. Numerically, he should have walked this, especially with Labienus on side. But Caesar's legions were veterans. They had never truly lost, and, given that, their victory should come as no surprise.

For the battlefield nuts among you I will give you my Munda. The actual location of Munda has long been disputed by historians and archaeologists. Cities such as Ronda and Monda have claimed it based on their names. Their connection goes no further. Montilla is even less likely. La Lantejuela has the best claim thus far. Geographically it is in a roughly appropriate position. Sling bullets apparently belonging to the rebel force have been found here. That, of course, is only suggestive of their military presence, not of the main battle. The area does not match up with the topography of the only account. I have done some research myself, and have settled upon a location not far east of La Lantejuela, just northwest of El Rubio. Here, Caesar's camp would lie somewhere on the A-388, with the army crossing the Rio Blanco and moving against a hill upon which sits the medieval tower of Torre Gallape which seems to incorporate materials from older Roman buildings. Oddly, while COVID once again got in the way of research trips, and this research was largely done from my office, I visited the site some years ago and can still picture it, as I did while writing the battle

For now, Labienus is dead. Sextus Pompey is dead. Gnaeus Pompey has disappeared. The war is over. The world can settle into peace. I suspect you will all know what is to come in book 15, and will not be surprised that there will be no war in it. I hope, regardless, it does not disappoint. The series could end no other way. Oh, and for the record, that last scene with Antonius and Trebonius is based upon recorded events. Given the portrayal of Mark Antony throughout history, it is interesting to note that, although he refused to go along with a plot against Caesar, he seems to never have made an attempt to bring that plot to the general's attention. Interesting, I would say.

Fronto is no longer a young man. Caesar is now 55, and Fronto is less than half a decade behind him. In the time of Rome that makes both men long-lived. Fronto is feeling his age. Aren't we all? I know that I am, some 18 years after inventing Fronto.

Still, he has legs left yet, especially if war no longer calls.

Caesar is on his way to Rome to confront his destiny.

Fronto is with him.

What will the winter and spring of 44BC hold?

Fronto will be back one more time next summer. Have a good year until then.

Simon Turney

October 2021

Printed in Great Britain
by Amazon